Please return this book on or before the last date
st.

ELIZABETH

Emily Purdy was born in Texas, where she still lives.

NEWCASTLE-UNDER-LYME
COLLEGE LEARNING RESOURCES

D0676448

By the same author:

The Tudor Wife

MARY &
ELIZABETH

EMILY PURDY

FICTION PUR
NEWCASTLE-UNDER-LYME
COLLEGE LEARNING RESOURCES
DCU40069

AVON

This novel is entirely a work of fiction.
The names, characters and incidents portrayed in it are
the work of the author's imagination. Any resemblance to
actual persons, living or dead, events or localities is
entirely coincidental.

AVON

A division of HarperCollins*Publishers*
77–85 Fulham Palace Road,
London W6 8JB

This paperback edition 2011

First published as *The Tudor Throne* by Kensington Publishing, New York, 2011

www.harpercollins.co.uk
1

Copyright © Brandy Purdy 2011

Brandy Purdy asserts the moral right to
be identified as the author of this work

A catalogue record for this book is
available from the British Library

ISBN-13: 978-1-84756-237-1

Printed and bound in Great Britain by
Clays Ltd, St Ives plc

All rights reserved. No part of this publication may be
reproduced, stored in a retrieval system, or transmitted,
in any form or by any means, electronic, mechanical,
photocopying, recording or otherwise, without the prior
permission of the publishers.

Mixed Sources
Product group from well-managed
forests and other controlled sources
www.fsc.org Cert no. SW-COC-001806
© 1996 Forest Stewardship Council

FSC is a non-profit international organisation established
to promote the responsible management of the world's forests.
Products carrying the FSC label are independently certified
to assure consumers that they come from forests that are managed
to meet the social, economic and ecological needs
of present and future generations.

Find out more about HarperCollins and the environment at
www.harpercollins.co.uk/green

Wonderful, dangerous, cruel, and wise, after thirty-eight years of ruling England, King Henry VIII lay dying. It was the end of an era. Many of his subjects had known no other king and feared the uncertainty that lay ahead when his nine-year-old son inherited the throne.

A cantankerous mountain of rotting flesh, already stinking of the grave, and looking far older than his fifty-five years, it was hard to believe the portrait on the wall, that was one of Master Holbein's finest and a magnificent, vivid and valiant likeness, that this reeking wreck had once been the handsomest prince in Christendom, standing with hands on hips and legs apart as if he meant to straddle the world.

The great gold-embroidered bed, reinforced to support his weight, creaked like a ship being tossed on angry waves, as if the royal bed itself would also protest the coming of Death and God's divine judgment.

The faded blue eyes started in a panic from amidst the fat pink folds of bloodshot flesh. As his head tossed upon the embroidered silken pillows a stream of muted, incoherent gibberish flowed along with a silvery ribbon of drool into his ginger-white beard, and a shaking hand rose and made a feeble attempt to point, jabbing adamantly, insistently, here and there at the empty spaces around the carved and gilded posts, as thick and sturdy as sentries standing at attention, supporting the gold-fringed crimson canopy.

There was a rustle of clothing and muted whispers as those who watched discreetly from the shadows – the courtiers, servants, statesmen, and clergy – shook their heads and shrugged their shoulders, knowing they could do nothing but watch and wonder if it were angels or demons that tormented their dying sovereign.

The Grim Reaper's approach had rendered Henry mute, so he could tell no one about the phantoms that clustered around his bed, which only he, on the threshold of death, could see.

Six wronged women, four dead and two living: a saintly Spaniard, a dark-eyed witch – or "bitch" as some would think it more apt to call her – a shy plain Jane, a plump rosy-cheeked German hausfrau absently munching marzipan, and a wanton jade-eyed auburn-haired nymph seeping sex from every pore. And, kneeling at the foot of the massive bed, in an attitude of prayer, the current queen, Catherine Parr, kind, capable Kate who always made everything all right, murmuring soothing words and reaching out a ruby-ringed white hand, like a snowy angel's wing, to rub his ruined rotting legs, scarred by leeches and lancets, and putrid with a seeping stink that stained the bandages and bedclothes an ugly urine-yellow.

Against the far wall, opposite the bed, on a velvet-padded bench positioned beneath Holbein's robust life-sized portrait of the pompous golden monarch in his prime and glory, sat the lion's cubs, his living legacy, the heirs he would leave behind; all motherless, and soon to be fatherless, orphans fated to be caught up in the storm that was certain to rage around the throne when the magnificent Henry Tudor breathed his last. Although he had taken steps to protect them by reinstating his disgraced and bastardized daughters in the succession and appointing coolly efficient Edward Seymour to head a Regency Council comprised of sixteen men who would govern during the boy-king's minority, Henry was shrewd enough to know that that would not stop those about them from forming factions and fighting, jockeying for position and power, for he who is puppetmaster to a prince also holds the reins of power.

There was the good sheep: meek and mild, already greying, old maid Mary, a disapproving, thin-lipped pious prude, already a year past thirty, the only surviving child of Catherine of Aragon, the golden-haired Spanish girl who was supposed to be as fertile as the pomegranate she took as her personal emblem.

The black sheep: thirteen-year-old flame-haired Elizabeth, the dark enchantress Anne Boleyn's daughter, whose dark eyes, just like her mother's, flashed like black diamonds, brilliant, canny, and hard, as fast and furious as lightning; a clever minx this princess who should have been a prince. Oh what a waste! It was enough to make Henry weep, and tears of a disappointment that had never truly healed trickled down his cheeks. Oh what a king Elizabeth would have been! But no petticoat, no queen, could ever hold England and steer the ship of state with the firm hand and conviction, the will, strength, might, and robust majesty of a king. Politics, statecraft, and warfare were a man's domain. Women were too delicate and weak, too feeble and fragile of body and spirit, to bear the weight of a crown; queens were meant to be ornaments to decorate their husband's court and bear sons to ensure the succession so the chain of English kings remained unbroken and the crown did not become a token to be won in a civil war that turned the nation into one big bloody battlefield as feuding factions risked all to win the glittering prize.

"Oh, Bess, you should have been a boy! *What a waste!*" Henry tossed his head and wept, though none could decipher his garbled words or divine the source of his distress. "*Why, God, why?* She would have held England like a lover gripped hard between her thighs and never let go! Of the three of them, she's the only one who could!"

And last, but certainly not least – in fact, the most important of all – the frightened sheep, the little lost sheep, the weak and bland little runt of the flock: nine-year-old Edward. So soon to be the sixth king to bear that name, he would be caught at the centre of the brewing storm until he reached an age to take the sceptre in hand and wield power himself. He sat there now with his eyes downcast, the once snow-fair hair he had inherited from the King's beloved "Gentle Jane" darkening to a ruddy brown more like that of his uncles, the battling Seymour brothers – fish-frigid but oh so clever Edward and jolly, good-time Tom – than the flaxen locks of his pallid mother or the fiery Tudor-red tresses of his famous sire. His fingers absently shredded the curly white plume that adorned his round black velvet cap, letting the pieces waft like snowflakes onto the exotic whirls and swirls of the luxurious carpet from far-away Turkey. He then abandoned the denuded shaft to pluck the luminous, shimmering Orient pearls from the brim, letting them fall as carelessly as if they were nothing more than pebbles to be picked up, pocketed, and no doubt sold by the servants. Like casting pearls before swine!

"Oh, Edward!" Henry wept and raged against the Fates. "The son I always wanted but *not* the king England *needs!*"

Catherine Parr rose from where she knelt at the foot of the bed and took a jewel-encrusted goblet from the table nearby and filled it from a pitcher of cold water. Gently cupping the back of her husband's balding head, as if he were an infant grown to gigantic proportions, and lifting it from the pillows, she held the cup to his lips, thinking to cool his fever and thus remedy his distress. But not all the cool, sweet waters in the world could soothe Henry Tudor's troubled spirit.

The black-velvet-clad sisters, Mary and Elizabeth, the rich silver and golden threads on their black damask kirtles and under-sleeves glimmering in the candlelight like metallic fish darting through muddy water, sat on either side of their little brother, leaning in protectively. But as they comforted him with kind, reassuring words and loving arms about his frail shoulders – the left a tad higher than the right due to the clumsy, frantic fingers of a nervous midwife and the difficulty of wresting him from his mother's womb – their minds were far away, roving in the tumultuous past, turning the gilt-bordered, blood-spattered, angst-filled pages of the book of memory. . . .

❧ 1 ❧

Mary

*All I have ever wanted was to be loved, to
find on this earth a love as true and everlasting as God's.*

As Father lay dying, I remembered a time when he had well
and truly loved me; a time when he had called me the most
valuable jewel in his kingdom, his most precious pearl, dearer than
any diamond. Those were the days when he would burst through
the door, like the bright golden sun imperiously brushing aside an
ugly black rain cloud, and sweep me up into his arms and ask,
"How fares my best sweetheart?" and kiss me and call me "the
pearl of my world!" Easter of the year I turned five, upon a whim
of his, to illustrate this, he had me dressed in a white gown, cap,
and dainty little shoes so densely encrusted with pearls I seemed
to be wearing nothing else, they were sewn so thick and close. And
when I walked into the royal chapel between him and my mother,
holding their hands, turning my head eagerly from left to right to
smile up at them, I walked in love.

On my next birthday, my sixth, I awoke to find a garden of fragrant rosemary bushes, one for each year of my life, growing out of
gilded pots, their branches spangled with golden tinsel and glowing mysteriously from within with circles of rosy pink, sunny yellow, sapphire blue, emerald green, and ruby red light, emanating, I
discovered, from little lanterns with globes of coloured glass concealed inside. My father had created a veritable fairyland for me,
peopled with beautiful fairies and evil imps, grotesque goblins and

mischievous elves, leering trolls, playful pixies, crook-backed gnomes, and gossamer-winged sprites, and the Fairy Queen herself, flame-haired and majestic in emerald green, all made of sugar and marzipan in a triumph of confectioner's art. I stood before them timid and unsure, hardly daring to move or breathe, in case they truly were real and might work some terrible magic upon me if I dared interfere with them, until Father laughed and bit the head off a hobgoblin to show me I had nothing to fear. And there were four gaily costumed dwarves, two little women and two little men, every seam, and even their tiny shoes and caps, sewn with rows of tiny tinkling gold bells, to cavort and dance and play with me. We joined hands and danced rings around the rosemary bushes until we grew dizzy and fell down laughing. And when I sat down to break my fast, Father took it upon himself to play the servant and wait upon me. When he tipped the flagon over my cup, golden coins poured out instead of breakfast ale and overflowed into my lap and spilled onto the floor where the dwarves gathered them up for me.

In those days we were very much a family and, to my child's eyes, a *happy* family. Before I was of an age to sit at table and attend banquets and entertainments with them, Mother and Father used to come into my bedchamber every night to hear my prayers on their way to the Great Hall. How I loved seeing them in all their jewels and glittering finery standing side by side, smiling down at me, Father with his arm draped lovingly about Mother's shoulders, both of them with love and pride shining in their eyes as they watched me kneel upon my velvet cushioned prie-dieu in my white nightgown and silk-beribboned cap, eyes closed, brow intently furrowed, hands devoutly clasped as I recited my nightly prayers. And when I was old enough to don my very own sparkling finery and go with them to the Great Hall, I cherished each and every shared smile, sentimental heart-touched tear, and merry peal of laughter as, together, we delighted in troupes of dancing dogs and acrobats, musicians, minstrels, morris dancers, storytellers, and ballad singers.

And we served God together. Faithful and devout, we attended Mass together every day in the royal chapel. My mother spent untold hours kneeling in her private chapel before a statue of the Blessed Virgin surrounded by candles, a hair shirt chafing her lily-white skin red and raw beneath her sombrely ornate gowns, and hunger gnawing at her belly as she persevered in fasting, begging Christ's mother to intercede on her behalf so that her womb might quicken with the son my father desired above all else.

When the heretic Martin Luther published his vile and evil blasphemies, Father put pen to paper and wrote a book to refute them and defend the holy sacraments. When it was finished he had a copy bound in gold and sent a messenger to present it to the Pope, who, much impressed, declared it "a golden book both inside and out", and dubbed Father "Defender of the Faith". To celebrate this accolade, Father ordered all the pamphlets and books, the writings of Martin Luther that had been confiscated throughout the kingdom, assembled in the courtyard in a great heap. In a gown of black velvet and cloth-of-gold, with a black velvet cap trimmed with gold beads crowning my famous, fair marigold hair, I stood with Mother, also clad in black and gold, upon a balcony overlooking the courtyard, holding tight to her hand, and clasping a rosary of gold beads to my chest as I, always short-sighted, squinted down at the scene below. I felt such a rush of pride as Father, clad like Mother and I in black and gold, strode forth with a torch in his hand and set Luther's lies ablaze. I watched proudly as the curling white plumes of smoke rose up, billowing, wafting, twirling and swirling, as they danced away on the breeze.

I also remember a very special day when I was dressed for a very special occasion in pomegranate-coloured velvet and cloth-of-gold encrusted with sparkling white diamonds, lustrous pearls from the Orient, regal purple amethysts, and wine-dark glistening garnets, with a matching black velvet hood covering my hair, caught up beneath it in a pearl-studded net of gold. I was being presented to the Ambassadors of my cousin, the Holy Roman Emperor, Charles V. Though he was many years older than myself, it was Mother's most dearly cherished desire that we would marry; she had always wanted a Spanish bridegroom for me and raised me as befitted a lady of Spain, and the Ambassadors had come to judge and consider my merits as a possible bride for Charles.

As I curtsied low before those distinguished gentlemen in their sombre black velvets and sharp-pointed beards like daggers made of varnished hair, suddenly the solemnity of the moment was shattered by Father's boisterous laughter. He clapped his hands and called for music, then there he was, a jewel-encrusted giant sweeping his "best sweetheart" up in his strong, powerful arms, tossing me up high into the air, and catching me when I came down, skirts billowing, laughing and carefree, for all the world like a woodcutter and his daughter instead of the King of England and his little princess.

"This girl never cries!" he boasted when Mother sat forward anxiously in her chair, a worried frown creasing her brow, and said, "My Lord, take care, you will frighten her!"

But I just laughed and threw my arms around his neck, his bristly red beard tickling my cheek, and begged for more.

The musicians struck up a lively measure, and he led me to the centre of the floor, took my tiny hand in his, and shouted that I was his favourite dancing partner, and never in all his years had he found a better one.

As the skipping, prancing steps of the dance took us past the Ambassadors, suddenly he ripped the hood and net from my hair and tossed them into their startled midst. He combed his fingers through the long, thick, rippling waves, then more gold than red on account of my youth – I was but nine years old at the time – and his pride and joy in me showed clear upon his face.

"What hair my sweetheart has!" he cried. "My Lords, I ask you, have you *ever* seen such hair?"

And indeed he spoke the truth. In my earliest years I had Mother's Spanish gold hair lovingly united with Father's Tudor red, blending beautifully into an orange-yellow shade that caused the people to fondly dub me "Princess Marigold". "God bless our Princess Marigold!" they would shout whenever I rode past in a litter or barge or mounted sidesaddle upon my piebald pony, smiling and waving at them before reserved dignity replaced childish enthusiasm.

Though it may seem vain to say it, I had such beautiful hair in my youth, as true and shining an example as there ever was of why a woman's tresses are called her crowning glory. But before my youth was fully past it began to thin and fade until its lustrous beauty and abundance were only a memory and I was glad to pin it up and hide it under a hood, inside a snood or net, or beneath a veil.

But oh how I treasured the memory of Father's pride in me and my beautiful hair! The day he danced with me before the Ambassadors became one of my happiest memories.

I would never forget the way he swept me up in his arms and spun me round and round, my marigold hair flying out behind my head like a comet's tail, as he danced me from one end of the Great Hall to the other.

I *never* thought the love he felt for me then would ever diminish or die. I thought my earthly father's love, like our Heavenly Father's love, was permanent, unchanging, and everlasting.

"This girl never cries!" Father had said. Little did he know I would make up for a childhood filled with unshed tears by crying whole oceans of them in later years, and that most of them would be spilled on account of him, the callousness and cruelty he would mete out to me in place of the love and affection he once gave so freely and unconditionally to me.

But that was yet to come, and in those early days I truly was a princess. I sat on my own little gilded and bejewelled throne, set upon a dais, and upholstered in purple velvet with a canopy of estate, dripping with gold fringe, above me, and a plump purple cushion below me to rest my feet upon. And I wore gowns of velvet, damask, and brocade, silk, satin, silver, and gold; I sparkled with a rainbow of gems, and snuggled in ermine and sable when I was cold; gloves of the finest Spanish leather sheathed my hands; I walked in slippers made of cushion-soft velvet embroidered with pearls, gems, or gilt thread, and when I rode, boots of Spanish leather with silken tassels encased my feet; and underneath my finery only the finest lawns and linens touched my skin. But it was not the prestige and finery I liked best; being my father's daughter was what delighted my heart most. And during the bad years that followed the blissful ones, I used to think there was nothing I would not give to hear him call me "my best sweetheart" again.

Having no son to initiate into the manly pursuits, Father made do as best he could with me. He took me with him to the archery butts, and when I was nine he gave me my first hawk and taught me to fly her. We rode out at the head of a small retinue, me in my velvet habit, dyed the deep green of the forest, sidesaddle upon my piebald pony, the bells on my goshawk's jesses jingling, and the white plume on my cap swaying. And Father, a giant among men, powerfully muscular yet so very graceful, astride his great chestnut stallion, clad in fine white linen and rich brown hunting leathers, with bursts of rainbow light blazing out from the ring of white diamonds that encircled the brim of his velvet cap, and the jaunty white plume that topped it bouncing in the breeze.

We were following our hawks when we came to a large ditch filled with muddy water so dark we could not discern the bottom. Father made a wager with one of his men that he could swing himself across it on a pole. But when he tried, the pole snapped beneath his weight, and Father fell with a great splash, headfirst into the murky water. His legs and arms flailed and thrashed the surface frantically, but his head never appeared; it was stuck fast, mired deep in the mud below.

Edmund Moody, Father's squire, who would have given his life a hundred times over for him, did not hesitate. He dived in and worked to free my father's head. I could not bear to stand there doing nothing but watching helplessly, praying and wringing my hands, fearing that my beloved father might drown, so I recklessly plunged in, my green velvet skirts billowing up about my waist, floating on the muddy water like a lily pad. As I went to assist Master Moody, the tenacious mud sucked at my boots so that every step was a battle, slowing me down and showing me how it must be holding Father's head in a gluelike grip.

But through our diligent and determined efforts, Father was at last freed. Sputtering and gasping, coughing and gulping in mouthfuls of air, Father emerged and, leaning heavily between us, we helped him onto the grass, and he lay with his head in my lap as I tenderly cleaned the mud from his hair and face. An awed and humble cottager's wife brought us pears, cheese, and nuts in her apron, and we sat in the sun and feasted upon them as if they were the finest banquet while the sun dried us. Father made a joke about how my skirts had floated about me like a lily pad and called me his lily. And when we returned to the palace he summoned a goldsmith and commissioned a special jewelled and enamelled ring for me to commemorate that day when I had helped save his life – a golden frog and a pink and white lily resting on a green lily pad. It was the greatest of my worldly treasures, and for years afterward a week scarcely passed when it did not grace my finger. Even when I did not wear it, I kept it safe in a little green velvet pouch upon my person so I would always know it was there with me, a proud and exquisite emblem of Father's love for me.

Those were the happy days before the sad years of ignominy and disgrace, penury, indifference, and disdain, the callousness and cruelty he learned under the tutelage of The Great Whore, Anne Boleyn, the threats and veiled coercion, followed by a sort of uneasy tolerance, a truce, when he offered me a conditional love wherein I must betray my conscience, my most deeply cherished beliefs, and my own mother's sainted memory, and capitulate where she herself had held firm, if I wanted to bask in the sun of his love again.

To my everlasting shame, though I would hate myself for it ever afterward, I gave in to their barrage of threats. The Duke of Norfolk himself took a menacing step toward me and informed me that if I were his daughter he would bash my head against the wall until it was as soft as a baked apple to cure me of my stubbornness. And haunted by accounts of those who had already died for their resistance, including Sir Thomas More and cartloads of nuns and monks, I signed the documents they laid before me. "Lady Mary's Submission," they called it. I signed and thus declared my mother's marriage a sin, incestuous and unlawful in the sight of God and man, and myself the bastard spawn born of it. Even though my most trusted advisor, the Spanish Ambassador, urged me to sign and save myself, assuring me that a victim of force would be blameless in God's sight, and that since I signed under duress, in fear for my very life, the Pope would grant me absolution, such assurances did not ease my conscience or assuage my guilt, and my body began to mirror my mind's suffering. My stomach rebelled against all food, my hair began to fall out, and I suffered the agonies of the damned with megrims, monthly cramps, palpitations of the heart, and toothache, and before I was twenty I was known throughout Europe as "the most unhappy lady in Christendom", and the tooth-drawer had wrenched out most of the teeth Father had once called "pretty as pearls", leaving my face with a pinched, sunken expression and a close-mouthed smile that was purposefully tight-lipped. It was a miracle I survived, and I came wholeheartedly to believe that God had spared my life so that I might do important work in His name.

I betrayed everything I held sacred and dear just to walk in the sun of my father's love again, but it was never the same, and that, I think, was my penance, my punishment. It wasn't the old welcoming, all-embracing warmth that had enveloped me like a sable cloak on a cold winter's day; it was a weak, wavering, watery-yellow sunbeam that only cast a faint buttery hue, a faltering wispy frail fairy-light of yellow, onto the snow on a bone-chilling day. Just a tantalizing little light of love that left me always yearning for more, like a morsel of food given to a starving man only inflames his appetite. It was never enough compared to what had been before. But when I signed I did not know this. I was full to overflowing with hope when, in a presence chamber packed with courtiers, I knelt humbly before my scowling, glowering father and kissed the wide square toe of his white velvet slipper, slashed through with blood-red satin, reminding me of all the blood he had spilled and that it was always in his power to take my life upon a moment's fancy. After I kissed his shoe I sat up upon my knees, like a dog begging, my tear-filled eyes eager and beseeching, and told him earnestly that I would rather be a servant in his house than empress of the world and parted from him.

But there were many years of pain and humiliation that preceded my surrender and self-abasement.

For seven years, and against all the odds, The Great Whore led my father on a merry dance that made him the scandal and laughing stock of Europe and turned the world as I had known it upside down. She swept through my life as chaotic, destructive, merciless, and relentless as the ten plagues of Egypt and *nothing* would ever be the same again. Like a mastiff attacking a baited bear, she tore away all that I held dear. "All or Nothing" was her motto and she meant it. She took my father's love away from me and worked her dark magic to transform it into hatred and mistrust; she broke my mother's heart and banished her to die in brokenhearted disgrace in lonely, neglected exile; she took my title of "Princess" and my place as heiress to the throne away from me and gave it to her own red-haired bastard brat; she even took my house away, my beautiful Beaulieu, and gave it to the brother who would loyally let her lead him to the scaffold after his own wife revealed details of their incestuous romance. I remember her sitting on the arm of Father's golden throne, with diamond hearts in her luxuriant black hair, worn unbound like a virgin as her vanity's emblem, whispering lies into his ear, poisoning his mind against me, exacting a promise, because she knew how much it meant to me, that in his lifetime he would never allow me to marry lest my husband challenge the rights of the children she would bear him. I remember how she laughed and threw back her head as he reached up to caress her swan-slender neck, encircled by a necklace of ruby and diamond hearts. The rubies glistened like fresh blood in the candlelight. The sight made me shudder and I had to turn away.

Like the "Ash Girl" in the story my nurse used to tell me, who was made to be a servant to her stepsisters, I was made to serve as a nursemaid to the puking and squalling "Little Bastard" who had taken my place in our father's heart and usurped my birthright, my title and inheritance.

Elizabeth. I saw her come into this world with a gush of blood between The Great Whore's legs at the expense of the heart's blood of my mother and myself. I was made to bear witness to her triumphant arrival as Anne Boleyn, even on her bed of pain, raised her head to gloat and torment me, the better to conceal her own disappointment at failing to keep the promise she had made to give Father a son. But Father was still so besotted with her that, though disappointed by the child's sex, he forgave her.

To please Anne, Father had heralds parade through the corridors of Greenwich and announce that I was now a bastard and no longer to be addressed or acknowledged as Princess; Elizabeth was now England's only princess. My servants were ordered to line up and Anne's uncle, the Duke of Norfolk himself, walked up and down their ranks, ripping my blue and green badge from their liveries. And Anne's father, Thomas Boleyn, announced that when they had been fashioned each would be given a badge of Elizabeth's to replace mine, to show that they were now in her service. As I stood silently by and watched, my face burned with shame and each time another badge was torn away I felt as if I had been slapped.

Elizabeth. I should have hated her. But Christian charity would not allow me to hate an innocent child. No, that is not entirely true; my heart would not let me hate her. And no child should be held accountable or blamed for the sins of its mother, not even such a one as that infamous whore and Satan's strumpet, Anne Boleyn.

At seventeen, the age I was when Elizabeth was born, I longed more than anything to be a wife and mother, and when I saw that scrunched-up, squalling, pink-faced bundle of ire, with the tufts of red hair feathering her scalp, my arms ached to hold her. I could barely contain myself; I had to almost sit on my hands to keep from reaching out and begging to hold her.

Even when I was stripped of all my beloved finery – even made to surrender the dear golden frog and enamelled lily pad ring Father had given me, and the little gold cross with a splinter of the True Cross inside it that had belonged first to my grandmother and then to my mother before she had given it to me on that oh so special sixth birthday – and forced to make do with a single plain black cloth gown and white linen apron, and to tuck my hair up under a plain white cap just like a common maidservant, and made to sleep in a mean little room in the servants' attic, cramped and damp, with stale air and a ceiling so low, even petite as I was I could not stand up straight, still I could not hate Elizabeth. Even when I sickened and wasted away to skin and bones for want of food – I dared not eat lest The Great Whore send one of her lackeys to poison me – I could not hate, blame, or resent Elizabeth. Not even when I was wakened from a deep, exhausted sleep and brought in to change her shit-soiled napkins, I did not protest and wrinkle my nose up and turn away fastidiously, but humbly bent to the task and did what was required of me. And when her teeth started to come in – oh what pain those dainty pearls brought her! – I went without sleep and walked the floors all night with her in my arms, crooning the Spanish lullabies my mother had sung to me. Even when I was forced to walk in the dust or trudge through the mud alongside, but always three steps behind, while she rode in a sumptuous gilt and velvet-cushioned litter, dressed in splendid little gowns encrusted with embroidery, jewels, and pearls, while I went threadbare and wore the soles off my shoes as I stumbled and stubbed my toes over ruts and rocks or got mired in the mud, still my heart was filled with love for Elizabeth.

I relished each opportunity to bathe, feed, and dress her, to change her soiled napkins, rub salve onto her sore gums, tuck her into bed, coax and encourage her first steps as I held on to her leading strings, promising never to let go, and the wonderful afternoons when I was allowed to lead her around the courtyard on her first pony. And when she spoke her first word, a babyish rendition of my name – "Mare-ee" – my heart felt as if it had leapt over the moon. I loved Elizabeth; her leading strings were tied to my heart. Serving her was never the ordeal they intended it to be, for I *knew* who I was – I was a princess in disguise, just like in a fairy tale, and someday the truth would be revealed and all that was lost restored to me.

Sometimes I told myself I was practising for the day when I would be married and a mother myself, but I was also lying to myself as with each year my hopes and dreams, like sands from an hourglass, slipped further away from me even as I strained and tried with all my might to hold on to them until I felt all was lost and imagined I was watering their grave with my tears. For what man would have me? My father had declared me a bastard when his minion, the so-called Archbishop of Canterbury, Thomas Cranmer, dissolved his marriage to my mother. And though I dreamed, I never really dared hope that someday someone would fall in love with me. Love was the stuff of songs and stories and, for me, as elusive as a unicorn. Sometimes, I know better than any who has ever walked this earth, no matter how much you want something, you still cannot have it.

And the promise of beauty I had, as a child, possessed had failed to ripen into reality; it had deserted me in my years of grief, fear, and peril. My first grey hair sounded the death knell to my last lingering hope that I might someday attract a suitor. I was seventeen, and a scullery maid who was secretly sympathetic to my plight was brushing out my hair before I retired to my comfortless cot for another miserable night. She gave a little gasp and stopped suddenly, and I turned to see a stricken, sad look in her eyes. Mutely, she brought my hair round over my shoulder so I could see the strand of grey, standing out starkly like a silver thread embroidered on auburn silk. I nodded resignedly. What else could I do but accept it? "Bleached by sorrow," I sighed, and thanked her for her kind ministrations and went to my bed, but secretly, after I had blown the candle out, with the thin coverlet pulled up over my head, I cried myself to sleep as I said farewell to and buried one more dream.

But I had my faith to keep me strong. My mother always inspired great loyalty and love in those who knew her, thus she was able to find someone willing to take the risk and carry secret words of comfort to me. "Trust in God and keep faith in Him and the Holy Virgin and you will *never* be alone," she lovingly counselled me. "Even though we are divided in body, remember whenever you kneel to say your prayers, I will *always* be right there beside you in spirit. Faith in Our Lord and the Blessed Virgin are the ties that bind. Always remember that, my darling daughter. And God *never* gives us more than we can bear. Sometimes He tests us, to show us how strong we really are, and that, as we have faith in Him, so too does He have faith in us, and wants us to have faith in ourselves."

I was holding Elizabeth, then aged three, on May 19, 1536, when the Tower guns boomed to let Father, and all of England, know that he was free and the spell of the witch-whore had been broken. Elizabeth was now motherless, just like me. There we sat, a faded spinster in a threadbare black gown grown thin and shiny at the elbows and ragged at the hem, with a maid's plain white cap to hide her thinning hair, and a porridge-stained apron, and a vibrant, precocious toddler in pearl-embellished sunset-orange and gold brocade to complement the flame-bright curls tumbling from beneath a cap lovingly embroidered in golden threads by The Great Whore who had given life to her.

Now it was Elizabeth's turn to be a disgraced bastard accounted of no importance. And as fast as she was growing, soon she too would be in shabby clothes. Father wanted to forget, so I doubted money would be provided to keep her in fine array, so soon it would be goodbye to brocade and pearls. Our mothers were dead, mine a saint gone straight to Heaven and hers a whore and a witch gone straight to Hell – and our father had turned his back on us and called down the winter's gloom and chill to replace the warm sun of the love he had once given in turn to each of us. Now all we had was each other.

I wasn't with my mother when she died. When her body was laid open by the embalmers they found her heart had turned quite black and a hideous growth embraced it. I have often wondered whether it was some slow-acting poison administered by one of The Great Whore's minions or a broken heart pining for her Henry that killed her. She died declaring that her eyes desired my father above all things.

On the day my mother was entombed, Anne Boleyn's doom was sealed when she miscarried the son who would have been her saviour. Father's eye had already lighted on wholesome and pure, sweet Jane Seymour, a plain and pallid country buttercup to The Boleyn Whore's bold and tempestuous red rose. Her earnest simplicity and genuine modesty had completely won his heart, and it was only a matter of time; we all knew The Great Whore's days were numbered, and the number was not a great one. I saw it as divine retribution, an eye for an eye, a life for a life. Anne Boleyn, whether some lackey in her employ had administered a killing dose or not, was responsible for my mother's death, for which she dressed in sun-bright yellow to celebrate and insisted that Father do the same, thus, it was only fitting that her own life be cut short and a truly worthy woman take her place at Father's side.

As I sat there rocking Elizabeth, hugging her tight against my breast, I remembered the last time I saw my mother. Dressed for travel, in the courtyard, with her litter and a disrespectfully small entourage awaiting nearby, she knelt and pressed into my hands a little book of the letters of Saint Jerome and her own treasured ivory rosary, which had belonged to her own mother, the beads grown creamy with age and the caressing fingers of these two strong and devout Spanish queens.

"God only tests those He cherishes, in order to strengthen them and their virtues," she said to me, and then she embraced and kissed me. I never saw her again.

It was Jane Seymour who would work a miracle and persuade Father to see me. And as I knelt to kiss his foot, I saw from the corner of my eye her rust-red velvet gown and gold and black lattice-patterned kirtle as she stood meekly beside him. It was she who nodded encouragingly and looked at him with pleading eyes as I knelt there with bated breath awaiting my fate.

And then, after a tense glowering silence that seemed to hover like an executioner's axe above my head, he gave his hand to me, and I saw upon his finger the great ruby known as the Regal of France, famous for its brilliance that was said to light up even the dark, that had once adorned the now desecrated and demolished shrine of Thomas Becket at Canterbury. Father had had it made into a ring, and for the rest of his life would wear it as a symbol of his mastery over the Church, flaunting the fact that he had kicked the Pope out of England and had enriched himself with "Papist spoils" when the monasteries were dissolved and the lands parcelled out, sold or gifted to favoured courtiers, and the monks and nuns who had done so much good, dispensing alms, succouring the poor, and tending the sick, were turned out to become beggars and vagabonds themselves. I recoiled, sickened, at the sight of that glowing blood-red ring and feared I would vomit all over his feet; it took all of my will to take his hand and kiss it. I knew my submission was yet another betrayal of God, my mother, and our beliefs.

But I did it. And his face broke out in a triumphant smile. He raised me to my feet, embraced me, and kissed me. And, at his urging, Jane Seymour did the same. I was allowed to sit on the dais, on the top step, at their feet, and the woman Father called his "Gentle Jane" soon became one of the dearest friends I have ever had. She did much to further my cause. In time, all my manor houses and lands were restored to me, the jewels that had been taken from me were returned, along with some that had belonged to my mother that The Great Whore had stolen, my old servants came back, and Father personally selected fine horses for me. I was given pets, Italian greyhounds and a parrot, and even for my first birthday after my return to favour, a female fool to entertain me and enliven the dull hours, and Father also chose a talented band of musicians to join my household. Queen Jane helped me with my wardrobe; old gowns were refurbished, and many new ones ordered. We sat together for hours scrutinizing the wares the London mercers laid before us. And she gave me a diamond ring from her own finger that I would forever cherish.

She had a generous heart and was kind to everyone, even Elizabeth. Treading with great delicacy and care, she engineered Elizabeth's return to court and had her too-short-even-with-the-hems-turned-down bursting-at-the-seams gowns and pinching, parchment-thin-soled shoes replaced. What fun we had dressing her, each of us pretending that our deeply cherished dream of motherhood had come true and she was our very own little girl to clothe and choose pretty things for.

When I thanked Queen Jane for her kindness, she said to me: "Verily, I could not do otherwise. When I look at her I think if I had a daughter and some misfortune were to befall me, and I could not be there to see her grow up, I would hope that my successor, whoever she was, would be kind to her. There but for the grace of God, My Lady Mary, there but for the grace . . ."

When she was with child and craving cucumbers and quails, Father took care of the birds, sending as far away as Calais for them, while I sent her baskets brimming with cucumbers from my own country gardens.

I wept an ocean when she died. Even though her death gave Father his most heartfelt desire – a son, my brother, Edward – I still keenly felt her loss. Because of her kind heart, I was a princess again in all but name.

Other wives followed, but none stayed very long. And in between queens I was the first lady of the land, privileged to sit at

Father's side, presiding over the court, with everyone bowing, smiling, and deferring to me, and there was even occasionally talk that a marriage might be arranged for me, but, alas, nothing ever came of that.

After Jane Seymour came the Lady Anne of Cleves, a German Protestant princess, a heretic, but a merry soul with a heart of gold. One could not help liking her, even though the cleanliness and odours of her person and the dowdiness of her clothes left much to be desired. But Father could not stomach to lie with her and she obligingly, no doubt fearing the headsman's axe if she did not graciously acquiesce, exchanged the role of queen for that of adopted sister and a substantial income that would allow her to lead the life of an independent lady of means.

And after Anne came the one people chuckled behind their hands about and called "the old man's folly", pert and wanton Catherine Howard with only fifteen years to Father's fifty. I felt so embarrassed for him! I marvelled that he could not see how she demeaned his majesty. She made him the butt of jests and remarks that ran the gamut from pitying to lewd. She meant to be kind, I am sure, but she could not curb her exuberance; she did not understand that being a queen meant one must comport oneself with dignity. Though I was some years older than she, and to call her my stepmother felt supremely awkward, she tried to befriend me, being overfamiliar as though she were my own sister, one with whom I had grown up in close intimacy, sharing everything. She would brazenly and openly discuss the most intimate things with no regard for modesty or propriety.

She could not believe that I had reached the ripe old age of twenty-four without ever having had a sweetheart, and would prod me incessantly, over and over again, asking incredulously, "You mean you *never* had a sweetheart, *never?*" And when I answered, alas, God had not so deemed to bless me, she embraced me and bemoaned the tragedy of my fate, then, blinking away her tears and tossing back her auburn curls, determinedly said we must do something to remedy it.

She arranged a masque for my birthday wherein a number of particularly handsome young men, whom she had chosen herself, were costumed as various flowers, dressed in shimmering satins and silks of the proper colours festooned with lace and embroideries and intricate silk renditions of the blooms they had been chosen to represent.

"We need a little springtime even in the chill of February!" the hoydenish young queen declared as she whooped and kicked up her heels and bade this garden of living posies to encircle and dance around me.

I remember there was a graceful pink gillyflower, a deep red rose who was rather bold, a haughty regal violet, a jaunty daffodil, a bluebell whose costume was cunningly devised to include tiny tinkling bells, a marigold whose tawny locks brought back memories of my youth, a flamboyant heart's-ease pansy, a perky pink, a bashful buttercup, a profusely blossoming lavender, a rather indecent goldenrod who brushed me from behind to draw my attention to the prominent golden bloom sprouting from his loins, and a demure – by comparison to the rest – daisy. As they danced around me they each offered me silken flowers taken from their attire and sang, "Choose me, pretty maiden, do!"

Roses of vivid pink embarrassment bloomed in my cheeks and I desired nothing more than to break the dancing ring moving around me and escape to the privacy of my bedchamber. I disliked being the centre of such attentions, and there was a nagging suspicion at the heart of me that they were mocking and making cruel sport of me, the pathetic Lady Mary who was no longer young and had never been pretty like the Queen. Katherine crept up behind me and tied a kerchief over my eyes and spun me round and round until I staggered dizzily and feared I might disgrace myself by being sick, then gave me a shove into the arms of the nearest gentleman.

"Ah, heart's-ease, that brings back memories, does it not, my dear Derham?" she teasingly addressed the vividly costumed gentleman who held me in his arms and had just removed my blindfold so I could see him smiling down at me with a set of very fine, even white teeth.

She drew me aside for a moment before we paired off for dancing and whispered wicked but kindly meant words in my ear, telling me that if I were so minded to meddle with a man, she knew of ways to prevent conception. I was appalled that she would speak of such, and even more so that she would possess such knowledge, and with flaming cheeks I pulled away from her and fled, forsaking the chance to dance with Master Derham.

Time would later disclose that, despite her youth, Catherine Howard had been a rather enthusiastic gardener herself, and that of the bevy of handsome fellows who had danced around me that night, two of them were known to have been her lovers. Francis Derham was purposefully costumed as heart's-ease as a reminder of a silken flower he had once given his common-law wife – the Queen – a fact unbeknownst to Father, who called that wanton little guttersnipe his "Rose Without a Thorn". And even at that time she was dallying with the daffodil – Thomas Culpepper, Father's favourite bodyservant, who so tenderly ministered to his poor, sore and ulcerated legs.

She gave me a gold pomander ball studded with turquoises and rubies for my birthday, but I made a point of losing it. I wanted nothing from that foolish girl and hoped that perhaps some poor soul might find it and benefit from the sale of so costly a bauble.

It was only a matter of time before the truth came out and she died on the scaffold for her sins and Father was plunged into a deep, dark depression from which I feared he would never emerge.

But emerge he did, to take a sixth and final wife, the one who would nurse and care for him for the remainder of his life. He began and ended his married life with a Catherine. Both Catherine of Aragon and Catherine Parr were kind, clever, strong, and capable women. And though I liked her well, and she did much for my sister and me, seeing that Elizabeth received a formidable education every bit as good as that given to our brother, and persuading Father to reinstate us in the succession so we could both be called "Princess" again, still I mistrusted Kate on account of her Reformist beliefs. Though she kept it discreetly veiled, she was in truth a Protestant, a heretic, and encouraged my brother and sister to follow this path, which would lead them away from the *true* religion.

This made me both fearful and sad. I wanted to right the wrongs Father had wrought at The Great Whore's instigation. I wanted to go back in time to a place of greater safety, to the tranquillity and traditions of my childhood, and the indescribably blissful feeling of rightness and a well-ordered world. I remembered the love, the peace, the sense of security and serenity I had felt when I walked, dressed in pearls, between my parents, who loved each other and loved me, and went hand in hand with them to kneel and worship God, to witness the miracle when the priest held the Host aloft and the bread became the body of Jesus Christ, our Saviour. There was nothing better and nothing else like it in the world, and I wanted my siblings to know and share it; I wanted faith to unite us, not tear us apart. The comfort of the Latin litanies, the adoring hymns writ to praise Him, the Miracle of the Mass, the Elevation of the Host, the comforting clickety-clack of rosary beads moving smooth and cool beneath devout fingers, the swinging censers filling the chapel with fragrant incense, the sprinkling of holy water, the flickering candles that reminded us that God is the light of the world, the crucifixes and statues, the tapestries and jewel-hued stained-glass windows depicting scenes from the Bible, the embroidered altar cloths, the golden chalices, the embroidered vestments the priests wore, the beautiful things offered up to worship, glorify, and adore God and His saints and the Blessed Virgin, and the relics and shrines and the miracles they wrought: the blind made to see, and the lame to walk. I wanted my siblings to behold, marvel, and adore all these sacred things. And the knowledge, and the comfort it gave, that all who believed and followed the true faith walked with God, and walked in love, and never walked alone. More than *anything*, I wanted to give this special and most precious gift, this beautiful and blissful serene sense of well-being and peace, to my siblings and every other man, woman, and child who lived and breathed, to restore it to the people of England from whom it had been violently and most cruelly taken away. And as I sat keeping vigil at Father's deathbed, I *knew* then that this was my divinely appointed mission. I was ready and God would not find me wanting; I would dedicate my life to it.

2

Elizabeth

Nothing lasts forever, and everyone says "goodbye", even if they don't actually say it because they don't have the chance or choose not to out of cruelty, cowardice, or spite; it is not a question of "if", it is only a matter of "when". L'amaro e il dolce – the bitter and the sweet. Life is not a banquet; we cannot always pick and choose of which dishes we wish to partake; we have to take the bitter and the sweet, the bland and the savoury, the delicious and the detestable.

Sage? Philosophical? Poetic? Lofty? Call them what you will. These thoughts have often run like a raging river through my life. As my father lay dying they crashed violently against the rocks of my mind until I thought the pain would knock me to the floor, gasping and clutching my head in the throes of a violent megrim. He had, like a river himself, mighty and majestic, beautiful and horrible, tranquil or terrifying, the power to destroy any who dared cross him, sweeping them aside or pulling them down to drown. When I was a little girl I thought he was invincible, but by thirteen I was old enough to understand that Time and Death conquer all that live; kings are no exception to the rule, merely mortals God infuses with a little of His divinity and power. A crown is a God-given gift, and the one to whom it is given wields the power that comes with it for the good of all, not just for personal wealth and glory.

I could still remember a time before the very mention of my name, let alone a glimpse of me, was enough to make my father roar and lash out like a wounded lion. For the first three years of my life I was adored, a true princess, in title, and in the way others treated me, with bows and flattery and words spoken in soft, deferential tones.

I vividly remember a day when all the court was dressed in sunny yellow, all was jubilation and celebration, but I couldn't understand why. When I asked her, my lady-governess said, "No, My Lady Princess, today is not a holiday," but would not say more and sternly forbade me to ask my parents. I too was dressed in a gown of gaudy yellow, sewn all over with golden threads and sparkling yellow gems like miniature suns themselves that seemed to wink mischievously at me whenever the light struck them. I loved watching the big round yellow jewels set in golden suns on the toes of my shoes peep out and flash and wink at me with every step I took so that my lady-governess had to scold me to walk properly like a princess and hold myself erect instead of stooped over like a hunchback as she escorted me to the Great Hall where my great golden giant of a father, as big and bright as the sun itself he seemed to me then, swept me up onto his shoulder and paraded me about, showing me off to all his court.

My mother was there too, her belly bulging round like a ball beneath the sunshine-yellow brocade of her gown. My father smiled and patted her stomach and said this, at long last, would be the Tudor sun the soothsayers had predicted would come to shine over England.

"It was supposed to be you, Bess," he smilingly chided me. "My son has certainly taken his time in coming, but he is well worth waiting for."

He patted my mother's stomach again. "Herein sleeps your brother, Bess, England's next king. Guard him well, Madame, guard him well," he told my mother, and though the words were said in a laughing, jocular tone there was no laughter in his eyes; they were as hard as blue marble. And there was fear in hers when she heard them, racing like a frightened animal trapped in a room it yearns to flee, running frantically from end to end, across and back, up and down, even though it knows there is no escape. Though she tried to hide it behind her smile I saw the fear full plain even though I did not understand it at the time.

Then we were off again, parading round the room. My father tore the little yellow cap from my head and tossed it high into the air.

"Take off that cap and show the world that Tudor-red hair, Bess, my red-haired brat!"

And I shook my head hard, shaking out my curls to show them all that I was Great Harry's red-haired brat and proud of it.

Even the marzipan was gilded that day and he let me eat all I wanted. Then a big yellow dragon came prancing in, all trimmed with red, gold, and green, with the players' dancing legs in motley-coloured hose with bells on their toes peeking out from beneath the swaying yellow silk and gilded and painted body. But it was no ordinary dragon like I had seen at other revels. Instead of a fearsome, toothy gaping mouth and menacing red eyes, its painted papier-mâché face was a woman's, sadly serene like the face of Our Lord's mother, the face of a woman who would feel deeply the sorrows of the world and feel its weight profoundly perched upon her shoulders. I heard someone say her name was Katherine. I didn't know it then, I was too little to understand, that it was my sister Mary's mother, Catherine of Aragon, the proud princess from Spain who had died vowing that her eyes desired my father above all things. Instead of mourning a strong and valiant woman, who had been despite her petite stature a tower of strength and conviction, we were celebrating her demise by eating gilded marzipan, laughing, dancing, and cutting capers, while dressed in the brightest gaudy yellow imaginable. Years later when I discovered the truth about that day I felt sick; every time I thought of it after that I wanted to vomit up all the marzipan I had eaten that day even though it had all happened years ago.

My father swept me up and bounded over to the dragon. He drew his sword and gave me the jewelled dagger from his belt.

"Come on, Bess, let's slay this dragon!" he cried, and laughing, we both struck out at the dancing, capering beast until it fell with a great groan onto the floor, sprawling conquered at our feet.

"That's my girl!" He hugged me close and kissed my cheek, and buried his face in my bright red curls. "My Bess is as brave as any boy!" he declared. Then he threw me up into the air and caught me when I came down, my yellow skirts billowing like a buttercup about me. "Praise be to God," he cried as he spun us round and round. "The old harridan is dead and we are free from all threat of war! The Emperor Charles can kiss my arse!" he shouted, causing all the court to roar and rock with laughter. And I laughed too even though I did not understand.

But I wasn't just Great Harry's red-haired brat; I was Anne Boleyn's daughter too. I have seen her portrait hidden away in musty palace attics, and when I look at myself in the mirror, only my flame-red hair, and the milk-pale skin that goes with it, are Tudor. All the rest of me is Anne Boleyn – the shape of my face, my dark eyes and their shape, my nose, my lips, my long-fingered musician's hands, even my long, slender neck. That is why, I think, for so many years my father could not stand the sight of me, and even after I was welcomed, albeit reluctantly at first, back to court, I would catch him watching me, and there would be something in his eyes, as if he were a man who had just seen a ghost. I was the living, breathing shade of someone he had loved enough to change the world to wed and then hated enough to kill; in my parents' marriage the pendulum swung from love to hate without the middle ground of indifference in between. I think that was also why I had the ability to so easily provoke his rage, even when I did not mean to, thus giving him an excuse, when the sight of Anne Boleyn's living legacy became too much for him, to send me away from court, back to Hatfield.

"Back to Hatfield" was a phrase I heard many times throughout my childhood, spoken morosely by me, my lady-governess, or stepmother of the moment, or in a thundering roaring red-black rage by my father.

I'm not supposed to remember her, but I do. Everyone thought I was so young that I would forget. Most of my memories are blurred and fleeting, the kind where I strain and strive to hold on to them and bring them into sharper focus but, alas, I cannot. It is like gazing at one's reflection upon the surface of a still, dark blue-black pool onto which someone then abruptly drops a stone, caus-ing the image to break and blur. But there is one day I remember very well, though some of the details are lost or hazy. I cannot re-call it moment by moment, word by word, but what I do remember is vividly crisp and clear, etched diamond-sharp into my memory.

A spring day in the garden at Greenwich, my mother was dressed all in black satin, and her hair, long, thick, and straight, hung all the way down to her knees like a shimmering, glossy cloak of ink-black silk. She knelt and held out her arms to me, and I toddled into them, a baby still uncertain on my feet, learning to walk like a lady in a stiff brocade court gown, leather stays, and petticoats, with pearls edging my square-cut bodice "just like Maman!" I crowed happily when I noticed the similarity.

She laughed and swept me up into her arms and spun round and round. Suddenly she stopped, looking up at the window above, where my father stood frowning down at us, his face dark and dan-gerous, like a thundercloud. Even from far away I felt the heat of his anger. I whimpered and started to cry, the murderous intensity of his gaze having struck such terror into my little heart. And in my mother's eyes . . . a wild, hunted look, like a doe fleeing from a huntsman and a pack of hounds. In later years, when I first heard the poem by Thomas Wyatt, the poet who was said to have loved her, in which he likened her to a hunted deer, I would be cata-pulted back to that moment and the look in her eyes, and see my father as a mighty huntsman poised to strike the killing blow.

"*Never surrender!*" my mother said to me that day, an adamant, intense, ferocity endowing each word. "Be mistress of your own fate, Elizabeth, and let *no man* be your master!"

Uncle George, her brother, was waiting for her. She beckoned to my lady-governess and set me down and went to join him. He put his arms around her and she laid her head upon his shoulder, and leaned welcomingly into him as they walked away. I never saw her again.

Then there came a day when I heard the Tower guns boom, rat-tling the diamond-paned glass in the windows like thunder. I was sitting on my sister Mary's lap. She hugged me close and kissed my brow.

"We are both bastards now, poppet," she whispered, and told me that my mother was dead, but I didn't understand. Mary shook her head and refused to say more. "Not now, poppet, not now; later, when you are old enough to understand." Then she began to sing a Spanish lullaby as she rocked me on her lap.

But I knew something was very wrong, I felt it in my bones, and when the servants started addressing me as "My Lady Elizabeth" instead of "My Lady Princess", that confirmed my suspicions that something was very wrong indeed. And when they thought I was beyond hearing, some even referred to me as "The Little Bastard", though when I asked what that word meant, faces flushed and voices stammered and the subject was hastily changed or I was given candy or cake or offered a song or a story or a new doll to distract me.

My world had changed overnight but I could not understand why and no one would tell me. "Where is my mother?" I asked over and over and over again, but all those about me would say, with averted eyes, was that she was gone and I must forget her and never mention her again. She never came to visit me any more, when she used to come so often, and the gifts of pretty caps and dresses stopped, and when I outgrew those I had there were lengthy delays before other garments, nowhere near as fine and not crafted from a mother's love, finally came to replace them. I used to feel her love for me in every stitch, but now that was gone; these new clothes were made by a stranger's hands. I didn't understand it; did this mean she no longer loved me? And there were no more of the music lessons where either she or Uncle George – and where was he? – would take me on their lap and guide my fingers over the strings. And she had only just begun teaching me to dance. Where was she? Why did she not come to visit me any more? Why wouldn't anyone tell me?

Then one day I heard the chambermaids gossiping as they were making my bed. I had come back to get the pretty doll, the last one she had given me, in a gown made from scraps left from one of her very own dresses, its bodice and French hood trimmed with pearls just like hers. I stood there silent and still, with tears running down my face, unbeknownst to them, and heard it all. When they told how the French executioner – imported from Calais as a token of the great love my father had once felt for her – had struck off her head in one swift stroke, I screamed and ran at them, kicking and biting, pummelling them with my tiny fists, and scratching them with my little fingernails. The physician had to give me something to quiet me. That was the last time I let my emotions get the better of me; it was also the last time I mentioned my mother. I put my doll away, at the bottom of a chest, tenderly and lovingly wrapped in a length of red silk with a lavender and rose petal sachet, and vowed never to surrender and never to forget. I would never give any man the power to act as a living god and ordain my fate – life or death at his sufferance or fancy. *Never surrender!* I burned those words into my brain and engraved them on my heart.

Afterwards, a parade of stepmothers passed fleetingly through my life. Most had pity in their eyes when they looked at me, and tried, though it was not their fault, to atone for what my father had done, and give me their best imitation of a mother's love.

First pale, prim Jane Seymour, whose shyness made her seem cold and aloof. She died giving my father the son he had always longed for. When Mary took my hand and led me in to see our new little brother, lying in his golden cradle, bundled against the cold in purple velvet and ermine, Jane Seymour lay as listless and quiet as a corpse upon her bed, as still and white as a marble tomb effigy. Her skin looked so like wax I wondered that she did not melt; the heat from the fire was such that pearls of sweat beaded my own brow and trickled down my back. I was four years old then and fully understood what death meant. And in that moment my mind forged a new link in the chain between surrender, marriage, and death – childbirth. It was another peril that came when a woman surrendered and put her life in a man's hands.

When Mary and I walked in the funeral procession, two of twenty-nine slow and solemn ladies – one for each year of Jane Seymour's life – with bowed heads and hands clasped around tall, flickering white tapers, all of us clad in the simple, stark death-black dresses and snow-white hoods that meant the deceased had died in childbirth, I vowed that I would never marry. Later, when I told her, Mary shook her head and scoffed at this childish non-sense, hugging me close and promising that I would forget all about this foolish fancy when I was old enough to understand what being a wife and mother meant; it was something that every woman wanted. I bit my tongue and kept my own counsel, but I knew that my conviction would never waver; God would be the only man to ever have the power of life and death over me. And as I knelt in chapel before Jane Seymour's catafalque, I looked up at the cross and swore it as a vow, a pact between God and myself. He would be my heavenly master and I would always bow to His will, but I would have no earthly master force his will upon me.

Then came jolly German Anne of Cleves, always pink-cheeked and smiling, a platter of marzipan and candied fruits, like edible jewels, always within reach. She even wore a comfit box on a jew-elled chain about her waist so that she would never be without her sweets. I helped her with her English and she taught me German, and was the soul of patience when helping me with my much hated sewing. But I had no sooner learned to care for her than she was gone, supplanted by flighty, foolish, vain, but oh so beautiful Catherine Howard.

I was amazed to learn that she was but a few years older than me; I was seven and she was a tender fifteen to my father's half century when they married. When I heard that she was my mother's cousin I was so excited and eager to meet her, I bobbed on my toes like an ill-bred peasant child, bursting with impatience and craning my neck to catch a glimpse of her. Yet when at last I stood before her I looked in vain for any resemblance to my slim, elegant mother in that plump-breasted, auburn-haired, green-eyed, pouty cherry-lipped little nymph whom my father called his "Rose Without a Thorn" in token of what he saw as her pure, un-trammelled innocence. Though she was indeed beautiful, she had none of my mother's elegance, intelligence, and sophistication; she was more like an illiterate country bumpkin dressed up in silks and satins. And though the court looked askance at her impetuous, impulsive ways, my father adored her.

I remember once, one rare occasion when I was allowed to stay up as late as I wished for some court celebration – "Oh do let her!"

my flighty young stepmother implored, and my father was so besotted he could not resist her. As the dawn broke, Catherine Howard suddenly tore off her shoes and stockings, flinging them aside with careless abandon, not caring where they fell or whether the servants pocketed the pearls and diamonds that trimmed the dainty white velvet slippers, and ran out onto the lawn, like a great length of green velvet spangled with diamonds spread out by an eager London mercer, to dance in the dew in her bare feet, reveling in the feel of the blades of grass tickling her naked soles and tiny pink toes. She threw back her head and laughed and laughed, a silly, giddy girl taking joy in life's simple pleasures, twirling dizzily round and round, lifting her pearl-white skirts higher and higher, much more so than was proper, as she spun around, while my father slapped his thigh and roared with laughter at her antics.

"Come on, join me!" she cried, and some of the more daring ladies shed their shoes and stockings and ran out to dance with her, uttering delighted, startled little shrieks and piglet-squeals at the chilly nip of the dew on their naked toes.

Beside me, my sister Mary gasped, appalled, and looked fit to fall down dead of apoplexy when our stepmother's swirling white skirts rose high enough to give a glimpse of plump dimpled pink-ivory buttocks, but my father clapped his hands and laughed all the harder.

Dressed most often in virgin white dripping with diamonds and pearls so that she looked like an Ice Queen, my father's "Rose Without a Thorn" would sit, stroking her silky-haired spaniel or a big fluffy white cat, or idly twirling her auburn curls around her fingers, and daintily nibbling sweetmeats or languorously trailing her finger through some cream-slathered dish and lingeringly sucking it off, always appearing distant and bored, yawning and indolent, unless there was a handsome gallant nearby whom she could bat her eyelashes at and exchange coy, flirtatious banter with. Children and female company often seemed to bore her, though she was always kind to me. The only time she seemed to ever really stir herself was to dance, and oh how she loved to do that, artfully swirling about, high-spirited, young, and carefree, as she lifted her skirts high to show off her legs and garters, pretending it was an act of exuberant mischance when in truth it was carefully choreographed and practised for hours before a mirror in the privacy of her bedchamber. I knew this for a fact, for she had offered to teach Mary and me, but Mary had gasped in horror and dragged me out the door as fast as if we were fleeing the flames of Hell.

I noticed that a certain courtier, a particularly handsome fellow called Thomas Culpepper, had a most curious effect on her. Whenever he was near, a flush would blossom rose-red in Catherine's cheeks and her bosom would begin to heave beneath the tight-laced, low-cut bodice of her gown until I feared her laces would burst and her breasts spring out, and until he left her presence she would act more distracted and empty-headed than ever. Once when I sat embroidering beside her and Master Culpepper came in, she bade me go and play in the garden as it was such a lovely day when in truth it was pouring down rain.

Then she too was gone, like a butterfly fated to live only a season – her head stricken off just like my mother's, only by an English headsman's weighty, cumbersome axe; there was no French executioner with his sleek and graceful sword for my father's "Rose Without a Thorn". And Master Culpepper's head, I heard, and that of another man, one Francis Derham, adorned spikes on London Bridge, to be pecked and picked clean by the voracious ravens. And people began to tell tales about Catherine's white-gowned ghost running along the corridors of Hampton Court, uttering bloodcurdling screams, begging and pleading for mercy, pounding futilely on the chapel door, as she had done the day my father turned his back and a deaf ear on her.

And I saw again how men and sex and marriage had destroyed another woman who was close to me, in blood if not in affection. My father, acting as a vengeful god on earth, had ordained her death, showing none of the mercy or forgiveness our Heavenly Father might have vouchsafed wanton little Catherine Howard.

"I will never marry," I said to my best friend, Robert Dudley, whom I called Robin, who laughed at me and said he would remind me of my words when he danced with me on my wedding day.

Then, like the answer to a prayer, came Catherine Parr. Kind

Kate, capable Kate, we all called her, a mature, twice-widowed woman with the gift of making everything all right, of solving every problem and soothing every hurt. Fearlessly, she went like an angel into the lion's den and tended my father in his declining years. Never once did her nose wrinkle or disgust show upon her face when she tended his putrid, pus-seeping leg, applying herbal poultices of her own concoction and changing the bandages with comforting and efficient hands. Though it was an open secret that she harboured a strong sympathy for the Protestant religion, deemed heretical by many, including my staunchly Catholic sister, she won Mary's affection and became a loyal friend and loving stepmother to her. And to me . . . She was my saviour! She did more than any other to restore me to my father's good graces. And she took a personal interest in the development of my mind; she was passionate about education for girls, and took it upon herself to personally select my tutors and confer with them over my curriculum. Under her guidance, I studied languages, becoming fluent in a full seven of them, and also mathematics, history, philosophy, the Classics and the writings of the early Church Fathers, architec-ture, and astronomy. Nor were the female accomplishments neglected; equal time was given to dancing, music, and sewing, both practical and ornamental, and also to outdoor pursuits such as riding, hunting, hawking, and archery. But even she brushed her skirts perilously close to Death when she dared argue with my father, contradicting him about religion. A careless hand dropped the warrant for her arrest in the corridor and I found it and brought it to her.

Careful observation had already taught me that my father would always distance himself from those he meant to condemn; he would not deign to face them lest their tears and pleas for mercy sway him. I urged her to go, to save herself before it was too late. I begged her to swallow her pride and throw herself at his feet – so great was my love for her that I implored her to grovel, though the very thought of it sickened me – to claim that she had only dared argue with him to profit from his superior knowledge, to learn from him, and also, as an added boon, to distract him from the pain of his sore leg.

Though I was but a child, she listened to me, and was saved, but I would never forget how close she came to danger, or the power of life and death my father had to wield over her as her sovereign lord, husband, and master. Or the shame that she, one of the torchbearers of enlightenment and reformation, must have felt to have to lower herself in such a manner and humbly declare womankind, whose champion she was, weak and inferior, and that God had created women to serve men, and no female should ever presume to contradict, question, or disobey her husband, father, brother, or indeed any male at all.

Already I knew the value of dissembling for self-preservation. Once my father had favoured women with sharp, clever minds and the gift of intelligent conversation, but after my mother he put docility and beauty first and foremost, so that his last wife, Catherine Parr, must need stifle her intellect and bridle her tongue and play perpetual pupil to my father's teacher. I don't know how she stood it, but it only matters that she survived it.

Six wives . . . four dead and two living. Their history clearly showed me that marriage is the road to doom and destruction for all womankind and affirmed my conviction that never would I walk it; I would go a virgin to my grave. But I also knew, and feared, that there would be times in the years to come when God would test me.

❧ 3 ❧

Mary

"The King is dead. Long live the King!" Edward Seymour, the Duke of Somerset, pronounced in a voice both loud and sombre. Even as Father's minion, that heretical serpent Cranmer, leaned down to close Father's eyes, all other eyes were turning towards the future – pale and weeping little Edward, aged only nine.

He sat there mute and quaking between my sister and me. And then he turned away from me and flung himself into Elizabeth's arms, weeping more, I think, at the enormity of what lay ahead of him than for the loss of our father.

Though Edward had been his greatest treasure, the son he had spent most of his life longing for, Father had never truly taken him under his wing, never forged a bond of friendly father-and-son camaraderie with him; instead, like a priceless jewel, he had locked Edward away, safe under guard with every possible precaution, trying to protect him from any enemy or illness that might threaten the safety of his person and lessen his chance of surviving to adulthood and inheriting the throne. But in doing so, I fear, he made my brother unsympathetic and cold, immune to and unmoved by human suffering.

It hurt me, I confess, to have Edward turn from me instead of to me, and to hide my pain, I went to kneel by Father's bed, to pray for his soul and say a private farewell.

Though I tried hard to hide it, I gagged at the stench, and tears pricked my eyes, but I did my duty and knelt at his side with the ivory rosary beads my sainted mother had given me twined around my hands. Poor Father, he would have much to answer for and, I feared, would linger long in Purgatory.

Tentatively, I reached out and touched the mottled pink-and-grey flesh of his hand. I bowed my head and kissed it and let my tears cleanse it. How often I had prayed for his anger to end, and for his love for me to bloom anew, like the perfect rose it had once been, not the blighted blossom that had struggled along for years after sweet Jane Seymour broke The Great Whore's spell that had held Father captive like Merlin in the cave of crystal.

And now that he was gone, selfishly, I wondered what would become of me. Anne Boleyn's ambition had paved the way for heresy to take root in England. And those roots had grown into tenacious vines that already held those dearest to me – Edward, Elizabeth, and the Dowager Queen Catherine – in their deadly, soul-destroying grasp.

I knew I would be pressured to conform. Most of the men on the Regency Council had profited well by the dissolution of the monasteries. They would be loath to relinquish their ill-gotten gains, and return to Rome all that they had stolen; thus they would encourage this heresy to flourish whilst they stamped and rooted out the *true* religion.

But I would confound them; I would rather give up my life than my religion. And I knew then, with complete and utter certainty, as I knelt beside the corpse of my father, that it was my duty to save the soul of England and, like a good shepherdess, lead these poor lost sheep back to the Pope's flock. I prayed to God to give me, one lone weak and fragile woman, the strength to prevail against the virulent Protestant heresy that had come like a plague to blacken and imperil the souls of the English people, born of ambition and greed, not out of a true but misguided faith. And I knew then, as surely as if a holy beacon of pure white light from Heaven had just shone down upon me, that I had been chosen to guide my country back into the light. I felt a divine presence enfold and embrace me, as if angels knelt on either side of me, enveloping me in their snowy wings, and whispering in my ear that *this* was my purpose, my divine mission in life, the reason I had been born and survived all the perils and pitfalls that had marked and marred my life, and I would rather die a *thousand* deaths than fail our Heavenly Father!

I kissed Father's forehead and stood up. I promised him that I would make right his wrongs, that the sins he had committed out of Satan-sent carnal lust and the wiles of that witch-whore would all be undone. England would again become a nation of altars blazing with candles as a reminder to all that God is the light of the world. I would be His instrument, His light-bearer, and lead my people out of the dark night of heresy!

৵ 4 ৵

Elizabeth

Poor little poppet, I thought as Edward wept in my arms. They will dress you up, put words in your mouth, and make you dance to their tune. And there, intently watching his prey with the same greedy, carrion-hungry jet eyes of a raven, is the puppet-master – Edward Seymour, Duke of Somerset, the Lord Protector of the Realm, who will head the Regency Council, presiding over fifteen equally ambitious, power-hungry men, all of whom would not hesitate to pull him from his lofty pedestal and take his place. Poor little poppet indeed – I patted Edward's back and murmured soothing words – you will have nine years to contend with this before you come into your own and can tell them all to go to the Devil and leave you be to rule your kingdom as you please.

From the shadowy, candlelit gloom of the deathbed they began to step forward, slowly surrounding us, first Seymour, then the other members of the Council, like sharks closing in around a lone sailor clinging to some bit of flotsam as they circle around, hungry for his blood. And I wondered then if my little brother, who was not so robust as he and our late father liked to pretend, had the stamina and spirit to survive until he reached his majority.

Boldly, I stared back at Edward Seymour, meeting those beady, black bird-of-prey eyes, and hugged my brother tighter, wishing I had the power to protect him.

"Edward," I said firmly, pulling away from him. "Look at me," I commanded as I stood up.

"The King is dead," I said, calmly and straightforwardly. "Long live the King." With those words I sank in a deep curtsy before my brother and kissed his trembling hand.

"I am too young to rule!" Edward sobbed.

"But not too young to *reign*," I corrected.

With a gentle pressure of my hand, I urged him to stand beside me.

"You were born for this, Edward," I said, my mind harking back to the three lives, three wives, that had been lost to bring this pale, frail boy into the world. "Your Majesty, it is time for you to greet your Council. These" – I waved a hand to encompass the solemn and stern-faced men who belatedly knelt before the pale, sobbing boy – "are the men who will assist you to govern in your minority and help you acquire the wisdom and skill to rule alone when you are of age."

Edward Seymour came forth then and knelt before my brother, and I knew then that he was doomed. This ruthless man would never let go of the reins of power unless they were snatched from him by force. And my brother, God help him, had not that strength; he would never be more than a puppet king. A shiver snaked up my spine then and told me that Edward would never make old bones; either malaise or malice would send him early to the grave. And then the tears that I had fought so hard to hold back began to flow and, though I tried to stifle it, a sob broke from me.

"God's teeth, stop that blubbering, Bess!" Edward snapped, endeavouring to make his voice sound gruff and deeper as he struck a pompous pose in imitation of our father's favourite stance, hands on hips, legs apart. "I never could abide weeping women! Stop it, I say, I am the King and you must obey me; is that not so, My Lord?" he asked, turning to Edward Seymour for approval.

"Quite right, Your Majesty, quite right." Seymour smiled as the rest of the Council began to praise my brother's resemblance to his sire.

"My brother," I whispered, "though you do not know it, you have just stepped upon a snake in the grass."

"Do not vex me with riddles, Bess, I have not the time for them!" Edward glowered impatiently at me. "Come, gentlemen," he said to his Council and then strode, with them scurrying and smiling after him, in a pompous parody of majesty, from the room where our father lay dead.

Poor Edward, he thought playacting was enough to make him worthy to fill our father's shoes, and those about him would do nothing but encourage him to ape the king they had called "Great Harry". After all, playing and perfecting the part would consume much of Edward's attention, leaving them free to rule the realm as they pleased. It was as if they had taken a portrait of our father down from the wall, cut out the face, and bade Edward stand behind it, with his face poked through, parroting the lines they whispered, like a prompter in a theatre helping the actors to remember their lines. Edward would never be encouraged or allowed to be himself. He would grow up always pretending to be somebody else and in doing so would lose himself before he even knew who he truly was; that was the *real* tragedy of his life and reign.

❧ 5 ❧

Mary

In mourning for Father, I withdrew to the country to live quietly, though always in tense and wary expectation of the storm I expected to break at any moment when my brother and the hell-bound heretics who ruled him would officially outlaw the practise of the true religion in England.

Before he bade me farewell, Edward, with the Lord Protector, Edward Seymour, standing solidly behind him, told me that it was his dearest wish that I would purge my soul of Popish superstitions and cast out of my life all the Papist accoutrements and furbelows that went with it – the rosaries, crucifixes, chalices, candles, plaster saints, holy water, wafers, wine, relics, and censers, and such – and hear the word of God spoken in our own plain, good, wholesome, and unadorned English tongue, rather than the Latin that was the language of priests and scholars and mystified and muddled the minds of the unschooled and ignorant common people, making God more of an aloof stranger and mystery than a real and true presence in their lives. For what good were prayers learned by rote, phonetically, so that those uttering them could not understand? God and His Church did not need to be painted and perfumed and dressed up like a courtesan to be worshipped, Edward stoutly and pompously maintained, striking our father's favourite pose and standing with his hands on his hips and feet planted wide. Better that it be plain and unvarnished, he continued, and nothing but the pure and naked truth.

I was *horrified* to hear my brother comparing my Church to harlotry, and I could not put the shame and fear I felt for his soul into words; I was struck dumb with horror. I was so disappointed in him that I was glad to quit his presence, though not prepared to give up the fight to save his soul; it was clear that Edward needed me. But I knew now was not the time to argue, and that I must choose my battles with care, for if I were defeated at the very start I would fail God and the great work He had saved me for, and Edward's soul would be just one of the many that would be lost.

Though Edward liked to think otherwise, I knew my brother, though he now bore the title of "King" and "Supreme Head of the Church of England" was in reality only a little boy of nine, a child, and as such incapable of making decisions about such monumental matters as religion; he could not even govern himself, much less the consciences of others. I knew these thoughts were being put into his head, and these words, these blasphemies, put into his mouth by greedy, ambitious men who had grown rich off England's break with Rome and the plundered gold and lands of the monasteries. They taught my brother heresy as they would a parrot a repertoire of pretty phrases. The poor child was merely a fountain spouting their gibberish and, to make himself feel more mature and grown-up, he had persuaded himself that he understood and believed what he was saying. And to bolster his ego, those about him encouraged him to see himself as an authority on such matters, and to weigh and expound upon them like a hardened and seasoned judge whose mind brimmed with many years' knowledge and experience. They touted him as a theological scholar like Father had been, but a prodigy because of his tender years and "a virtuous marvel of learning and understanding". He was urged to regard himself as the torchbearer who would lead England into enlightenment and free his people from the shackles of superstition. And it all went to his head and puffed up his pride to bursting so that he became arrogant, overweening, and almost unbearable. He was a pompous little prig, to put it bluntly, who even chastised *me*, a woman of undisputable virtue, for sometimes dancing after dinner and for my enjoyment of card games. He even took me to task about my clothing, describing my dresses as "overly lavish and ornate as your gaudy, overdecorated Church is."

He was determined to start his reign like a great broom sweeping away all the Papist dust and rubbish that lingered in the land; out with the old and in with the new, he extolled like a cock crowing. And I began to hear reports of blasphemous and sacrilegious remarks he had made. "Holy water makes a good sauce for mutton if a little onion is added," he declared in a sage and worldly-wise voice as he presided over a banquet. I heard it direct from the Spanish Ambassador, who had the misfortune to be present.

And it was said that he took immense delight in masques wherein the Pope was portrayed as a villain, a devil in disguise, or even a fool. In one such, dancers costumed as the Pope and a monk were beaten to death with English Bibles and the Book of Common Prayer – that vile, detestable book of collected blasphemies written by that vile, detestable creature Cranmer, who had declared my mother's marriage legally invalid, an incestuous sin and abomination in the sight of God and man, and myself a bastard, and performed the marriage service for Father and The Great Whore. My poor misguided brother had had that evil, blasphemous book installed in every church in England to corrupt the souls of all who touched it. These wordy weapons were wielded by stern and serious Protestants clad in plain black who monotonously chanted, "The word of the Lord endureth for ever!" as concealed bladders of false blood burst and spurted from the prone, thrashing bodies of the Pope and monk, and my brother rocked on his throne and howled with glee and wished a similarly bloody fate to be visited upon all Catholics. And in another masque a dancing Pope suddenly threw off his bejewelled and embroidered robes and mitre to reveal the scarlet horns and tail of the Devil as he danced a rude jig replete with lewd gestures and loud belches and farts.

Such so-called "entertainments" were not for me, and I was glad not to be a part of my brother's court. I could not have sat there and watched such a sacrilegious spectacle; I would have been afraid God would strike me blind and deaf for bearing witness to such blasphemy or else send a lightning bolt hurtling down from the heavens to annihilate the entire court.

For a time, they did indeed leave me in peace; they had things of far greater import to occupy themselves with than "a sour old maid who devotes herself to God in the absence of a husband."

From Hunsdon, my haven in the Hertfordshire countryside, where I continued to celebrate the Mass with my household and any of the local gentry and common folk who wished to attend, I heard disquieting stories of churches being desecrated in London, denuded of all their ornaments and sacred treasures, and priests being violently attacked and even murdered. The beautiful jewel-toned stained-glass windows, depicting holy saints and stories from the Bible, were smashed, and paintings, tapestries, and statuary of like subjects were also destroyed. Holy books were defiled, often defecated or masturbated upon before they were cast onto the bonfires. And "pissing on the priest" became a favourite sport. Rough and uncouth men would corner some unfortunate man of God, beat him down, often with Bibles and prayer books, then whip out their masculine organs and ease their bladders upon his prone and injured person, laughing as their urine stung his bleeding wounds. I heard the tale of one poor priest who was forced to kneel as a man snatched up a golden chalice from the altar and urinated in it. The priest was held up and restrained and forced to drink the watery waste while those about him chanted, "Turn the water into wine!"

Those loyal to the true faith began to rally around me, like sheep frightened by a wolf running to their shepherd for comfort and protection. Though it was treasonous to speculate about the death of the sovereign, Edward was frail, and if he should die I was next in line for the crown. Some even came stealthily, cloaked and masked by night, to show me secretly and illegally cast horoscopes that affirmed Edward would not make old bones, to give me courage to endure my suffering and persecution as it would only be for a little while. Thus the greedy men on the Regency Council had great cause to fear me. I would make all the wrongs right and undo all the wrongs that had been committed against God and the true religion, and I would also have the power to punish the offenders. I would rid England of every taint and trace of heresy or die trying, and everyone knew it. And when they heard tell of like-minded people rallying around me, it was no wonder they quaked in their shoes and rested uneasily in their beds, but not more uneasily than I did, for I knew that I must with good cause fear for my life when a dagger or a poisoned cup could so easily rid them of these worries. There was even some talk of marrying me off to some foreign prince to rid the realm of the nuisance that was Catholic Mary.

Around this time a rather strange individual, a tall, shapely-limbed, fine-figured man with a long, auburn beard, dressed in a rainbow of silken fool's motley, with gaily coloured ribbons tied in his bushy beard so that it seemed a nest of bows and silken streamers, intruded – mercifully briefly, but nonetheless disturbingly, upon my life.

It was my custom to take a daily walk whenever the weather was fine and circumstances permitted. I started this when I first became a woman; I found that it helped ease the cramps and pains of my monthly affliction, and from there it evolved into a habit, which I particularly delighted in whenever I was residing in the country. It was on one of these outings, when I and two of my ladies were on our way to visit a poor family I had taken an interest in, and bring them a basket of foodstuffs, and some blankets and clothing, when this man of mystery first made his presence known.

Suddenly a boisterous, but I must admit very fine, baritone voice boomed out of nowhere, shattering the quietude of the countryside, startling the birds, and nearly causing me to jump out of my skin and drop my basket. My heart beat at an alarming rate, and I pressed my hand over it as the mysterious voice belted out with great gusto:

> *I gave her Cakes and I gave her Ale,*
> *I gave her Sack and Sherry;*
> *I kist her once and I kist her twice,*
> *And we were wondrous merry!*

I gave her Beads and Bracelets fine,
I gave her Gold down derry.
I thought she was afear'd till she stroked my Beard
And we were wondrous merry!

Merry my Heart, merry my Cock,
Merry my Spright.
Merry my hey down derry.
I kist her once and I kist her twice,
And we were wondrous merry!

Then a tall motley-clad man sprang out from behind a flowering bush, with a basket of what appeared to be little golden cakes in one hand and a large cork-stoppered green flagon in the other, or so said my ladies, Susan Clarencieux and Jane Dormer. Being extremely short-sighted, I could never discern anything not directly before my face, and this bizarre character was always a rainbow-coloured blur to me; I never saw him close enough to discern his features.

Leaping from behind the bush, with his cakes and ale in hand, he began to merrily give chase, skipping and prancing after us, loudly singing all the while, but never presuming to actually catch up with and accost us. Sometimes he would pause and break into a wild wanton jig, throwing back his head and laughing, kicking his legs up high, or taking a honey cake from his basket and throwing it at me, though I leapt back from them as though they were cakes of cow dung. I didn't know whether to be flattered, frightened, or amused, and Susan and Jane and I quickened our pace in consequence and hurried onward on our errand of mercy, though not, I must admit, without looking back often over our shoulders to track the fool's progress.

When we departed after dispensing alms and aid to that poor family, enjoining them to "always trust and fear God" as we went out, he sprang from behind a tree and was there to chase us all the way back to Hunsdon in the same eccentric manner, singing, skip-

ping, prancing, dancing, throwing cakes, and going through many
loud repetitions of that ribald song until we were safely behind
closed doors again.

After that I never knew when he might appear, always trailing
after me but never daring catch me, singing that increasingly irri-
tating song and flourishing a basket of cakes and a flagon of ale.
Sometimes as I sat reading or sewing, a lone honey cake would fly
through the open window and land on my open book or lap. And
he began to leave me gifts of cakes and ale in all manner of places.
One morning I awoke and swung my feet over the side of my bed
only to have my bare toes sink into a platter of warm, moist honey
cakes, sticky with drizzled honey, that gave every sign of being
fresh from the oven. I found them in my pew at chapel, upon my
desk, on my favourite garden bench, and even in the privy as if I
might wish to partake of them while I eased my body of its waste,
and once as I climbed into my coach I almost sat down upon a platter. And even, most alarmingly, I awoke some mornings to find
them beside my head on the pillow. Another time when I prepared
to take my bath I found the tub filled with ale instead of water
with light golden honey cakes bobbing in it while that voice belted
out that nerve-grating song outside the window.

Then, one night I was awakened from a sound sleep by an anguished male voice crying out, "I can't stand it any more – I want
to taste *your* honey cake!" as a head thrust beneath my bedcovers
and a pair of strong masculine hands closed round my ankles and
tried to spread wide my legs. I struggled free and ran screaming, in
my bare feet and nightgown, down the stairs to the Great Hall.

"There is a man in my room!" I shouted as my guards and various servants swarmed around me. "He . . ." I paused suddenly,
casting my eyes down and lowering my voice as I felt the heat of
shame burn my face. I hugged my arms tight over my breasts, in
that moment intensely aware that I was naked beneath my nightgown. "He . . . attempted indecencies upon my person!" I at last
blurted out as I burst into tears and fell into Susan's arms as Jane
hastily brought a cloak to drape about my shoulders.

My guards raced upstairs to investigate and found my bedcovers upon the floor and a number of honey cakes arranged in the

shape of a heart upon the white linen sheet, the outline filled in with red rose petals. And upon the table beside my bed, lit by a pair of rose-perfumed candles tinted the most delicate shade of pink, were a flagon of ale and two golden goblets adorned with a rich, glittering pattern of garnet hearts and diamond lovers' knots. But of the intruder there was no sign.

Returning to my room on the heels of my guards, with Susan and Jane keeping close on either side of me, I went to the window and squinted out into the dark night. And there below me that familiar voice boomed out that annoyingly familiar bawdy tavern tune again.

> *I gave her Cakes and I gave her Ale,*
> *I gave her Sack and Sherry;*
> *I kist her once and I kist her twice,*
> *And we were wondrous merry!*
>
> *I gave her Beads and Bracelets fine,*
> *I gave her Gold down derry.*
> *I thought she was afear'd till she stroked my Beard*
> *And we were wondrous merry!*
>
> *Merry my Heart, merry my Cock,*
> *Merry my Spright.*
> *Merry my hey down derry.*
> *I kist her once and I kist her twice,*
> *And we were wondrous merry!*

"Unleash the hounds!" I ordered, bristling with outrage. But he merely laughed at me, throwing back his head as he broke into a jig, kicking his legs up high and blowing kisses to me, before he had to flee with a bevy of barking dogs at his heels. After that night, I never saw him again.

Some weeks later the Spanish Ambassador came to dine with me. He told me he had heard that the Lord Protector's brother, the

Lord Admiral, Sir Thomas Seymour, had petitioned the Council for my hand in marriage, and that he had already most presumptuously begun to woo me until he was ordered by his brother to desist as neither of them was meant to marry a king's daughter.

"If such is true, I know nothing about it," I answered. "As for his courting me, I have only seen the man once or perhaps twice at court celebrations, and I have never spoken a word to him in my life."

Later that evening as she helped me to undress, my faithful Susan ventured to inform me, in the most deferential terms of course, that such was not exactly the case, and that I had seen Thomas Seymour several times in the guise of that mad fool stranger we had called "The Cakes and Ale Man".

"I naturally assumed you knew, Ma'am," Susan said.

"No, indeed I did *not* know," I assured her, "and I doubt I would have even if I had seen him close enough to discern his features. But if that is his way of wooing, his technique leaves *much* to be desired."

"I quite agree, Ma'am," Susan replied, "though he is said to have quite a way with the ladies, I think the rumours give him more credit than he deserves, as do the London moneylenders."

After "The Cakes and Ale Man" had come and gone, all lapsed back into normality, but it was only the quiet before the storm.

❧ 6 ❧

Elizabeth

I could not remain at court, for the Lord Protector had decreed
that during the King's minority, while Edward was unmarried, it
would not be seemly for single ladies, including the King's sisters,
to reside at court. I thought I was destined to go, yet again, back to
Hatfield, and languish there for many years to come, with only occasional visits to Mary and the court at Christmastime to relieve
the tedium, but Catherine Parr came to my rescue once again. I
was like a daughter to her, she said, and she dreaded so to part with
me, and asked me if I would like to come and live with her.

It was a dream come true to be at cheerful Chelsea, Katherine's
redbrick manor house set in a verdant green heart of woodlands,
parks, and gardens overlooking a usually placid expanse of the
Thames. The mullioned windows welcomed in the sun as if to
dare the gloom to intrude, and everyone, even the lowliest servant,
always went about with a smile on their face; everyone was happy
at Chelsea. And I settled happily into a quiet routine of study and
pleasant pastimes in Kate's company.

And there was a mystery to spice up this bland but nonetheless
pleasant existence – titillating gossip that Kate had a lover. And so
soon after my father's death! It was as unexpected as it was scan-
dalous. Who would have believed it of Kate? I had always thought
of Kate as such a practical, prim, level-headed, decorous lady, alto-

gether lacking in passion, but apparently she had hidden depths. Even though her beliefs about religion and education were new-fangled and excitingly bold, I never once thought of her as the sort of woman who would fling herself into a lover's embrace, especially not before the official period of mourning for her husband had expired.

My dearest, darling Kat, my plump, fussy, mother hen of a governess, Katherine Ashley, and I would crouch on the window seat in my bedchamber at night, bundled in our velvet dressing gowns, and watch by moonlight as Kate crept out cloaked and veiled amidst the night-blooming jasmine to the gate at the back of the garden to let him in, a tall, dark shadow stealthy as a phantom.

He would take her in his arms, bend her over backwards, and kiss her with a scorching passion that even we, sitting there watching from the window above like a pair of giddy, giggling housemaids, could feel as we tried to guess his identity. Then she would take his hand and lead him to the house and, presumably, up the back stairs to her bed.

And with the dawn's first faint light, when Mrs Ashley still slept soundly, snoring in the small room adjoining mine, I would sometimes creep from my bed, the stone floor cold beneath my naked toes, making me shiver, to watch them, arms about each other's waists, leaning into one another, as they walked slowly back to the garden gate, pausing to steal one last, lingering kiss before he took his leave, as the jasmine closed its petals for the day.

And then came the day when it wasn't a secret any more. I received a summons bidding me to come to Kate's chamber. And there he was – the rash and reckless, hotheaded and handsome, Lord Admiral Thomas Seymour of the winning smile and ready laugh. Handsome beyond words and measure, with sun-bronzed skin, wavy auburn hair, a long luxuriant beard, twinkling cinnamon-brown eyes, and a voice like a velvet glove on bare skin, he moved with a bold, larger-than-life, confident swagger that suggested he had never in his life known a moment of self-doubt, and wielded his charm like a weapon. Every woman who crossed his path seemed to succumb to that charm. Even staid and proper matrons were reduced to giggling, giddy schoolgirls simpering and blushing in his presence, with hearts aflutter and knees like butter, hanging on his every word, and men were enraptured and enthralled by his tales of adventure and derring-do upon the high seas and his dealings with the pirates who plied the Scilly Isles. He was the complete and contrary opposite of his icy, calculating, meticulous cold fish of a brother, the Lord Protector. Tom Seymour was the man every woman wanted to wed or bed and every man wanted to be.

When I walked in he was standing before the fire in Kate's bedchamber, stretching his hands out to the welcoming warmth of the fragrant applewood logs as raindrops dribbled from his cinnamon velvet cloak onto the bearskin rug upon the hearth.

The moment I saw him my heart felt a jolt as if it had been struck by lightning and unaccountably I began to blush and tremble. I could not speak; my lips could not form the words to utter even a simple greeting. I felt as if my tongue had become a useless pink ribbon all tied up in tenacious, impossible knots. For the life of me, I couldn't understand why. Then he was crossing the room. His hands were on my waist and he was lifting me up high, my feet dangling uselessly above the floor. My long red hair swung down over my shoulders to tickle his face as I gazed down at him and he in turn fixed me with an intense, penetrating gaze. Then, very slowly, he lowered me, and pressed me close against his strong chest – I felt sure he could feel my heart pounding as if there were a wild, bucking horse trapped inside my breast – and then . . . *he kissed me!* Long and lingeringly upon my lips, he kissed me! I surprised myself, even as I knew I should shove him away and slap him for his impertinence, and instead I wrapped my arms around his neck and clung to him.

"My Lord!" I gasped, blushing and befuddled, when his lips left mine.

"Well met, My Lady Elizabeth." He smiled at me, displaying a set of perfect pearl-white teeth, sparkling from amidst his bushy beard, as he released me and his hands reached out knowingly to catch my elbows and steady me as my knees threatened to give way beneath my black damask and velvet mourning gown.

"I thought it only fair that since I have swept you off your feet at both our previous meetings I should continue in the same vein," he said teasingly.

As he spoke his eyes roved over my body and I felt as if every stitch I wore was being peeled away, leaving me stark naked before his piercing gaze.

"Do you not remember?" An incredulous little frown creased his brow before he shook his head to chase it away and smiled again. "No, you cannot have forgotten! I am a man who *always* makes a lasting impression! The first time was on the occasion of my dear sister Jane's first, and sadly last, Christmas as Queen . . ."

"Y-Yes, M-My Lord, I . . . I . . . remember . . ." Blushing and tongue-tied, I stammered, as my mind hurtled back in time to that Christmas of 1536 when Tom Seymour, dressed in motley coloured silks and ribbon streamers all trimmed with tiny bells, and a gilded tin crown, had presided over the Yuletide celebrations as the Lord of Misrule. All of a sudden he had swooped down on me and swept me up high into the air and demanded a kiss from me. Laughing, I threw my arms around his neck and complied wholeheartedly with a hearty smacking kiss that made all those about us laugh. I was but three at the time and not so mindful of my dignity, and everyone is apt to let decorum slip when the jolly, cavorting Lord of Misrule holds sway and the wine and wassail are flowing freely. Everyone looked on smilingly, observing that "Jolly Tom" had such a way with children, they naturally responded to him, and what a shame it was that he was still a bachelor and had none of his own. Then he set me down, and taking out a flute, called the other children to gather round, and bade us follow him, forming a living serpent of gaily garbed little bodies, weaving our way through the adults amassed in the Great Hall.

"And the second time," he prompted, "was when I carried you in the procession for . . ."

I gulped and nodded. ". . . my brother Edward's christening."

"Yes! God's teeth, you *do* remember!" He smiled broadly. "I *knew* you could not have forgotten! My brother Ned was supposed to have the honour of carrying you, but you took an instant dislike to him – and who could blame you? – and kicked his shin and ran to me and threw yourself into my arms and said as regally as a little queen, 'You may carry me,' and when he tried to take you from me you bit him."

I blushed at the memory and hung my head; I could not meet his eyes knowing my face was all aflame, and my stomach felt as if it were aswarm with thousands of anxious bees.

"Y-Yes, M-My Lord," I said quietly, "I . . . I remember."

"And now . . ." Tom smiled, oblivious to my embarrassment. "Here I am, to sweep you off your feet every day for many years to come! What, can it be? Have you not guessed, my clever Princess?" He threw back his head and laughed at my befuddled countenance. He spread wide his arms to show off his fine manly physique and the equally fine clothing beneath his sodden cloak. "Your new stepfather stands before you! – Here I am! Come, embrace me, Bess!"

I felt the most peculiar feeling then, a breathlessness that left me reeling, as if the breath had suddenly been knocked violently from my lungs. I couldn't understand it then, my mind churned with confusion, but knowing that he was married made me feel as if a crushing blow had been dealt me and made me want to rage against fate, to shriek and strike out with my fists and tear with my nails. "He *can't* be married!" I kept wailing despairingly over and over in my mind, "He just *can't* be married!" I cried without understanding why the news should so distress me. Tom Seymour was a grown man about to cross the threshold of forty; he had remained a bachelor long past the age when most men are many years married, and the gossips had long wondered why he tarried so long without taking a wife. Now he had only done what society had always expected of him. So why should the news leave me reeling and ready to burst into tears? God's bones, I hardly knew the man, so why was I ready to curse and shriek at the Fates that he should have been mine?

He took a step toward me, reaching out, as if he would draw me back into his arms again. I stepped back, even as I longed to run forward and hurl myself into them. I stumbled as my limbs tangled in my skirts, and only the quick grasp of his hand around my elbow kept me from falling.

"Tom!" a soft, gentle voice behind me said, and I started, unaccountably feeling a hard jolt of guilt, as if I had been caught doing something illicit, as my stepmother quietly entered the room and stepped past me to lay a gentle hand on her husband's arm.

"For shame, Tom! You have broken the news too abruptly! Can you not see you have nearly felled her with the shock? Tut, tut, you are too impulsive, My Lord Husband! And take off that wet cloak, before you catch a chill; I want to be a wife this time, not a physician in petticoats. Sit down, please, Bess" – she turned back to me, smiling gently, encouragingly – "and I shall tell you all about it."

Seeing me rooted there, my distress plain, Kate instantly took pity on me and guided me into the chair nearest the fire and knelt down before me, rubbing my hands.

"*Please*, dear, do not think unkindly of me – of us – for marrying in haste. I assure you no insult was intended to the memory of your father. I know many will think we have done wrong by not waiting a full year, until the mourning period had ended. But, dearest, the truth is, we were in love and planned to marry before your father's eye lighted on me. But when it did, I renounced my own desires and did my duty to my King and country, and now . . . I am a woman five years past thirty and I *long* to be a *true* wife, and a mother, if God will so bless me. As you know, Bess dear, I was married twice before I wed your father; my youth was spent caring for husbands far older than myself with children older than I was. I thought it was my lot to go through life as a caretaker for the old and infirm and other women's children. When I married your father and met you and Edward, and your little cousin Jane Grey, all in dire need of a mother's love and guidance, it reawakened my desire for motherhood, to have a child of my own, and stirred such a longing in me I know not words great enough to convey the urgency and strength of it; there were times I wanted it so much it hurt me, as I thought it was a hunger that would never be sated. Please, judge me not too harshly, Bess, for grasping greedily at my last chance to fulfil my heart's most ardent and deeply felt desire. Few of us are fortunate to marry where our hearts lie; do not condemn me for grasping at Fortune's blessing, the chance to have happiness in this life, to not have to wait, to live in expectation of Heaven's promise."

"I . . ." I shook my head to clear it as I struggled vainly for composure; I heard her words but I was having trouble putting them together in coherent fashion. "Indeed, Madame, I . . . I do not blame you! I . . . It was just a surprise, that's all," I said abruptly, snapping my mouth shut and lowering my eyes as I could not bring myself to meet her loving and concerned gaze for fear that she might divine the truth that even then I was still floundering and grappling to understand. "Have I your leave to retire now, Madame? The surprise has brought on one of my headaches."

"Of course, my dear!" I surrendered gladly to her gentle ministrations and let her help me from my chair and put her arm about my shoulders to guide me to the door.

Then he was there again, bounding in front of us, barring our way.

"But I've not told you how the deed was done!" he protested, taking my arm and leading me back to my chair.

"Tom!" Kate protested. "Let Bess go; there will be time aplenty for you to tell your tale later!"

Laughing, he wrapped his arms around her waist, scooped her up, and spun around and plunked her down into the chair opposite mine.

"Sit you down too, woman, your Tom has a tale to tell, and he'll not be thwarted!" He chuckled as he plopped himself down beside my chair and his fingers began to play with a loose silver thread on my black damask kirtle.

"Now, Bess, how do you suppose I came to marry your fine stepmother?" he asked.

"I daresay you petitioned the Council, My Lord," I said, surprised that I was able to speak so coolly when inside I was a raging inferno.

"*The Council!*" he sneered. "*The Council?* I, Thomas Seymour, petition that bunch of mutton-headed dolts?" He slapped his thigh and threw back his head and laughed. "A pox upon the Council, and that includes my *dear* brother, Ned, the Lord Protector of the Realm! The Council can kiss my fine white arse and thank me for the honour! Nay, pet" – he patted my knee – "I'm a man who knows how to get what he wants; and, as a rule, I shoot straight for the heart, of the lady or the problem. And why should I waste my time with that bunch of fools and knaves? Nay, Bess, the King himself gave our marriage his blessing; did he not, my buxom, kissable Kate?"

"Indeed he did, My Lord." Kate smiled softly, indulgently, her cheeks rosy and her hazel eyes radiant and full of love. She was clearly a woman so deep in love she risked losing herself and drowning in it.

"Now, let me explain how I did it." He gave my knee another pat. "My fool brother Ned has no more idea of how to win friends and make himself liked than a fish has. He dares to short the King of pocket money through some fool notion of teaching him economy and restraint! Fancy that, Bess. Did you ever hear such a foolish thing? *Economy and restraint!* God's wounds, the boy is the King of England! Economy and restraint be damned. We are not talking about some lowly clerk who has to pinch his pennies to make ends meet!"

I sat up straighter in my chair, acutely aware that a war was raging inside me. My mind saw full plain that this man was a braggart and a fool, a complete stranger to common sense, who thought himself above and exempt from all the rules. But he was a handsome knave, a reckless rascal, with a winning smile, and a way with him that made me want to fall at his feet and offer myself to him like a pagan sacrifice. I felt my body, and my heart, lurch and tremble, wanting to be possessed by him, while my mind tried to pull them back, as if it were yanking on the reins of a runaway horse. No good can come of this, I told myself; but the parts of me that needed to listen were deaf to reason. The moment I had seen Tom Seymour standing before the fire, I too had cast common sense aside and embraced danger even as I embraced him. "Step back from the precipice and save yourself while you still can!" my conscience warned; but my rash, passionate, impetuous side shoved reason over the cliff to silence it.

"So I decided to step in and save my nephew from penury," Tom was saying. "Since Ned had already cast himself as the bad uncle the stage was set for me to play the good one; jolly Uncle Tom, with his pockets always ajingle with coins, who never comes to court without a gift for His Majesty! I put my man Fowler at the King's service, to keep little Neddy in ready money in my bsence, and praise me to the skies whenever he can, and I had him ask a favour on my behalf. I had him say to the King that I was of a mind to marry, and asked him if he would do me the very great honour of choosing a bride for me. I thought the poor little puppet would relish the chance to name the tune instead of just dancing to it. And I was right, I tell you, Bess. It gave his pride such a puffing up, plumping it up fat as a new-stuffed goose-down pillow it did! Was that not good of me? Well, Bess, first he suggested the Lady Anne of Cleves" – Tom wrinkled up his nose – "but, no, that would not suit me at all! I like my women with breath sweet as perfume, not stinking of sauerkraut! So my man tactfully put him off that. So, next, little clueless Neddy suggested his sister Mary, to wean her from the papist teat. But my mind and heart were set elsewhere, so Fowler, who knew in whose bed my inclinations lay, suggested the Dowager Queen, my beloved, bonny, buxom Kate here" – he blew her a kiss – "and little Neddy said, 'Oh yes, that is a fine idea!' And as a loyal subject to the King it was both my duty and my very great pleasure to obey his royal command! Now is that not a grand tale, Bess?"

"Audacious and amazing, My Lord." My reason reasserted itself, slowly clawing its way back up from the sharp and painful rocks onto which I had impetuously shoved it.

Grasping the arms of my chair, I levered myself up. "Now I really must beg leave to retire. . . . My head . . ."

"Of course, my dear!" Kate leapt up and rushed to my side. "We have delayed you too long already." She began to shepherd me toward the door again and her lips pressed a tender, motherly kiss onto my throbbing brow. "You do look pale, my dear. Shall I send you a soothing posset of chamomile?"

"No, thank you, Madame. I just need to rest," I said as I bobbed a hasty curtsy and quickly fled.

I forced myself to walk swiftly but sedately, as becomes a princess, down the corridor to my chamber, but once inside I flung myself onto my bed and wept until the stars came out.

❧ 7 ❧

Mary

I was *appalled* when word reached me that my eminently sensible stepmother, Catherine Parr, had married "The Cakes and Ale Man". Indeed, I was surprised that she had married anyone at all so soon after Father's death; it showed a wanton and selfish disregard for his memory, and I had never taken her for one who would so brazenly and callously flout propriety. Father's body was barely cold in the tomb before she was in another man's warm bed; it was the height of disrespect and I could *never* forgive her for it.

I wrote to my sister and implored her in the most urgent and heartfelt words to forsake that unprincipled den of heretical wickedness and moral laxity and come and make her home with me, where both her body and soul would be safe in my household where the light of God's goodness shone warm and ever-bright and all comported themselves with the utmost virtue and decorum. But Elizabeth declined, saying that she could see both sides of the matter, and both had equally valid points to make. And, to her mind, Father was as dead as he was ever going to be whether six months or six years had passed; Kate was well past the first flush of youth and desirous of motherhood before it was too late; and as for herself, she thought she would tarry there for a time as she liked it well enough, and she had good company and her studies to occupy her and did not feel herself morally endangered.

I felt a phantom slap of betrayal sting my face as I read Elizabeth's words. My own sister had wilfully chosen to dwell in an immoral household, a place as wanton and unprincipled as a brothel, to wilfully let her morals and soul be corrupted, rather than make her home with me, a virtuous and righteous woman who permitted no indecorous mischief beneath her roof. I crumpled her letter in my hand and flung it into the fire, telling myself I should have expected nothing less from The Boleyn Whore's bastard brat who probably was not even my sister anyway; I had always thought she had the stamp of the lute player, Mark Smeaton, about her features.

Meanwhile, despite my pleas that I was not a well woman and thus should be left in peace, Edward's Councillors incessantly hounded and bombarded me with stern reprimands for "making a grand show" of my celebration of the Mass and throwing my chapel doors wide in welcome to all and sundry who wished to attend. Edward, they said, had only intended that I myself alone be allowed the privilege of the Mass until I could be persuaded from the folly of my ways; he only tolerated my misguided ways because I was his sister. I repeatedly informed the Council that I could not bar my chapel doors against the faithful; denying them the Mass would be the same as condemning them to Hell, and I would not have that upon my conscience. "I am God's servant first," I declared, "and the King's second. I can put no earthly master above our heavenly one, and His Majesty must understand and accept that or take my life, for I would rather die than give up my religion."

They sent letters to explain to me as though I were a simpleton that the Act of Uniformity was meant to unite the whole of England under one religion, but by flaunting my beliefs and making myself appear as a candle in the dark to the Catholic rebels I was doing the country more harm than good; because of me, bloody civil war might erupt. Did I want to see England torn apart by religious strife? they asked, stressing that it was integral that I, the King's sister, conform to the laws of the land. I should not hold myself up as above them or exempt, but instead set a good example for the common folk and nobly born alike to follow.

"I would rather lose my life than lose my religion!" I exclaimed time and time again, imploring them to understand that it would be my death to deprive me of the consolations of the faith I had been brought up in, but they had closed their hearts and were deaf to my soul's anguished cries.

And so it continued, back and forth, to and fro, the same argument, again and again, but I knew it could not go on for ever. I prayed to God to give me strength to withstand it as I continued to live in fear of assassins or being walled up alive to die a lonely death in a crumbling old castle in the middle of nowhere, where no one could hear my screams or rescue me.

Every day I thanked God for my cousin, the Emperor Charles. The Spanish Ambassador kept him well apprised of my plight and brought diplomatic pressure to bear upon the Council, hinting that if I were harmed in any way or forced to forsake my faith the Emperor would declare war on England. That threat, for a time, at least, would keep me safe, as England could not afford a war, but, I also knew, many a murder had been arranged to mimic illness or natural death, and my health had never been robust, so none would greet the news that I had died of some malaise with great surprise. So I continued to live in fear, knowing that God was the only one I could truly trust to safeguard me, and into His hands I commended both my life and spirit.

❧ 8 ❧

Elizabeth

"He is your stepfather, Bess," I kept reminding myself. But it did no good. "No good can come of dallying with such a rash and reckless knave," I told myself times too numerous to tally. "Ambition is the star that guides him, and in following it he forgets to watch his feet; he will stroll right off the precipice someday, and if you go along hand in hand with him, gazing rapt like lovers do, so too will you." But all he had to do was smile at me and I was deaf to reason and all serious thoughts went scurrying out of my mind like rats fleeing a burning building.

He would saunter in as I sat upon a velvet-upholstered stool, embroidering or reading aloud with Kate, with his arms overflowing with great bouquets of wildflowers. He would draw up a chair behind me and nimbly pluck off my hood and take my wavy waist-length Tudor-red tresses in his confident hands and weave them into a braid. Inserting the sunny yellow daffodils, deep purple violets, orange-yellow marigolds, sky-coloured bluebells, pinks, buttercups, daisies, gillyflowers, and the vibrant multi-hued pansies called heart's-ease into the plait he had fashioned, he would marvel breathlessly at the golden strands amongst the red, picked out by the fire's or the sun's light, "like gilded threads worked into red damask." And when I stood it would look as though I had a garden growing down my back. Sometimes he would come bearing only daisies and would lie at my feet, idly weaving them into chains and crowns to adorn both me and his "bonny, buxom Kate", pausing sometimes to slowly, deliberately, pluck the petals, gazing at me, hard and bold as his lips mouthed the words: "She loves me, she loves me not, she loves me . . ." And a fire as red as my hair would ignite in my face, and the words would crash and pile into a hopeless jumble upon my lips or else stick in a tangled heap in my throat, and I would feel that for the life of me I could not sort them out again.

Another day he joined us for a picnic under the shady trees in the park. And I noticed, marvelling yet again, at how my step-mother had changed from the days when she had been my father's wife. Nowadays Kate seemed to walk in a dream, with her head lost in the clouds. Though Kate personified autumn in her colours, her red-gold hair and hazel eyes reminiscent of autumn leaves, marriage to Tom had brought spring back into her life and rejuvenated her, making her more girlish and giddy and less matronly and dignified. At that particular picnic, she grew giddy, then just as quickly drowsy as Tom plied her with cup after cup of malmsey, until she fell asleep.

As she slumped against the trunk of an old oak tree, snoring softly, Tom stealthily removed her hood and plucked the pins from her hair so that it fell down about her shoulders. Next he took off her shoes and, reaching up under her skirts, with a sly wink at me, rolled down and peeled off her stockings. It struck me, like an arrow in the heart that, as he lifted her foot to his lips and delicately nibbled her little pink toes, Tom's eyes never once left my face. Indeed, his eyes fixed on mine, almost tauntingly, as if he meant to torment me by behaving thus with his wife right in front of me, as if he were flaunting privileges that were hers by right but could never be mine.

Kate awoke with a cry at the feel of his teeth nipping at her toes, and Tom leapt up, laughing like a madman, brandishing her shoes and stockings high above his head, shouting if she wanted them back she would have to catch him as he took off at a fast run across the park. And I was treated to the most unlikely spectacle of the barefoot Catherine Parr, a woman renowned for her dignity, racing after him like a barefoot peasant girl shrieking and shouting with laughter as she ran across the grass, with her skirts bunched up about her knees and her hair streaming in the breeze.

I kept telling myself he was my stepfather and that it was wrong that I should have such thoughts about him. I kept reminding myself that he was Kate's husband. Kate who had been the kindest woman in the world to me, taking me under her wing and nurturing me as if I were her own natural-born daughter. And yet . . . his behaviour towards me contradicted the facts. He behaved like a boisterous young swain hellbent on wooing and winning me.

One morning, just as the sun's gentle butter-yellow fingers were beginning to whisk the dawn away, and I lay still in slumber, safe and warm inside the dark haven of my bedcurtains, I heard my door creak open. Drowsily, I thought I must remember to ask Mrs Ashley to have the hinges oiled, then rolled over, burrowing deeper into the feather mattress, and thought no more about it.

Suddenly, my bedcurtains were wrenched open wide, and there, to my astonishment, stood the gardener, with the old battered wooden bucket he used to carry manure to fertilize the roses that bloomed so beautifully at Chelsea.

I bolted up in bed, outraged, clutching the covers over my bare chest, as I often slept naked in those days, and my dressing gown was draped over a chair, nearby, but still beyond my reach. A sharp retort was primed to blast like a cannonball from my mouth, when suddenly his lips spread in a wide pearly smile that I recognized instantly as Tom's, and he tilted back the brim of the battered old hat that had cast a dark shadow over his face. I gasped and braced myself as he raised the pail and flung its contents at me and I found myself sitting in the midst of a flurry of red rose petals.

Carelessly, he flung the pail aside, the bearskin on the hearth muffling the thud, then dived onto the bed right on top of me. I gave a little startled cry as I lay pinned beneath his weight, but his hand clapped quickly over my mouth stifled it newborn.

"Lady," he said smiling, "I come to you in the guise of a gardener to tend my rosy buds."

And with those words he raised himself and pulled the bedclothes down to my waist, pinning the downturned covers with his knees, and holding my arms pinioned at my sides to prevent me from pushing him away or covering myself.

"Slow-blooming posies need nurturing and encouragement in order that they might grow and thrive," he explained in a mockingly sage tone, ignoring the blush that dyed my face as red as the rose petals he had spilled on my bed, and the tears of shame that shimmered in my eyes. He ducked his head down and began to kiss the pallid pink nipples that sat in pools of rosy flesh upon my flat white chest.

Though I was thirteen, my body was indeed slow to blossom; my courses had only begun to flow and were as yet an irregular trickle rather than a full-blown crimson gush, and only a few sparse red tendrils curled around my nether lips.

I squirmed and struggled beneath him, caught between resistance and surrender. One moment I gasped and struggled hard, and the next I arched my back, offering up my paltry bosom for more of his exquisite kisses, sighing at this newly discovered delight.

With a lascivious grin and a last serpentlike flicking little lick, he abandoned my little pink paps, now throbbing and stiff, no longer pale but flushed a much rosier hue, and left a trail of meandering hot kisses down to my waist. Then he tore back the covers and let loose an exclamation of surprised delight.

"Pink petals amongst the red!" he cried, and promptly lowered his mouth to kiss my nether lips.

I nearly swooned as I squirmed and sighed beneath his questing, teasing tongue, exploring every nook and cranny of my most intimate parts, which no man had ever seen before. I was lost in a new world of bliss, a dream from which I never wanted to awaken, when suddenly a scream pierced the dawn, jolting me up in a rude awakening.

Mrs Ashley stood in the doorway of her room, which adjoined mine, her eyes wide and her mouth agape.

With laughter twinkling in his eyes, Tom raised his head and winked at her.

"Careful, Mistress Kat, remember, curiosity killed the curious cat!" he chided playfully as he leapt off the bed and bounded out the door, pausing only long enough to pat her plump posterior and provoke an indignant cry from her.

I lay taut, in dead silence, too stunned and ashamed to even cover my nakedness, and Mrs Ashley stood likewise stricken as we listened to his footsteps and laughter retreating down the hall.

"*Bess!*" she exclaimed, an expression of horror spreading across her round, full-moon face. "*How could you?*"

"*Get out! Go away!*" I cried, the spell suddenly broken, yanking the covers up over my head, and turning onto my side, turning my back on my beloved governess, and wrapping them tight about me, as close as I could, like a cocoon, as I burst into angry, confused tears.

"Oh my darling girl!" Instantly contrite, wringing her hands and looking as if she too were about to cry, Kat wailed as she ran to me and tried to take me in her arms. I struggled free and refused to let her embrace me and, finally, she let me be, saying only that we must talk soon, for there were things that she, in a mother's stead, must say to me. And at those words I wept all the harder.

Tom was a man brimming over with charm and winning ways and he began to woo Kat too, to overcome the rightful objections a governess should make when amorous advances are directed at her charge, especially one of royal blood – and a princess's virtue and virginity must never be in doubt. He brought her bouquets of flowers, and baskets of berries he picked himself. He kissed her cheeks and twirled his fingers and stuck violets, pinks, and daisies in the frizzy, flyaway brown-grey curls escaping from the prim prison of her black French hood. Oftentimes he would creep up behind her and smack and pinch her ample bottom, saying he liked a full-hipped woman with great pillow-plump buttocks, and give her gifts of cakes and sweets to further fatten them up. "I am fattening Mrs Ashley's great buttocks as if they were a Christmas goose!" he would jestingly declare, making her giggle and exclaim, "Oh, you are a *naughty* man!" waggling a finger at him as if he were a naughty schoolboy, and he would playfully snap his fine teeth at it as if he meant to bite it, and make her laugh all the more. There would always be an affectionate undertone to mar the severity of the scolds and reprimands she addressed to him. "A *very* naughty man!" she would repeat as she simpered and preened, blushed, and giggled, before she fluttered away, putting a little more sway into her steps and swing into her hips, darting a furtive glance back over her shoulder through coyly fluttered lashes to make sure that he was watching.

But Tom had achieved what he set out to do – he had won an ally – and Kat began to sing his praises to me at every turn. And every night thereafter when she tucked me into bed with a peck upon my cheek she would wish me "sweet dreams of the Lord Admiral, my pet". She seemed to forget that she was a governess, not a matchmaker, and that Tom was married to our hostess, my own dear stepmother. She would spin elaborate, fantastical dreams, castles in the clouds in which Tom and I dwelled as man and wife in wedded bliss, and she proudly presided over a nursery filled with our fine, handsome children. Her dreams were so vivid I could feel his ring upon my finger, the weight of the gold, the flashing green fire of the emerald that stood symbol for his everlasting love, and his naked body, muscular, hard, virile, and strong, spooned around mine beneath the covers of our marriage bed, with the warmth of his breath against the nape of my neck, the tickle of his beard, and his hand lovingly cupping my breast, the hardness of his manhood pressed against my bare bottom. I could even smell and taste the food and wine on our table, and hear the merry chatter of our guests. And there were our daughters, Emily and Cassandra, playing with their dolls, dressing them up and talking to them like little mothers, and our sons, Christopher and Mark, cantering about on hobby horses and fighting mock battles with wooden swords, shouting with laughter and crying when they took a tumble and scraped their knees, all under the watchful eye of their governess, Kat, of course.

Though reason tried to hold me back, Kat dragged me into her dreamworld, and they became my dreams as well. And oh how my heart leapt and soared each time he called me his, and melted at each endearment, each "darling", "sweetheart", "dear heart", and "dear one".

But what about Kate, his wife and my stepmother – where was

she in all this? She had no place in our realm of dreams, though I loved her dearly and wished her no ill, certainly not the cruel fate of a forsaken wife like my father's first bride and Mary's mother, Catherine of Aragon, had been, nor the cold bed of the grave where my own mother, Jane Seymour, and Catherine Howard now reposed. My heart felt a sharp twinge of guilt whenever I thought of Kate, vying emotions of resentment and regret. I knew I wronged her, and part of me was sorely sorry for it, yet another part of me did not care one whit.

In times of quiet, away from Kat's chatter and fantasy prattle, I fought at times to face and at other times to stave off stone-cold reality. Tom was a married man. I was a royal princess, with my reputation to guard as if it were a priceless treasure. If we gave in and surrendered to our passion, what kind of life could we have together? My warring emotions reminded me of my long-held conviction that I did not want to be a wife, yet a part of me deep down and buried kindled to that urge. But did the role of mistress suit me? Could my proud spirit buckle to and accept a life lived in waiting and longing and hoping for stolen moments, treasuring each tryst, prizing each pilfered hour as if it were a precious, perfect pearl pried from the heart of an oyster? And to know that I was a luxury, a pastime, a private pleasure to be enjoyed in strictest secrecy and the utmost discretion, fated always to come second, never first, to live on crumbs from Tom's wife's table. To always temper passion with precaution lest I face the deathly perils of pregnancy and the ignominy and disgrace of bearing a bastard. To dwell forever in the shadows, while Kate walked openly in the sun at his side, unless the Wheel of Fortune spun in such a way that fate would one day let me take her place, but that was far too cruel and horrid to contemplate, for I truly did love Kate and never for a moment wished her in her grave. And to never be able to take up my pen and write to him the words *I love you*, lest they fall into the wrong hands, and our secret be betrayed, and he, for the presumption of dallying carnally with a royal princess, face the headsman's axe that was the penalty for high treason. Could I? Would I? *Yes!* In defiance of all risk and reason my heart sang out like a whole choir of fallen angels, *Yes, yes, and again yes! Anything* to be with and belong to Tom! For him I would play Love's prisoner and Love's fool! Oh, and I was indeed a fool for him!

Every night, when the time came to say good night, I would watch Kate take Tom's arm and ascend the stairs, clinging lovingly to him, the perfect picture of the devoted wife. And he, with his free hand, holding a candle to light their way. I would lag behind, my steps as leaden as my heart, my mind in an agony of torment as I watched their bedchamber door close behind them. Sometimes, Tom would wink back at me and then seize hold of Kate and sweep her up in his arms saying, "Did you not promise to be buxom and bonair in bed and at board? Well, tonight's the night to make good on your promise, wife, then on the morrow we shall see how you do at board!" And, kicking the door shut behind him with his boot heel, he would carry her, giggling and snuggling in his arms, in to bed.

Alone in my bed, I would toss and turn as I imagined them locked together in a naked embrace, all caressing fingers and hungry lips. Every male organ I had ever seen started to thrust itself into my mind, a parade of phalluses, crude woodcarvings of cocks, illustrations in scholarly tomes pertaining to medicine and anatomy, paintings and statues, naked peasant brats howling at the roadside or playing in the mud, and my brother Edward as an alabaster-skinned infant being bathed in warm rosewater poured into a golden basin. And in the privacy of my bed, shrouded in the dark of night and drawn bedcurtains, my fingers began to stray more and more often down to the secret place between my thighs, to delve and explore where Tom's ardent lips and tongue once had, but my own efforts were a poor proxy for his bold, practised touch. In a fever of frustration, seething with a jealousy that verged on hatred for my good stepmother, I would roll onto my side, pound my pillow with an angry fist and sometimes bite it with my teeth to stifle my frustrated sobs, and weep until at last I fell asleep.

Then morning would come, and with the dawn came Tom. Sometimes striding in garbed in the gardener's guise, ready to tend his "rosy buds", others fully dressed for the day in fine velvet court attire gleaming with golden braid, or booted and gloved in riding leathers with a jaunty plume swaying in his cap, brandishing his riding crop and announcing, "I have come to spank my slug-abed!" But no matter what he was wearing he was always ready to rouse me. Sometimes he would come to me naked and bare-legged beneath his garnet velvet dressing gown with his cock pro-truding like a cannon at the ready to introduce to my eager, inquisitive hands and hungry mouth, to make me believe that I had some heady, intoxicating power over him.

I tried, albeit halfheartedly, to resist and do the right thing. Some nights I leapt into bed, gloriously and wantonly nude, wig-gling and writhing sensuously against the sheets, impatient for the dawn and Tom to come and rouse me with his caresses. Other nights I forced myself to show more restraint and donned a proper form-concealing white linen nightgown or gossamer-thin cobweb lawn night-shift to tantalizingly veil my burgeoning woman's body, so that he would tease me out of it, shouting, "Be gone, virtuous raiments!" and chastise me for my false modesty and pull me naked and squealing across his knees to spank my bare bottom until it bore a matching set of smarting red handprints and he could truly say, not just in jest, that he had left his mark on me.

Some mornings, to give myself the illusion of being in control, in full command of my body and emotions, I rose before the dawn, and bade Kat lace me into a severe high-collared black mourning gown with a stiffly boned bodice, and sat myself down upon the window seat with my head bowed over a book, so that when Tom arrived he found a proper paragon of virtuous and modest maiden-hood waiting for him.

And there were other mornings when he would catch me in the act of dressing. He would come in determined to play lady's maid, and shoo the tittering, blushing Mrs Ashley out of his way with a swat at her "great buttocks". He would help me draw the sheer cobweb lawn shift over my head, and help me with my stays and bodice laces, always letting his fingers dally most familiarly, stand-ing behind me, pressing his loins close, as his hands roved over me, often lingering to caress the bones at my hips as he held me and his lips pressed a kiss onto the nape of my neck, or nuzzled my ears and shoulders. He would kneel at my feet to put my stockings on, pausing first to playfully nip and nibble my naked toes, before rolling the stockings up and tying my silken garters in pretty bows just below my knees. And he would brush my hair, one hundred long, luxuriant strokes, over my scalp and down to my waist, before his deft fingers began to braid and nimbly insert the pins before he crowned me with my crescent-shaped French hood, darting in to steal a swift kiss if there were a chin-strap that required fastening. As he tilted my chin up and trailed his fingers slowly over my neck, pretending to examine the strap, to make sure it was neither too tight nor too loose, oh how I would shiver and my knees would feel deliciously weak and it was all I could do not to fall at his feet and pull up my skirts and open my legs, begging him to take me. At such times, I was as shameless as a bitch in heat.

To my surprise, I revelled in being naked before him. I felt a hot and happy wanton pride and a surge of intoxicating power when I finally admitted it to myself and stopped pretending to a modesty I didn't truly feel.

Throughout the day, whenever Tom was away – and oh how bereft and empty the house seemed without him! – I was often sullen and listless, weary as though I hadn't slept at all, and prone to be short of temper and tart of tongue, to snap at those about me who innocently and unintentionally irritated my frayed and passion-inflamed nerves, as sensitive as a rotten tooth is to sugar. Shadows hovered beneath my eyes and Cupid's arrow shot away all appetite for food. I hungered only for Tom, to greedily swallow down love's nectar when his cock-cannon fired inside my eager mouth. But when Tom was near, all it took was a touch of his hand or even a look would suffice and my heart would go *zing!* like the sharply plucked strings of a harp, and what he called "the pink petals amongst the red" would grow moist with the dew of lust as I yearned for my gardener to come and tend my rosy buds, growing well now under his care. And I lost all trust I had ever had in my knees; I felt as if the whole of me would turn to water upon which a pulsing, throbbing, vibrant pink flower would bob like a lustily beating heart. As such fanciful thoughts assailed me, my whole body would quiver as if I were one of the wobbly fat ladies the pastry cook fashioned out of jelly for Tom's amusement, and Kate would voice concern that I had caught a chill and order another applewood log thrown upon the fire, so solicitous was she for my welfare and blind to the truth before her eyes.

Then suddenly a strange lethargy began to steal over Kate, sapping her energy. She grew listless and pale and often queasy, and began to shun her breakfast tray, and lie abed late. She took frequent naps throughout the day and retired early at night as if she could not wait to fall into bed and sleep. Sometimes she would even nod off over her embroidery or beloved English translations of the Scriptures. Heedlessly, Tom and I would laugh and off we would scurry for long rides, galloping across the countryside with the wind in our hair, or sometimes, when the fancy seized us, and Kate bade us go and enjoy ourselves while she went early, yawning, droopy-eyed and leaden-footed to bed, to sail in her barge beneath the silvery moonlight upon the smooth sparkling sapphire-black river.

While Kate slumbered peacefully and obliviously in her bed, we would lounge by the fire, late into the night, lolling together on the bearskin rug, dipping strawberries into wine or cream and feeding each other, with Tom's head resting in my lap or mine in his. Once he even dared take a strawberry and reach beneath my skirts with it, pressing it gently between my legs, against the pink heart of my womanhood. And, drawing it out again, the ruby-red heart-shaped fruit glistening with my juices, he looked up at me, deep into my eyes, as he slowly savoured it. I shivered and quivered and felt as if the core of me were slowly melting and soon all that would be left of me was a hank of red hair and a puddle of flesh-coloured wax at his feet. He made even something as simple as eating strawberries a sensual delight.

One night he recited a poem to me:

> *They flee from me that sometime did me seek,*
> *With naked foot stalking in my chamber.*
> *I have seen them gentle, tame, and meek*
> *That are now wild and do not remember*
> *That sometime they put themselves in danger*

> *To take bread at my hand; and now they range*
> *Busily seeking in continual change.*
>
> *Thanks be to Fortune, it hath been otherwise*
> *Twenty times better; but once especial,*
> *In thin array, after a pleasant guise,*
> *When her loose gown did from her shoulders fall,*
> *And she me caught in her arms long and small,*
> *And Therewithall so sweetly did me kiss,*
> *And softly said, "Dear heart, how like you this?"*
>
> *It was no dream, for I lay broad awaking.*
> *But all is turned now through my gentleness*
> *Into a strange fashion of forsaking,*
> *And I have leave to go of her goodness,*
> *And she also to use new-fangleness.*
> *But since that I unkindly so am served,*
> *"How like you this," what hath she now deserved?*

Afterwards, he told me that the poet, Sir Thomas Wyatt, had written it for my mother, each stanza heart-heavy with longing and regret for their lost love, the chance fate had cheated them of when my father, the determined hunter and mighty Caesar of Wyatt's most famous poem, marked her out as his and fastened a black velvet choker about her neck like a dog's collar set with diamonds spelling out "Noli Me Tangere", making it plain that she was his.

By firelight, Tom resurrected, just for me, the fascinating creature that was Anne Boleyn. Through his words he made her live again, letting me see her as, in a moment of triumph, she danced and waded through red rose petals which my father had ordered suspended in a golden net beneath the ceiling to be released, to rain down, upon her entry into the Great Hall. And how she had laughed and spun around, her black hair swinging gypsy-free all the way down to her knees, with my own unborn self making her belly into a proud little round ball beneath her crimson gown. The gold cord laces on the back of her bodice had been left unfastened, for her personal comfort and to better accommodate me, and the tasselled ends bobbed and bounced, mingling with the blackness of her hair as she danced, and also to boast, to flaunt her success in the faces of her enemies and the naysayers who had dared declare that Anne Boleyn would never be queen. Giddy with triumph, she threw back her head and laughed and laughed as she spun round and round, stirring up rose petals and, watching her, my father smiled with joy.

Tom was a man who loved to live on the slicing edge of danger's razor. As time passed, he grew bolder and more flagrant in his attentions to me, touching or looking at me in such a suggestive way right in front of Kate and other members of the household that I feared the truth would be revealed.

Once when my tutor had stepped momentarily out of our schoolroom, Tom seized the chance to run in, drop to his knees, and crawl beneath the table where I sat absorbed in my Greek translations, and duck his head beneath my skirts. I gave a startled cry and Master Grindal opened the door just as Tom was backing out from beneath the table and standing up. He made some excuse about having come to see how his stepdaughter's lessons progressed only to discover me in a state of fright because of a spider, which he had just killed, but my flaming hot blush, and the absence of a dead spider, betrayed the truth, I am sure. And Master Grindal knew it took much more than a spider to frighten Elizabeth Tudor.

Another afternoon we were strolling in the garden with Kate when Tom decided that I had been overlong in wearing mourning for my father; he was tired of seeing me in black all the time, and so saying, unsheathed his dagger and, bidding Kate hold my arms behind my back, he began to cut my black velvet gown away from me until it was reduced to nothing but a pile of useless ribbons curling round my feet.

But he did not stop there. As the jagged ribbons fell and twined round my ankles like ebony snakes, his dagger rose and thrust down again and again, slicing through my starched white petticoats and soft lawn shift, his hands snatching and tearing away the frayed white strips, baring my limbs and privy parts.

My face burning with shame, I struggled against Kate's grasp. I was surprised by her strength; her graceful white hands were suddenly as strong as shackles. Turning to try to see her face, I thought I glimpsed a gloating malice lurking in her eyes before it disappeared so swiftly I was never truly certain if I had seen it or merely imagined it. I twisted hard against her, with all my might, and finally succeeded in wresting my wrists free. I twisted around and grasped and clung to her, my face flaming crimson as the roses that bloomed nearby, as I felt a breeze caress my now newborn-naked buttocks. My whole body felt on fire with shame, and yet . . . there was something else, something that made my knees grow weak. There were distinct threads of excitement and desire plaited so intricately with the humiliation, shame, and fear that I could not for the life of me tell where one ended and the other began. I couldn't understand it, and it frightened me; it undermined my illusion of being in control, mistress of my own mind and body. I was in such a state of turmoil; peace of mind became akin to the Holy Grail to me!

As I clung entreatingly to Kate, begging her to have mercy and shield me, to take off one of her petticoats and give it to me to hide my nakedness, Tom roared with laughter, smacked my buttocks, and sliced through the laces at the back of my stiff leather stays and tore them away, flinging them carelessly into the rosebushes. He then sliced nimbly through the little that was left of my shift, baring the pert, firm, little pink-tipped white mounds of my breasts, leaving me wearing only my black velvet slippers, white stockings, and black silk ribbon garters tied in bows below my knees.

"Look, Kate!" he exclaimed, grabbing hold of my shoulders and pulling me away from her, pinning my arms back, as I continued to plead with my stepmother to spare me just one petticoat to cover myself as impassionedly as ever a starving beggar cried for a crust of bread. "Our Bess has acquired a bosom at last! Just look at those dainty pink buds blooming proudly on those creamy little hillocks!" He jabbed a finger at my stiff, rosy nipples, actually daring to tweak them right in front of Kate! "And look there, Kate" – he pointed down between my tightly clenched thighs – "what a fine crop of carroty curls our Bess has got!"

A dam burst within me then and tears of shame poured from my eyes and, shielding myself as best I could with my arms and hair, I broke free of them and raced across the seemingly endless expanse of velvety green lawn while behind me Tom and Kate whooped and howled with laughter, doubling over and slapping their thighs and clinging to each other in their mirth. The gardeners and their helpers stopped their work, dropped their hoes and rakes and pruning shears, and stared wide-eyed as I ran past, blinking and rubbing their eyes in disbelief. I daresay it was the first and only time in their lives they had ever seen a naked princess running across a lawn.

As I burst into the house, I could not bear to meet the stunned faces of the servants, or their hastily turned backs or averted eyes, as I bolted up the stairs. How could I ever bear to face them again knowing they had seen me thus? Like a babe in the throes of a tantrum, I howled for Kat at the top of my lungs as I hurled myself through my chamber door and straight into her arms.

"How could she do it?" I demanded, when I told her what had happened and the part Kate had played in it.

"Aye, my little chick, it is unlike her to indulge in such unseemly sport," Kat concurred, concern creasing her brow. "She was never a one to take pleasure in another person's pain or discomfort but to always step in and try to remedy it. 'Kind, capable Kate,' your father always used to call her; he swore there was never such a one as her for making things right. More than once I heard him say had Lucifer hurt his knee when he fell and Kate had been there she would have slapped on a poultice and bound it up for him, just as she always did his own sore leg."

"Then why?" I wept. "*Why* would she do this to me?" I sobbed as I laid my head on Kat's pillow-plump bosom and she hugged me close and stroked my hair.

"It can only mean *one* thing, pet," Kat said, pausing meaningfully, and I raised my head to look at her. "She is jealous of you; the Lord Admiral fancies you and she knows it."

I stood up straight and blinked. It had never occurred to me that Kate even suspected; I thought her well and truly blind to what went on behind her back and beneath her own roof.

"Try to see it her way; she's but five years shy of forty, a fair gracious lady she is to be sure, but" – Kat looked me up and down – "not a nubile young lass like you, pet. She sees the difference, mark you, my pet, and she *feels* it too, like a lance through her heart every time she sees him look at you. A ring on her finger doesn't always make a woman safe where her husband is concerned. A betrothal band doesn't come with a tether to keep him always at her side and in her sights or right next to her in bed at night. A man's a man, love, even if you put a gold ring on his hand and have a churchman say words over it. Aye" – Kat beamed broadly, like a cat licking its whiskers over a bowl of rich cream – "she's *jealous* of you, that she is, and with good cause, eh, pet? The Lord Admiral certainly is a handsome rascal, is he not, my bonny Bess?"

She giggled and nudged me knowingly, until I blushed and looked away, too embarrassed by the stark naked truth to meet her eyes.

The awkward moment was broken when there was a knock upon the door and Blanche Parry, the wife of my steward, called out in her cheery, lilting Welsh voice that she came bearing a gift for me.

Kat snatched up my dressing gown and hurriedly bundled me into it as the door swung wide and in marched Blanche leading a procession of serving maids, each with her arms outstretched, carrying a complete new gown – bodice, over- and under-sleeves, skirt, and kirtle – in a rainbow of colours, all the best ones to suit my flame-bright hair, dark eyes, and milk-pale skin. There was a whole gamut of greens as bright as emeralds, to the more subdued shade of moss, pease porridge, and the deep green of the forest. And tawny trimmed with gold, garnet, russet, and sunset orange, sunshine yellow, regal purple, peacock blue trimmed with peacock feathers, cloth-of-gold, delicate pink, and crimson. As it was the fashion for gowns to be made in detachable parts, so that kirtles and sleeves could be mixed and matched with different bodices and skirts, dozens of eye-catching combinations were possible, and I need never appear dressed the same way for many a day. And behind them all came Tom Seymour, sauntering audaciously into the room, whistling a lively tune, as if he had not just moments before humiliated me by stripping me stark naked in the rose garden.

Like an indignant mother hen, flapping and squawking in defence of her chick, Kat rushed at him.

"For shame, My Lord Admiral, stripping a princess of England naked . . ."

"But see, Mrs Ashley," he said with a broad smile, and a wave of his hand to take in the bounteous array of new gowns, "now I have come to clothe her!"

"Oh!" Kat cried, affection fighting a losing battle with outrage being played out across her face, "you are a *wicked, wicked* man!" She waggled a finger at him, then convulsed in blushing giggles like a schoolgirl when he playfully snapped at it with his fine white teeth.

He caught her to him in an embrace, and drummed his hands playfully upon her plump buttocks. "Come now, Kat," he cajoled. "Now that you've forgiven me – and I know you have, woman, it's as plain as that pretty nose on your face! – will you not intercede with Her Highness there and persuade her to forgive me? Remind her that just as forgiveness is a divine quality, 'tis a worthy virtue for royalty as well!"

"Oh!" Kat cried and threw up her hands and rushed back to my side, rosy-cheeked with her face wreathed in smiles. "Come now, pet," she turned to me and cajoled, as I continued to hold myself aloof, back straight and nose in the air, looking anywhere but at Tom. "See what pretty things the naughty man has brought you to atone for his naughtiness! It would be most unkind not to forgive him! And he is right about forgiveness being a fine, princely quality! And it would not be meet to stand on your dignity and hold a grudge when the *dear* naughty man has brought you all these pretties!"

The smiling servant women formed a circle round me, each holding her arms outstretched, offering the gorgeous gowns to me, as Tom came and put his arm around my shoulders and drew me close to kiss the top of my head. And in that instant I was conquered, my knees melted like wax over an open flame, and I crumpled into his embrace.

"Oh, Bess! My darling Bess!" he cried, burying his face in my wild, disarrayed hair.

"Are all these *really* for me?" I asked.

"Every one! And all chosen by me, just for you, my bonny Bess!" he declared proudly. "I meant what I said – it's high time we got you out of mourning. Youth and beauty deserve colour, not crow black! So I have come to tempt you! Look at this one, Bess!" He reached out to caress a gown of pink brocade. "Cunny pink!" he said, causing all the women to giggle and blush. "What?" he protested. "It is very close to the colour of cunny lips; is it not, ladies? Here!" His hand shot out to snatch the sash from my dressing gown, causing it to fall open. "Let us compare!" He held a fold of the pink gown close to the cleft between my thighs. "Indeed it is!" he beamed. "Upon my soul, I declare, I have a fine eye for colour, haven't I, ladies?" He looked round the room for affirmation and all agreed that indeed he did as I blushed furiously and gathered my robe close about me. "And look!" He held the skirt of the pink gown up. "Is there not something suggestive of the shape of a woman's cunny in the pattern of the weave?" he asked mischievously, sparking another round of blushes and giggles all around.

"This one!" he exclaimed suddenly, darting forward to snatch a gown of bright robin's egg blue silk exquisitely embroidered with sunny yellow daffodils around the cuffs, bodice, and hem, with gold brocade under-sleeves and kirtle. "I want to see you in it now!" And so saying he shucked the robe from my shoulders, and even though Mrs Ashley protested that to be properly dressed I needed proper undergarments – shift, stays, and petticoats – he tugged the dress over my head, then set to work adjusting the ties that attached the sleeves and bodice, before turning me round and lacing up the back, while I found myself nearly swooning at the exquisite sensation of silk against my naked skin, without the lawn and linen of shift and petticoats, and the prison of the stiff leather stays, posing a barrier between. I blushed hotly as I felt a burst of wetness between my thighs and my nipples stiffen, making their presence known through the beautiful blue silk, and lowered my eyes, shamed by the knowing smiles, titters, and whispers of the serving maids and wished Tom would dismiss them.

"There!" Tom beamed. "Didn't I tell you? It's high time you leave off those melancholy weeds; there's no point in such vibrant beauty going around dressed like a storm cloud in black and shades of grey all the time!"

And then he was on his knees before the clothespress, fishing out the black mourning gowns and sombre-hued satins and silks and damasks of ash and cinder, a whole gamut of greys from the most delicate to the darkest, and flinging them out.

"Away with this! Away!" he ordered. "I hereby banish you from My Lady Princess's wardrobe! In with the new and out with the old!" he said to the serving maids and they obligingly laid down their armloads of peacock finery upon my bed and began gathering up the discarded garments of grief and mourning. "And now" – Tom smiled at them – "out with you all!" He pinched and patted their bottoms as they obediently filed out, blushing and giggling, a smile on every face.

"Now then." He turned smilingly to me. He started towards me but then made a detour to my bed, where he snatched up a deep crimson satin gown trimmed with glittering jet spangles, beads, and black Spanish lace. "Wear this for me tonight, Bess. It reminds me of the dress your mother wore the night she danced in rose petals. Wear it for me tonight, Bess, and we too shall dance in rose petals!"

Then he enfolded me in his arms and kissed me long and lingeringly, then let his lips trail down the curve of my neck, and over my shoulder, down my arm to my hand, to the fingertips, before he backed slowly out the door.

"Oh what a man! A fine lusty fellow, is he not, Bess?" Kat enthused. "If he weren't married already I am as sure as sure can be that he would look to have you, to be buxom and bonair in bed and at board!"

"But he *is* wed already," I reminded Kat and myself, though in truth it seemed not to matter. Indeed, I was often surprised by just how little I cared.

That night, after supper, before he took the already yawning, bleary-eyed Kate's arm to escort her upstairs, he brushed a good-night kiss onto my cheek and whispered one word – "Midnight."

At the appointed hour, I descended the stairs, wearing the crimson gown he had requested. He was waiting for me. And while his wife slept obliviously in a room above our heads, a lute player began to softly strum a pulsing, sensual Spanish melody and Tom led me out to dance. "You dance as light as a dust mote on a sunbeam," he said as his manservant leaned over the banister and tossed handfuls of red petals down on us.

I laughed, threw back my head, and spun round and round beneath the fluttering, fragrant red petal rain. Tom stood back and watched me, and then he reached out his hand and pulled me into his arms, and kissed me passionately, holding me so close it felt as if our two bodies had fused into one.

Yet things were never quite the same after that day in the garden. Kate seemed to grow colder, to hold herself more guarded and aloof around me. A layer of thin but impenetrable frost had frozen over my warm stepmother – just enough for me to see that she was still the same person she had always been, but that her feelings for me had changed. And another seemed now to have replaced me in Kate's heart – my nine-year-old cousin, Lady Jane Grey, a shy little scholar who loved learning above all things, who had recently come to live with us at Chelsea. Though I did not begrudge Jane, whom I knew to be much maltreated and beaten for the slightest mistake or most trivial imperfection by her cruel and ambitious parents; this child sorely needed affection, kindness, and encouragement. I confess, my stepmother's coolness hurt me, and because of it I was not always as kind to Jane as I should have been. She looked up to me, in a kind of awe, as if she admired me, with her mouth agape, and I would snap tartly in passing that she had best close it before a fly flew in, and go on my merry way without a thought for her feelings. And whenever Tom gave the poor little mite so much as an iota of his attention I reacted harshly, meting out even more rudeness and unkindness, so jealous was I of his time and affection, and I would sulk until he teased me out of my dark, pouting mood.

Though always proper and deferential, the servants' behaviour towards me seemed also to be rimed with frost. Sometimes I would come upon two or three of them unawares, huddled together in conversation, and hear my name and my mother's and such remarks as "bad blood will tell," knowingly asserted. And tales of my mother's trial and the crimes she had been accused of – adultery and incest – were dredged up again with gossipy relish and assurances that I was bound to go the same way.

And Kat . . . Someone must have spoken sharply to my Mrs Ashley, for of a sudden a bolt of mighty lightning seemed to demolish the castles in the clouds she had built. She awoke from her dreams with the troubling realization that she had erred in her duties as governess to a royal princess by encouraging her virgin charge to dally with a married man, and set about trying to remedy the situation and scrub away the tarnish she had allowed to blacken my name and reputation.

But against Tom Seymour's fatal charm we were all powerless. Kat found herself in the same quandary as I did myself – her heart saying one thing and her head another. She made an effort to arise earlier to rush me out of bed and into my clothes before Tom came sauntering in for his early morning visits.

"Must I sleep fully clothed to thwart him?" I groused at having to rise before the dawn.

"Nay, lovey," Kat said, her words contradicting her actions as she laced me into my gown, "you are even more comely in only your hair and bare skin. The Lord Admiral his naughty self told me that when you blush you are like a statue of pink ivory sprung to life!"

And on mornings when she was loath to drag herself out of her warm bed, Kat did manage to come in before matters went too far, to shoo "that naughty man" out and to scold him for coming barelegged in his nightshirt and slippers into a maiden's bedchamber. "It is a most improper way to come calling, My Lord!" she chided as sternly as she could against that dagger-sharp deadly charm.

I had yet to grant him the ultimate favour, and Kat was determined that my virginity, a woman's most precious commodity, and vital to a princess in the royal marriage game, should be preserved until my wedding night whether my bridegroom be the Lord Admiral or someone else – a fine prince perhaps? – as yet unknown to me.

But Tom had a way of getting the better of her, and if he was inclined to tarry, there was nothing Mrs Ashley could do about it. I remember him once dropping to his knees and scampering about the room on all fours, barking like a dog, as he gave chase to my flustered governess, running her round and round the room, before he pounced and sunk his teeth into her "great buttocks" through her voluminous billowing white bedgown. Kat yelped and clutched her bottom. "Oh you *wicked, wicked* man!" she cried as she fled back into her bedchamber and bolted and barricaded the door behind her. And muffled by its thickness we heard her repeat again that Tom was a "*wicked, wicked* man" and never had she seen the likes of him, whilst I fell back on my bed, convulsed with glee, and he, still playing the fool, bounded up onto the bed and began to kiss and lick me from head to toe, like a great big, playful puppy.

Another time, when she walked in just as he was lifting the hem of his nightshirt, to mischievously show me what I had done to him, Kat gave a squeal of horror and Tom turned smilingly to her and lifted his nightshirt still higher and began to walk towards her, holding his cock like a weapon. "Lift up that skirt, woman," he smilingly commanded. "I want to see if those great buttocks of yours are truly the stuff of dreams and then, perhaps, I shall indeed stuff this between them!" With a terrified shriek, Kat fled, again to lock and barricade herself in her room, leaving me, her charge, to fend for myself, as Tom shucked off his nightshirt and leapt laughing onto my bed and into my arms.

The fear that she would bear the full brunt of the blame should the whole sordid story come out still needling at her, Kat went to speak with Kate. Time had revealed that pregnancy was the cause of my stepmother's strange lethargy, and, though it was obvious she was troubled by suspicions herself, she rounded on my Mrs Ashley, scolding her soundly for troubling her with such wicked accusations, staunchly defending her husband as a great overgrown boy, always playing and making merry, a great one for jests, sometimes of the bawdy sort, but *never* meaning any harm, and to insinuate such things against him was an insult she took personally to heart. And to prove her loyalty and belief in her husband's innocence, and to try to silence the servants' gossip, she began, for a time, to accompany Tom on his morning visits to me.

With his wife at his side, cloaking her concern with a strained smile, Tom curtailed his attentions to me, restricting himself to playful smacks and ticklings, and chasing me and Mrs Ashley around the room, and kisses and hugs of the kind that none could call unsuitable, the sort that any fond stepfather or uncle might give to a young girl. Sometimes he still played at lady's maid, but only as a jester would, swapping silliness for sensuality, until, satisfied that nothing was amiss, Kate resumed lying abed late and left her husband to play whatever games he pleased.

"It's all perfectly innocent, child's play, boisterousness and high spirits, and I will hear no more about it," she said firmly and turned her back on my governess's wringing hands and worried eyes.

So Tom and I continued on the same as always. We would wave a lighthearted goodbye to Kate and off to picnic beneath the trees we would go, mocking her constant craving for cheese tarts. Even though they bent her double in a bloated agony that resulted in loud, stinking farts that greatly undermined her dignity, still she could not resist them. They called to her like a siren's song, and the cook was kept busy baking batches of them almost daily. Giggling like naughty children, Tom and I would roll on the grass in each other's arms, laughing and making up silly rhymes about tarts and farts.

But it was all about to end. Tom himself would cure me of all my dreams and delusions about love and passion. He would douse the flame even as he sought to bank it up into a soul- and sense-consuming inferno that would destroy the last vestiges of reason and restraint and leave me lying shattered at his feet, a weak and foolish woman enslaved and entirely in his power.

❧ 9 ❧

Mary

I was so delighted when my little cousin, Lady Jane Grey, accepted an invitation to come and stay a week with me in October. She always held herself so stiff and aloof; I was afraid she didn't like me. When I kissed, embraced, and touched her or reached out to stroke and pet her beautiful hair, she would flinch and stiffen, and pull away from me, but I loved children and was determined to win her.

I had not seen that shy little lady in ever so long, though I remembered well the delicate beauty of her heart-shaped face, milky white with a smattering of freckles, like cinnamon sprinkled on cream, and her wealth of wavy chestnut hair. *Elfin* was a word that always sprang to my mind when I thought of her; she was so diminutive, small-boned and slender, tiny for her years, like one of those unobtrusive household sprites that are said to help tidy the house if a treat is left out for them at night. She was one of the most striking children I had ever seen, though shy beyond measure, morose and unsmiling, and incapable of meeting anyone's eyes. She rarely spoke above a whisper except in the presence of like-minded scholars; she was so besotted with learning that in the schoolroom she quite forgot her shyness and spoke up boldly, parading her intelligence like a peacock strutting to show off his tail feathers.

Her dainty, pallid ghost still stalks my dreams; I see her as a forlorn little figure in her stark black, brown, or grey gowns, and equally plain hoods, devoid of ornamentation except for a discreet border of jet or silk braid. I can see her standing there, assuming that stiff stance, with her hands clasped, and her sorrowful brown eyes downcast. There was something always so sad about her.

I remembered being her age and how I had always loved and longed for pretty things. I wanted to banish the blacks and chase the dull greys and mud-dingy browns out of her wardrobe and replace them with rainbows and glitter; I wanted to make her smile, sparkle, and shine. I wanted to change the greys to silver and the browns to copper and the blacks to gold, to coax out the glints of red and gold hiding in that abundant, wavy mass of chestnut hair.

Though envy is a sin, I confess I was guilty of it, for I did envy Jane Grey the glory and abundance of her hair. My own had grown distressingly thin and faded. When grey begins to take a tenacious foothold, encroaching more every year, in some women's hair, it has a lovely silvery hue, but not so with mine. On me it was dull and made me appear haggard and older. When I was a little girl everyone loved my hair. How sadly I had changed! All is vanity!

But Jane was, alas, misguided in matters of religion. She was a rabidly fervent Protestant, like a mad dog afflicted with the rabies of heresy, and had a distressing tendency to sometimes be rude and obnoxious in expressing her beliefs and mocking those of others, even if they were her elders. It was not a becoming trait in one so pretty.

One night, after a quiet supper, as we walked past the open doors of my chapel I curtsied low and crossed myself. Jane watched me with a puzzled expression and then asked, "To whom do you curtsy? I see no one within."

"I am curtsying to the Host, my dear," I gently explained, gesturing to the holy wafers that lay upon a golden plate on the beautifully arrayed altar, draped with embroidered gold-fringed cloth and adorned with a large bejewelled crucifix, all illuminated by a number of tall, perfumed tapers. "The bread is consecrated and represents the body of Our Lord and it becomes thus indeed when it is elevated by the priest during Mass; that is why it is called the

Miracle of the Mass. And it is such a *wondrous*, *glorious* thing to behold, to gaze up reverently and feel that one is in the presence of the Lord and He is performing a miracle for our benefit, to reward us for our faith!"

"I see." Little Jane nodded gravely. "Pray tell me, Cousin Mary, do you also do obeisance to the baker who baked the Lord in his oven? And do you think it a fit expression of your love of Our Saviour to champ Him between your teeth?"

I was so outraged I wanted to slap her, but I curtailed my wrath, remembering that violence was a familiar and commonplace fixture in Jane's sad life. Her parents thought it their bounden duty to beat her raw with a riding crop for the tiniest infraction or imperfection of appearance, conduct, speech, or demeanour. Servants gossiped of Jane's mother, the robust, rawboned, red-haired Frances, Duchess of Suffolk, beating Jane until she collapsed exhausted, florid-faced and panting, and had not the strength to raise the crop or cane again and had to be helped from the room by her maids, leaving her daughter lying weeping and bleeding on the floor.

So I suppressed my rage, and instead said quietly, "You have much still to learn, little Cousin Jane. For one so wise in book-learning you are surprisingly bereft of tact and human sympathy and understanding. But now is not the time to discuss it; come with me" – I determinedly took her hand – "I have a surprise for you. . . ."

Though I still harboured grave reservations about Chelsea and those who lived there, and particularly disliked the idea of impressionable young people such as my sister and Jane being brought up in an environ of moral laxity by a widow who had failed to properly honour her late husband's memory and leapt lustily and straightaway into another man's bed before the requisite mourning period had passed, I was, for the sake of Jane's physical wellbeing, grateful that Catherine Parr had taken her under her wing. Vowing that he would make a grand marriage for her, the Lord Admiral had purchased her wardship from her parents, who were no doubt glad to have more time to devote to their shared great passion for hunting instead of having to beat their eldest daughter bloody, black and blue.

So instead of chastising Jane for her blasphemous impudence as she sorely deserved, I took her hand and led her into her bedroom where, spread out upon her bed, lay an opulent silver tinsel gown festooned with heavy gold parchment lace, little twinkling diamonds, and delicate seed pearls. And there was a matching French hood, sparkling with an intricate braided edging of gold, pearls, and diamonds, with a waist-length gold lace veil at the back.

"There!" I said, beaming down at it. "Now what do you think of that, Cousin Jane?"

The poor, pale little thing was overcome, struck speechless at the sight of that sumptuous gown, the likes of which I am sure she had never seen. And, in truth, I could not blame her. It was *magnificent*.

"It is . . . it is . . ." She gulped, then blurted out quickly, "It is very grand, Madame!"

"Oh sweeting!" I smiled down at her and stroked her cheek. "Not Madame. Call me what I am – your Cousin Mary! And yes, it is indeed *very* grand! I had it made just for you, to wear when we go to court to celebrate the King's birthday. I remember how when I was a little girl I always loved pretty things; and it is time we got you out of those drab and boring clothes. And I *long* to see my plain little Jane transformed into a beautiful butterfly! Oh but I can see you are overwhelmed!" I hugged the poor little thing, standing there gaping and, I could tell, on the verge of tears. "And the hour grows late, so I will leave you to your rest," I said as I withdrew, admittedly feeling a little hurt that she had not expressed her gratitude more enthusiastically; she had not even hugged me back, and I had taken such time and lavished so much care upon the creation of that beautiful gown. She had not, it occurred to me afterwards, as I settled myself into bed, even said "Thank you."

The next day, Jane and I left for Hampton Court, to be with Edward on his tenth birthday. I had a special gift for him and could not wait to see the smile that would light up his face when I gave it to him. I had worked my fingers to the bone, stabbing, blistering, and scraping them, all out of love for my little brother, to create a gift born of my own heart and hands, so that I had to resort to slathering them in creams and ointments and sleeping in white linen gloves so that they would be soft, ladylike, and presentable when I knelt before my brother to wish him a happy birthday.

I did not know it then, but it would be the last time we would all be together – Edward, Elizabeth, Jane, and I.

My brother's court was far different from Father's. It was marked by a frowning severity interspersed with occasional bursts of gaiety, like loud fireworks lighting up the night sky and quickly fading in a shower of sparks that sank into the dingy dark water of the Thames. Edward's face habitually wore a frown, despite his youth; he personified the words *priggish* and *pompous*. He dressed in clothes greatly puffed and padded that mimicked the garments Father had worn in his later years, and pronounced oaths and struck poses also in imitation of him, but it was more a pathetic caricature than a true likeness. Though none would dare admit it, everyone could see it, even those who encouraged him. Though sired by a king, Edward simply was not meant to be one, though his handlers treated him like liquid candy and saw themselves as the confectioners who poured him into a mould shaped like the late, great Henry. Something was wrong in the mixture, recipe, or technique, and it would *never* turn out right.

Edward was a stickler for ceremony and had changed the rules regarding entering and exiting the King's presence from what they had been in Father's day. I was now required to curtsy not thrice but a full *five* times upon entering his presence, and five times again when I reached the foot of the dais where he sat upon his gilded throne, and then I must kneel, and stay thus, until he either bade me rise or withdraw, and upon leaving I must walk backwards and again twice repeat the five requisite curtsies. I thought it over-much, especially for a sister of the King, but, since it was his birthday, I chose not to speak up.

Instead, dressed in a splendid new black gown lavishly embroidered in red silk, with full puffed under-sleeves and a kirtle of red embroidered in black, with a large, ruby-studded crucifix pinned boldly and proudly at my breast, I knelt humbly before him, staring down at his square-toed red-silk-slashed white velvet slippers resting on a velvet cushion, and holding out my carefully prepared gift, wrapped in cloth-of-gold and tied at each end with silver cord, and waited for Edward to acknowledge me.

"Sister," Edward intoned grandly, giving me his hand to kiss, "you have brought us a present for our birthday, I see."

"Yes, Your Majesty," I answered, feeling the bite of the step's edge through my skirts and wishing he would give me leave to rise, but I kept smiling and offered up my gift to him.

With childish delight that revealed his true age, Edward cast aside his grown-up pretensions as he eagerly undid the wrappings and lifted out the most *beautiful* hobbyhorse the world has ever seen. His head was cloth of gold dappled with regal purple embroidered silk spots, and his mane made of long bright red silk fringe. His black eyes were fashioned of glittering jet, and his silver bridle sparkled with jewels – I had dismantled a necklace and a pair of earrings to provide them – a procession of which continued down the silver stick, upon which was affixed a small quilted purple velvet saddle so that Edward could ride in comfort.

"Do you like him, Edward?" I asked eagerly, with an earnest, childlike smile. "You can ride him in the gallery when the weather is foul and outdoors in the garden when the weather is fine. Though it was bold of me, I know, to name him, I call him Golden Gallant. I made him with my own two loving hands!" I held up my hands for Edward to see, half wishing now that I had not gone to such pains to heal my blisters and restore my skin to its usual ladylike softness so that he could see proof of how hard I had laboured out of love for him.

"*A hobbyhorse, Mary?*" Edward frowned down at me and queried in pompous disbelief. "You have given the King of England a *toy* meant for *babies*, Mary?"

Edward arrogantly thrust my gift aside, and the Lord Protector, Edward Seymour, took it and, with a malicious smile lurking about his lips, broke my beautiful hobbyhorse over his knee and tossed the two pieces contemptuously over his shoulder, then brushed his hands together and resumed his vigilant pose beside Edward's throne.

"*Go!*" Edward leaned his cheek sulkily on his hand and slouched down in his throne as he waved me away. "The very sight of your snivelling face vexes me!"

"But, Edward, my dear brother, I . . ." Tears pricked my eyes as I vainly tried to find the right words to explain that I had meant no harm or offence, I just wanted my brother to have the luxury of being a child while he was still a child, and playing like one, instead of always being burdened with the weighty duties and pomp and ceremony that came with a crown.

"By this gesture you have shown me *exactly* what you think of me, Mary," Edward informed me coldly. "And my Councillors have told me that you have often expressed your opinion that I lack the maturity and years to make important decisions. You see me as a child, not a king!"

"Edward, my dear . . ." I tried again.

"My Lord Protector." With an impatient gesture Edward cut me off and turned to address Edward Seymour. "Did I give my sister leave to address me by my name?"

"Not within my hearing, Your Majesty," Edward Seymour deftly replied.

"Then please instruct the Lady Mary to use the *proper* form of address when she speaks to me, and also remind her that she is not to speak at all unless I give her permission to do so."

"With pleasure, Your Majesty," Edward Seymour purred with a deferential bow before he turned to address me. "Lady Mary," he began in a strict, formal tone, "please conform to the requisite etiquette of this court and address the King as 'Your Majesty', and do not be so free and bold with your words as to speak them without first being given leave to by our gracious sovereign. Do not presume on your close familial ties to take liberties; that would be a *grave* mistake."

Stung by this public rebuke, which had been delivered before the eyes of the entire court – I could hear their titters and whispers behind my back – I bowed my head low and humbly tendered my apologies before retreating, bobbing the required five curtsies twice more, before I backed out the door and fled to my apartment, fighting back tears all the time.

When I returned later that afternoon after I had lain for a time with a cold compress on my head and composed myself, I was in time to observe a most startling scene – the Lord Protector and his wife were arriving just ahead of Catherine Parr and her husband, the Lord Admiral, Sir Thomas Seymour. I knew there had been some discord between them about the jewels that had been given Catherine Parr when she was queen and whether they were Crown Property or not, and also regarding matters of precedence. As the Queen Dowager, until Edward married and England had a proper queen-consort, she should have enjoyed precedence over every other lady in the land, but since she had remarried, it was argued that she had forfeited this right. The Lord Admiral and his brother had argued bitterly over this and, apparently, judging by what I witnessed, the matter had not been settled.

Just as the Lord Protector's wife, the Duchess of Somerset, a dear friend of mine whom I fondly called "my good gossip Nan", was about to sail majestically across the threshold in her rust-red velvet gown, Tom Seymour sprang forward, caught hold of her train, and yanked it back so hard that I heard stitches pop and she tottered backward, flailing her arms, and most assuredly would have fallen had her husband not caught her in time.

At a nod from the Lord Admiral, and wearing a placid smile to match the serene blue silk of her gown, Kate walked calmly into the royal Presence Chamber.

"Wait, Kate!" Tom cried, causing her to turn back. "Are those not your pearls around that fat sow's neck?" he demanded, pointing at the Duchess's necklace.

Kate hesitated, obviously not wanting to quarrel further, especially not in such a public place with so many eyes upon them. "Tom, *please* . . ."

But the Lord Admiral was not listening; already he was darting forward to snatch the pearls from Nan's neck and fling the broken strand, with pearls flying every which way, at his brother's feet.

"*See!*" he bellowed triumphantly, standing tall and proud with his hands upon his hips. "*I have cast these pearls down before a swine!*"

"Tom, *please* . . ." With a worried frown creasing her brow, Kate came and took his arm. "Come, husband, let us go in and wish Edward a happy birthday."

"We shall see who is liked best here!" Tom tossed back defiantly over his shoulder as he gave in and let Kate lead him into the
King's Presence Chamber.

Ignoring the proper etiquette, Tom bounded up to the dais
where Edward sat, pouting and pompous in white velvet, cloth-of-
silver, and rubies. "Edward, my boy! How fares my favourite
nephew?" He swooped the arrogant little king up, swung him
round, high in the air, as if he were a tot still resident in the nursery instead of a young man teetering on the verge of adolescence,
and then, to the astonished gasps of all, plopped himself down
onto the throne as if it were his favourite fireside chair, with Edward on his lap.

"I have brought you a new pony and a suit of shiny silver armour beautifully enamelled with Tudor roses, and a falcon. His
name is Hercules; I trained him myself to ensure that he was fit for
a king – for you, my fine boy! Ho there! Bring in that pony!" Tom
shouted and with a startled, indignant cry I leapt aside as the inquisitive snout of a black-and-white pony nuzzled the back of my
skirts. The Lord High Chamberlain ran towards the door, loudly
protesting, "You cannot bring a pony into the King's Presence
Chamber!" but the Lord Admiral ignored him. "Bring him in, Bar-
ney, and the hawk too!" he commanded as if he were himself king,
and another servant followed with a hooded falcon perched on his
leather-gauntleted arm.

As it passed me, the hawk screeched and nervously flapped its
wings, causing the bells on its jesses to jangle. I gasped and
clasped a hand to my heart, which was beating far too fast from the
various assaults and indignities I had been subjected to throughout the course of the day.

"Susan!" I called, looking round for my chief lady-in-waiting.
"Have you my smelling salts? I am not well!"

As I clutched the little crystal vial to my nose and inhaled
sharply I saw my little brother whisper something into the Lord
Admiral's ear and Tom Seymour produced from the folds of his
doublet a blue velvet purse bulging no doubt with coins of silver
and gold, which Edward, his eyes agleam with joyful avarice,
hastily concealed beneath the folds of his ermine-edged surcoat.

Elizabeth was the next to arrive, making quite an entrance, cheered by the common folk and servants alike who thronged the gates and courtyard just to catch a glimpse of her. She wore amber velvet delicately embroidered with swirls of golden thread and furred at the sleeves with tawny, with a necklace of amber hearts and gold filigree about her slender white neck, as long and swan-like as The Great Whore's had been. And with a haughty spirit instead of humility she made the requisite series of curtsies, then knelt to present Edward with her birthday offering. It was a book she had made and bound herself. The covers were beautifully embroidered, and the inside filled with "certain passages from Your Majesty's Book of Common Prayer that particularly touched my heart and made a great impression upon me, so that my soul finds solace and my mind turns to them again and again to ponder both their wisdom and their beauty," Elizabeth explained. All were elegantly inscribed in her bold and elaborate Italianate script, all curlicues and flourishes, as if she had actually embroidered each word upon the paper, like black silk on white linen, reminiscent of the Spanish blackwork embroidery my mother had taught me. She had, like the monks and nuns of the good but sadly gone days, illuminated the borders of each page with gilt and coloured inks, drawing various fruits, flowers, designs, and symbols.

Overjoyed with this gift, Edward ordered a cushioned stool brought so that Elizabeth might sit beside him as he perused its pages, nodding over it sagely and enthusiastically, excitedly reading aloud certain passages that he particularly favoured. The courtiers nodded approvingly and proffered compliments on how well the King read and understood Scripture, praising God for blessing them with so devout and erudite a king who had been born free of the shackles of Rome and papist superstition. And Elizabeth was invited to sit again on the dais with him for that evening's entertainment.

Before she kissed his hand and took leave of him, Edward declared her his "favourite sister" and remarked on how she "glowed with the inner radiance of one who has embraced the Reformed Faith."

Having failed so dismally with Edward, I again sought out my little cousin Jane. I knew it would both delight and soothe me to dress her in the gown I had given her. Dressing that pretty child would be just like being a little girl again and dressing up my dolls.

Modestly, she tried to put me off, blushing and stammering, unable to get the words out, at times almost verging on tears, but I insisted, and in the end, she let me have my way. As I undressed her, we both averted our eyes and pointedly said nothing about the ugly bruises marring her pale flesh and the silver-white scars up and down her back, buttocks, and the backs of her thighs. And soon she stood before the looking glass sumptuously arrayed in silver and gold, as I drew the brush through those luxuriant chestnut waves, then set the French hood in place.

"See, Jane, we shall be dressed in reverse!" I smiled, spinning around before her to show off my gold tinsel gown trimmed with silver lace, pearls, and diamonds that was an almost exact mirror image of Jane's gown. I even had a silver lace veil down my back to contrast with her gold one. "But wait, I have one more surprise for you!" And I took from a concealed pocket in my overskirt a velvet box and opened it to reveal a dainty necklace of pearls set in gold rosebuds. "Let me put it on you, my dear!"

When I kissed her cheek and left her she was still standing before the mirror in a state of speechlessness, pale-faced and wide-eyed with amazement. Poor dear, with all her plain dresses and cruel parents, I am sure she never expected to see herself dressed so finely. I am sure that until then she never realized just how pretty she was. And such a dress was indeed the stuff of dreams; indeed, I had told my dressmaker to make a dress that would make those dreams come true, and she had excelled beyond my wildest expectations. With my gift I had pulled Jane out of her cocoon and I could not wait for the court to see the beautiful butterfly that had emerged, so with a glad heart I hastened to the Great Hall so I could be present to see the reaction when Jane arrived. I just knew she would take everyone's breath away!

An hour later Jane walked in wearing a plain black cloth gown, its square neckline filled in with a partlet of plain white lawn without even a stitch of embroidery or a brooch. Her beautiful hair was drawn severely back and pinned up tight, out of sight, beneath the plain black veil of her equally plain black hood. Her only adornment, if it could be accounted such, was a little black velvet-bound prayer book that hung from a black braided cord about her waist. I was so hurt that she had rejected my gift that at first I failed to notice that she was walking very stiffly and her eyes were red as if she had been crying.

I would later hear from my good Susan – who heard the tale direct from Mrs Ellen, Jane's much harried and vexed nurse – what had happened after I left Jane's room. Jane had burst into tears and begun to claw at the dress, calling it "tawdry and vainglorious", and declaring that she "would rather go naked as God made me than offend His eyes with such a decadent and wanton waste of skilled hands that would have been better occupied in sewing simple garments to clothe the poor than in creating such Papist fripperies!" Ripping the gown from her body as if it burned her, Jane flung it into the cold fireplace, onto the ashes. Then, overcome by the enormity of what she had just done, she was assailed by a sudden nervous loosening of the bowels that sent her running for her chamberpot, which Jane afterwards recklessly emptied onto the dress, to render it completely unfit to ever wear again. When her mother came in and saw what she had done, she sent for her riding crop and provided a series of raw ruby-red stripes to adorn Jane's back, bottom, and thighs, which accounted for her slow, stiff gait.

I watched as Thomas Seymour left Kate's side and crossed the room to sweep Jane up high in the air and spin her around, just as he had done earlier with Edward. Smiling broadly, he loudly declared, "I see big things in store for you, little Jane! Bigger than you can even begin to imagine!"

When he put her down, he took her hand and led her to the banquet table. I watched Jane hesitate and try to pull away when he showed her where she should sit, but Tom Seymour bent low and whispered something in her ear, and when Edward came in and we all sat down, Jane gingerly lowered herself into the seat of honour at Edward's side.

A great cake had been prepared to celebrate my brother's birthday, a towering confection of currant cake slathered in waves of pink-tinged whipped cream, with a profusion of red and black berries riding the crest of the waves. It was crowned by a marzipan subtlety depicting his late mother's device – a woman with a crown atop her long flowing yellow tresses emerging from a red and white Tudor rose, whilst behind her a gilded phoenix rose proudly into the sky.

Like a village matchmaker, Tom Seymour leapt up from his chair and went to lean and whisper into Edward's ear when the cake was being served. Edward nodded and bade one of the servers bring Lady Jane, along with her slice of cake, the little head-and-shoulders figure of his late mother. Edward presented it to our blushing, diminutive little cousin himself, saying that since she was named after his late mother it was only fitting that she should have this, her likeness, while the court smiled and, led by a broadly beaming Tom Seymour, applauded the gesture and declared it charmingly romantic.

As the evening wore on, I became more certain of Tom Seymour's intentions. When, at his direction, Jane was again seated at Edward's side, this time upon the dais to watch the entertainments, the pieces began to fall into place – Edward and Jane were the same age, born in the same month and year and, as Edward himself had stated, Jane had indeed been named in honour of his mother, and they were both misguided children wrongly reared up to walk the road of heresy. Tom Seymour was obviously grooming Jane to be England's next queen, a home-grown Protestant queen in lieu of a more dynastically and financially beneficial foreign bride. And when Elizabeth, who had been invited to sit with our brother, started to join them, the Lord Admiral caught her arm, whispered something in her ear, and drew her away, no doubt urging her to leave the young couple alone so that romance might blossom unchecked. This only confirmed my suspicions.

When the evening's entertainment began I was so horrified I found myself stricken with a stunned and sickened paralysis; I could not stir, only sit there staring in horror and outrage at what was happening right before my eyes.

A troupe of tiny chattering monkeys was led in by their handler. Each little figure was garbed as a Roman cleric; there were monks, bishops, cardinals, priests, and the female monkeys were dressed as nuns. The largest monkey, a great shaggy orange-haired beast, wore the white robes and mitre of His Holiness, the Pope, and carried a staff topped by a jewelled crucifix. At the sight of them the whole court erupted in gales of delighted laughter. And Edward so forgot his dignity that he roared with laughter, rocking back and forth upon his throne, until tears ran down his face, and he clutched his sides, as the monkeys capered and danced before him.

"What could be more apt?" he asked Lady Jane beside him, who, in her mirth, had forgotten the pain of her latest beating and also rocked with laughter.

"Yes, Your Majesty," Jane replied, "the papists are a lot of posturing apes, so this is very apt indeed!"

And then the monkeys began to misbehave. One of the little nuns pulled the skirt of her habit up over her head and began to dance round in circles, exposing her privy parts to the males until one of the monks leapt on her and the two began to copulate quite shamelessly at the foot of the throne.

The whole court roared with laughter, cheered them on, and called out encouragement and crude and bawdy remarks, and began to pelt the monkeys with little jewel-coloured candied fruits, nuts, dates, grapes, and raisins as one by one, the monkey nuns flipped up their skirts and presented their private parts to the monks, priests, bishops, and cardinals, until only a few were left without a mate. And the hideous little beasts not preoccupied with carnal congress greedily fell on the sweets, and some even snatched them up and threw them back at the guests. I heard a woman shriek and turned to see my friend Nan in a state of great distress. Apparently some of the sweetmeats thrown by the monkeys had gone down the front of her gown and one of the horrid little monsters had gone bounding greedily after them and was now reaching his tiny furry black paw down between her creamy ample breasts to grope for them. Nan shrieked and tried to beat him off with her fan. Her husband abandoned his post beside the King and ran to assist her, slapping at and cursing the shrieking monkey, which snapped at and tried to bite him whilst those around looked on and laughed uproariously instead of coming to their aid.

There were monkeys everywhere now; some of them were

swarming over the great cake prepared for my brother's birthday, gobbling up handfuls of the moist cake and creamy frosting or else slinging globs of it at the courtiers. Others raced along the banquet table sampling wine and food from the gold and silver plates or flinging it about. One little fellow, entranced by a jiggling fat jelly-woman in green and yellow skirts with a jolly, smiling apple-cheeked face sculpted from coloured marzipan, sought to embrace and carnally unite with her, but instead fell from the table with the jelly lady plopping down on top of him with a loud splat.

Their harried handler, not knowing which of his charges to try to curtail first, ran back and forth and round in circles, starting off first in one direction and then turning and going in another, rather like a dog running round in circles after his own tail.

The court was torn between mirth and panic now; some screamed with laughter and others screamed in fear, racing towards the doors or else climbing up onto the tables and chairs, trying to evade the monkeys run amok. Upon his great gilded throne my brother watched it all, and slapped his thigh and rocked and roared with laughter, as the now frightened Lady Jane Grey cowered against him, now unable to share his amusement; the joke had got out of hand and was no longer quite as funny.

As the big ugly orange ape playing the Pope lifted his white robes and began to fondle himself enthusiastically, my limbs at last recovered their ability to move and I bolted from my chair and fled the Great Hall as a wave of nausea fanned up in my stomach. As I went, I passed Elizabeth, leaning against the wall, calmly watching it all, nonchalantly sipping from a golden goblet, as cool as the cucumber-coloured silk of her gown.

With my hand clasped over my mouth, I hurried along the torchlit corridor until I found a secluded spot and vomited into the rushes. As I was still bent over, gasping, and bracing myself against the wall, I felt someone brush against me and a hand reach round to cup my breast.

With a gasp, I bolted upright, but before I could turn round to confront my molester, a second arm stole round my waist and I felt through my full, layered skirts the hard physique of a man pressed close against me as a voice sang softly in my ear:

I gave her Cakes and I gave her Ale,
I gave her Sack and Sherry;
I kist her once and I kist her twice,
And we were wondrous merry!

A warm, wet tongue flicked out to lick the nape of my neck and a hot voice that made my skin crawl as if someone had just walked over my grave whispered, "Just think, Lady Mary, you could have had me!" And with a mocking, somewhat sinister, little laugh, Tom Seymour released me and returned to the brightly lit Great Hall.

I left court the very next morning without even saying goodbye to my brother or sister, leaving Jane to travel back to Chelsea with Elizabeth, Kate, and that rogue Tom Seymour. It didn't really matter; I knew I would not be missed. But I could no longer bear to witness such sacrilegious atrocities, and it only confirmed that I was correct – young people, such as my brother, sister, and little cousin Jane, lack the wisdom to make decisions in such important matters as religion and are easily led astray. But they are not without hope; with kind and proper guidance, they could just as easily find their way back to the true faith and become good and devout Catholics. Why could they not see that just as that big ugly orange ape had put on white robes and pretended to be the Pope, when they attended their stark, unadorned Protestant services and listened to the preacher's sermons, delivered in English, not priestly, sanctified Latin, they were listening to Satan showing off how skilfully he could quote Scriptures? Why could they not see that as clearly as I could? As I rode back to Hunsdon, weeping in my litter, I prayed that God would cure their blindness and let them see the truth before it was too late and their souls were damned and lost for ever.

❧ 10 ❧

Elizabeth

One afternoon I idly traversed the paths of the garden, just happy to be outside. I had spent the morning forcing myself to stand still for the portrait painter. The moment he was done with me, I ran straight out into the fresh air and sunshine, still wearing the gown Tom had chosen for me. It was a bright red damask, of a shade popularly known as "Lusty Gallant", with a deep square bodice cut low off the shoulders and edged with large white pearls and gold-framed wine-dark garnets that appeared almost black until the light struck them and the red came bursting out like a spontaneously delivered kiss. It had long, full, bell-shaped sleeves, worn over puffed and padded wrist-length under-sleeves and a kirtle of pease-porridge green and gold brocade. And there was a red French hood trimmed with pearls and gold-set garnets to match.

Catching me unawares, Tom crept up behind me and slipped a silken kerchief over my eyes, blindfolding me. He pulled me close and kissed me, then, laughing, spun me round and round and, leaving me reeling, scampered off, his boots crunching upon the gravelled path. He bade me follow the sound of his voice and began to sing.

> *I gave her Cakes and I gave her Ale,*
> *I gave her Sack and Sherry;*

> *I kist her once and I kist her twice,*
> *And we were wondrous merry!*

> *I gave her Beads and Bracelets fine,*
> *I gave her Gold down derry.*
> *I thought she was afear'd till she stroked my Beard*
> *And we were wondrous merry!*

> *Merry my Heart, merry my Cock,*
> *Merry my Spright.*
> *Merry my hey down derry.*
> *I kist her once and I kist her twice,*
> *And we were wondrous merry!*

With my arms outstretched before me, I followed him blindly. When I brushed against a wall of greenery I knew he was leading me into the hedge maze.

"Tom, wait! Stop!" I begged as I bumped and bumbled my way after his song.

> *I gave her Cakes and I gave her Ale,*
> *I gave her Sack and Sherry;*
> *I kist her once and I kist her twice,*
> *And we were wondrous merry!*

> *I gave her Beads and Bracelets fine,*
> *I gave her Gold down derry.*
> *I thought she was afear'd till she stroked my Beard*
> *And we were wondrous merry!*

> *Merry my Heart, merry my Cock,*
> *Merry my Spright.*
> *Merry my hey down derry.*
> *I kist her once and I kist her twice,*
> *And we were wondrous merry!*

Sometimes he would dart back and take me in his arms, and steal a swift kiss, then, with a laugh, he would be off again, bidding me to follow him as he sang and skipped along, leading me deeper and deeper into the emerald-green heart of the hedge maze.

I knew that at the centre stood a pair of white marble benches, half-moon in shape and facing each other, with a white marble statue of Cupid upon a pedestal with his bow raised, poised to fire a heart-tipped arrow, in the centre between them.

When Tom stopped singing I sensed we had reached the heart. He came to me then, took my hands, and guided me to Cupid's statue.

We stood facing one another – though I was blindfolded still and could see nothing – across Cupid's arrow.

Tom pressed something against my lips, something soft, moist, slightly warm, and smelling of honey.

"Taste, Bess," he instructed, and I bit into the delicious golden warmth of a fresh-baked honey cake sticky with drizzled honey.

Next he pressed the cool metal rim of a cup against my lips, and I obediently took a sip of ale.

Leaning across Cupid's arrow, Tom's lips grazed my ear. I shuddered and felt my knees go weak at the warmth of his breath, and the very nearness of him, as he softly sang:

> *I gave her Cakes and I gave her Ale,*
> *I gave her Sack and Sherry;*
> *I kist her once . . .*

He paused to kiss me.

> *. . . and I kist her twice,*

A second time, he kissed me.

> *And we were wondrous merry!*

I heard a rustle of clothing, as if Tom were riffling about inside his doublet, searching for something as he sang.

> *I gave her Beads and Bracelets fine,*
> *I gave her Gold down derry.*
> *I thought she was afear'd till she stroked my Beard*
> *And we were wondrous merry!*

"It's not beads or a bracelet, Bess." He took my hand and, raising it to his lips, turned it over, and pressed a kiss onto the blue vein pulsing beneath the milk-pale skin of my wrist. "A bracelet would only slip off such a slender wrist as this. No, rather a ring to adorn these beautiful, long white fingers!" And so saying, he slipped a ring onto the third finger of my left hand, the one upon which tradition and custom decreed a woman should wear her betrothal ring.

"Now," he directed, "stroke my beard, Bess, like the song says, and I shall lift up your blindfold for just a moment and let you glimpse how this love-token glitters against it."

As he spoke, he did just that and I saw upon my finger a garnet heart ringed by fiery rubies set upon a golden band of lovers' knots sparkling against the luxuriant auburn of his beard. As my hand stroked, the jewels seemed to give off sparks in varying shades of red, from wine-dark to the colour of new-spilt blood, with teasing, fast, fleeting glimpses of orange and pink, all coaxed out by the light and the movement of my hand. But it was, as he said, only a glimpse, for my eyes had barely taken it in before he lowered the blindfold and I was in the dark again.

"Touch his arrow, Bess, for luck," Tom said, taking my hand, "and love," he added in a caressing whisper as he guided my fingers along the smooth, straight, hard white marble shaft of Cupid's arrow. Then he sang another verse.

> *Merry my Heart, merry my Cock,*
> *Merry my Spright.*
> *Merry my hey down derry.*
> *I kist her once . . .*

He paused to brush a kiss, swift and feather-light, against my lips.

. . . and I kist her twice,

Again, he kissed me, this time lingering a moment longer.

And we were wondrous merry!

He sang the last line low and slow, and even as the last word lingered on his lips he guided my hand down, to another shaft, this one made of pulsing hot flesh and blood. I curled my hand around it, savouring the heady empowering sensation, the knowledge that desire for me had caused this.

Across Cupid's arrow, we kissed, then Tom pulled me round, past the point of Cupid's arrow, and into his embrace. He eased down my bodice, baring my breasts. I shivered at the cool air upon them, feeling my nipples stiffen and the rosy halos of flesh about them pucker. Tom's tongue and teeth teased the pert pink nubs, and I sighed and arched my neck and clutched tight his head as I moaned and revelled in the blissful sensations. Then he reached down to gather up my full skirts, my starched petticoats rustling as his practised fingers gently delved into the warmth and wetness between my thighs. I gave an anguished, disappointed little cry as I felt his fingers withdraw.

"You taste as sweet as honey," he said. I felt his fingers brush my lips. My nostrils quivered at the scent of my own juices. "Taste!" he whispered, his beard and warm lips grazing my ear, and I did.

He took my hands again and led me over to the nearest of the two benches, where he sat down. I stood before him, at once tense and trembling, excited, eager, and afraid, as his hands reached down to gather up the folds of my full skirts and petticoats once again. Clasping my naked hips, he drew me down astride his lap, slow and straight onto his arrow of flesh, aimed straight at my maidenhead, poised to shatter the Shield of Hymen.

I gasped at the brutal assault of pain. I had expected only pleasure, rolling, intense waves that would engulf and threaten to drown me in the love Tom and I made together, not this sharp stab that at once made me think of the Hungarian prince infamously called Vlad I had heard tales of, who delighted in torturing his victims by having them impaled upon stakes so that the weight of their bodies would drag them down the wooden shaft in a slow and agonizing death. The pain shook me so I cried out.

I tried to push him away, but Tom, intent on his own pleasure, groaning and thrusting, his fingertips digging bruisingly hard into my naked hips, was oblivious to my pain and distress, and continued to hold tight. And then, deep within me, his manhood shuddered, and a warm, sticky, wetness filled the raw, sore, and torn place inside me. And it was over.

Tom's hands, still clasping my hips, eased me off his lap. He reached out and pulled the blindfold from my eyes and used it to wipe himself. And I was left standing there, watching him, with my blood and his seed dripping out of me.

I found the act itself curiously hollow. Though his seed had filled me I felt empty inside. *Is that all there is to it?* I wondered. Was there to be no pleasure for me?

Instinctively, I knew that everything was different now. When Tom looked up at me and smiled I had the distinct feeling that I was no longer the centre of his attention but merely an afterthought.

When he reached out for me I leapt back. As suddenly as it had flared up, the flame of passion had burnt out, and I had lost all desire for his touch. I gathered up my skirts and ran as fast as I could, fleeing from the infatuation – I knew now it would be a lie to call it love – that had almost devoured and destroyed me.

Tom ran after me, snatching up the basket of honey cakes and the flagon of ale, crying out for me to stop and wait, to come and sit and sup with him on the cakes and ale he had brought just for me, and that he longed to lap up ale from the hollow of my throat, and that he would dip the honey cakes in my own honey to make them taste all the sweeter. To him, it was as if nothing of any importance had just happened, and we were only having a high-spirited game of chase, and as he ran after me he began to sing.

> *I gave her Cakes and I gave her Ale,*
> *I gave her Sack and Sherry;*
> *I kist her once and I kist her twice,*
> *And we were wondrous merry!*

> *I gave her Beads and Bracelets fine,*
> *I gave her Gold down derry.*
> *I thought she was afear'd till she stroked my Beard*
> *And we were wondrous merry!*

> *Merry my Heart, merry my Cock,*
> *Merry my Spright.*
> *Merry my hey down derry.*
> *I kist her once and I kist her twice,*
> *And we were wondrous merry!*

With an anguished cry, I tore his ring from my finger. They say the vein in that finger connects directly to the heart – that is why the wedding ring is worn upon it – and it felt as if that garnet and ruby heart were burning my own heart like a red-hot brand, marking me as Tom Seymour's property, like a prized piece of cattle. I turned and flung it back at him as hard as I could before I gathered up my skirts and ran even faster, wishing I could cover my ears against that infernal song, but knowing that even if I did it would still ring like an eternal echo within my ears, and that as long as I lived, I would never be free of it; it would haunt me like a ghost. I would never be able to hear that popular ditty sung and not think of him even as every honey cake proffered me from now on would conjure him up like a necromancer's demon to torment me.

> *I gave her Cakes and I gave her Ale,*
> *I gave her Sack and Sherry;*
> *I kist her once and I kist her twice,*
> *And we were wondrous merry!*

I gave her Beads and Bracelets fine,
I gave her Gold down derry.
I thought she was afear'd till she stroked my Beard
And we were wondrous merry!

Merry my Heart, merry my Cock,
Merry my Spright.
Merry my hey down derry.
I kist her once and I kist her twice,
And we were wondrous merry!

I was in the house and halfway up the stairs when Tom thrust the cakes and ale into the arms of a startled maidservant and bolted up after me.

On the landing, he caught up with me, and roughly grabbed my wrists and whirled me round to face him. There we stood, awash in the scarlet and gold light pouring in through the stained-glass windows. Recklessly, not caring who might see, Tom wrestled me into an embrace. Even as I fought to free myself, Tom clutched me close to his chest and pressed his lips hard against mine in a bruising kiss, such as a man gives to prove himself the master and the woman his chattel or slave, bound to serve and obey.

My fists pummelled him, and I struggled to break free, but he only held me tighter and kissed me harder, determined to conquer me, to prove his supremacy, his masculine might and power over me.

It was thus that Kate came upon us in a stealthy whisper of sky blue and creamy satin with her clasped hands folded benignly over her big round belly. All she saw was the kiss, not my struggle to resist and pounding, pummelling fists and the hellcat fingernails that tried to claw and rake his face. She said not one word. She didn't have to; the pain of our betrayal was in her eyes, and writ plain across her parchment-pale face, and in that instant I saw her heart break. But she, an erstwhile queen, was too proud to shriek and strike out and scream at me like a tavern wench bawling and brawling over a man. She merely drew her spine up straight, summoned forth all her dignity, and turned her back on us and walked away, back upstairs.

"Kate, wait! You don't understand!" Tom let go of me as if I were a flame that burned him, and ran after her. "It's not what you think! I can explain! The conniving little minx is sick with love for me! Have you not seen her mooning about, flaunting herself and making eyes at me? What else can you expect from Anne Boleyn's daughter? She was born with harlotry coursing through her veins! She threw herself at me! She took me unawares upon the stairs! It was not my fault! Kate! Wait! Look! I have brought you cakes and ale! You down there!" He leaned over the banister and bellowed at the maid, who all this time had been standing with her mouth agape, dumbly clutching the ale and honey cakes. "Bring up that basket of honey cakes and that flagon of ale. They are a gift for my lady wife! Kate! Wait!" He continued on up the stairs after her, protesting his innocence all the while.

I waited until their bedchamber door had closed behind them, then went slowly up the rest of the stairs to my own room. I sat upon the window seat, staring out without seeing, as the twilight fell, then full darkness, and the stars came out. To save himself, Tom had lied and branded me a harlot and thrown me into the lion's den. What a fool I had been, as is, in that moment I realized, any woman who puts her trust in a man. Love is just a lie men tell that women want to believe, and sincerity is the liar's dressing gown.

Later, Kat came in, her shoulders hunched in shame, and, without a word to me, began to pack my things. Kate wanted no open scandal, but we were being sent away; she wanted me out of her house. We were to go to stay with Kat's sister, Joan, and her husband, Sir Anthony Denny, at their country manor, Cheshunt, in Hertfordshire. There were to be no goodbyes. Kate would not see me.

I slept not at all that night. My shame was as sharp as a dagger embedded to the hilt in my breast, and gave me no respite or rest, yet I could not weep; there was a strange numbness that enshrouded me.

As dawn broke Kat mutely helped me into a travelling gown of moss-green velvet. Tom crept softly to my locked door as I was dressing and entreated entry, but I spoke not a word to him, and when Kat, compassion written plainly across her face, started toward the door, I shook my head sharply to stay her. I was done with Tom and all his lies and games. He had played with my heart, body, and head as if they were tokens on a gameboard, and there was no forgetting or forgiving that. Trust is a fragile thing and once broken can never be seamlessly put back together again; the cracks will always show and be ever vulnerable to fresh fractures and doubt. And I had no desire to glue what Tom and I had shared back together again. It was finished.

With his lips against the door, Tom began to recite another of Wyatt's poems, this one also, it was said, written for my mother.

> Forget not yet the tried intent
> Of such a truth as I have meant
> My great travail so gladly spent
> Forget not yet!
>
> Forget not yet when first began
> The weary life ye know, since whan
> The suit, the service none tell can,
> Forget not yet!
>
> Forget not yet the great assays,
> The cruel wrong, the scornful ways,
> The painful patience in delays,
> Forget not yet!
>
> Forget not! O, forget not this,
> How long ago hath been, and is,
> The mind that never meant amiss –
> Forget not yet!

I sat stiff-backed and still, listening to the rhythm of the rain on the tile roof, while Mrs Ashley brushed out my hair and tucked it up inside a net of gold then set atop it a round, flat moss-green velvet cap with a jaunty white plume.

"*Please,* Bess, open the door!" Tom begged, but I ignored him. The spell was broken. I stood up and imperiously held out my hand for my gloves.

I waited until he gave up and I heard his footsteps retreating before I left my room. As I descended the stairs I held my body stiff and my head high and proud, ignoring the whispers and speculative glances of the servants.

Kate's door was, like her heart, closed to me, but at the last moment, much to my surprise, she came out to bid me a formal farewell. The ice in her eyes and the steel in her spine pained me so much to behold that it was all I could do not to break down and cry, to fall in a heap weeping at her feet and beg her to forgive me.

And then, as I stepped into the barge, impulsively, she stepped forward, heedless of the cold rain, and caught my hand in hers, freezing Tom with a glance at once smouldering and frigid when his face broke into a smile and he took a step forward as if he meant to bid me adieu and kiss my hand. But at her look he stopped cold and stepped even farther back.

"Bess," – the old compassion came flooding back – "my heart has been dealt a powerful, great wound, that is true, but I am not sending you away to punish you, but to safeguard you. A woman's honour is above rubies, and you, my dear, are a princess, and may even be queen someday. And as your stepmother it is my duty to protect you and, to my everlasting shame, I have failed most grievously, and must belatedly take what measures I can now to atone for it." She leaned in swiftly and kissed my cheek. "Be well, Bess, and be *happy!*" she said, giving my hand a quick, reassuring squeeze, and then she was gone, clasping her belly and waddling back inside, shoving aside the hand Tom proffered to assist her.

I managed to retain my composure until we could no longer see the house. Because of me, Chelsea was now a house of sorrows instead of smiles. Then I could bear it no more; I yanked the velvet curtains closed about me and flung myself down on the velvet cushions and cried my heart out, pushing Kat away when she tried to hold and comfort me. Kate had loved me like a daughter, and I, to my everlasting shame, had betrayed her. I had stolen what she valued most – the husband of her heart, a match she regarded as heaven-sent, made out of love, not duty. And after I had stolen it, I had exposed it for the lie it was, an illusion, not worth the price she placed on it. All that glitters is not gold, and Kate's marriage was clearly base and false, and I had been the one to flake the gilt off and show her the ugly reality lurking beneath.

❧ 11 ❧

Mary

When I heard that Elizabeth had abruptly left Chelsea, suddenly and unexpectedly amidst a swirl of rumours, I wrote and again invited her to come to me. But she rebuffed me.

From Cheshunt, where she was staying with her governess's kin, she wrote back that she wanted to be alone, she craved quietness and seclusion.

She could have had all the peace and quiet she wanted at Hunsdon, so I knew what she was saying; I could read it between the lines. She did not want to be with me, she did not desire my company.

❧ 12 ❧

Elizabeth

In the weeks that followed I kept my own counsel, I refused to confide in Mrs Ashley and unburden my heart of the fear that held it fast. I had not bled since that day in the deep green secrecy of the hedge maze when I was jarred so rudely and abruptly out of love with Tom Seymour. I knew that there were herbs that women in such predicaments sometimes made use of, but I did not know what they were or the recipes to brew such concoctions, and I dared not seek the counsel of others. Women are prone to gossip, and I, as a princess, heiress second in line to the throne, faced great peril if what I feared indeed came to pass and my belly quickened with Tom Seymour's unlawfully, treasonously begotten bastard. Oh the scandal! I shuddered at the thought and prayed God to let this cup pass me by.

Some days I could not get out of bed. I would lie prostrate or else curled upon my side with my knees drawn up tight, viciously assailed by the four demons named Megrim, Stomachache, Nausea, and Fever. Kat would kneel worriedly beside me, applying cold compresses to my head, and saying over and over until I screamed and ordered her from my room: "Oh my darling girl, I don't know how I shall ever forgive myself! But it was a match made in heaven; I think it was the Devil's doing that he was married already when the two of you belonged together!" Alone, I would wail in agony and clasp my privy parts and belly; my courses had dried up, leaving

my always slender body painfully sore and bloated with the retention of the vile monthly blood I needed so desperately to expel. I
could feel it trapped inside me, bursting for release, but unable to
flow.

Though Kat implored me to remain inside and keep to my bed,
there were days when I was so restless that it drove me from my bed
to walk in the garden, pacing back and forth like a sentry. Even
though the autumn winds nipped at me and tugged tenaciously at
my cloak and hair, I preferred my solitary walks to Kat's inane prattle and attempts to cheer me or coax the rest of the story – the parts
I had not shared with her – out of me.

And then one day, as I walked distractedly in the misting rain,
cooling the fever that left a pearly sheen upon my brow, I felt a
pain, like a hand clutching tight, as if to wring dry my womanly
parts, and a warm trickle trailing down the inside of my thigh. And
I knew I was safe.

I saw now full clear that the fear, and the sickness brought on by
it, that I had suffered these hellish weeks was a warning, a stern rebuke issued by God, to remember and never again forget my
mother's warning – "*Never surrender!*" I had failed to heed it once,
I had dared put myself in a man's power and let myself fall under
his charismatic spell, and it had almost destroyed me. Should I forget or fail again, I would not be so fortunate.

In gratitude, I fell to my knees, heedless of the sharp bite of the
gravel through my skirts, and turned my face up to the leaden grey
sky, and gave my wholehearted thanks and assurances to God, and
my mother, that I had truly learned my lesson, and that from the
bottom of my heart to the depths of my soul I was grateful for the
second chance that had been given me. Though I had been a very
foolish girl, I was wise enough to know that not everyone is given
a second chance no matter how much they pray and long for it.
Passion had come like an infectious fever and scorched and almost
burned away my reason. Next time I might not be so fortunate;
therefore, there must not be a next time.

And then a letter came, like a blessing, from Kate, and further
strengthened my resolve.

My dearest daughter,

Time, contemplation, and prayer have shown me that I was overly harsh, and I pray that you will forgive me and allow me to speak to you as your own mother would have done had she lived.

Though few of us have the good fortune to marry as our heart dictates, there comes a time in each of our lives, sometimes, as with you, in the first flush of youth, and, to others, like myself, when we have already ripened into maturity, but sooner or later a time _always_ comes when we feel the stirrings of passion, and we let our heart overrule our head, and romance take precedence over reason, and sensuality over sense. And, for a young woman without a mother to counsel and guide her, such a time can be most perplexing and even frightening. The uncharted waters of first love are perilous, and I, preoccupied with the precious gift of motherhood God had at last vouchsafed me, was unforgivably remiss, my vigilance fell by the wayside, and I failed to be there for you when you needed me most of all. And for that I most humbly beseech _your_ pardon. Forgive me, Bess, for it is I and _not_ you, who should kneel and humbly pronounce those two heartfelt words – Forgive _me!_

You see, Bess, I fell under his spell too, though I was already a woman grown, mature, and past my youth, and already two times a widow, so how could I fault or blame you, an innocent young girl, for succumbing to the same blandishments?

After I was, for the second time, a widow, he came calling. He braided wildflowers into my hair, took me riding and sailing, and made me feel young again, though I had never done such things in my youth. I never had a sweetheart when I was young, but went instead straight into wedlock with the husband my mother chose for me, and then, when he died, the process was repeated. But Tom was different. He was like no one I had ever known before. He made life exciting and fun. Everyone always thought I was

*so serious, so proper and prim. A scholar and physician in
petticoats was how they all saw me. Everyone always expected me to do the right thing, but with Tom . . . I could
laugh and be free, let down my guard and forget all the
world expected of me! I could let down my hair, bunch up
my skirts, and run over the grass in my bare feet! He showered upon me a hundred little attentions that I had never
known before from either of my husbands and made me feel
as if I were the most special and important person in the
world. He made me feel alive, and – dare I confess it? –
sensual. He awakened a part of me I never knew existed before. So, you see, Bess, I <u>do</u> understand!*

*Tom is a man who wields his charm like an expert
swordsman does his weapon, and never have I encountered
a woman strong enough to withstand or defeat it. I remember the day he first won me. He bound my eyes with a kerchief and led me out, guiding me with his voice, as he sang a
bawdy song better suited to a tavern than courtship. "I
gave her cakes, I gave her ale," the chorus went, but I shall
spare you the rest. And he led me out across the meadow to
a great oak tree on my late husband's estate, underneath
which a blanket was spread and a picnic laid out of honey
cakes and a flagon of ale, and strawberries, which we ate
dipped in wine and cream. And that day, for the first time,
I submitted to him as I would to a husband, which is what
I believed he would soon be to me. Had your father not set
his sights upon me, we would have been married shortly
after. So you see, Bess, I know well the power and allure of
my husband, and I forgive, and fault you not one whit, for
succumbing. <u>Never</u> think for even a moment that I love you
any less, or that I am any less proud of you. Bess, my darling girl, I hold you in my heart as I always have, and in
the greatest esteem. Your intelligence and learning are an
example to our sex that I hope many young girls will aspire
to emulate. And I pray God that a day will come, when I
am past my travail, when we can be as mother and daugh-*

*ter again. Until then, my dear, may God keep you in His
care.*

Your Ever-Loving Stepmother,
Kate

A million times I must have read her letter, even after I had
committed every word to memory. What good it did my heart, and
what comfort and ease it brought my mind, to know that she understood and had forgiven me. And I saw again, full plain, the duplicity and unworthiness of Thomas Seymour, and was glad to be rid
of him. He had scorched me, but I had survived the flames,
scorched yet wiser for it.

When Tom wrote me, I scanned his letters for news of how Kate
fared in her pregnancy, then tore them into shreds and let the
winds disperse them. The memory of his touch now left me cold.
Reason had at last sucked all the venom of Cupid's dart from my
wounded heart and I was now entirely cured.

But tragic news soon followed fast on the heels of mercy. Kate
was dead, after being delivered of a baby girl, burned up from the
fever that often follows childbirth. She died on September 7, 1548,
my fifteenth birthday, wild and raving, accusing Tom of putting
poison in the guise of medicine into her cup to speed her to her
grave and leave him free to marry me. "The one whom I loved
best is my murderer!" she sobbed, tossing on the sweat-soaked
sheets of the bed that had been her marriage bed, where the child
she had so longed for had been conceived in connubial joy, and
was also fated to be her deathbed. I wondered if it were indeed
true. Such a one was Tom that even if he swore with his hand over
his heart that it was all a fancy wrought by the fever, still I would
never know for certain; a part of me would always wonder. And the
fact that Tom had forced her to sign a will dictated by, and leaving
all to him, further fueled my, and other's, suspicions. As she lay
burning up with fever, weeping in anguish, and feebly crying out
her accusations, Tom had grasped her hand and guided it to sign

her name for the final time. It all left me feeling as though a part of my soul were stained with the blood of my stepmother.

I mourned Kate in my own quiet way, but Kat began to build her cloud castles again, for Tom and me to dwell in marital bliss, before my stepmother was even laid in her grave.

"*He's free!*" she jubilantly sang out as if it were a hallelujah the moment she heard the sad news. "You may have him now! It is the Lord's doing! You see, Bess? It *was* meant to be! All in God's own good time! Oh He *does* move in mysterious ways, He *does*! We should have had more faith! Now my – I mean your – dream can come true! God has willed it. He has taken the Dowager Queen up to Heaven, and that is clear proof that this marriage was meant to be! Oh, Bess, I am *so happy* for you!"

She was deaf to my entreaties to cease her foolish prattle. "I will not have him," I told her, but she merely laughed and nodded knowingly and sometimes even winked, convinced that the moment he came calling I would melt.

There was also a maze, though a more modest one, at Cheshunt. The day I heard that Kate had died I walked alone to its centre. There wasn't a bench like at Chelsea, and no statue of Cupid or lover bearing cakes and ale awaited me there. Instead, I sat on the gravelled ground, my back against the dense wall of living green, hugged my knees against my heart, feeling my stays bite into my skin like a penance, and howled out my grief until I had no tears left.

Now, even though she had forgiven me in her letter, I would never have the chance to kneel at Kate's feet and beg her forgiveness as a part of me still needed to do, then sit beside her and talk it all out, listen to her kind, patient, and wise counsel, and make everything all right between us. Knowing that she had died in agony, coupling my name with her husband's as our bodies had once coupled, and most likely had been murdered to make way for me to wear Tom's ring, made it all so much harder to bear. In a way, Tom's passion had burned her up too, for it was in the throes of passion that the seed was planted. Had Kate not conceived a child, childbed fever could not have killed her or provided a likely guise to conceal her murder. And if it truly was murder, though I had no part in planning it, I was still in part responsible for her death. Just as my own mother had died because I had not been the prince she had promised my father, my most beloved stepmother had died because her husband lusted after me! Lust kills, as does the loss of it! After his passion for my mother burned out, it was easy for my father to condemn her, a woman he had no further use for, to make way for another. Desire is the antechamber of Death.

I returned to my childhood home, Hatfield, hoping I would find peace there. My gowns were barely unpacked before he came calling. I knew he would. I was in my bath when he arrived. My hair caught up loosely atop my head lest the pins bring on a headache, and trailing down my neck in damp red tendrils, I sank low in the steaming water, just as hot as I could stand it, drowsily watching the drifting ever-changing patterns of dried rose petals, crushed lavender, and chamomile floating upon the surface, and yawning as clouds of steam caressed and flushed my cheeks bright pink.

He bribed his way into my private sanctum where none should have been allowed to disturb me. Though I had said many times that I would not see him, and had even refused to write him a letter of condolence on the death of his wife, his manly charm still held such sway over my Mrs Ashley that she could deny him nothing. All it took was a smile from him, a peck on the cheek, and a pinch and a pat to her "great buttocks", and he was sauntering in, smiling in triumph, like a conquering hero, singing the same old song.

> *I gave her Cakes and I gave her Ale,*
> *I gave her Sack and Sherry;*
> *I kist her once and I kist her twice,*
> *And we were wondrous merry!*
>
> *I gave her Beads and Bracelets fine,*
> *I gave her Gold down derry.*
> *I thought she was afear'd till she stroked my Beard*
> *And we were wondrous merry!*

Merry my Heart, merry my Cock,
Merry my Spright.
Merry my hey down derry.
I kist her once and I kist her twice,
And we were wondrous merry!

True to form, he was carrying a flagon of ale and a basket of honey cakes. When the scent of honey reached my nostrils the memory of what had happened the last time he served me cakes and ale felt like a slap across my face.

I bolted upright in my bath and snatched the linen sheet Kat had left for me to dry myself with, but Tom just laughed as he yanked it from my grasp and made some silly jest about chaste Diana being surprised by Actaeon in her bath.

"Come now, dear one, I've seen you before. I've seen *all* of you before. Remember your devoted gardener who used to come to you early each morning to tend your rosy buds? And how well they have blossomed!" he said ardently, his gaze and voice full of admiration as he bent to teasingly tweak one rosy nipple.

He knelt behind me and draped a string of pearls about my throat and whispered, his lips grazing my ear, "For the life of me, I cannot tell which is fairer – your skin or these pearls!"

My whole body tensed and I shut my eyes and willed my heart to stay shut, for the locks and bolts I had placed upon it to hold fast. "Do not go back, Bess," the voice of reason whispered urgently inside my head, "do *not* go back!"

He took my hand, tugging my fingers from their tight, trembling grip on the tub's rim, and kissed it before he slipped the garnet and ruby heart ring back onto my finger again.

"Here is your betrothal ring, my bonny Bess, my soon-to-be bride!" he declared, kissing my hand again. "But I would dive for an even more precious pearl – a pink one!" And, careless of his fine, gold-embellished black velvet sleeve, he plunged his arm into my bath, his determined fingers avidly seeking the pink pearl of flesh between my thighs even as I backed away and shoved at him, all the time ordering him to get out.

"I do not want you here or your ring on my finger!" I insisted.

Ignoring me, Tom began to dream aloud; he was a man ever in love with his own voice.

As his fingers deftly stroked that sensitive little nub, making my own body betray me, I squirmed and sighed, even as I gripped the sides of the copper tub so hard, my knuckles trembled and stood out white, and gritted my teeth, willing myself to resist. He talked about what our life together as husband and wife would be like – "passion and bedsport galore!" But then his touch changed, growing harder, as if there were anger behind it, and there was a strange faraway look in his eyes, as if he had forgotten where he was and what he was doing. Ambition, his guiding star – I saw it light a fire in his eyes.

He was so lost in his dreams that he did not hear my pleas that he was hurting me. As I squirmed, trying to free myself, my hair tumbled down into the water, and his other arm rose up to circle round my throat so that my chin rested in the crook of his elbow – it was almost as if he meant to strangle me! – as the pressure of his finger on that most private and vulnerable part of me increased.

His finger digging in, hurting me, pressing hard, as if it would rub that tender pink bud red and raw, he spoke of vengeance, of casting his brother "the high and mighty Lord Protector of the Realm" "down onto the dung-heap." He would make him pay for denying him a place upon the Council, "hogging all the power for himself like a greedy hog at trough!" He would snatch the reins of power from the Regency Council and rule alone, Tom swore, as his finger continued to dig in cruelly, even as I squirmed and gasped and tried to push his hand away. "I will be king in all but name!" he declared, and revealed that he planned to marry Edward to Lady Jane Grey. And, being frail, Edward might not live to adulthood, which would leave Jane alone on the throne. Jane's own parents dominated her with physical brutality, with harsh words, slaps, and pinches, and by lashing her bare buttocks with a riding crop to make her docile and malleable. "But I," Tom boasted, "I can control her with kindness; she will be so grateful to me that she will do *anything* I ask. I can even make her fall in love with me if I have to." Then he spoke of the dynasty we would found, my regal Tudor blood blending with his in a powerful mix of ambition and strength. Or things might work out so that I sat upon the throne as England's Queen, with Tom at my side, of course. And, failing that, one of our sons was certain to be king someday, and he would be there, the power behind the throne, putting words in his mouth, and guiding his every move. "All England shall be my chessboard and I alone shall manoeuvre the pieces!"

As my mind absorbed his words like a sponge, my horror rising like vomit in my throat, the very last morsels of desire I felt for him shrivelled up and died, like grapes left too long upon the vine. I knew then that Tom, in spite of his words, had never really loved me, only my rank as royal princess, my place in the succession; I was only a stepping stone along the path to power and England's throne where Tom aimed to either sit or lurk behind, either openly or stealthily, wielding *all* the power. Oh no, I vowed, I will not be your, or any other man's, stepping stone!

Somehow I found the strength to pull his arm away from my throat, and I stood up and tore the string of pearls from my neck, letting them fall into the bath and onto the floor as I leapt from the tub. I wrenched that accursed ring from my finger again and flung it too into the bathwater and ran, naked and dripping, into my bedchamber.

Tom ran after me and, just as I was about to cross the threshold, he caught hold of me.

"Bess, listen to me! I know you are upset, aye, Kate's loss shook me too, but I must tell you . . . Listen to me!" He shook me hard and slapped my cheek to stun me into silence. "*Listen!* I *never* loved Catherine!" he insisted as I stood there clutching my smarting cheek and reeling. "I only married her because I couldn't have you. I asked the Council for your hand, but they just laughed at me, damn and pox them all, so I did the next best thing, I married her to be near you, because I knew you would come to live with her after your father died."

"*Liar!*" I screamed. "I know how you courted Kate before she married my father! You courted her with cakes and ale and braided wildflowers into her hair!"

"Elizabeth! You wound me!" he cried, slapping a hand over his heart. "I thought you a young woman of passion and intelligence far beyond your actual years, but now you behave as a child and reason like one still in the nursery and not out of leading strings! Don't you know I have been in love with you ever since the day you kicked Ned's shin at your brother's christening? For years I have been as one standing still, patiently enduring the ebb and flow of Time, trying to make do as best I could, while I waited for you to grow up. Aye, I dallied with Kate – I am a man after all and that is what men do. When I met her she was a widow, twice married to toothless old dotards. She had never known a *real* man, lusty, young, and vigorous between her thighs, and I gave her that. I was doing her a favour! She was ripe for it, *begging* for it, hot as a bitch in heat! And what man could resist that? But she took it for more than it was; she fell in love with me. I suppose it was only natural that she should; what woman wouldn't fall in love with me? If I were a woman I would fall in love with me! But I swear to you, Bess, I swear to you on Kate's grave, I was only dallying, waiting for you to grow up!"

Over his shoulder, in the steam rising from my abandoned bath, I thought I saw Kate's ghost take shape, mournfully mouthing these words of wisdom and warning: "Never give your heart lest it be betrayed!" It was the memory of the woman who had knelt at my feet and bared her heart and soul to me, telling me how after three times marrying for duty she was, at long last, free to follow her heart and marry for love, speaking to me from beyond the grave. She thought God had blessed her, and never realized until it was too late that the love she believed true was in fact false. Cupid had played my clever Kate for a fool and felled her with his dart fired by proxy from Tom Seymour's cock to impregnate her and steal her life away even as she gave birth to the child she had always longed for. Kate had died. Whether it was childbed fever or poison that had ultimately taken her life, the result was the same: Kate died, but I was alive and determined to survive. I would *not* let Tom Seymour, by cock or concoction, be the instrument of my demise! *He* will *not* destroy me! I swore.

"She loved you; I saw it in her face every time she looked at you!" I reminded him as shame flooded my heart. I had seen Kate's heart upon her face but I had chosen to be heartless and ignore it.

"As did you!" Tom reminded me. "I saw your love for me in your face, plain as the light of day!"

I nodded, for I could not deny it. "And that is a cross I shall carry for the rest of my life. She loved me like a daughter, and I, to my everlasting shame, betrayed her."

Summoning forth all my strength, I shoved him away from me, and slammed and bolted the door in his face.

Tom began at once to pound and demand entry. And when I ignored him, he once again resorted to poetry, thinking with the romance of Tom Wyatt's words that he could blind me to the truth and bring me back into his arms again.

> *And wilt thou leave me thus?*
> *Say nay! say nay! for shame!*
> *To save thee from the blame*
> *Of all my grief and grame.*
> *And wilt thou leave me thus?*
> *Say nay! say nay!*

> *And wilt thou leave me thus,*
> *That hath loved thee so long*
> *In wealth and woe among?*
> *And is thy heart so strong*
> *As for to leave me thus?*
> *Say nay! say nay!*

> *And wilt thou leave me thus,*
> *That hath given thee my heart*
> *Never for to depart*
> *Nother for pain nor smart?*
> *And wilt thou leave me thus?*
> *Say nay! say nay!*

And wilt thou leave me thus,
And have no more pity
Of him that loveth thee?
Alas, thy cruelty!
And wilt thou leave me thus?
Say nay! say nay!

I ran to my bed, shivering, and feeling as if the water still running in rivulets over my naked skin, and plastering my hair down my back, were turning into ice. I tore the covers back and dived onto the feather mattress, tarrying only long enough to blow out the candles on the table by the bed that I had meant to read by, before I tugged the covers up over my head, curled my body into a ball, and burrowed down, to fall asleep to the tune of my teeth chattering and the feel of the hot tears turning to ice upon my cheeks, as I ignored the passion-infused poetry that Tom Seymour lingered to recite outside my bolted door.

The castle in the clouds which lust masquerading as love, like a wolf in sheep's clothing, had built out of the bricks of a young girl's dreams and illusions, had now, once and for all, been demolished, wrecked to ruins forevermore, never to rise again. I was free of Love's chains; the truth and Tom Seymour's shallowness, callousness, and lies had set me free.

❧ 13 ❧

Mary

The seventh day of September, 1548, the day my sister turned fifteen, Catherine Parr breathed her last. The sad news came first with lurid rumour following fast on its heels. Thus I learned the whole sordid truth about Elizabeth and Thomas Seymour.

I had known all along that with Anne Boleyn's whore's blood coursing through her veins, Elizabeth must tread very carefully in carnal matters and not let her passions get the better of her. And here was certain proof that I was right, clear evidence that bad blood tells – like mother, like daughter. Elizabeth had embarked on a harlot's progress and she had started young.

But it was worse than that, *much* worse. Catherine Parr had gone to her grave raging against her husband's and Elizabeth's duplicity. And Tom Seymour was said to have administered poison in place of medicine to hasten her demise. And afterwards, instead of dismissing her maids and sending them home to their families after the funeral service with a generous purse to reward their service and loyalty, he bade them stay as they would soon have a new mistress to serve. And the "grieving widower", supposedly shut away behind locked doors alone with his grief, had crept out, like a thief in the night, and ridden straight to Elizabeth. I had heard he had disdained me as a "dried-up old maid" and described Elizabeth as "born for bedsport; as ripe and juicy as a cherry, a Tudor wench, perfect for a man who should be king and, God willing, one way or another, would be." There really was no end to the man's audacity; he lived and breathed treason as naturally as a fish does water.

Oh what a banquet "The Cakes and Ale Man" and Elizabeth provided for the gossipmongers! I flushed with shame every time I heard their names spoken, and it was all I could do to hold my head up. My "good gossip Nan" even wrote to me that Elizabeth had been sent away from Chelsea because she was purported to be carrying the Lord Admiral's child, a child that had been secretly born and disposed of, foully murdered according to the midwife who swore upon the Holy Bible that she had been taken blind-folded to attend a milk-fair redheaded young lady and had fought hard to save that slim-hipped girl from the clutches of Death. It was testament to her skill, she proudly asserted, that my sister still lived and breathed, and her child would have as well had it not been murdered.

I burned with shame and could not even bring myself to write to Elizabeth, a bastard who had borne a bastard and then suffered it to be killed to hide her shame. Every time I passed her portrait in the gallery I saw a redheaded version of Anne Boleyn. How apt that she had chosen to wear harlot-scarlet, and that neckline, ex-posing the curves of her shoulders, was immodestly low! I prayed for her soul – that was all I could do – beseeching the Holy Virgin to intercede with Our Lord so that He might show my sister the light and point her back onto the right path, the road to redemp-tion and salvation, and save her from a life of sin and harlotry.

The next I knew Tom Seymour was in the Tower as, one by one, his brazen schemes came to light and crumbled into fairy dust. He was arrested after stealing into the palace late one night and trying to abduct Edward. He intended to carry him off and marry him to Lady Jane Grey. Fortunately the valiant actions of my brother's spaniel, combined with the pistol shot Tom Seymour fired right between its eyes to silence it, alerted the palace guards in time to save Edward.

But in the end, I found I could not keep silent; I had to say something. It was my Christian duty. So I spoke to Elizabeth's vanity, and sent her a large ruby brooch set round in heavy gold which I had the goldsmith engrave boldly around the great glittering harlot-coloured stone with the words:

WHO CAN FIND A VIRTUOUS WOMAN?
FOR HER PRICE IS FAR ABOVE RUBIES.

And suspended below it, I had the jeweller attach an enamelled oval medallion depicting the Magdalene drying Jesus's feet with her long scarlet hair, and, dangling beneath it, a golden crucifix set with smaller rubies and diamonds.

I was confident that Elizabeth, clever as she was, would get the message. I hoped when she saw it her tarnished soul would smart with shame and want to be scrubbed clean, and that she, like the Magdalene, would see the error of her sinful ways and repent and redeem herself before it was too late.

But for nights after I sent it, I was plagued by the most disturbing dreams in which I saw myself suspended stark naked upon a wooden cross whilst Elizabeth, in a penitent's white gown, with her head and shoulders draped in a mantle of Our Lady's Blue, knelt at my feet, staring up at me with sad and pleading eyes. And then, out of a silver river that suddenly appeared as objects often inexplicably do in dreams, walked the nude and dripping form of Tom Seymour, his male organ greatly engorged and protruding like a battering ram. Seeing him, Elizabeth stood up, threw off her mantle, and stripped off her gown, letting it fall round her feet in an abandoned puddle of white to be sullied by the dust.

As she went to him she shook out her scarlet hair and paused for a tantalizing moment to teasingly cup her pert pink-tipped breasts and wiggle her hips at him. Then she was in his arms, and they were kissing passionately, and she began to sensuously slide her body up and down his as she used her hair to mop up the river water.

Bound helpless to the cross, I watched in horror, unable to cover my eyes, and acutely aware of my own nakedness, and the sudden humiliating hardness of my nipples, like brown pebbles upon my chest, and, even worse, the warm and wanton wetness between my legs as I struggled against my bonds, my thighs rubbing together in a way that only made it worse, but I couldn't stop. And then, as if he could read my mind, Tom Seymour looked up at me and winked as he grasped Elizabeth by her hips, lifted her up, and lowered her onto his fleshly lance. I unloosed a bloodcurdling scream upon my cross as I began to bleed all at once from my eyes and ears, my hands and feet, and between the thighs I clenched so tightly, as if by doing so I could hold the blood back. It was always at that moment that I woke up, bolting out of bed with a scream on my lips that sent me running straight into my private chapel to fling myself onto my knees before the altar, never caring that the skin split and bled.

❧ 14 ❧

Elizabeth

It was past the midnight hour and we were all sound asleep, snug in our beds, except for my steward, Mr Parry, who was burning the candles late over the account books, when the fists came pounding, incessant and demanding, upon the front door of my London house.

Mr Parry, who had fallen asleep at his desk, grumpily descended the stairs, rubbing the sleep from his eyes and barking at them to stop that infernal pounding. It was loud enough to wake the dead as well as the occupants of this house and those on either side, he said. His wife, Blanche, her greying blonde curls sleep-rumpled, followed him down, clutching a pale pink shawl over her modest white nightgown. And Kat and I straggled after, yawning, with our steps still leaden with slumber. In my sleep-befuddled state, I had forgotten to pull on my dressing gown, and Kat, her braids fuzzy beneath her ruffled nightcap, did not think to remind me, so I descended the stairs with my hair flowing loose about the shoulders of my white long-sleeved winter nightgown to confront a representative from the Council and a detachment of armed guards.

It was then that I learned that all Tom Seymour's schemes had gone fantastically awry, their destruction as fabulous and outlandish as the schemes themselves had been. It had all ended in a comedy of errors. Tom was in the Tower now, charged with High

Treason, and we – Mrs Ashley, Mr Parry, and I – stood accused of conspiring with him.

Despite their heated, increasingly frightened and hysterical protests of ignorance and innocence, the guards roughly seized hold of Kat and Mr Parry, wrestling their arms behind their backs, as they hustled them out into the icy January night to where a barge waited to take them to the Tower for questioning.

In a panic, Mr Parry broke free of them and threw off his gold chain of office from around his neck and wrenched the rings from his fingers and flung them higgledy-piggledy into the air, as he burst into frightened tears and wailed, "Would that I had never been born, for I am now undone!" before the guards again caught hold of him.

Kat and I tried to cling to each other but the guards tore us apart. And when Blanche Parry pleaded for them to tarry just long enough for her to run upstairs to fetch some proper warm clothes for Kat, shivering with cold and fear in her nightgown and cap, she was refused and soundly rebuked for trying to give comfort to one who was possibly a traitor.

"You have no right!" I heatedly exclaimed. Conjuring up the memory of my father and calling forth all my royal dignity, I stamped my foot indignantly, drew my spine up straight, thrust my shoulders back and my chin up high. "We know *nothing* of the Lord Admiral's schemes! How *dare* you disturb the peace of *my* household in the middle of the night and manhandle my servants? My brother, the King, shall hear of this!"

With chilly eyes, and an even colder voice, Sir Robert Tyrwhitt turned to me.

"My Lady Princess," he said with a mocking half bow, "in deference to your royal station, I offer you a choice – you may either walk out to my barge or be dragged and carried out by these guards and dumped into it like a sack of grain."

Eyes blazing, I tossed my head defiantly, whipping my hair back over my shoulders, and turned to plant my velvet-slippered foot firmly on the bottom step. "I will walk without the *chivalrous assistance* you so kindly offer me, My Lord, but *first*, I *will* dress."

His hand shot out to stay me.

"Mrs Parry can pack what you need; I shall send word back of where to send it. But *you must* come *now*, My Lady Princess. We shall *not* tarry."

Contemptuously, I jerked my arm free, shook back and smoothed down my hair and, clad in only my nightgown and slippers, walked boldly out into the frigid black night, with my head held high as if I were entering the King's Presence Chamber in my finest array. Appearances are everything, and those who show their fear and weaknesses are most vulnerable.

Perhaps something in my demeanour impressed him, or some hint of compassion stirred him, or maybe he was trying to win my trust and, by extension, my gratitude, I really cannot say, but as I paused on the jetty before stepping into the barge, the icy wind, that seemed to burn and freeze at the same time, tugging viciously at my hair and gown, Sir Robert removed his own velvet cloak and draped it most solicitously about my shoulders. Contemptuously, I shrugged it off just as quickly and let it fall into the dirty, dark waters of the Thames as I stepped, unaided, into the barge and settled myself upon the velvet-cushioned seat.

I held my chin up high and stared straight ahead of me, biting my lips to prevent their quivering lest they think I shivered from fear as well as from the cold. Nor did I give them the satisfaction of asking where they were taking me; I would know soon enough. And if it happened to be the Tower, where my mother had gone before me, my body would not betray the truth that inside I cowered and cried like a frightened child, like the three-year-old I had been the day the French executioner's sword ended my mother's life. I was not only Great Harry's daughter, I was Anne Boleyn's as well, and, by heaven, I would show them all that that was a combination to be reckoned with! And, come what may, I would hold my head up high until the moment the executioner struck it off, if such was to be my fate!

But it was not to the Tower that they took me, but to my own house of Hatfield. But rather than let me go upstairs to resume my so rudely interrupted rest, or to dress or even don a robe, ease my bladder, or partake of a morsel of food or a warming drink, instead

I was ushered immediately into the downstairs study by Sir Robert Tyrwhitt to begin the first round of questioning.

I knew what his game was; keeping me thus, he expected me to behave like what I was – a frightened and friendless fifteen-year-old girl, her nerves sorely jangled by an abrupt awakening and seeing her beloved governess dragged off to the Tower, with its numerous tortures and horrors, where the man she allegedly loved already languished. And as an added boon they hoped that my nakedness beneath my nightgown – one lone layer of white cloth without the rigid and respectable confines of tightly laced stays, stiff layered petticoats, covered by a proper gown – would make me feel even more vulnerable, and perhaps even conjure up memories of the wanton romps I was said to have indulged in with my stepfather, the Lord Admiral. Well, Sir Robert had met his match in Elizabeth Tudor. He might strip me naked, and leave me without sustenance until my belly howled like a banshee, but he would *never* take away my dignity! Stark naked I still had more backbone than the most rigorous corset either tailor or torturer could devise!

My chin shooting up as if my nose would bump the moon out of the sky to make way for the sun, I swept past him and settled myself in the most comfortable chair by the fire, flipped off my damp, cold slippers, and stretched out my toes to the toasty warmth.

"You have questions, Sir Robert? Well, let us get on with it then since they are apparently *so urgent* that you must roust me out of bed without tarrying even long enough for me to dress myself properly against the cold." I paused and coughed meaningfully into my hand. "If I have caught cold, rest assured, I shall know *exactly* where to fix the blame." To emphasize my point, I levelled accusing eyes straight at him.

"Urgent indeed, My Lady Princess," he began. "Your paramour . . ."

"My what, Sir?" I instantly interrupted.

"The what is your paramour, My Lady Princess," Sir Robert retorted sharply. "And before you interrupt me again to ask who I mean I shall tell you that it is the Lord Admiral, Sir Thomas Seymour, to whom I refer."

"You are misinformed then, Sir Robert. I have no paramour. Furthermore, I am a princess of royal blood, the daughter of Henry VIII" – I gestured to the majestic portrait of my scowling, seemingly invincible sire hanging above the mantel, his meaty, bejewelled hands curled into fists as he glowered out at the world from the confines of the gilded frame – "and as such I may not entertain suitors without the consent of the Council, as surely you know, being a member of said Council and, unless you know more than I do, none has ever sued for my hand."

"The Lord Admiral *did* ask for your hand, My Lady Princess," Sir Robert informed me, "and was refused, rebuffed actually, to be quite candid. He did not take it well. He also petitioned for the hand of your sister, the Princess Mary, and was refused permission to court her as well. And was 'laughed out on his arse', to use the crude expression that was bandied about when after the Council's rebuke he went courting the Lady Anne of Cleves. I was told he was actually chased away by a barrage of onions hurled from the windows by that lady's servants when he attempted to infiltrate her bedchamber in the guise of a footman bringing her an early morning repast of cakes and ale."

I did not let Sir Robert see that this was news to me. Tom had never mentioned Mary or the Lady Anne of Cleves except in passing when he told me about how my brother had once suggested them as possible brides for him when he connived, with the devious assistance of his man Fowler, to secure royal approval of his marriage to Kate. Nor had Mary in her rigidly polite letters ever mentioned any such dealings. There had been, much to my regret, a coldness between us since I had chosen to remain at Chelsea with Kate and Tom after their surprisingly sudden marriage which had outraged Mary's inflexible sense of propriety. I had meant to write to her, to try to thaw the coldness, but in my reckless passion for Tom I kept putting it off.

"The Lord Admiral was my stepfather," I calmly explained to Sir Robert, "the husband of my late lamented stepmother the Dowager Queen Catherine, and I was never privy to what business he had with the Council. If he ever asked for my hand, he never deigned to discuss the matter with me personally, so you might add presumption to his list of alleged crimes."

"He already stands accused of three-and-thirty counts of High Treason, Princess; do you not think that sufficient?" Sir Robert parried.

"*Three-and-thirty!*" I arched my brows. "How flamboyant! One would think an Englishman would show more restraint! It shows a want of good taste, to say nothing of good judgment! Do you not agree, Sir Robert?"

"Yes, Princess, I entirely agree; a most apt assessment for one so young." He nodded grudgingly.

"Oh my lord, how you do flatter me!" I cried, slumping back in my chair with my hand upon my heart in parody of a swoon.

He fixed me with a cold, stern, and reproachful stare. "I do not have time for flattery, Princess, or levity either."

He then went on to enumerate Tom's various crimes as I shook my head, clucked my tongue, and feigned surprise at his foolishness, interjecting from time to time a litany of amazed comments.

"A Lord Admiral of England consorting with pirates?"

"Allowing them free rein in exchange for a share of their spoils?"

"For shame!"

"The dread pirate Thomessin was his boon companion?"

"They actually sat at table together for a moonlit banquet on the pirate's flagship and the Lord Admiral *sang* bawdy English tavern songs and danced for him?"

"Surely not 'Cakes and Ale' again, Sir Robert? Verily, the Lord Admiral seems to sing but one song!"

"This reflects badly upon England and our navy as well as upon the Lord Admiral!"

"Embezzling the Royal Mint? Coin clipping? Oh my! How brazen!"

"The keys were not pilfered but given to him by the royal locksmith? Well, apparently the Lord Admiral's charm must extend to locksmiths as well as ladies and pirates!"

He went on to tell me that my mad, rash-brained Tom had been apprehended after sneaking into the royal apartments at Hampton

Court in the dead of night to put in motion a harebrained scheme in which he planned to sneak my brother from his bed, to carry him away and marry him to the Lady Jane Grey before anyone noticed he was missing. He had intended not to return him to the palace until the marriage had been consummated so none could annul it. But his scheme had been thwarted by my brother's spaniel, Hector, who roused the guards by barking. The faithful canine paid for his loyalty with his life when Tom discharged his pistol right between its beautiful brown eyes, thus rousing those in the palace who had not already been awakened by the dog's barking, and causing my brother to burst into tears and fly at his once favourite uncle, pummelling him with his fists and screaming, "You killed my dog, now I will kill you!" before he collapsed on the floor cradling the lifeless body of the only one whose loyalty he never doubted, staining his white nightshirt with its faithful fast-cooling blood.

Tom was dragged away by the palace guards, shouting back over his shoulder that he would bring Edward "a new dog tomorrow! Don't despair, Nephew, I shall bring you a whole kennel full of dogs – brown dogs, and black dogs, white dogs, and red dogs, yellow dogs, parti-coloured, striped, and spotted dogs! Dogs with long hair and dogs with short, dogs with bristly hair and silky soft! Stop crying now and smile for Uncle Tom," he cajoled, "and tomorrow I shall bring you dancing dogs and singing cats, all dressed in clothes and funny hats!"

"Poor Edward!" I sighed. I could see him in my mind's eye, weeping as he hugged his murdered pet, wondering if there was even *one* honest man in England who would gladly and selflessly see him to his majority without being blinded by self-interest and ambition or the honeyed words and bribes of court factions.

"There is more, Princess, much more," Sir Robert said, and went on to tell me that Tom was also under suspicion of having poisoned his wife. Witnesses claimed that he had added a mysterious white powder to her wine, and the way he had forced the dictation and signing of her will was most suspicious, to say nothing of callous and unkind. I learned that he had also planned to invite the entire Council and their wives to a lavish banquet at his London house that would also turn out to be their last supper. In a dark-humoured touch, he had even procured a large tapestry depicting the Last Supper to be hung overlooking the banquet table. The banquet was to be held ostensibly to make peace with his brother, but at the last moment Tom had planned to have his cook fall ill, thus necessitating him to send an urgent message to his brother, begging to borrow his own cook for the night else the dinner be ruined. The plan was to administer poison and lay the blame on his brother's cook and, by extension, upon the Lord Protector himself, thus neatly disposing of all Tom's enemies in one fell stroke.

Sir Robert also told me that Tom had three lists, which he would whip out at a moment's whim and show to anyone, even strangers on the street or people passing him in the palace corridors. The first list consisted of the names of Tom's friends as well as acquaintances who liked him, the second list included the names of men who disliked Tom and favoured his brother instead, and the third were those whose preference was either uncertain or for neither. Tom saw it as his mission to move as many names as possible from the second and third lists onto the first. He also kept a map that denoted in solid black ink the parts of England where he was more popular than his brother, and in black spots those where his brother was preferred, and in stripes those areas where neither held sway, so Tom could clearly see the parts of the nation he needed to work on winning over to his side, his goal being to someday see the whole map painted solid black.

My amazement showed clear upon my face, and Sir Robert hastened to assure me, "I know for a fact these documents exist. Sir Thomas unwisely showed them to several men at court who, in their dedication to assuring the safety of the King and realm, brought it to the Lord Protector's attention. They were also upon his person when he was taken."

With every word I was discovering more and more what a fool Tom was. His efforts to obtain more supporters were . . . childlike, to put it bluntly. I could easily imagine him saying to his brother, "More people like me than like you!" and putting out his tongue to punctuate it.

But I had little time to ponder this as Sir Robert was now telling me that, whenever he was in London, Tom frequented a particular tavern, where, after a few cups of their finest brew, he would leap up onto the bar, throw off his codpiece, and flamboyantly flaunt his well-endowed masculinity. Brandishing his cock as he strutted back and forth along the bar like a proud cockerel, he would belt out at the top of his lungs a boisterous ditty of his own composition that seemingly consisted of countless repetitions of the same two lines:

> *O My cock is bigger than my brother's!*
> *O diddle diddle diddle all the day!*

He would vigorously urge the other patrons of the tavern to join in. "Everybody sing!" he would shout, waggling his cock at them and declaring, "He deserves a serenade!"

When he tired of singing, Tom would empty his purse into his hands, fling the coins up into the air, letting them fall where they would, and invite all the women in the tavern to "Come and get it, my pretty whores!" and launch himself from the bar onto the nearest table occupied by women of dubious repute, causing the table to splinter and collapse beneath his weight, not that the proprietor particularly minded; Tom was so free with his gold that they could not help but be fond of him and look forward to his visits, and by the time his reign of table-diving was ended by his arrest, he had furnished the Jolly Mermaid with a whole new set of tables and chairs. In fact, so well-regarded was he by the proprietors that they had even painted him onto the shingle-sign outside, embracing the mermaid from behind, cupping a bare breast and kissing her cheek.

It angered me that I blushed, for I knew that was Sir Robert's aim in telling me this; he wanted to shock me, to provoke some visible reaction. He wanted me flustered, angry and confused, perhaps even jealous and hurt over Tom's philandering. But I was past that. I was embarrassed for Tom, as I would have been for any fool who comported himself in such a manner, but I was past caring about what he did and whom he did it with. The Lord Admiral's ship was sinking, and my only goal now was to save myself and my servants from going down with it.

"The man is obviously quite mad," I said. "Heaven help him, for no one else will."

I knew that Tom's madness would not save him; my father had repealed the law against executing the insane for High Treason for the benefit of the vengeful and treacherous Lady Rochford, who had falsely accused my mother and Uncle George of incest, when she lost her wits in the Tower after her role in abetting that poor silly girl Catherine Howard's adultery was discovered.

"I daresay he will soon stand before a higher judge than Parliament." Sir Robert nodded. "But now, let us concern ourselves with you, My Lady Princess," he continued in a crisp, businesslike tone. "Now that you know what the Lord Admiral stands accused of, you must answer for your role in it."

"That I can do in one word, Sir Robert – *none!* I had *no* part in it whatsoever, no part at all!" I firmly declared. "Do you honestly think, My Lord, that I would be involved in anything so absurdly foolish? The man obviously had more courage than cunning, but it was not enough to carry the thing off!"

"Everyone plays the fool sometime, Princess. *You* are no exception to the rule." Icicles hung from every word Sir Robert uttered. "However" – he clapped his hands and came to stand before the fire, rubbing them together and holding them out to warm – "you are young, and be grateful for it, for therein your salvation may lie . . ."

"In my youth, My Lord?" I queried. "Not in my trust and faith in God and the following of His commandments?"

"Youth excuses much, Princess. Those with more experience of life may be, in some instances, more tolerant of the foibles and follies, the mistakes and missteps made by persons of more tender years, including the breaking of God's commandments as well as Man's laws. And, my fine lady, I have reason to believe that you may have broken some of both. Adultery, for instance; the Lord Admiral was another woman's husband when he first became your lover." He walked to a table nearby and brandished a sheaf of papers. "I have many reports from the late Dowager Queen's household at Chelsea . . ."

"*Tittle-tattle? Servants' gossip?*" I exclaimed. "With that you would condemn me? Surely, Sir Robert, you do not take *that* as gospel truth! Servants *love* to gossip about their betters. I daresay your own kitchen maids and laundresses have their share of tales to tell!" I said boldly, brazenly trying to fight down the red tide of shame that was rising inside me as I remembered all that had passed between Tom and myself beneath my stepmother's roof.

"Alas, they are too numerous to be entirely discounted as gossip. I even have here" – he riffled through the pages – "a report from a midwife who claims she was brought blindfolded to attend you when you gave birth to the Lord Admiral's child, which was then most foully disposed of, thrown living into the fireplace and burned to ashes, she claims. Many have heard this tale and believe it to be true."

"*How dare you! How do you dare?*" I leapt to my feet and boldly gathered the loose folds of my full, shapeless white nightgown behind me, drawing the fabric taut against my slender body to outline my flat belly and small, firm breasts. "Do I have the look of a woman who has ever borne a child, My Lord?"

"Looks, like words, can be deceiving, Princess." Sir Robert shrugged, unmoved by my display.

I snatched the papers from him and flung them high, letting them fly and fall where they would. "And these are words that *lie!*" I shouted. "Bring me pen and paper!" I commanded. "*Now!*" I stamped my foot so hard it bruised the sole. "I *will* write at once to my brother, and the Council, and I shall *demand* that a proclamation be published far and wide throughout the land giving the lie to this false and base slander! I shall *not* have my name sullied by some slack-jawed, loose-tongued, slandermongering midwife telling tales to lift herself out of obscurity and get the town gossips and her neighbours to treat her at the alehouse! It is the attention she thirsts for, and it is this *lie* that provides the brew to slake it! And I *will* have my innocence proclaimed from one end of England to the other so that every man, woman, and child knows of it!"

Sir Robert went to the desk and pulled back the chair, indicating that all writing implements I might need awaited me there.

I crossed the room in three long strides and sat down and took a sheet of parchment and selected a quill and bent diligently to my task, letting my outrage take flight as my pen flew back and forth over the page, the quill biting deep and shaking like the wings of an avenging angel as I wrote. When I had finished I did not bother to seal it but simply thrust it at Sir Robert and asked him to convey it immediately to the Lord Protector.

"I *will* have my innocence proclaimed from one end of England to the other! I shall have it shouted into every nook and cranny of this realm until *every* man, woman, and child knows that Elizabeth Tudor is no man's doxy!" I declared, and then, with my head held high, I swept grandly from the room and upstairs to my bedchamber without waiting for Sir Robert to give me leave to retire.

When I burst through the door I nearly collided with the curtsying black-clad figure of Sir Robert's grim, sour-faced wife, still clad in deepest mourning for her beloved former stepmother, Catherine Parr.

Lady Tyrwhitt was also Kate's stepdaughter by her first marriage, and by her expression clearly believed the rumours swirling about myself and the Lord Admiral.

"My Lady Princess," she said in a voice as hard as her face, "in the absence of Mrs Ashley, I am commanded to serve you as your lady-governess."

"*Get out!*" I stamped my foot at her. "If I can't have Kat I will have no one, and certainly not *you*, My Lady *Gaoler!*"

"It is the Council's pleasure that I remain," she said frostily, drawing her back up full straight.

"But not yours!" I challenged.

"No, Madame, it is most certainly not *my* pleasure, but . . . duty calls." She turned her attention to turning back my bed, giving the pillows such shakes and slaps as she plumped them that I had the distinct impression that she wished them my head instead so that she might box my ears and slap and pummel me. "Bad blood tells!" she hissed harshly, each word coinciding with a slap to the pillows. "Like mother, like daughter! You stole Kate's husband the same as Anne Boleyn stole Katherine of Aragon's!"

Furiously, I yanked the pillow from her hands and flung it across the room.

"*Get out!*" I said in a voice low and murderous. "Else you regret it, Madame, for I am not only Anne Boleyn's daughter but Henry VIII's as well and you would *never* have dared be so free with your opinions in my father's presence! And if you are to serve me, even though we both dislike it, then you *will* bridle your damned scold's tongue and treat me with the respect that is due a king's daughter!"

She took a step back and I saw the shadow of fear flit across her face before she lowered her head and bobbed a brief curtsy. "As you wish, Madame. Good night," she murmured as she hastily backed out and shut the door behind her.

Once she was gone, I let my façade of bravado and strength crumble, like an aged and decayed marble pillar, and collapsed, face down and weeping, onto my bed.

I slept through a whole day and night until the following dawn. Then I rose and dressed to do battle with Sir Robert again. Did St George feel this exhilarating yet daunting mixture of courage and fear, determination and dread, when he went out to slay the dragon? I wondered as I descended the stairs.

In the difficult and trying days that followed, Sir Robert continued to try to wile and beguile a confession out of me, repeating often that my youth excused much, as did my weak and fragile female sex. I was, he opined, more sinned against than sinning. The lion's share of the blame lay rightly upon Mrs Ashley's shoulders, he claimed, for as my governess she had charge of me and should have known better than to encourage a scoundrel like the Lord Admiral to court me.

Even Mary seemed to believe the worst of me and sent a brooch of the penitent Magdalene to speak for her as a silent but nonetheless stinging rebuke. I was tempted to throw it in the river, but in the end good sense prevailed and I buried it at the bottom of my jewellery casket so I would not have to look at it. The ruby was a large one with much sparkle and a deep, rich colour, and perhaps one day I could have it reset into a design less pious and more pleasing.

This experience had taught me a valuable lesson – that I could neither trust nor depend on anyone, not even the governess who had loved me like a mother for most of my life. For she betrayed me too, I discovered, when they laid her rambling hysterical confession before me, setting it all down in black and white how Tom had come to dally with me so many mornings at Chelsea and had even once cut the dress from my body leaving me almost as naked as Eve in the Garden of Eden.

I realized now that the only person I could truly trust and depend on was myself. I must learn to stand and walk alone, *Semper Eadem*. "Always the same," and trust no one: That would be my motto for the rest of my life. Henceforth, I could never lean on anyone, or let my guard down, never confide in a friend, or set down on paper that which might harm or damn me if it were read by others. Even though as a princess, and perhaps someday a queen, I would live my life surrounded by others, I would always be alone. Even if I did not like it, I must learn to accept and bear it, for it was the reality of my life. *Semper Eadem*. I, Elizabeth, Elizabeth I – if Destiny ever decreed it – would always be alone.

But shining through the treachery was one bright beacon of hope. We had acted foolishly, unwisely, and indiscreetly, but none of us had committed actual treason. Somehow, even in the terrible place that was the Tower, surrounded and perhaps even confronted with the hellish implements of torture, Kat had had the wit not to admit that she had ever encouraged me to marry Tom, for to do so, without the Council's consent, was indeed treason.

"These are my loyal and faithful servants," I said calmly to Sir Robert as I laid aside Kat's and Mr Parry's equally damning and rambling confessions, "and I will not have them coerced by fear of torture into making false statements. Yea, My Lord, we have all played the fool where the Lord Admiral is concerned. We were all, I admit, gulled by his charms, but the question of matrimony was never broached. Mrs Ashley, from the time I was of an age to understand such things, was always at great pains to impress upon me that I must *never* even *think* of a man as a suitor for my hand unless he came with the approval of the Council. And, indeed, My Lord, I never have; I have never thought, either seriously or frivolously, of marrying anyone, least of all Thomas Seymour. Though he fooled and flattered me for a time, which doth, even with my youth, reflect badly upon me and my brains, I never could suffer a fool in the real world and out of motley, and certainly not, even if the Council had allowed or even encouraged it, in the marriage bed."

Tom believed that he would best his brother, but in the end it would be the other way around and Fortune's Knave would break Ambition's Fool as the Wheel of Fortune spun round. And all too soon my vain, handsome, cocksure Tom would lay his head on the block, and the mouth that had once rained hot kisses upon me and sung to me of cakes and ale would be silenced for ever.

When they brought me word that he had died, they watched me very closely, thinking that when confronted with such news my face would betray the truth inside my heart. They thought that grief would loosen my tongue and all my most deeply guarded secrets would come pouring out on a torrent of tears. But I refused to oblige them.

I stood up straight, my eyes fever-bright but my flesh marble-pale, like a tall, slim, white taper in my virgin white gown, my flame-coloured hair appearing all the brighter against my pallor, and shook my head and sighed, "Today died a man of much wit but very little judgment." Quotable, succinct, and true; I daresay no poet could coin a more apt epitaph for Thomas Seymour.

Sir Robert flinched before me as if a wasp had stung him, and his lady wife shook her head and heaved a sigh. "As cold as ice" she called me, as I walked out into the orchard where I could be alone, awash in a late-afternoon sunset that painted the sky with streaks of crimson, as if the very sky was bleeding for Tom, with the buttercups nodding knowingly and whispering against my white skirt.

It was true, my heart had frosted over, and I was cold; a core of ice had come to replace the fire of passion that had once burned so bright within me.

He died and I survived. And that day a part of me died too. Blinded by passion, like the blindfold Tom had tied over my eyes the day he led me to the heart of the hedge maze, I had nearly followed him blithely and blindly through the gates of Hell. I had walked into a trap, and I had had a narrow escape, jumping clear just moments before the trap snapped shut. But I hadn't escaped unscathed. My virtue was maimed and marred, my honour was scarred, but I had survived – that was the important thing! Unlike my mother, I had been granted a second chance and I would *never* take that for granted. Sex, I had discovered, enslaves the female and empowers the male. When a woman surrenders to a man she becomes like the fly ensnared in a spider's web, and it is only a matter of time before she dies. But this fly had broken free and flown away while the spider instead had died, strangled by his own web.

Tom had stained my honour like a virgin's bloodstain on a clean white sheet. And when people looked at me I feared that they could see that stain. I wanted my virginity, and my honour, back. Thus, from the day the scandal broke like a storm cloud above my head, pelting me with a heavy relentless rain of shame and suspicion, I began to affect plain white gowns, the virgin white of new-fallen snow and eggshells, lily white, the perfect white of a pearl, the shimmering nacreous flash of a fish's belly, white – the unstained, unsullied colour of purity, the emblematic colour of virginity with which I would whitewash the bloodstain. I vowed to always keep my body straight and slender, to never let it grow womanly and round with the curves that bespoke fecundity, and to wear pearls about my neck, in remembrance of both my mother, whose favourite necklace had been a simple strand of white pearls with a golden *B*, and of the lustrous rope rash and reckless Tom had put briefly about my throat, and which I had broken before it could choke me like a noose. Now with pearls of my own choosing coupled with a straight, reed-slender form and a wardrobe of white dresses I would symbolically reclaim what had been taken from me – my virginity.

In that moment I said farewell to my dreams – there would never be a husband or children or lovers for me, only the flirtation, the dance, the prelude to romance but never the climax or fulfilment.

At midnight there was a knock upon my chamber door. I rose from my bed and drew on my dressing gown, and opened it to behold the sorrowful face of Tom's manservant, the very one who had once stood above us on the staircase at Chelsea and showered us with red rose petals.

Wordlessly, he handed me a small square of black velvet, and vanished into the night.

I knew before I unfolded it what it contained – the garnet and ruby heart on a band of golden lovers' knots, the rubies the colour of freshly spilt blood and the garnet the hue of dried, dark, and clotted blood.

All of a sudden I felt as if I were indeed holding Tom Seymour's heart in my hands. I swayed upon my feet as the truth sank in. Tom was dead. Never again would he hold me in his arms, never again would I feel the warmth of his body, his hot kisses and bold caresses, and the molten liquid thrill they kindled between my thighs. I would never again see him smile or hear him laugh or singing lustily of cakes and ale.

With an anguished cry, my fist closed tight around the ring, feeling the hard bite of the metal and gems, and clutched it to my own heart. I fell in a dead faint as, from beyond the grave, the ghostly voice of memory sang inside my head:

> *I gave her Cakes and I gave her Ale,*
> *I gave her Sack and Sherry;*
> *I kist her once and I kist her twice,*
> *And we were wondrous merry!*
>
> *I gave her Beads and Bracelets fine,*
> *I gave her Gold down derry.*
> *I thought she was afear'd till she stroked my Beard*
> *And we were wondrous merry!*
>
> *Merry my Heart, merry my Cock,*
> *Merry my Spright.*
> *Merry my hey down derry.*
> *I kist her once and I kist her twice,*
> *And we were wondrous merry!*

❧ 15 ❧

Mary

Things did not get better, only worse, as I continued to flout the Council's edict banning the Mass, throwing my chapel doors open wide in welcome to all faithful Catholics who wished to come, and celebrating Mass as many as six times a day. Those noble families that, despite fear of persecution, still clung to the unravelled true faith, vied to send their daughters to serve me, quite correctly praising my household as "a true school of virtuous demeanour and the only safe harbour for honourable young gentlewomen given to piety and devotion." I knew it was only the threat of war from my cousin, the Emperor, that kept me safe, and I clung to the ultimatum he had issued to Edward's Council as if it were a talisman. But living in constant fear took a drastic toll on me; my nerves frayed and unravelled, dreams of assassins lurking in the shadows kept me awake at night or disturbed my sleep with violent and terrifying dreams, and my mind began to turn seriously to the thought of escape.

Finally, I took up my pen and wrote adamantly to the Emperor, stressing the dangers of my situation. "If my brother were to die," I wrote, "I should be far better off out of the kingdom, because as soon as he were dead, before the public knew it, they would dispatch me too. There is no doubt of that, because you know there is nobody in the government who is not opposed to me."

I showed my letter to Charles's ambassador, the good Francis van der Delft, before I entrusted it to him to deliver, but he urged me to wait. "Act in haste, repent at leisure," he recited like a schoolmaster, adding that to run away would seem to some the same as renouncing my claim to the throne, and if my brother were to die I might have great difficulty in recovering what I had, by my actions, appeared to renounce; the people might not take to a queen they thought ready to bolt like a frightened rabbit running back to its hole at the slightest sign of danger or difficulty.

But I pleaded with him, knowing that he was about to retire due to failing health, to take me with him, to make conveying me to safety his last loyal act of service.

"The men who sit upon my brother's Council fear no God and respect no persons, but follow their own fancy. The most dangerous crime a person can commit in England today is to be a good Catholic and lead a righteous life. And I would rather die than give up my religion! My cause is so righteous in God's sight that if His Imperial Majesty favours me, I need take no further justification in delaying, until I am past all help! When they send me orders forbidding me the Mass, I shall expect to suffer as I suffered once during my father's lifetime!" I cried vehemently as I clung to his arm, my tears making damp spots upon the velvet. "I must fly beyond their clutches before the blow falls, as when that time comes they will order me to withdraw thirty miles from any navigable river or seaport, and will deprive me of my most trusted servants and, surrounded by strangers and reduced to the utmost destitution, they will deal with me as they please. They know I would rather suffer death than stain my conscience. I beg you to help me, so that I may not be taken unawares. I am like a little ignorant girl, and I care neither for my goods nor for the world, but only for God's service and my conscience. If there is peril in going and peril in staying, I must choose the lesser of the two evils! As soon as I am safe in my imperial cousin's dominion, I trust him to act in my best interests and see that I am not cheated or thwarted of my just right to reign if it so pleases God to take my brother's life!"

Quaking with tears, my knees gave way, and I collapsed sobbing at Ambassador van der Delft's feet.

Moved by my plight, he chivalrously bent to raise me. "Madame, I give you my solemn promise that I will deliver you from this lions' den," he said. "Weep no more, My Lady, your sorrows and fears will soon be past and your smile will be lighting up the imperial court."

Gallantly, he led me to the window seat and, thick as thieves, we began to plot my escape. In the following month of May, he was to officially take his leave of my brother's court and board ship for Brussels. Before that time, I must withdraw to my Essex estate, Woodham Walter, which lay near Maldon, and await the arrival of a Dutch corn merchant in a small boat to sell his wares to the town and also my household. Disguised as a man I was to switch places with one of the men who accompanied the merchant or else I was to be smuggled out bundled in a coarse cloth grain sack. Once in the merchant's boat, I would be borne out to sea where an imperial ship was anchored ready to convey me, and Ambassador van der Delft, back to the comfort and safety of my cousin's court.

It seemed like a fine plan, foolproof, and I was confident of its success. For the first time in months, I felt able to breathe easily and to sleep soundly as I counted the days until I would be free.

But then it all began to unravel. First, Ambassador van der Delft took to his bed and died suddenly, but not without having the foresight to entrust the completion of his mission to his loyal secretary, Jehan Dubois.

It was he who put all into motion, and accompanied by his brother-in-law, Peter, saw to it that an imperial ship was anchored off the coast in readiness, waiting for me, and then, upon the first day of July, in the guise of a corn merchant come to transact some business, he came prepared to whisk me away to safety.

He found me in quite a state. A raging fever of commingled uncertainty, anticipation, and dread plagued me, made all the worse by a raging throbbing megrim and a queasy stomach that felt all aflutter and made me nervous of my dignity and bowels. Before, I had been so convinced that leaving was the right thing to do, but now I was not sure, an inkling of doubt tugged at my mind. My steward, Master Rochester, urged me to stay, claiming that horoscopes cast secretly by learned London astrologers known for their accuracy portended an early death for Edward. And the rumours from London seemed to confirm this with reports of ill health, an attack of measles following hard on the heels of a mild bout of smallpox, from which he had failed to bounce back. These combined illnesses had left him with a loss of strength and vigour, in a perpetual state of listlessness and lethargy, having a constant waxy pallor, a loss of appetite and weight, and a persistent cough that would not be eased by herbal lozenges or soothing syrups or depart in the natural course of things. While my loyal ladies, Susan and Jane, the only two I had entrusted with my secret plans, cried and clung to me, contradictorily begging me not to forsake them yet nobly urging me to go and save myself, I wept and wrung my hands; I did not know what to do.

Herr Jehan found me ill-prepared. I had packed nothing. And Susan, Jane, and I ran back and forth stuffing shifts, gowns, and petticoats, shoes and stockings, into grain sacks and then taking them out again, whilst Herr Jehan and his brother-in-law Peter looked on in horror at the mounting pile of bulging sacks and implored me to take only the bare necessities.

"As you can see, I am ill prepared," I said sadly, gesturing to the sacks, even as one fell over and a carnelian-coloured kirtle sewn with seed pearls tumbled out even as Susan and Jane busied themselves with stuffing two others. "I do not know how the Emperor would take it if it turned out to be impossible for me to go now after I have so importuned him on the subject!"

In a rumpled, mismatched welter of my possessions, I sank down and pressed my hands to my aching brow.

"I cannot leave tonight!" I gathered up the carnelian kirtle and hugged it tight against my breast. "I need more time! I pray you, Herr Jehan, return tomorrow night and you will find me better prepared, or better yet if you could wait until Friday, my ladies and I could meet you on the beach before dawn and you can row us out to the ship."

"Madame, what you suggest is impossible!" Herr Jehan exclaimed, giving me the distinct impression that he was growing irritated with me.

"Impossible!" Peter affirmed.

"But . . ." I tried to think of words that would persuade them.

"Madame, we are leaving England tonight," Herr Jehan said forcefully. "If you prefer to stay, you know best your situation, and the Emperor will be content with that and think no less of you. But if you desire to accompany me, you must come *this instant!*"

I got shakily to my feet and began to wrench off my rings. "If I do not accompany you this time, will you at least take my jewellery to safety?" I tremulously asked as I held them out to him.

"Madame!" Herr Jehan sighed in a vexed and irritable manner. "If I am to take your rings, you might as well go with them!"

"I could go to my house at Newhall in a few days' time, and we could rendezvous at Stansgate and . . ."

The stern frowning faces and shaking heads of Herr Jehan and Peter stopped the words on my lips.

"Madame, I am obliged to point out to you that there is danger in delay!" Herr Jehan said most emphatically, and Peter nodded in agreement. "It is *imperative* that we sail with the *next* tide. If I remain any longer, there is grave risk that all we intend will be brought to light."

"And I must add," said Peter, "that I see no better opportunity than the present one. This undertaking is passing through so many hands" – he glared reproachfully at each of my servants in turn – "that it is daily becoming more difficult, and I fear it may not remain secret much longer."

"Great danger threatens us if we tarry," Herr Jehan continued. "Already the countryside is in a state of unrest. They are wary and suspicious of the imperial ships anchored off the shore, and of me, a foreigner, a Dutchman, though I have given it out that I travelled with the imperial ship only to enjoy their protection against pirates. Now that I have sold my corn and have no other reason for remaining in Maldon, it will look highly suspicious if I linger. If we are to do this thing, Madame, we must go *now!*"

"Yes, Madame." Peter nodded. "Leave everything." He swept a disdainful hand at the grain sacks, some bulging near to bursting and others sagging half empty, surrounded by a jumble of scattered and rumpled garments and shoes strewn all across the floor from one end of the room to the other. "Leave all this, and come with us. You are the Emperor's beloved and much esteemed cousin, the daughter of Henry VIII and Katherine of Aragon and the true and rightful heiress to the English throne, and you will be provided for as befits your station, as a queen in exile. You will only have to make do without these comforts and luxuries for a few days; a very *minor* inconvenience surely when your very life is at stake!"

"No, Madame, stay!" Master Rochester fell to his knees and begged of me. "For the very reason that the countryside is so unsettled. The constables and armed men are out on watch, there is not a back road or even a creek that is not under observation, and any person seen out at night is stopped and questioned. If you are stopped, even in disguise, you will be recognized, and it will not go well for you when the King's men learn that you have tried to flee the realm."

There was a knock upon the door then and in came a wild-looking character with bushy ginger hair who was introduced to me as Master Schurts, one of Herr Jehan's men.

"This affair is going very ill, sir," he announced, coming straight to the point without taking time for the polite conversational niceties. "The bailiff and other folk of the town wish to detain and search your boat; they suspect your involvement with the ship offshore. You had best leave right now. Already they have doubled the watch and posted men on the church tower, whence they can see all the country roundabout, and they have never done that before. And there is talk in the town of lighting a great bonfire on the hill to warn the people of the surrounding villages that there is trouble afoot and to be on the lookout. Come now, I implore you, before it is too late!"

Herr Jehan threw up his hands and heaved a defeated sigh. "We have let our chance go by!"

"But what is to become of me?" I wailed. Now that the chance was lost I longed to turn back the clock and seize it.

"Madame," said Herr Jehan, "the best service we can render you now is to leave your house immediately and as inconspicuously as possible."

"There is a way through the woods," said Master Rochester. "I can show you . . ."

Herr Jehan nodded and motioned to Peter and Master Schurts to follow him, and with a curt bow to me they hurried out.

"But what is to become of me?" I cried after them, but they never looked back or answered, and instead left me weeping on the floor, crushing the carnelian kirtle to my breast, keening with despair, repeating over and over, "But what is to become of me?" as Susan and Jane knelt beside me and tried to console me.

The next day brought a troop of the Lord Protector's men galloping into Maldon "to stop the Lady Mary from going away", and I knew I must abandon all thought of escaping.

❧ 16 ❧

Elizabeth

In time, the scandal abated. And I resolved to live quietly in the country and devote myself to my studies. I had no desire to play a larger role in the drama of life at the moment and I knew I was better off out of the thick of things.

England had a new Lord Protector now, John Dudley, the Duke of Northumberland. While the Seymour brothers were busy battling each other they had failed to notice the threat of Northumberland lurking in the background, biding his time, making plans and winning supporters, until it was too late, and Edward Seymour soon followed his brother to the block, and my brother had a new puppetmaster to pull his strings and put words into his mouth.

When Kat came back to me, we flew into each other's arms. Kat sank down onto her knees before me and vowed "never again to speak or even whisper of matrimony, not even if it would win the world for me!" and bathed my hands with her tears and humbly begged my pardon for betraying me in her darkest hour of fear when she had heard the bloodcurdling screams of the tortured and seen the bodies stretched in mortal agony upon the rack.

I was so glad to have her back that, of course, I readily forgave her all. Though Anne Boleyn had given me life, Kat Ashley had given me the mother's love I otherwise would have gone without; she had stood proxy for my real mother, and that counted much with me. But when I beheld the effects her stay in the Tower had wrought upon her person, I felt our roles shift. Though Kat would always love me like a mother, I had grown up. I would no longer be the child. On the contrary, I would now be the one who would take care of Kat for the rest of her life, though she would always see it as the other way around. The Tower had changed and aged my dear Kat beyond her years and, I feared, taken away years from her life. She was gaunt and greyer now, the rounded flesh Tom Seymour had so admired had melted away, and there was a wild, haunted look that hung about her eyes, a tremor in her hands that would remain always as a permanent reminder of the terrors of the Tower, and she jumped and started at every sudden and unexpected sound, and often I would hear her cry out in her sleep. For the rest of her life she would suffer greatly from the cold, bundling herself in layers as if she could never get warm enough, unable to dry out the dampness that had crept into her bones and eventually gnarled her hands and produced untold agony in her hips, knees, and feet.

Our first night together again, Kat brushed out my hair before bed as she had always used to do. Kat was silent now, where before she would have been all chatter, but as she finished the final strokes she heaved a long sigh over the loss of the poor Lord Admiral, lamenting, "We shall not see his like again."

"We can only hope," I answered, "but I fear the world is full of handsome, charming, foolish, and reckless men willing to risk anything to see their ambitions fulfilled."

"You've hardened your heart against him, poor man!" Kat sighed as she put down the brush and eased the dressing gown from my shoulders. "Such hardness does not become you, Bess; you are a flesh-and-blood woman with a heart, not a statue of white marble."

"Without his shell the tortoise is too vulnerable to survive for long, Kat," I said sagely as I slid between the sheets and bade her good night.

"But you're not a tortoise, love," Kat said softly as she drew the bedcurtains about me, shutting me in darkness, "you're a woman."

I would never admit to her, or anyone else, how many nights after Tom died that I started awake after a dream in which Tom as a lasciviously leering satyr with a huge, throbbing phallus, and a wild, wicked laugh, chased me through the forest, reaching out and ripping away my diaphanous white gown as it billowed out behind me as I ran, until I was running stark naked through the forest. When he caught me he laid me down upon the sun-dappled ground and ravished me upon a bed of wildflowers, with ferns like green lace fans hanging over us. Trembling uncontrollably, I would bolt up in bed only to find my face wet with tears, my nipples hard, and a throbbing molten wetness between my thighs, as the memory of Tom's hands and lips burned my body and scorched my soul, setting me on fire all over again, making me weep for what might have been even though I *knew* it never could have been. And I knew that long after Tom Seymour's bones had mouldered into dust inside his tomb I would still be fighting the war between practicality and passion, fighting against myself in a war that would never end until I drew my final breath.

❧ 17 ❧

Mary

Come what may, whether it meant the best or the worst for me, in England I must remain, so I decided to be brave. I assembled all my household, my servants, guards, and loyal retainers, and every staunch Catholic who would follow me, and bade them dress in deepest black velvet and bloodred satin, and hang round their necks their crucifixes, and either carry in hand or wear at their waist their well-fingered rosaries, and mount their horses and ride with me to London. And all six of my priests, despite the great risk to them, took up staves topped with gleaming gold and silver crosses, and donned their godly vestments, and accompanied us to serve as God's standard-bearers. And so we took to the road, a thousand strong and devout Catholics.

The common folk lined the parched and dusty roads to watch us pass, stiff-backed and unyielding. Despite the sweltering August heat and our heavy velvets and stultifying satins, we never for an instant faltered, and rode with calm dignity to London. The humble people could not fail to be impressed and raised their voices to bless and cheer us as we passed. Some would later swear that they saw in the clouds above us a phantom army of medieval Crusaders, wearing armour and the red cross on their white tunics, riding right in step with us. When I heard, it gladdened my heart, and I hoped fervently that it was true. Surely it was a sign from God, and it gave me comfort and courage to believe that those brave men and women who had gone to the Holy Land, some never to return, were with us in spirit.

"If God is for us," I told my people in proud, ringing tones, "none can be against us!"

And with those words I nudged my mount with my booted heel, stiffened my spine, held my head up high, and rode through the gates of Whitehall to meet my brother and settle this matter once and for all. I was weary beyond words of living in fear, and of being harassed, hounded, and threatened by godless men whose only religion was gold, who tried to mould my conscience as if it were made of clay to suit their avaricious ambitions.

They did not want to let me see Edward, but I insisted. Curiously, the royal bedchamber stank of rotting fish, but the moment I spied my brother I forgot all about it. He looked so small lying there in that great bed, the one that had belonged to Father. His face was nearly as white as the pillows his head lay upon. Up close, I could see the fading marks of measles and smallpox standing out starkly against his pallor. He wore a gold-embroidered nightcap to hide the fact that he had lost all his hair.

My nose crinkled and my stomach lurched; the rotting fishy odour that pervaded the room was stronger about the bed and impossible to ignore. Forcing myself to sniff it out, to discover its source, I moved around the bed, and at the foot I braced myself and turned back the covers. I gasped and leapt back, clutching both my hands over my mouth to stifle my scream. I staggered and swayed and had to clutch one of the great gilded bedposts to keep from falling. I feared I would vomit at the sight that lay before me. Tied tight to the soles of my brother's feet with rough twine that bit most cruelly into his flesh were a pair of rotting fish, so far gone that in places I could actually glimpse the white of bone. And there was worse, much worse – the condition of my brother's feet made me gag and want to turn away and run. What were the men entrusted with the care of him thinking? Every toenail had fallen out and against the pale white skin there were red streaks and mottled black and green sores rimmed in red and oozing yellow pus, and there was dried blood caked around the twine.

Edward opened his eyes and looked at me, and I was startled to see how large they looked; the fever lent them an unexpected brightness and made them seem even bluer than they ever had before.

"Oh my *poor, poor* brother!" I wailed, and, heedless of the proper ceremony due his station, I rushed to his side, and sank down onto the bed beside him, facing him. When I reached beneath the purple velvet coverlet and white sheets and tried to take his hand in mine I discovered that he was wearing white silk gloves, stained with the same telltale yellow pus.

My eyes must have looked like pools of pity for he said to me, "I do not want your pity, Mary."

A fit of coughing convulsed him, and he struggled to pull himself up higher upon the pillows, scowling at me when I came to help him, proudly disdaining to proffer any thanks. His hand flailed out blindly to grope for a handkerchief on the bedside table. When I picked it up and offered it to him he glared at me and snatched it from my hand but nonetheless clutched it to his lips. When the coughing subsided and he lowered it I saw it was stained with blackish-red bile.

"And do you also disdain your sister's love, Edward?" I asked gently. Then, without waiting for an answer, I continued, gesturing down at his ruined feet, "Oh, Edward, what have they done to you?"

"When the doctors failed to cure me with medicines and herbs, blistering and bleeding, Northumberland, in desperation to save my life, and to save England from *you* and your papist ways, sought the advice of others – quacks, charlatans, miracle workers, wise men and women, even witches in the service of Satan – all tempted by the promise of riches if they could effect a cure and sworn to secrecy on pain of a horrible and lingering death. And it was the opinion of one wise woman Northumberland consulted that a pair of fish should be bound live, one each, to the soles of my feet, securely with twine lest they in their death throes thrash free, and as they rotted the pestilence and putrescence that afflicts my lungs would be drawn down through my limbs and out through the soles of my feet into the rotting carcasses of the fish as like attracts like, and then, when nothing but bones was left, I would be cured."

"But that is absurd!" I cried, horrified to learn that any quack who wished to was allowed to attempt to restore the King's health.

In a peeved, angry tone, Edward went on to tell me that he had also been made to eat thrice daily a broth made from a black cat thrown into a kettle and boiled alive and left constantly to stew and simmer. He had even been given minute doses of poison in the theory that it would murder the disease and save, rather than take, his life; unfortunately one of the effects of this had been the loss of all his hair and nails. And to cure the resulting gangrene, a blood-charmer had been brought in who had danced newborn-naked, with his skin painted like a heathen's with strange symbols, round and round Edward's bed, shrieking some shrill gibberish, and then bathed my brother's ruined feet and hands with the urine of fair-haired virgins that had been collected at dawn on May Day morning and bottled and saved to treat conditions such as this. Another suggested drinking nightly before bed a large goblet of red wine with twenty or so crickets floating and drowning in it. Another put my poor brother on a strict diet of nothing but boiled carrot mush for each of his three daily meals to restore his strength and vigour augmented by a spoonful of honey in which a little brown mouse was preserved every hour upon the hour to cure his cough. Another tried to burn his fever out by packing his frail little body in slivers of boiled onions so densely that only his eyes, nose, and mouth were left uncovered. And when that failed, another quack insisted that a sure cure for consumption could be wrought by swallowing seven live baby frogs each morning before breakfast. One afternoon my brother even awoke from a drugged slumber to find a circle of smiling nude men and women wearing antlers and animal masks and garlands of wildflowers surrounding his bed holding hands and chanting. Before they departed, they propped Edward up in bed and gave him a sweet, soothing drink with a very pleasant taste and showered him with flowers and festooned his bed and chamber with wreaths and garlands until it looked a very garden and threw wide the windows to let the sunshine in. Another time, a more sinister naked coven cut the throat of a black cock at the stroke of midnight and drained it into a chalice which Northumberland, almost weeping and begging God to forgive them all, implored Edward to drink for England's sake. And two of their members lay down naked beside Edward in his bed and copulated, explaining that to save his life they must make a new life which, out of their devotion to the King they would, when the time for its birth drew nigh, come to have birthed in this very chamber, in Edward's bed beside him, just as it was conceived, so the moment it emerged from the mother's womb Edward might lay his hands on the infant and let it absorb his illness so that he might recover and reign happy, prosperous, and long over England; for the King and the gold Northumberland was paying them, they were willing to make the sacrifice. And on the advice of yet another the Duke of Northumberland himself had tenderly taken up my brother's weak, emaciated body in his own arms, as Edward was no longer able to walk, and carried him through a flock of sheep as they left their pen in the morning to go out to graze and laid him down to rest in their hay, still warm from their woolly bodies. And later that day, after he had slept, Edward was made to suckle the milk directly from a sheep's teats as if he were indeed a little lamb. But all to no avail. My brother was clearly dying and the remedies they subjected him to were barely better than torture.

As I sat and listened to this catalogue of horrors, tears poured down my face.

"Oh, Edward!" I shook my head and the lump in my throat prevented me from saying more.

"So, Mary," Edward said, "you have come to vex me further about that papist pother you cling to so tenaciously. My Council tells me that you refuse to obey and conform to my laws, and have, by your example, encouraged others to likewise ignore and flout my laws. By doing so you deny my sovereignty . . ."

"Edward, no, I . . ."

"*Silence!* I am King and I am speaking and you *will* listen!" Raising his voice brought on another bout of coughing and he grudgingly accepted another handkerchief from me, which, like the other, came away stained black and red. Trying to pretend nothing had happened, he went on speaking. "Your nearness to us in blood, your greatness in estate as a daughter and sister of kings, and the tumultuous and precarious conditions of our time, make your fault all the greater. And now I will say no more" – he shut his eyes and leaned back, looking all the more pale and weak – "because my duty would compel me to use much harsher words, which you deserve, but which I, out of love for you as my sister, will spare you, suffice it to say that I am king of this realm and I will see my laws obeyed and those who break them shall be punished if they do not mend their ways."

"But Edward, dear, it was the faith I was raised in, and I am too old and ill to change my ways!" I insisted.

"*Ill?*" He arched his brows at me and with a movement of his eyes indicated the condition of his body, then glared hard at me.

I shut my eyes at my ill-chosen words; indeed, compared to Edward I was in glowing health, even with my megrims, toothaches, and cramping monthly agony. I knew nothing I could say would erase them, so I pressed on. "Brother, you did agree not to take the Mass away from me!" I reminded him.

"But only temporarily," Edward insisted, "so that you might be weaned from your imbecility while you learned to embrace the Protestant faith."

"That I can *never* do! Brother" – I softened my tone and reached out for his hand, which he jerked away – "although Our Lord has blessed you with greater gifts and knowledge superior to others of your tender years, it is not possible that at your age you can be a judge in matters of religion. When you have attained riper and fuller years . . ."

I gasped, realizing what I had just said, as Edward glared at me. Gulping hard and inwardly kicking myself for the insensitivity of my words, I rushed on. "In the last resort there are only two things that matter: the body and the soul. And my soul belongs to God, but I gladly offer my body to Your Majesty, better that you take my life than take away the religion I was brought up in and desire to live and die in."

"Go away, Mary. You weary me!" Edward sighed, making a shooing motion with his hand as he slumped back against the pillows and closed his eyes. "You may have your Mass if you must, provided you go about it quietly and without grandiose show and display. Later, when – if – " he hastily amended, "I am better and have attained riper and fuller years" – there was a cruel mockery in his voice as he repeated my poorly chosen words – "we will discuss this further, but for now, go and leave me in peace."

Softly I tiptoed back and bent over the bed and pressed a gentle kiss onto his feverish brow. "Thank you, brother dear," I whispered. "Rest assured, you are in my thoughts and prayers; I shall pray every hour for your recovery. Please, give no credit to any person who might desire to make Your Grace think evil of me. I am, as I have always been and always will be, your humble, obedient, and unworthy, but *always* loving, sister."

"*Go away, Mary!*" Edward groaned feebly.

And then I left him to sleep, knowing that soon, no matter how hard or often I prayed, unless it pleased God to work a miracle, Edward would soon be sleeping eternally in his grave.

The next morning, before I embarked on the return journey, I went to bid Edward farewell, but the Duke of Northumberland was there, barring the door against me with his own stocky determined body.

"Madame, I fear you may not see the King. It would do him more harm than good. You make him sad and melancholy, for in your person he sees all his good work undone."

"No," I challenged boldly, squaring my shoulders and meeting Northumberland's cold, lying snake's eyes, "he sees a strong woman who will not be cowed and ruled by greedy, soulless men like you, who do not fear the wrath of God because their greed for gold and earthly wealth and prominence blinds them to all else. No, in me he sees a woman who will, when she is queen, if God so ordains it, put all the wrongs right!"

"Oh, Madame!" Northumberland said mockingly, widening his eyes and bending and shaking his knees in a parody of extreme fear, "My knees are already shaking with fear!"

"And well they should!" I declared in all seriousness, and spun on my heel and strode briskly from the palace, slapping my riding crop sharply against my full black velvet and red satin skirts, a warrior queen-to-be in the service of God like my grandmother, the great Isabella, who had ousted the Moors from Spain, just as I would one day oust the heretical Protestants from England. That was my destiny!

❧ 18 ❧

Elizabeth

"My Lady, you must come at once!" Kat's frantic cries from the foot of the stairs brought me at a run. There was a messenger from the Lord Protector saying that Edward was mortally ill, dying, and I must come at once if I wished to see him before he departed this life.

I ordered my horse saddled – my trunks could follow later by cart – and threw on my riding clothes. But then, inexplicably, just as my booted foot crossed the threshold to step out into the courtyard where my horse and the small retinue that would accompany me awaited, I felt as if a hand had reached out and forcefully yanked me back, adamantly shouting the word *"No!"* right into my ear.

So strong was the feeling, I could not ignore it. I had always had an instinct for self-preservation and I knew that my very life might hang upon heeding that warning voice regardless of whether it came from my conscience or some other source.

I gave a little cry and began to sway. I dropped my riding crop, and raised a hand to my brow as I staggered and slumped in the doorway before I let myself fall in a swoon cushioned by my skirts. My servants, led by a hysterically shrieking Kat, fidgeting and anxious to undo my stays so I could breathe unimpeded, rushed to bear me up, back upstairs, to my bed, and summon a physician.

From my bed, where I complained loudly of pains in my head and stomach to such an extent I easily persuaded my physician to send word to London that I was too unwell to travel, I heard the news that my cousin, Lady Jane Grey, had been married to Northumberland's youngest son, Guildford, that petulant, gilt-haired pretty boy who was his mother's preening pet peacock.

My poor little cousin had tried to resist the match, but had been beaten into submission by her parents, and forced to eschew her plain garb for a splendid wedding gown of gold and silver trimmed with pearls, diamonds, and gold lace, and walk sore-backed and stiff-legged to the altar where a vain golden bridegroom more in love with himself than he would ever be with her or anyone else awaited her. Curiously, neither Mary nor I had been invited to the wedding.

That was enough to tell me that these were the ingredients of a new stew Northumberland was brewing. Better to stay here, safe in my bed, I reasoned, and contemplate the position of the pieces on the chessboard of the nation before I made my move.

❧ 19 ❧

Mary

I was on my knees in my private chapel at Hunsdon, praying for my brother, when Susan and Jane burst in to tell me that a messenger had arrived from court. Edward was dying, and begged me to come to him; he didn't want to die with harsh words hanging between us.

Giving orders for horses to be saddled, and for a small retinue of four guards, a priest, and the more hardy Susan to accompany me, I raced up the stairs to don my riding clothes. As Jane helped me dress, while Susan went off to likewise prepare herself, I gave orders for her to follow with my trunks and a more suitable escort befitting my station. But right now I must travel light; speed was of the essence. Then down the stairs I ran, and out into the courtyard. Disdaining the proffered assistance of my groom, I sprang into the saddle astride – now was not the time to be ladylike – dug in my heels, plied my crop, and took off at a gallop, leaving the rest of my startled and amazed entourage to recover their wits and hasten after me.

I was frantic to reach Edward in time so that he could die in peace. And perhaps, on the threshold of death, between Heaven and Hell, he would listen to me and embrace the true faith with his dying breath; for this reason I had asked one of my priests to accompany me. As I galloped through the night towards London, my deep crimson skirts flapping up and down like red wings with the motion of my mount, my limp, thin hair slipping from its pins beneath my feathered cap, I prayed in time to the rhythm of the hoofbeats. *"Please don't let it be too late, please don't let it be too late . . ."*

Suddenly I spied a dark figure standing in the road ahead, faintly lit by a lantern held in his left hand, while he extended his right to me, palm emphatically outward, fingers stiff and pointing up straight to the sky, in a gesture that screamed the word *halt!*

I reined in my mount so sharply to avoid colliding with him that I nearly went flying over my horse's head. My heart began to race and pound and my mind teemed with lurid and frightening tales of highwaymen who waylaid travellers and divested them of all their valuables and sometimes left them lying dead or dying in pools of blood in the dusty road while they galloped off with their ill-gotten gains.

As he came toward me, I saw he wore a dark hooded cloak and beneath it a scarf was wound so that it concealed the lower portions of his face, whilst the hood and a black mask hid the rest so there appeared to be only blackness where a face should have been.

"Who are you?" I demanded in a commanding tone, drawing myself up straight in the saddle. "How dare you waylay me like this? Do you know who I am?"

Silently, he came towards me and thrust a folded square of paper up at me. He wore no rings, I saw, so there was no signet ring bearing a family crest that I could identify him by, if he were indeed of a noble family as his commanding bearing seemed to suggest.

Puzzled, I bent my head and, in the orange glow of the lantern he held for me, I unfolded the paper and read:

> *The king is dead.*
> *Turn back NOW!*
> *You are riding into a trap.*
> *Northumberland lies in wait for you.*
> *His son Robert is leading an army to arrest you.*
> *Prepare to fight for your throne.*
> *Do NOT let them take you!*
> *God save Queen Mary!*

"*Who are you?*" I demanded. "Is this . . . can this be true?"

He nodded his head once, most emphatically, and I knew the words written on that paper did not lie.

"Why do you not speak? Are you mute?" And then the truth suddenly dawned on me. "You don't want me to recognize your voice!"

He stood before me in the road again and lifted his arm and jabbed his finger in an adamant point back in the direction I had come, over and over again, the gesture urgently screaming "*Go! Now!*"

"Thank you," I said falteringly, as the enormity of the words written on that piece of paper sank in. Edward, my poor dear little brother, was already dead – he had died a heretic instead of in the true faith – and Northumberland and his hell-bound lackeys were already moving to keep me from the throne that was my right by birth. I must not let them do it! "Whoever you are, I thank you." And, fighting to hold back my tears, I turned my mount round, dug in my heels, and galloped back the way I had come, with my bewildered and mystified entourage following after.

Whoever the mysterious dark man who came out of the shadows to warn me was I never did discover.

❧ 20 ❧

Elizabeth

Lying in the quiet of my bed, with the curtains drawn, the pieces of the puzzle began to fall into place.

I had always known Edward would never make old bones. A recent attack of smallpox following hard on the heels of a virulent case of measles had fatally undermined his constitution, and a consumption of the lungs had set in. I heard he was worn to a shadow by a constant racking cough and often brought up blood.

Northumberland clearly relished his role as the power behind the throne and was loath to relinquish it as he surely must with Edward's death.

Mary was next in line to the throne, and as an ardent Catholic, would undermine the Protestant regime, reverse it out of existence in her vain attempt to turn back the clock to the happy days of her youth, and root out what she saw as heresy with all the zeal of a pig after truffles. She would never suffer Northumberland to continue in his current role or any other. He wanted to rule, not be ruled, and it would be folly to place him in any position of power. No, Northumberland would have to go first into the Tower and then up the thirteen steps of the scaffold. It would not be safe to let him live, even if sent into exile he would never stop plotting to regain power. And Northumberland knew that if I came to the throne instead of Mary he could not control me; no puppetmaster would pull my strings or put words into my mouth.

But, if, by some means, both Mary and I were excluded from the succession, then the next logical heir would be Cousin Jane – fifteen, meek, weak and, most importantly to Northumberland and her power-hungry parents, malleable. Easily intimidated, devoutly Protestant Lady Jane Grey might be an intellectual power to be reckoned with when it came to scholarship, but when it came to her own life, was a spineless quivering heap of fear who had been intimately acquainted with cruel words and physical brutality from babyhood; she would not be able to fight those who would force her onto the throne and cram onto her head a crown I knew she did not want. She had recently been forced into wedlock with Northumberland's youngest son.

Now it all made sense. Northumberland was setting himself up as a kingmaker, to found a ruling dynasty of Dudleys with his youngest, fairest son, Guildford, to wear the crown on his gleaming crop of perfect golden curls.

Jane was just the means to an end, and might even afterwards be disposed of if she became too bothersome once she had provided Guildford with a son or two, an heir and a spare to assure the succession. And it did not take a mind of astounding brilliance to see who would in reality rule the realm; vain Guildford had more interest in his wardrobe than in politics. Thus his father, Northumberland, the Lord Protector, would continue to hold the reins of power, king in all but name. Guildford would just be the pretty figurehead who so becomingly wore the crown.

But Northumberland did not look beyond the glittering façade of glory. His vainglorious concoction was in truth a recipe for disaster. He did not reckon on the English people.

Jane was all but a stranger to them. Some might have a vague notion of who she was, but they had not watched her grow up and suffer all manner of trials and tribulations as they had Great Harry's daughters; Mary and I were the last remaining vital links to our father, that majestic figure of awe and fear, the king they had for so long known and loved, and they knew and loved us too.

And Jane, poor Jane, lacked the confidence to command. She

was gifted with great intelligence, yes, but she did not have the quality of queenship, that aura of supreme confidence. She could never harness the hearts of the common people; the poor girl could not even meet the eyes of whomever she talked to. The people would see her at once as a usurper, Northumberland's puppet, and they would rise up against this new regime and fight for what they knew was right – the ascension of the rightful heiress, Queen Mary.

I knew I had assessed the situation correctly when Northumberland sent a messenger to me, offering me a weighty bribe to formally renounce my claim to the crown.

I informed him that he must first make this agreement with my sister before he petitioned me, for as long as she lived I had no claim to renounce. Then I fell back against my pillows, assailed by the most violent head pains, and Kat shooed Northumberland's lackey out and told him sharply to tell his master to bother me no more.

Left in peace, my privacy ensured by a physician's certificate that I was too ill to be disturbed or to travel, and comfortably co-cooned in my bed with the curtains drawn, and a comfit box filled with my favourite fruit suckets, I waited to see which way the winds of fortune would blow. Would Mary prevail or would it be the unwilling and unwanted usurper Queen Jane?

❧ 21 ❧

Mary

"We ride for Kenninghall!" I called back to my entourage, now less by one, as I sent one of the men galloping back to Hunsdon with a brief note to my steward, telling him what had occurred, and to muster the rest of my people, and all the loyal folks thereabout who would follow their true queen, and come straightaway to Kenninghall, my well-fortified manor in Norfolk, more like a moated castle-keep than a house, as fast as they could.

I *must* fight for my throne! When I sent little Jane Grey a ruby necklace to wear on her wedding day – a wedding I received no invitation to attend despite my beautiful and costly gift and kindness in overlooking the dress incident – I never realized that a conspiracy directed against me was unfolding. Even as Jane was sulking at the altar in a gown that was an exact replica of the one I had given her that she had destroyed – as an apology to me, her mother had asked my dressmaker to recreate it for Jane's wedding gown – and tugging at the ruby necklace I sent, ungraciously complaining that it cut her throat, Northumberland was already moving to cement his place as the power behind the throne by persuading a dying boy, for the good of England and the Protestant religion, to alter our father's will and name our cousin Jane as his successor. And by marrying his spoiled brat of a son, Guildford, to her, Northumberland's position of power was solidified.

When the horses were foaming at the mouth and we were so weary we feared the need for sleep would pull us from our saddles, we stopped to rest at Sawston Hall, the home of Sir John Huddlestone, a devoutly Catholic country gentleman.

He and his wife welcomed me warmly despite the lateness of the hour. I was taken at once to the best bedchamber. A model of efficiency, Lady Huddlestone ordered the fire lit and plates of meat, cheese, and bread, bowls of stew, and cups of ale brought in for Susan and me. Fresh sheets were put onto the bed and it was turned down in readiness for me, and a trundle bed was pulled out from underneath for Susan. Servants carried in a tub and pails of steaming water to fill it so that I might wash away the dust of the road, and Lady Huddlestone's maid even sprinkled dried flower petals into it. And since I had no spare clothing with me, Lady Huddlestone gave me one of her nightgowns and took away my dust-caked and sweat-stained clothes and went to roust her best laundress out of bed to see that my clothes were ready by morning. When I thanked her, Lady Huddlestone knelt at my feet and kissed my hand. "My life and my home and all I possess are at Your Majesty's service," she solemnly declared. It felt so good to be so honoured, to know that I was capable of inspiring such devotion.

We were roused from a deep exhausted sleep a few hours later by shouting and pounding on the front door. In my borrowed nightgown I stepped out onto the landing only to discover that some zealous Protestants from nearby Cambridge were on the march, having learned of my whereabouts, and the great golden bounty Northumberland had placed upon my head, for my capture, dead or alive.

"Madame, for your safety, you must leave at once!" Sir John said anxiously.

I nodded, and turned to go, tarrying only long enough to ask for my clothes to be sent, clean or not, back upstairs so I could dress, when Sir John stopped me.

"If I might presume to suggest it, I think Your Majesty would fare much better if you travelled in disguise."

"Yes!" I fervently agreed, my eyes darting about until they fell on a serving woman downstairs. "You!" I pointed down at her. "Come up here now! Make haste! I want your clothes!" And without waiting to see if she followed, I turned and went back into my bedchamber.

All modesty forsaken, as soon as she shut the door behind her, I tore off my nightgown.

"Well? Don't stand there gaping, girl! Give me your dress!"

When she just stood there, staring and blinking, her mouth hanging open, Susan gave an irritated sigh and went and lifted off her linen cap and untied her stained and patched apron and set them aside, then took her rough brown homespun gown by its hem and yanked it up and off over her head and helped me into it, with an apology for there being "no petticoats, Ma'am. I would gladly give you mine," she continued as she briskly put up my hair and covered it with the coarse linen cap and knotted the apron about my waist with its frayed, dingy strings, "but I fear it would give the charade away as it is longer than this girl's dress and would show, and it is also of a quality beyond her station."

"Shoes!" I cried suddenly, gazing down at my bare feet then over at my fine Spanish leather boots sitting by the fire. No serving girl would possess their like, at least not if she had come by them honestly. If I put them on, even though they were my own, I risked drawing attention to myself and perhaps even being detained as a thief.

"Off with them, girl!" Susan pointed at the crude and clunky wooden clogs the now nude but still dumbstruck maid was wearing on her dirty bare feet.

I winced as I stepped into them. I had never worn anything like them, and feared both blisters and splinters, but, for my throne, I would stoically endure this hardship.

"Follow at first light with the others," I quickly told Susan as I headed for the door, "to Kenninghall, as planned."

"A moment, Ma'am!" Susan stayed me as she ran to the hearth and scooped up some ashes. "You have just had a bath, Ma'am, and no serving girl in clothes such as these would be so clean of person. May I?" And at my nod she gently but swiftly rubbed her hands over my face and hands. "There!" She nodded approvingly. "Go with God, Ma'am!"

I hugged her quickly and kissed her cheek. "God keep you in his care, my faithful Susan!"

And I flew down the stairs in those cumbersome, clunky clogs and out into the darkened courtyard where Sir John himself and one of his men waited with fresh horses.

I paused uncertainly, seeing that there were only two horses. Then a third man came forward and took me off guard by suddenly boosting me up into the saddle behind Sir John.

"Hold tight, Your Majesty!" he said, before I had time to properly arrange my skirts, and I hastily wrapped my arms around his waist as he spurred his mount onward and tore out of the courtyard at a thundering fast gallop.

We rode hard for I know not how long. As we crested a hill, the horses were lathered in sweat and foaming white at their mouths, so we stopped to rest. Looking back, I spied a blaze. I hesitated, being so short-sighted, I wasn't sure, but the groom raised the alarm with a despairing wail. "Oh, Master, your house! It's Sawston Hall that is a-burning!"

I saw proud Sir John's face fall and his shoulders wilt. He looked near to tears. Clearly he was torn between going back and staying with me.

"My friend, you have served me well. I swear to you that when I am proclaimed queen of this realm I shall build you a finer house than the one you have lost. Go now, and see to the safety of your family, and, if you will, leave your man with me."

"Your Majesty! Thank you and may God preserve you!" Sir John bowed over my hand and kissed it fervently before he flung himself back into the saddle and galloped back down the hill in the direction we had just come.

The groom, whose name I learned was Daniel, doffed his cap and respectfully addressed me. "We'd best be off, Your Majesty, before they catch us up; not meaning to alarm you, Your Majesty, but they're not that far behind."

"Let us go then." I nodded, and riding behind him, holding

tight to his waist, we took the road to Kenninghall, the horse's hooves loud as thunder in the quiet night as they struck the hard-packed dirt road, stirring up clouds of billowing dust that stung my eyes and made me want to cough and sneeze.

Holding tight to Daniel's waist, I leaned my throbbing, aching forehead against his strong back and shut my eyes and tried to ignore the rough cloth of my borrowed skirt chafing my thighs, rubbing them raw, and the feel of the breeze upon my buttocks as my skirt billowed out behind me, constantly reminding me that I was quite naked underneath; it was the first time in my life I had gone without a shift, petticoats, and stays. I had given up trying to tuck the coarse skirt under me, for as I bounced up and down with the motion of the horse it always came untucked, so I tried to ignore it and think of something else instead, and found myself remembering the last time I had worn servants' garb. . . .

I was seventeen and forced to serve at Hatfield as Elizabeth's nurse. I was in disgrace. Because of his feud with my proud mother, who would not bow to his will and let herself be divorced, and because the Great Whore despised me, whenever Father came to visit Elizabeth, to dandle her upon his knee, pet her, give her gifts, and listen to her baby prattle, I was locked away lest I try to see him and throw myself upon his mercy. But there came a day, when Anne Boleyn was losing ground, and someone forgot to lock the door; whether it was intentional or not I cannot say. I had to see Father again; I had to remind him of my love, and my existence. I knew if I tried to go downstairs to the nursery I would be stopped, taken back by force and locked in, so I must forgo a face-to-face encounter.

Instead, I gathered up my skirts and ran to the door leading up to the roof. Up and up, despite the pinch of my stays beneath my drab and worn servant's gown and nursemaid's apron. My weakened condition made me pause at times, feeling light-headed and faint, to gasp for air, with my heart beating far too fast, and a throbbing, drumming in my head and ears, and pearls of sweat adorning my brow. I feared my body would fail me and I would collapse and die there upon those dark and winding stairs. But I didn't give up. On and on I ran, up and up and round and round the winding, twisting, dizzyingly steep stairs of the tower turret, barely able to see my hand before my face in the dim light of the far-spaced pitch-tipped torches bracketed to the stone wall.

And then – it was like a miracle! – I reached the top and burst out into the fresh blustery air of daylight, onto the roof overlooking the courtyard. I was almost too late. Father was just about to swing himself up into the saddle of his great white horse.

Desperate to attract his attention, I snatched off my cap and raked the pins from my hair. With my fingers, I combed my long, faded and thinning tresses out, trusting the distance to work on my behalf and keep any from spying the skeins of grey, and, with the wind whipping my hair wildly around my head, I frantically waved my white linen cap in the air, hoping to attract Father's attention.

Below me in the courtyard a number of courtiers and attendants noticed and began to point up at me, and then he looked up right at me. Being so short-sighted, I could not discern his features, so I could not tell whether he smiled or frowned. I stopped waving my cap, absently letting the wind snatch it from me, so that it flew away like a white bird with the strings trailing and fluttering behind it, and fell to my knees, holding my hands out to Father, clasping them in a gesture of entreaty, murmuring a fervent *"Please!"*

Finally he raised his hand and waved briefly at me, then he mounted his horse and rode away. . . .

When we arrived at Kenninghall, I spoke briefly with my steward so that he might give the necessary orders to ready the manor to make a stand and fend off the attack I feared would be forthcoming. Then I went to bathe and dress myself, for when I addressed my people I must look every bit a queen. After I had bathed and donned a gown of deep purple velvet with a high white satin winged collar, and a white satin kirtle embroidered in purple and gold with matching under-sleeves, puffed and padded with horsehair, and positioned a pearl-and-diamond-edged purple velvet hood on my head, I pinned a large diamond crucifix to my breast and, with my rosary in hand, went out to address my household.

Standing at the top of the stairs, looking suitably regal but sombre enough to mourn my brother's passing, with a series of tapestries depicting the Passion of Christ behind me, I proclaimed myself Queen of England "by divine right and human law" and explained all that had occurred to them. I told them that Edward was dead, and we grieved for him and prayed for his soul, and though I was now, by right and the will of both God and my late father, Queen of England, Northumberland had sought to cheat me of my birthright by putting another in my place and a bounty on my head. I asked them all to stand by me and uphold my rights, to help me claim my throne.

One by one, each and every man, woman, and child sank to their knees, hand over heart, and gave a heartfelt cry of "God save Queen Mary!"

I went next into my study and took up my pen and addressed myself in very stern and formal terms to the Duke of Northumberland, asserting my rights and that I was prepared to fight for them.

> *My Lord,*
>
> *We greet you well, and have received sure advertisement that our dearest brother the King is departed to God, which news, how they be woeful unto our heart, He wholly knoweth to whose will and pleasure we must and do humbly submit us and our will.*
>
> *But in this lamentable case, that is to wit now after his death, concerning the crown and governance of this realm of England, what has been provided by Act of Parliament and the last will of our dear father, the realm and all the world knoweth, and we verily trust that there is no good true subject that can or will pretend to be ignorant thereof. And of our part, as God shall aid and strengthen us, we have ourselves caused, and shall cause, our right and title in this behalf to be published and acclaimed accordingly.*
>
> *And albeit this matter being so weighty, the manner seemeth strange that, our brother dying upon Thursday at night last past, we hitherto had no knowledge from you thereof. Yet we considered your wisdoms and prudence to be such that, after having amongst you debated, pondered and well-weighed this present case, we shall and may conceive*

great hope and trust and much assurance in your loyalty and service, and that you will, like noble men, work the best.

Nevertheless, we are not ignorant of your consultations and provisions forcible, there with you assembled and prepared, by whom, and to what end, God and you know, and Nature can but fear some evil. But be it that some consideration politic hath hastily moved you thereto, yet doubt you not, My Lord, we take all these your doings in gracious part, being also right ready to remit and fully pardon the same freely, to eschew bloodshed and vengeance, trusting also assuredly you will take and accept this grace and virtue in such good part as appeareth, and that we shall not be enforced to use the service of our other true subjects and friends, which in this, our just and rightful cause, God, in whom our whole affiance is, shall send us.

Wherefore, My Lord, we require and charge you, for that allegiance which you owe to God and us, that, for your honour and the surety of your person, you employ yourself and forthwith, upon receipt hereof, cause our right and title to the crown and government of this realm to be proclaimed in our city of London and such other places as to your wisdom shall seem good, not failing hereof, as our very trust is in you. And this letter signed with our hand shall be your sufficient warrant.

Given under our signet at our manor of Kenninghall, on the 9th day of July in the year of Our Lord 1553,
Mary

I then assembled a number of messengers and sent them galloping off with verbal messages to the local gentry, telling them Edward was dead and it was time for them to do fealty to me, as their rightful sovereign, and help me claim what was my birthright – my throne.

As the day wore on, and word spread, people from all walks of life – rich men, poor men, and those in between – began pouring in to pledge their allegiance. Peasant farmers came brandishing their scythes and pitchforks for want of proper weapons, and the gentry came with lines of armed men equipped with the weapons of war. Those who could not come because of age or infirmity sent gifts of money, carts piled high with provisions to feed or weapons to equip my burgeoning army, twenty thousand strong and growing by the hour. They came from Norfolk, Buckinghamshire, Hertfordshire, Suffolk, Berkshire, Gloucestershire, Oxfordshire, and even London. From every nook and cranny of the kingdom, they came to rally beneath my banner, ready to fight for me, "Great Harry's daughter", their one true queen. And the air was rife with cries of "God save Queen Mary. Long may she reign!" and "Down with Northumberland and the false queen Jane!" "Death to all traitors!" "Long live Queen Mary!"

Every time I showed myself, at the windows, or walking on the battlements, or when I went out to mingle with the troops and tender my personal and most heartfelt thanks, the cries grew in number and intensity. Men all around me fell to their knees, hands on their hearts, and swore they would give their lives to see me on the throne where I belonged. They kissed the hem of my gown and even the ground I had walked upon. I had never before felt so loved and wanted. I prayed it would always be like this, that my people's love for me would never die.

A few days later I had a reply to my letter from Northumberland, writing on behalf of the Council.

> *My Lady Mary,*
>
> *Madame, we have received your letter declaring your supposed title which you judge yourself to have. Our answer is to advise you forasmuch as our sovereign lady Queen Jane is invested and possessed with the right and just title to the imperial crown of this realm, not only by good order of old ancient laws of this realm, but also by your late sovereign's Letters Patent signed with his own hand and sealed with the Great Seal of England in the presence of the most part of the nobles and councillors, judgers and diverse other grown and sage persons assenting and subscribing to the same.*

*We must profess and declare unto you that by divers Acts
of Parliament you be made illegitimate and unheritable to
the imperial crown of this realm. You will, upon just consideration thereof, cease your pretence to vex and molest any
of our sovereign lady Queen Jane's subjects, drawing them
from the true faith and allegiance due unto Her Grace.*

*Assuring you that, if you will for respect show yourself
quiet and obedient as you ought, you shall find us all ready
to do you any service, that we with duty may be glad with
you to preserve the common state of this realm, wherein you
may otherwise be grievous unto us, to yourself, and to them.*

*And thus we bid you most heartily well to fare, from the
Tower of London, Your Ladyship's loving friends, showing
yourself an obedient subject.*

It was signed by Northumberland and twenty-one members of
the Privy Council, including that heretic in archbishop's robes,
Thomas Cranmer, the man who had as his first official act upon
being appointed Archbishop of Canterbury annulled my parents'
marriage and declared my mother a whore and myself a bastard
and Anne Boleyn queen.

In a fury, I crumpled it and flung it at the wall, then stormed out
to call my people to assemble in the Great Hall. I had decided that
it was best that we move to Framlingham Castle in Suffolk, made
of solid, impregnable stone with eight sturdy towers. It was larger
and better fortified to withstand a siege, and as the loyal and faithful continued to swell the ranks of my makeshift army we would
have need of larger quarters. There, at Framlingham, I had decided,
I would make my stand.

As Susan and Jane helped me into my riding clothes and fastened a gleaming silver breastplate over my chest, I thought of my
mother and grandmother, both of whom had donned armour at one
time or another during their valiant lives, and I vowed that I would
not shame myself and would prove myself worthy of them. I also
wanted to be remembered as a queen who had donned armour,
fully prepared to ride out into battle.

After Susan had set the silver helm, plumed in green and white, the royal Tudor colours, upon my head, I nodded approvingly at my reflection in the mirror. "Let us be off then," I said, "and fear not, my dears." I kissed each of my dear devoted ladies on the cheek. "God is with us, so none can be against us!" And I went briskly down the stairs and out into the courtyard to mount my horse and lead my people to Framlingham and, God willing, on to victory.

Every step of the way, I knew I was not alone; I felt as if my mother and grandmother, the strong Spanish warrior queens, were riding right alongside me, in spirit, in proud armour and conviction, once again. And I felt the benevolent and serene presence of the Blessed Virgin infusing my soul with comfort and courage. And God, God was *always* with us. Every step of the way I felt His presence and He freed me of even the slightest twinge of fear. I knew then that, though the days to come would be difficult, in the end, I would prevail.

And then, a few anxious days later, the miracle happened – I won the battle without a drop of blood being shed. It was over just like that, in the time it takes to snap one's fingers.

Young Robert Dudley's men began to desert him and come to me, as did the men manning the warships anchored off Yarmouth to keep me from fleeing the country to seek foreign aid. They threatened to throw their captains into the sea if they did not declare for me, and they did, and to a man, they came marching out to me. And the furious Northumberland, fuming no doubt that if he wanted something done right he must do it himself, assembled his army and rode out himself, leaving the unhappy, unwilling, and unwanted Queen Jane at the mercy of her cruel parents, mother-in-law, bridegroom, and the remaining members of the Council. Then the Treasurer absconded with the money, hurrying hotfoot to me, followed fast by the rest of the Council. And soon they were kneeling, to a man – with the notable exception of Northumberland, of course – with their hands over their hearts, vowing that they were loyal to me, England's one true queen, and all they had done had been unwillingly at the behest of Northumberland, whose vengeful and violent nature they feared.

Then Northumberland, despised and deserted by all his men,

muddy and bedraggled, tried to save himself by ripping down the proclamations declaring Jane queen and flinging his cap and all the gold coins he was carrying into the air as he ran through Cambridge crying, "Long live Queen Mary!" Thus he was captured. The people pelted him with excrement, rotten eggs, and abuse as he was marched back to London. He would later try to save himself by converting to Catholicism in the Tower, but I knew it was just another of his tricks, and he was not to be trusted. He was the one person I could not afford to be merciful to; he was the one traitor who absolutely had to die.

And on July 19, standing before the Eleanor Cross, which Edward I, the venerable and mighty "Hammer of the Scots", had erected out of love for his deceased wife, the Lord Mayor of London officially proclaimed me queen, and the whole city went mad and merry with rejoicing. Wine flowed in the city fountains, banquet tables with free meat, bread, and cheese were set up throughout the city, bonfires were lit, church bells rang nonstop, and the people cheered and danced, sang, and threw their caps in the air, and strangers embraced strangers in the streets. "God has worked a miracle!" over and over they declared, heaping blessings upon my name, and wishing me a long and prosperous life and reign.

Then I, God's chosen instrument, the happy recipient of this miracle, this victory without bloodshed, was riding triumphantly towards London along roads lined with cheering, smiling people, weeping with joy, and shouting out their love and blessings to me. Children even climbed trees to get a better look, and called out and waved at me. "God save Queen Mary, long may she reign!" Over and over again they shouted, and all the way to London there was not one moment of silence. That day it was all love and blessings.

Midway to London, Elizabeth rode out to me, riding at the head of a splendid mounted entourage of five hundred ladies, gentlemen, knights, and servants all clad in the green and white Tudor colours. She dismounted and I saw her through a haze of sizzling, shimmering heat, kneeling there in the dusty road in a white gown so blindingly bright a white that I had to shield my eyes. Flaunting her supposed virginity like a banner! I thought, clucking my tongue at the sight of her; I found such emphatic, overzealous display most suspicious, the way she kept pressing and underlining the point, and I could not help but wonder how far Tom Seymour had truly gone with her. Had his fleshly lance indeed shattered the Shield of Hymen? Bareheaded, with her head humbly bowed, with her long red hair shining like scarlet silk in the sun, and the ends trailing in the dust, she spread her hands in a gesture of supplication.

Traveling in white, how utterly impractical! I observed as I dismounted and went to her. Whether they be simpleton or scholar, or somewhere in between, everyone knows how white shows the dirt so. I hope for Elizabeth's sake, and mine as well – for I will *not* have her disgracing me with a slovenly, unkempt appearance – that her Mrs Ashley has brought along the clothes brushes and has them close at hand.

"Well met, sister," I said as I embraced and kissed her once on each cheek. She was rigid in my embrace now, no longer the little girl who used to nestle into me, begging for bedtime stories. Now she was nineteen, and the survivor of a scandal, with a bold question mark hanging over her virtue. "Come, ride beside me. This is the happiest day of my life, and I want you there beside me, to share it."

Elizabeth sank into a deep curtsy. "Your Majesty does me great honour."

As she mounted her white horse and instructed her people to fall in line behind mine, I could not help noting, seeing her there all in white, with her vibrant flaming tresses, at the head of half a thousand men and women clad in green and white, that she was like the herald of spring. Whilst I, in my sombre high-necked plum velvet and deep crimson satin under-sleeves and kirtle, with a veritable rainbow of gems flashing blindingly in the summer sun on the large crucifix at my throat and edging the purple velvet hood atop my grey-streaked auburn hair – to distract the people's eyes and compensate for my own faded charms and lined face – was, at thirty-seven, well into the autumn of my life.

I shivered, despite the July heat and heavy velvet, feeling for the first time the hard stamp of mortality. Whether I liked it or not,

Elizabeth was the future. Unless I married and God blessed me with a son, Elizabeth would follow in my footsteps up the dais to the throne and wear the crown of England on her head. Thus it was all the more vital that I turn her heart from heresy and persuade her to embrace the true religion, else all the good I was going to do would be undone by The Great Whore's red-haired brat.

After a brief stop to refresh and tidy ourselves – Mrs Ashley had indeed had the foresight to bring the clothes brushes – we made our triumphal entry into London. When the people saw us riding side by side, their cheers redoubled and hundreds threw their caps in the air.

I glanced over at Elizabeth, with her white skirts flowing like milk as she sat sidesaddle on her horse, straight-backed and holding confidently to the green leather reins with one hand and waving to the people with the other. I thought it was rather common and undignified the way she smiled so broadly and waved so enthusiastically back at them, sometimes even calling out to them, thanking them for their compliments and goodwill. It was as if she saw them not as a great churning mass of humanity but as individual people; she met their eyes and made them feel as if each one were the special recipient of her attention! Father had been like that. "Bluff King Hal" they had called him because of the magical touch he had with the common people. But while it was acceptable in a man, I thought it altogether unseemly for a lady, especially one of royal blood, to behave so. A woman should be virtuous, above rubies, as the Scriptures said; she should hold herself aloof and reserved, not lower and demean herself by coarse and common manners. If a lady behaved as common as the masses, she became as common as they were, and no one would look up to her or respect her. It was not just her title, jewels, and fine clothes, but her dignity and bearing that set a lady apart and above the humble and lowborn people. Had no one ever explained this to Elizabeth? It seemed to me that as a governess Mrs Ashley had been most remiss.

I myself preserved a queenly dignity, holding my back straight as an iron poker and nodding and smiling graciously, serenely, benignly, as best becomes a queen, giving only the briefest, most cursory glances, lifting my hand in a controlled and placidly regal wave.

I paused and glared pointedly at Elizabeth, hoping she would read my disapproval in my eyes and, chastened, strive to emulate me, but she only smiled back at me and called to me above the great din of rejoicing that surrounded us, "This is indeed a *glorious* day, Mary!"

"It is indeed!" I said crisply. Then a little girl ran up, eager and bouncing on her toes, to offer my sister a posy of violets, which she smilingly accepted and tucked into her horse's bridle, then took from her sleeve a white silk ribbon and gave it to the child in exchange as a memento of this happy day. The little girl thanked her profusely and in a rush of prattle promised she would treasure it all the rest of her life, and even when she was an old woman with hair as white as that ribbon she would still cherish it and pass it on to her children or grandchildren when she died.

I turned and stared straight ahead, startled to feel the sharp bitter bite of jealousy, like the first tart taste of a green apple.

Suddenly the day didn't seem so bright or the people's voices quite so loving any more. I listened more closely to what they were saying now.

"Look at that red hair!"

"Aye, it's just like Great 'arry's was in 'is youth, it is!"

"No Spanish blood there, she's *all* Tudor, that one is!"

"A *true* English rose!"

"English through and through, to the core our Elizabeth is – blood, bone, and gristle, and amen for it!"

"God bless our Princess Elizabeth!"

"*Vivat Elizabetha!*"

Though there were still cries aplenty of "God save Queen Mary!" they seemed all of a sudden muted, to lack the clarity and enthusiasm of those who sang my sister's praises. Suddenly I was stricken with the fear that though they accepted and acknowledged me as their rightful queen, they loved Elizabeth more; I was Queen of England, but she was Queen of Hearts.

And then a handsome young man, with the eyes of a poet, ran

up to Elizabeth and kissed the hem of her white gown as if she, and not I, were queen. "The fairest of the fair," he called her, and vowed he would write a sonnet in "The Fair Eliza's" honour.

My fingers clenched around the reins and I bit my bottom lip and forced myself to breathe deeply and count to ten, and then I counted to ten again, as I fought down the urge to lean over and rip that red hair out by its roots and shove my sister from her saddle to be trampled beneath the horses' hooves as we rode on past. I wanted to shout at the people, *"My sister is the bastard of that whore Anne Boleyn!"* and remind them that as such she did not deserve their love and adulation. *I* was the one who deserved, and needed, their love; *I* was the Queen, not she. The glory and praise should be mine, *all* mine. They should be writing songs and sonnets about me, not about that baseborn red-haired temptress, who smiled at me even as her mind hatched plots against me. She was going to steal my throne, I *knew* it. This day had shown her her power; she had it within her to harness the hearts of the people and command all!

It was not a Christian thought, I admit, and I would later confess and do penance for it. It was most unworthy of me, and shamed me before God and the mirror of my soul, but in that moment it was what I felt, and I cannot deny it, for to do so would be a lie, and that would further compound my sin.

And then, just as suddenly as this pall of suspicion and dread had fallen over me, it was whisked away. A choir of angelic blond-haired little boys in white silk robes trimmed with golden lace appeared singing joyously, praising God for sending a virgin called Mary to sit upon England's throne. When the song was done the youngest and prettiest of those exquisite little children came forward and, cupping it in his little hands, shyly presented me with a heart fashioned of solid gold engraved with the words:

THE HEART OF THE PEOPLE

I was overcome, and as I held that golden heart within my hands I almost believed I could feel it beating and pulsing as if it were real and I did indeed hold the very heart of England.

Then a toothless old man, with tufts of white hair sticking up around his bald pate, broke through the crowd and dashed up to me.

"Princess Marigold! Princess Marigold!" he cried as he thrust a scraggly bouquet of marigolds up at me. I almost tumbled off my horse, I was so astonished that anyone remembered. My heart was beating so fast that I had to press my hand over it, but I did not let emotion overwhelm me and, smiling graciously, I leaned down and accepted that poor little bouquet. The words slightly garbled in his toothless mouth, he continued, "I remember when Your Grace was just a wee thing and your da', Great 'arry, 'e called you Princess Marigold 'cause your hair was just like 'em in colour, it was."

"Yes." I nodded, flashing a brief, bittersweet smile down at him as I gazed at the orange-yellow blossoms. "That was a long time ago, but I remember it well. Thank you, my good man; God bless and keep you in His care," I added, as I passed the flowers back to Susan, riding behind me, to put in her saddlebag with the golden heart and all the other keepsakes I meant to save as reminders of this joyous day.

As I nudged my horse onward, I darted a swift glance at Elizabeth as if to say, "See? You are not the only one who can play to the masses!" But she just smiled back at me, a born actress, to look at her anyone would have thought that she was genuinely happy for me, but *I* knew better!

When we arrived at the Tower, to resounding cheers and the deafening boom of a hundred-gun salute, I found the Lieutenant of the Tower, Sir John Bridges, waiting for me. With him, kneeling humbly on the grass, were the last four remaining prisoners from my brother's reign.

The first was the Duchess of Somerset, Edward Seymour's widow, my "good gossip Nan", who had been imprisoned when he followed "The Cakes and Ale Man" to the scaffold. She was trembling and pale as white chalk in her widow's weeds.

Then, the most important political prisoner in the realm, the tall, handsome, golden-haired young man they called "The Last Sprig of the White Rose", the last surviving Plantagenet, Edward

Courtenay. Now twenty-seven, he had practically grown up in the Tower, and I doubted he could remember any other home. He was a naïve and guileless young man whose blue eyes radiated angelic innocence and sweetness and, I must admit, a want of wits. I knew many would expect me to marry him, as he was the only Englishman alive worthy of me in rank, but here I must confess, I had always desired a man stronger than myself, a pillar of strength I could lean on whenever I had need, a man who would be to me like the shell that protects and shelters the snail's vulnerable flesh, and Edward Courtenay I knew at a glance was *not* the man for me. But he did not deserve to remain a prisoner, and I would see that he was compensated for his lost years and set him at liberty.

The third prisoner was Stephen Gardiner, the aged Bishop of Winchester, who had been imprisoned years ago for championing my mother's rights against The Boleyn Whore, and for staunchly resisting the Protestant regime. I would see to it that his loyalty to the true faith was amply rewarded.

And lastly, the elderly Duke of Norfolk, who had been destined for the block, only Father had died before he could sign the death warrant. Although he was Anne Boleyn's uncle, he was no friend to her, and had presided over her trial and, without hesitation, had condemned her. Though he had been cruel to me at her instigation, I could be merciful like Our Lord Jesus Christ and forgive one who truly repented their past sins and misdeeds.

One by one, I went to them – raised, kissed, and embraced them.

"These are my prisoners," I proclaimed, "and I declare them prisoners no more! My Lords, and Lady" – I nodded to Nan – "you are now at liberty!"

Hearing my words, oh how the people cheered; they called me "Merciful Mary" and I could not think of a more wonderful, beautiful name to be known by. I saw it as a sign. It was as if God were speaking through those thousands of voices, and in that moment I vowed "Merciful Mary" I would always be until the day I died. My people gave me that name out of love, and I vowed then and there that I would never give them cause to call me anything else.

In gratitude, the quartet of liberated prisoners vied to kiss my

194   *Emily Purdy*

hand. I felt their tears drip down onto my skin; later I would notice
the water spots this emblem of their hearts' gratitude left on my
rings, which would, of course, require polishing, but after such a
dusty, tumultuous day, they would have anyway.

When the aged Bishop of Winchester tried to bow over my
hand, I stopped him and instead kissed his, honouring him as a
man of God, and asked him to honour me by serving as my Lord
Chancellor.

With tears running down his grizzled cheeks into his long white
beard, he raised his gnarled and trembling talonlike hands to
heaven and cried: "God has taken pity on His People and Church
in England through the instrument of a virgin called Mary whom
He has raised to the throne!"

And from every side the people cheered, "Long live Queen
Mary! God save Queen Mary!" and hats by the hundreds flew up
and down in the air.

And Nan, falling to her knees and kissing the hem of my skirt in
deepest gratitude, declared, "There never was a queen in Christendom of greater goodness than this one!"

Not to be outdone, Edward Courtenay dropped to his knees
and commandeered my other hand and covered it with kisses.
"Your Majesty's kindness has only one rival – your beauty!"

The wily old Duke of Norfolk just watched it all with a be-
mused smile and bowed. "I owe Your Majesty my eternal gratitude. I thought the last fresh air I would ever breathe would be as
I walked to the scaffold."

Oh what a happy, joyous day that was, when everyone seemed
to love me! And as I pardoned my prisoners, Elizabeth was all but
forgotten; she could not snatch or surpass my glory here! I watched
her cheering me with all the rest of them and marvelled yet again
at her ability to dissemble. If women had been allowed to tread the
boards of the London theatres she would have been among the
greatest.

The first time I met with my Council, I knew that as one lone
woman against so many men, seasoned statesmen all, I must not
let my nervousness and weakness show; I must prove to them that

I was strong enough to hold, and control, the reins of power.

Sitting at the head of the long oak table, in a gown of deep crimson velvet, with my white silk under-sleeves and kirtle embroidered in golden pomegranates and red and white Tudor roses, to remind all who saw me of my proud and illustrious heritage, I chose not to mince words, and instead shot like an arrow straight to the heart of the matter.

"My mother called England a land of ruined souls and martyred saints," I began. "She said this after Anne Boleyn cast her dark spell over my father and unloosed a plague of heresy on England that caused the break with Rome. I intend to do everything in my power to undo The Great Whore's reign of destruction. I will give the true religion back to the people; I will bring England back to Rome."

"Madame," the Earl of Arundel said, "that is a laudable goal, but I beg of you as you go about this great work, be both cautious and slow lest you frighten the people by acting too precipitously. In the years since the break with Rome and your venerable mother's death, much has changed here in England, and this new religion, this Reformed Faith, whether we as good Catholics, like it or not, has put down firm roots . . ."

"Then they shall be uprooted!" I cried, banging my fists down hard on the table. "Heresy shall *never* thrive in *my* country – *God's country!* And well that the people should be frightened – for the sake of their souls they should be *very* afraid indeed!"

"Madame, with all due respect," Sir William Paget said patiently, almost condescendingly, as if I were an ignorant little girl, "it already flourishes here as a healthy living presence and many have embraced it, quite willingly, not through force. It has taken the place for many of the true faith, which has now changed places with the Reformist religion, which was once practised secretly, underground if you will. Now it is thus with the Roman faith. What was once publicly celebrated is now hidden away in secret, whilst what was once hidden is now openly espoused. And if you begin your reign like a great broom seeking to sweep all the changes the years have brought out, you will frighten many of your subjects, and there will be panic and acts of violence and rebellion if you try to take their faith away from them. The Protestants will not creep away meekly like whipped dogs with their tails tucked between their legs, they *will* fight; just as you yourself have fought for your own beliefs and the freedom to worship as you please. A little tolerance – and I say this as both a devout son of the Church and as a statesman – will go a long way to keeping the peace in England."

"*No*, Sir William" – I shook my head emphatically – "I am not taking anyone's faith away from them! I am returning it, restoring it, to them! Do you not see? I am giving them back what they lost, what was taken from them. In its absence they were misguided, misled, and embraced a false religion to fill the void left by the true. But now, I am going to give it back to them. I am going to make everything all right!"

"Madame" – the Earl of Throckmorton shook his head dolefully – "I fear a great many of your subjects will not see it that way. We are all loyal Catholics here" – he gestured round the Council table and all the men nodded in affirmation – "but England has changed since the break with Rome . . ."

"But God hasn't!" I cried, slamming my hands down on the tabletop for emphasis. "*God has not changed!*"

"Madame, what you seek to undertake shall not be easy and *will* be met by opposition," Arundel warned, "and therein are the bare bones of the situation."

"My sainted mother taught me patience and perseverance and I shall lead *all* my people back to God and the *true* religion!" I declared. And with those words I stood up and swept grandly from the Council chamber.

I began then to see that I was surrounded by enemies, wolves in sheep's clothing; even those who claimed to be my friends and to serve and support me were in their hearts against me.

And yet, after prayer and careful reflection, I decided to take the cautious course. I had not yet been crowned, and many, I knew, were nervous, so whilst I openly proclaimed my devotion to the Catholic faith – the *true* religion – and set in motion its restoration, letting the priests come out of hiding, repairing the desecrated churches, bringing the beautiful adornments that glorified

God and His Saints back to decorate the walls and altars, and, of course, allowing the faithful to again hear the Latin Mass and bask in the miracle of the Elevation of the Host, I let it be known that I would make no sweeping changes until Parliament had met and officially restored the laws of the land to their proper and rightful state. And, as a compromise, I allowed my brother two funerals – a stark Protestant service in English and a grand Requiem Mass in Latin with all the requisite pomp and ceremony.

My coronation was a radiant and glorious God-blessed day. I felt important, cherished, loved, and adored. I felt vindicated and victorious – for myself and my sainted mother, and I wished with all my heart she could be riding beside me this day, in the flesh, not just in spirit, though I could still feel her loving presence always right there beside me. It made me feel good to know I had done her proud.

The people lined the streets, crowded the rooftops, hanging like bunches of grapes from the chimneys, and leaned from the windows to shower me with flower petals. There was not a voice amongst them that was not raised to wish me well and bless me as I rode past in a golden chariot, gowned in gold-embroidered deep blue velvet. I had refrained from wearing my hair loose and flowing down my back, as was customary for queens on their coronation day, as I did not want to disappoint those who remembered the famous orange-gold tresses of Princess Marigold by letting them see how thin, dark, and faded it had grown, with a rusty auburn replacing the orange, marred by ugly grey streaks. Instead, I wore it caught up in a fringed gold tinsel net studded with precious gems beneath a beautifully crafted wreath of jewelled flowers. As I had stood before my mirror that morning, Susan had brushed out my hair and crowned it with that exquisite jewelled wreath and tried to persuade me to wear it thus, but I was so dismayed to see how the bold beautiful colours of the gems made my tresses seem all the more faded and paltry, that I insisted that she pin it up tightly inside the tinsel-fringed gold net.

Elizabeth, and Father's only surviving wife, the Lady Anne of Cleves, as the two highest-ranking ladies in the land after me, rode behind me, each in a silver chariot. Elizabeth was all in white again, but the Lady of Cleves, plump and jolly as always despite her years, wore a grand crimson and gold gown. And behind them, to represent the restoration of our nation's badly debased currency, the noble ladies and gentlemen of my court walked in stately procession all clad in silver and gold. They were followed by my servants in new liveries, trumpeters, archers, guards, and knights in shining silver armour. And lastly, in chariots draped with banners emblematic of their countries, the foreign ambassadors and their retinues.

It was a grand show and the people loved it so! All along the route the fountains and conduits ran with free wine, and there was singing and dancing, and the cheers never ceased. And at intervals, the procession paused, so that my subjects might honour me with poems, pageants, speeches, and songs, many of them performed by little children, which delighted my heart. As I watched those sweet little souls striving so hard to please me, tears filled my eyes. If only I could have a child of my own, then my happiness would be complete!

At Westminster Abbey, my ladies helped me change into an austere, unadorned gown of royal purple velvet, cut purposefully, and I thought, rather immodestly, low at the neck and shoulders, which was necessary for the anointing. But I was comforted by the thought that I would, for most of the ceremony, be covered by regal robes of crimson velvet furred with ermine. And then, as the choir sang the familiar and oh so dear Latin hymns to God's glory, the bells rang, and priests in embroidered vestments sprinkled me with holy water and swung gilded censers, I walked solemnly up the aisle with Elizabeth behind me bearing my train, wearing a silver surcoat edged with ermine over yet another white gown – I really would have to do something about that, it was absurd the way she went about waving her supposed virginity like a flag! – and a silver coronet crowning her hair that hung glossy and free like a cloak of flames down her back.

When I reached the altar, we withdrew behind a screen and Elizabeth helped me remove my heavy robe and jewelled headdress and smiled reassuringly as I shivered nervously at the idea of showing myself with my shoulders and so much of my bosom bare. Truly, I felt naked, and it was all I could do not to go out with my arms folded across my chest.

"You are Queen, and this is *your* day, Mary," Elizabeth whispered. "Do not let fear or nervousness trespass upon it!"

I was so grateful for her kind and reassuring words that I embraced her and kissed her cheek. Then, with a deep breath, I squared my shoulders, held my head up high, and boldly stepped out from behind the screen.

As I knelt before the altar and the Archbishop anointed my head, shoulders, and chest with the holy oil, I felt all the fear leave me. Never before had I felt so truly blessed. I was God's instrument and He had made all this possible so that I might do His work; by divine right, and against all the odds, I had won the crown. God would not have given me this if I had been unworthy. I had nothing to fear; it was meant to be. I was meant to be Queen!

And then I lay prostrate, face down before the altar, as the Archbishop prayed over me in the solemn, sonorous Latin that was like a comforting and soothing balm to my soul. I felt the blue velvet carpet soft against my face and closed my eyes and breathed deeply of the incense even though it made me feel a little sleepy. And then he raised me to my feet and Elizabeth was there to help me into my crimson and ermine robes again, and the Archbishop led me to the great gilded, velvet-cushioned throne. As I stood before it, gazing out at the crowd, Elizabeth knelt to arrange the folds of my train so I would not stumble over them. The Archbishop took my hand and slid the coronation ring, "the wedding ring of England", a band of heavy gold and blackest onyx, onto my finger, the one the doctors said had a vein inside that ran directly to the heart. And then he held aloft the heavy golden and bejewelled crown, letting the people see, and, after a long, solemn moment, lowered it and set it gently upon my head, and I sat down upon the throne as the anointed Queen of England, and he placed the sceptre and weighty golden orb in my hands. At that moment the people leapt to their feet, cheering wildly, and the choir lifted their voices in song again as white doves were released into the air.

Tears of the purest joy I had ever known flowed down my face.

I was Queen, Queen of England; I had triumphed over all the odds and all my enemies. I would thank my loving subjects for their loyalty and devotion to me by giving them the greatest gift any sovereign could give – I would make *everything* all right. I would restore peace and harmony and the true religion and make England a bastion of faith where all were united under God, His Church, and their loving queen – Merciful Mary. My reign would be an era of happiness unsurpassed, an era of smiles instead of tears!

❧ 22 ❧

Elizabeth

As I rode beside Mary the triumphant day she entered London and witnessed the great outpouring of joy with which the people greeted her ascension, I noticed her watching me with a wary alertness from the corner of her eye as I smiled and waved and returned the people's greetings. The coldness that had grown between us had never truly thawed. And with this realization came the sharp stab of fear. I knew that nothing would ever be the same again. The days when we were loving sisters were long past; the links in the chain that held us together had grown weaker through the years and I feared they might, at any moment, break. And I was afraid, very afraid, that my own sister was destined to become my enemy.

I loved Mary. I remembered the tender care she had taken of me, how she used to comfort, teach, and play with me when I was a child, and I mourned the loss of closeness that had accompanied the passage of years. I wanted us to be friends; I wanted us to love each other as sisters should. But I knew that there was an inflexible intolerance about Mary that had been building a wall between us that only grew higher as time passed, and I feared I might never be able to surmount it.

It quickly became apparent that Mary thought she could turn back time, to undo what she saw as the damage my mother had done, to erase the advent of the Reformed Faith in England, and bring England and Rome back together again. She was determined to be the good shepherd who brought the Pope's lost flock back to him, chastened and contrite over the folly of their having strayed. She was hellbent on saving souls, but it was too late for that. Mary was doomed to wilful blindness; she could not and would not see that the new ways had already become established – the Reformed Faith was not just some passing fad or fancy. Though there were many who still remained true to the old Roman ways, the Protestants were not just going to hang their heads like naughty children faced with a scolding and apologize, mend their ways, and become good Catholics. But Mary must have all or nothing – that was the one thing she had in common with my mother, whose motto had been "All or Nothing" – and like a crazed gardener she set about trying to rip the tenacious weeds the Reformation had planted out of her garden, out of her England. She seemed to have forgotten there was such a word as *tolerance* or that she had once been forced to beg for it herself during our brother's brief reign.

She began her campaign of correction with me. For I, in my virgin-white gowns and elegant, discreet pearl embellishments, was the beacon of hope the Protestants turned to. I was the living spirit of Tolerance who believed there was but one Jesus Christ and Ten Commandments and the rest was just disputes about trifles. I believed that all people should be left in peace to worship their Heavenly Father as they pleased as long as they showed proper respect and reverence to their earthly sovereign. I represented freedom to follow one's own conscience, I believed God heard us whenever we spoke to Him, whether it be in Latin, English or even Turkish, and the people loved me for it.

She began first with my clothes. She had ordered herself a magnificent new wardrobe, one befitting a queen, all ornate and overembellished, encrusted with embroidery, pearls, precious gems, with gilded fringe or braid borders, in sumptuous shades of rich reds, regal purples, stately dignified blacks, sombre dark, or muted oranges and greens, and the glitter of silver and gold, and she wanted to do the same for me.

"It is unseemly that the sister of the Queen should appear so devoid of ornamentation," she said. "People will talk."

She sent for me to come to her when she was in her petticoats and stays surrounded by seamstresses and dressmakers and bade her attendants strip me down to the same state. She then began to drape me in swathes of fabric in shades of amber, garnet, orange, russet, tawny, purple, green, deep crimson, sapphire, and cinnamon as she chattered on about embroideries and trimmings.

I felt like a doll; as if she were playing dress-up with me as she used to do when I was a little girl. I remember she used to save pretty scraps of fabric and snippets of lace and gilt braid, and stray gems and beads, to make dresses for my dolls. Mary had such a passion for clothes; had she not been born a princess I am sure she would have excelled at the dressmaker's craft and been famed throughout Europe for her creations. She was more interested in my dolls than I ever was. In truth, I felt a little awkward and embarrassed for her, this woman who seemed so old to a child's eyes, playing with dolls, spending hours dressing and undressing them, making them walk and talk and devising little dramas for them to act out and trying to cajole serious little me to join in while I sat watching her with a stormy face and my arms folded across my chest. She would spend hours fastidiously designing and sewing exquisite little dresses for them, with all the proper accoutrements and accessories, even fashioning stays out of buckram and cord. I remember how crestfallen she was the day I petulantly informed her that I was too old to play with dolls.

Now here we were, playing dress-up again, only I was a real living and breathing person, a grown woman nearing twenty, not a child, and most certainly *not* a doll. But Mary was Queen of England, and to oppose or disappoint her was to dance and dice with danger.

I wanted the people to know that no matter what I wore on my body, and even if I were compelled to kneel beside my sister in the royal chapel as the Host was elevated, that I was true to myself and them, so I ordered the goldsmith to fashion a little book with golden covers that I might wear hanging from a cord or chain about my waist, and inside it, upon the ivory pages, I inscribed my brother's deathbed prayer, and let it be known that I wore it on my person always.

> *Lord God, deliver me out of this miserable and wretched life, and take me amongst Thy chosen; howbeit, not my will but Thy will be done. Lord, I commit my spirit to Thee. O, Lord, Thou knowest how happy it were for me to be with Thee; yet, for Thy chosen's sake, send me life and health, that I may truly serve Thee. O, My Lord God, defend this realm from papistry, and maintain Thy true religion, that I and my people may praise Thy Holy Name, for Thy Son Jesus Christ's sake, Amen.*

Though it was rather strongly worded and placed one faith above the other rather than embodying the tolerance that was my personal creed, still I wore it to convey a silent message. Thus, even on those occasions when gold-embroidered butterflies swarmed across my bodice or bands of ermine snaked up the front of my gown and over my shoulders and down my back, the people would see that little gold book swinging from a chain or cord against my skirts, bouncing and flashing with every step I took, and know where my loyalties truly lay, and that the spirit of Tolerance would remain alive and well in England as long as Elizabeth Tudor drew breath.

After my wardrobe, it was my soul's turn. Mary summoned me to her private apartments again. Squinting her short-sighted eyes at me, she set aside her sewing, the beautiful Spanish black-work embroidery she had learned from her mother, and bade me sit beside her.

She began with gentle persuasions and the gift of an ivory rosary to try to coax me to attend Mass. Nothing could make her happier, she declared, than to have her dear sister kneeling beside her there as the priest held the Host aloft.

I played for time. I asked for instruction, for learned men and books to teach me and guide me, and then . . . if my conscience were so moved . . . then I *might* embrace it. I could promise only to do as my conscience dictated.

"I was brought up another way," I explained. "I do not believe."

"But attend Mass with me and the belief *will* come!" Mary cried, clasping my hands so hard it hurt. "Just come, sit beside me, open your mind and heart, and God *will* fill it with belief!"

"I want to believe," I assured her.

In the end, for my own safety, I felt I must concede a little or else lose all. But I let the people see that I went unwillingly, as a move meant only to mollify Mary. In a white gown – saving the new finery Mary had gifted me with for court occasions – with Edward's deathbed prayer dangling from my waist, I began to accompany Mary to Mass. Sometimes I feigned illness, complaining loudly of pains in my stomach or the violent pangs of a megrim assailing my poor head as I went unwillingly into chapel. Sometimes I even fell faint in the corridor so that I must be picked up, revived, and carried back to my rooms. Sometimes, when I did attend, I had to leave hurriedly before the Elevation of the Host, rushing out with my hand clapped over my mouth, else I disgrace myself, and my sister, the Queen, by being sick right there in the chapel.

Mary grew even colder towards me. When she looked at me there was the glint of suspicion in her eyes and an icy chill in her rare embrace. She was alert and vigilant, watching and waiting for me to make a grave mistake, like a serpent watching and waiting to corner and strike down its prey. And I knew in both my head and heart, though it hurt so much to acknowledge it, that my sister was now my enemy.

Religion, that eternal bone of contention, had pitted sister against sister, and made us rivals, and only one of us could emerge the victor. And therein Mary made a fatal mistake that would cost her dear; Catholicism was her religion, and she would fight for it to her last breath even if it cost her everything, whereas I, whilst I called myself a Protestant, my *true* religion was England and its people.

∂ 23 ∂

Mary

I was seven years past thirty, no longer a girl in the first radiant glow of youth with pink roses in her cheeks and the whole of life before her. I was far past the age when most women are many years married and mothers many times over. Had I been a private gentlewoman, I would have reconciled myself to the spinster's lot, but as Queen of England I owed my people an heir. I knew I could not trust Elizabeth to uphold the true faith and fight to stave off the infectious plague of heresy. No, it was far more likely that she would welcome and embrace it. No, to safeguard the soul of England, I needed a child born of my own body, who would be loyal to me as both mother and queen, and, for that, I needed a husband.

Some thought I should marry Edward Courtenay, that my Tudor blood and his Plantagenet would breed a fine race of English kings, but I could not suffer the thought of that fool in my bed. I needed a *real* man, a strong and commanding virile presence, someone I could turn to, lean on, and rely on. I needed a man who was born to hold the reins of power in his hands; a man who was born to be a king among men.

Then one day, as my Council hotly debated the matrimonial issue, and I sprang from my chair at the head of the table and fled from them in embarrassment, my cheeks burning at the thought of all these men sitting around discussing who should share my bed and my chances of successfully conceiving at my age, with my own doctors at hand to answer their questions, the Spanish Ambassador, Señor Renard, sought me out. He said he had something to cheer me. He had brought me a present from his master, my cousin, the Emperor. It was a portrait painted by the master artist Titian.

As I stood, rapt with curiosity before the canvas, tantalizingly veiled in blue velvet, Ambassador Renard delivered a most flattering message from my imperial cousin.

"Your Majesty, my imperial master bade me tell you this: Since age and infirmity now render him ill-equipped and rob him of the pleasure of becoming himself your bridegroom, a chance he lost once before, and deeply regrets to this day, he offers you the finest and a far superior substitute – his son, Prince Philip of Spain."

With those words, Renard ripped away the blue velvet and there before me, staring out at me from inside the gilded frame, was the handsomest young man I had ever seen.

His hair and short, pointed little beard were like burnished gold silk, his eyes were the blue of a placid ocean, and his mouth wore the tiniest little smile that seemed to me so sensual and inviting that I was startled by the realization that I wanted to kiss it. Beneath my velvet skirts, I felt my knees tremble and go so weak that I had to grope behind me for a chair and sank down into it with my hand going up to clasp my pounding, racing heart. I could not take my eyes off him. He was *so* beautiful! He stood turned slightly to the side, not fully facing me, which put him half in shadows, and gave him an air of mystery, his slender form encased in rich midnight blue velvet trimmed with pearls and delicate but fine silver and gold beading and embroidery. He was the sun and the moon all at once, and I *knew* then that he would be the whole world to me.

My face burned with a red-hot blush as I felt the most exquisite little tingling, the like of which I had never felt before, between my legs, accompanied by a sudden burst of warm wetness. This, I rather poetically fancied, was what a rose must feel like before it first unfurled its petals in full bloom to the morning dew.

"I . . . I . . ." I tried to speak but my heart was pounding so that it proved most distracting; it was as if I could hear it echoing in my ears. I swallowed hard and tried again. "I thank the Emperor for suggesting a greater match than I deserve, but . . . is he not . . . rather . . . young?"

"Madame, a man of twenty-six can hardly be considered young!" Renard protested. "I would instead call him a middle-aged man, for he is settled and stable in his ways, and nowadays a man nearing thirty is considered as old as men formerly were at forty, and few men survive to more than fifty or sixty."

"But a man of twenty-six is likely to be disposed to be amorous," I persisted, "and, at my age, such is not my inclination. I have never felt that which is called love," I confided, "nor have I harboured amorous thoughts. I never even thought of marriage until God was pleased to raise me to the throne, and as a private individual I would not desire it," I continued, whilst inwardly chastising myself for this untruth, for denying my lifelong dream of marriage and motherhood. "I must, therefore, look to the Emperor for guidance, and leave all in his hands, as if he were my father, and indeed I have long been accustomed to think of him and honour and respect him as such."

"Madame" – Renard came and knelt beside my chair – "the Emperor regards you with the same affection as he would a daughter and indeed, if you were his very own daughter he could not hope to discover a better match for you. Prince Philip is unparalleled! He is so admirable, so virtuous, so prudent, so wise beyond his years, and modest in his person and demeanour as to appear too good to be true and too wonderful to be human. Many have gone so far as to call him divine. Far from being young and amorous, I assure you, His Highness is a prince of stable and settled character who deplores lasciviousness and licentiousness in others. And if you accept his proposal, the burden will be lifted from your shoulders; you will be relieved of the pains and travails which are meant to be a man's work and not the profession of ladies. And His Highness is a puissant prince to whom this kingdom could turn for protection and succour against your enemies."

"I . . ." My head began to swim and I closed my eyes and

clasped my hands tight around it. "This is all so sudden! Señor Renard, *please*, I need time! I *must* think! I must pray and reflect on all that you have told me."

"Of course, Madame," he said kindly, standing, and sweeping me a low bow. "I understand; forgive me, it was not my intention to overwhelm you. With your permission, I shall withdraw."

I nodded absently and waved him out, but as he neared the door I called out to him to wait and rushed and took his hand in mine and stared intently into his dark eyes.

"Tell me truthfully," I implored, "is Prince Philip *really* as you say?"

"Madame, in truth, he is even better! I confess to you now that I have been minimizing his qualities so that he would not sound too good to be true. I assure you, His Highness is the most virtuous prince in this world, and such that one would be tempted to pinch him to make sure he was not a dream, and then to pinch oneself to make sure one was not dreaming to be in the presence of such a man."

"So you are not speaking out of duty, or fear, or affection for the Prince or my imperial cousin the Emperor?" I pressed again for reassurance.

"Your Majesty, I beg you to take my honour and my life as hostages for the honesty of my words!" Renard exclaimed.

I wanted to believe him, I wanted it all to be true, and yet . . . whether it was something in me, or something about the Prince, still I hesitated.

"Would it be possible," I timidly inquired, fearing to give offense by my request and shatter all hope of dragging this dream into reality, "for the Prince to visit me first, before I accept his proposal?"

Renard shook his head. "I fear not, Madame, but I am certain that as soon as his proposal is accepted he will come to you on the fastest ship. Having heard so much about you and your great and many virtues – I tell you this confidentially – the Prince is already quite smitten."

"*Really?*" I gasped, clutching my chest as my heart fluttered so I thought it had sprouted wings and was about to fly up my throat and out my mouth. Prince Philip smitten, with me? Praise God, it was too good to be true!

Renard nodded, and lowered his voice to a whisper. "In strictest confidence, Your Majesty – *yes*, he is indeed quite smitten, and not an hour passes that he does not think of you, nor a night in which he does not dream of having you beside him as his bride. I cannot count the number of times he looks upon your portrait each day. If I may be so bold . . ." He hesitated until I nodded eagerly for him to continue. "Your concern about the difference in age is utterly unnecessary. His Highness relishes the thought of a mature bride, an intelligent woman of dignified and regal bearing and strong faith. He has no liking for the idea of sharing his life with a silly green girl who giggles and blushes and simpers and thinks of nothing but dancing and new clothes."

Blushing, I turned away. "Thank you, Señor Renard. That will be all. Leave me, please; you have given me much to think on. And I must pray; I must ask God for guidance."

"I understand, Madame," he said gently. "And I too shall pray, as I know His Highness does every day, that this happy union shall come to pass, for it is like a match made in Heaven under the smiling gazes of God and His angels."

"I hope, but yet . . . I dare not!" I breathlessly confided.

"Hope, Madame, hope!" he urged as he drew the door shut behind him.

I shut myself away from the prying eyes of the court, and had Susan give out that I was ill, and for two days and nights, I fasted and prayed. Forsaking slumber, I paced my rooms like an animal caged and restless. I scrutinized the face in the portrait, and knelt at my altar. I occupied every moment with deep, intense thought and fervent prayer. And then, my decision made, on Sunday evening I sent Susan to bring Ambassador Renard to my private chapel.

He found me kneeling before the candlelit altar.

"I have not slept for the past two days," I confided, solemn and weary, as I held out my hand to him with a nod that conveyed he should kneel down beside me. "I have spent every moment in

thought and prayer, asking God, as my protector, guide, and coun-
sellor, to help me make the right decision regarding this marriage.
And He, who has shown me so many miracles and favours, has
shown me the way and performed yet one more miracle on my behalf." My Bible lay open upon the altar and I laid my hand upon it.
"He has inspired me, now, before you, to make this unbreakable
vow. My mind is made up and I can never change it; I will marry
Prince Philip and love him perfectly and never give him cause for
jealousy."

"Oh, Madame!" Renard kissed my hand in a most passionate,
heartfelt manner. "I am so happy! May I say on behalf of His
Highness the words that I know will be in his heart and on his lips
the moment he hears of your decision? You have made him *the happiest man in the world!*"

"And I," I said fervently, as tears rolled down my face, "knowing that he wants me, am the happiest woman in the world! I never
thought that I would feel that which is called love, but now . . .
God has blessed me with another miracle! He has opened my
heart! And for the first time in my life, I am in love! I am to be a
wife, and God willing, a mother! And now" – I turned my smiling
face, in joyous expectation, to Renard – "there is nothing to stop
His Highness from coming to me on the fastest ship!"

Ambassador Renard frowned and lowered his eyes.

"*What?*" I gasped and reached out to grasp his hand. "Is something wrong? Tell me!"

"There is *one* thing, Your Majesty – the Protestant usurper, the
Lady Jane Grey. There is great unrest in the land, and I fear those
who will, out of fear and ignorance, oppose this marriage, might
rise up and try to restore the Lady Jane to the throne."

"But Jane does not want to be Queen!" I protested. "She never
did. It was forced upon her; so surely there is nothing to fear from
her?"

"Madame, your kindness is commendable, it is a goodly and
godly feminine virtue, but a sovereign must think first and foremost of the good of their kingdom. They cannot always follow
their personal inclination to be merciful. I regret, the Lady Jane's
very existence is a *serious* threat to the life and security of the

Prince, and as long as she lives, Prince Philip cannot set foot in England; the Emperor will not allow it."

"But I swear upon my life, Prince Philip shall be safe!" I cried.

Renard shook his head sadly. "I am sorry, Madame, but I regret . . ."

I felt my heart shatter. Happiness had been in my grasp and now it had been most cruelly snatched away and in the tussle fallen and shattered like a fragile glass bauble.

"Leave me!" I motioned for Renard to withdraw as I fell weeping before the altar, begging the Blessed Virgin to help me. I had come *so* close to having *all* my dreams come true. And now . . . now I must choose between the life of my innocent cousin and my personal happiness; my chance to be a wife and mother as I had always dreamed of and enjoy the God-ordained purpose and fulfilment of all womankind. It was *too* cruel! I didn't know what to do.

I was determined to be merciful. She was *only* sixteen, *just a child*, a battered and badly used *child*. She had not taken my throne on purpose, it was not done out of spite or malice or a belief that it was her right; she had been beaten and forced and even as she accepted she admitted she did wrong and it was mine by right, not hers. Of course, I would have to sentence her to death, as a formality and a warning to others, but I fully intended to pardon her. I had thought to keep her safe in the Tower, out of harm's way, away from the immediate personal peril of her parents, and her vain and vapid, but also reputedly quite cruel, peacock of a husband, as well as beyond the reach of the Protestant rebels, until I married and had a child to safeguard the succession. Then I would set her free. After all, it was not a cruel imprisonment and she seemed to be quite content, holed up with her beloved books. But now . . . her very existence put my dreams, and England's future, in peril. In the end, it all boiled down to her death or the death of my dreams. One or the other must be sacrificed.

I took from a drawer a miniature likeness painted of the Lady Jane and drew up a comfortable chair before Prince Philip's portrait, and for a long time I sat there gazing first at one and then at the other, knowing that I must sacrifice one of them. Losing Philip would be like death to me; I knew I would never find another man who would suit me even half so well, and time was not on my side. I was closer to forty than I was to thirty; I needed to bear an heir before it was too late and Mother Nature's hourglass ran out for me, but having Philip would mean death to Lady Jane.

Life had not been kind or fair to that little lady. I could picture it all in my mind, like a series of tapestries on the wall, woven together from the various threads of gossip, letters, and reports I had received.

She had been wakened from a sound sleep and ordered to dress. She was taken in the grey light of dawn to Syon House. Northumberland himself escorted her, and Guildford, preening his golden hair and pouting at being woken from the sound sleep that was so necessary for him to look his best, to the Presence Chamber where a bevy of noble men and women awaited them. Since Edward's death the throne had sat empty beneath the gold-fringed canopy of estate. As Jane entered, the gentlemen knelt and the ladies curtsied, doing reverence to the startled and confused girl.

Dazed and uncomprehending, Jane faltered and seemed about to bolt. Northumberland's hands shot out to stay her. His eyes boring commandingly into hers, he took her hand firmly in a grasp that threatened to crush the delicate little bones beneath the snow-white flesh and forcibly dragged her, shaking with fright, up the steps of the dais to the throne and, with steely hands on her frail shoulders, made her sit, speechless and stunned, as he read out a proclamation announcing the death of King Edward VI and that before his death he had altered the succession to disinherit both his sisters and name his cousin, the Lady Jane, Queen of England.

At these words, Jane sprang up then, just as suddenly, fell down in a dead faint. There she lay in a crumpled heap of grey velvet skirts and wavy chestnut hair. No one made a move to tend or assist her; impatiently they waited for her to recover. Even her own husband made no move to help her; instead he made a great show of polishing his nails against his velvet doublet and admiring them and the flash of his rings in the candlelight. When Jane came to, she burst into tears upon realizing that this was really happening and not some hellish nightmare.

She lay sobbing on the floor, whilst the nobles looked away, embarrassed, pretending not to see. Not a one of them was moved to pity that poor frightened, helpless girl, alone and misused, with no one to turn to for assistance, comfort, or advice. At last her mother, the irascible and impatient Frances, Duchess of Suffolk, strode over, as powerful as a plough horse, and leaned down and grasped Jane's arm and yanked her to her feet and shoved her back onto the throne. The crown was waiting for Jane to try on and, slapping down the feeble little hands, like frightened, flapping white doves, that rose and tried to push it away, Frances crammed it down on Jane's head and thus crowned her daughter Queen of England.

"The crown is not my right! This pleases me not!" Jane sobbingly protested. "The Lady Mary is the rightful heir!"

"Shut up, you stupid little girl!" Frances hissed, giving her cheek a swift stinging slap and the soft flesh of her upper arm a savage pinch that made Jane yelp and cower back against the velvet cushions of her unwanted throne.

Then, smiling broadly at the assembled courtiers and Councillors, Frances smilingly declared, "It is most becoming, is it not?" gesturing to the crown glittering upon the tousled head of her tearstained and trembling daughter.

And all agreed that it was indeed most becoming and a perfect fit for their beautiful young queen. And Guildford Dudley declared that he wanted one for himself set with sapphires fine enough to rival his beautiful eyes. Beside him, his doting mother agreed that would look breathtaking.

Then at first light they were forcing Jane's bruised and battered body into an elaborate gown of Tudor green and white furred with ermine and adorned with gold embroidery, emeralds, diamonds, seed pearls, and enamelled Tudor roses of red and white, and brushing her hair out to a gleaming, glossy shine, and crowning it with a jewelled hood to match her gown. About her neck they fastened the ruby necklace I had given her for her wedding day, which made her again tug and fidget and complain that it cut her throat. Then her nurse, Mrs Ellen, knelt to strap a pair of chopines with high, cork-platformed soles onto Jane's tiny feet to lend her the illusion of height. And they were on their way, with the domineering Frances, glittering murderously in cloth-of-gold and blood-red rubies, acting as her daughter's trainbearer, and Guildford, his golden hair shining like waves of molten gold, resplendently jewelled and costumed in green and white velvet, roughly taking her arm. Thus, Jane most unwillingly tottered out, teetering on her unaccustomed high heels, to board the barge that would carry her to the Tower of London where she was to lodge in the royal apartments until her coronation. It was deemed safer to convey her there by barge instead of in the traditional procession through the streets thronged with stony-faced and silent people, not a one of whom raised their voice to wish her well. They all sulked and glowered and longed for me, their one true queen. And as Guildford smiled to show off his perfect teeth and waved to the crowd, Jane stared down at the floor, her chin quivering with the tears she was trying not to shed, and tugged nervously at the ruby necklace that encircled her throat, complaining that it cut her and she couldn't breathe.

That night in the royal apartments, Guildford insisted on a crown of his own. Jane refused him, whereupon Guildford burst into tears and threatened to go home to his mother. In his nightshirt, he ran to fetch her and she came barging in, in indignant haste, with her nightgown flapping about her bountiful form, and delivered a harsh tongue-lashing to her daughter-in-law, "so ungrateful for the gift she had been given in Guildford," then took her son's hand and said, "Come, Guildford, you shall not lodge with such an ungrateful wife!" Smarting with humiliation, Jane sent guards to bar them from leaving the Tower. "I have no need of my husband in my bed," she explained, perhaps, as some suspected, intending it as a slur upon Guildford's masculinity, "but by day his place is by my side."

In the days that followed, Jane became sick with fear and worry. Unable to keep food down, and with her glorious hair starting to come out in clumps, she became convinced that Northumberland was poisoning her, to get rid of her, so that he might make his son, Guildford, reigning king instead of mere consort.

Then the people rose up in favour of me, the Treasurer absconded with the money, and the Council deserted, all running as fast as they could to me. When it was all over and she heard the distant sounds of rejoicing in the city, Jane breathed a sigh of relief. She was alone in the Presence Chamber when her father came in and ripped down the canopy of estate from over her head.

"You are no longer Queen," he brusquely informed her. "You must put off your royal robes and be content with a private life."

"I put them off more willingly than I ever put them on," Jane replied. "I gladly relinquish the crown. May I go home now?"

Her father ignored the question and turned on his heel and left, abandoning her like all the rest, hurrying back to the London town house where his wife was hastily restoring the chapel to full Catholic splendour and getting out of storage their rosaries and crucifixes. On his way home, he paused on Tower Hill to wave a hastily procured rosary in the air and shout at the top of his lungs, "God save Queen Mary, our one true queen! Long may she reign!" He tossed a few coins in the air for good measure and the benefit of the common folk standing nearby.

Alone in the Presence Chamber, the weary Jane gladly got up from her unwanted throne and went back to her bedchamber to doff the splendid gown of jet-spangled mulberry velvet she had been laced into that morning.

"I am glad I am no longer Queen," she said to her nurse, Mrs Ellen, as she unlaced her. "No one can ever say I sought the crown or was pleased with it."

And then, exhausted, thin as a reed and pale as her shift, Jane fell into bed, believing that her ordeal was over.

The next morning she arose, dressed in plain black, and wrote a letter of apology to me, explaining that though the crown was forced upon her, she knew she had done wrong to accept it. "It did not become me to accept it," she admitted. "It showed a want of prudence." Then, letter dispatched, she took up her Greek Testament, and settled herself on the window seat to resume her studies.

How could I send such an unfortunate creature to the block? I thought of summoning her, to talk with her privately, but I knew that if I did, I would *never* be able to do what I feared I must. If I saw and spoke with her, I would never be able to condemn her. It had been the same with Father. Once he had decided upon a death, he never saw the condemned again, lest their pleading words and tears turn his heart and sway him to mercy. And what good would it do? I knew I had nothing to fear from Jane – she did not want my crown. It was those Protestant rebels who would espouse her cause, whether she wanted them to or not, whom I had to fear and worry about, not Jane herself. Jane, the fervent Protestant, was the figurehead for the Protestant warship. It was as simple as that. And as such, it was not safe to let her live; she was a weapon that would be used against me again and again. Unless . . . A smile lit up my face and my hand rose to clasp the jewelled cross at my breast. Unless I could rob the weapon of its ammunition. If Jane embraced the true faith, she would no longer be a threat!

I would send a good and kindly teacher – I knew just the one: Dr Feckenham, the Abbot of Westminster – and give her every opportunity to save herself. Now Jane's fate would be in her own hands, and no longer in mine; she herself would decide whether she was to live or to die and, whatever happened, my conscience would be clear and blameless. I fell to my knees and thanked God for shining a beacon to show me the way. "Thou art indeed the light of the world – my world!" I breathed in fervent gratitude.

❦ 24 ❦

Elizabeth

That stupid fool jackanapes Courtenay lost whatever wits he had – if he ever had any to start with – in the Tower, and when he was set free, rather than be grateful and keep a firm grasp on his head, he seemed determined to risk losing it at every turn.

First he courted Mary, behaving as if she were the sun, moon, and stars, and made the world move and the tides ebb and flow for him.

He chose to make his feelings known in a particularly spectacular fashion. To celebrate "the ascension of this heavenly beauteous queen to an earthly throne", he chose to replicate the tournament that our father had arranged to celebrate Mary's birth.

Courtenay, who had spent his formative years in the Tower and thus had been denied the proper tutelage befitting his quasi-royal station, had never in his life sat a horse, and all, if anything, he knew about horsemanship and the arts of war came from stories and books. But he decided not to let his deficiencies stop him. Thus, I suppose, for sheer determination, he must be applauded.

As Mary sat in the royal box overlooking the tiltyard, politely applauding, "The Last Sprig of the White Rose" rode out to the centre of the tiltyard mounted on a white horse. Both Courtenay and his snowy mount were splendidly arrayed in golden armour and crimson silk embroidered with the golden pomegranates of

Spain, and both the rider's helm and his horse's head were adorned with graciously swaying plumes. And as Henry VIII had done thirty-seven years before, Courtenay sported a badge identifying himself as Sir Loyal Heart.

Alas, this beautiful tableau was spoiled when Courtenay tried to bow to the Queen from the saddle and first his golden helm, followed by the gilt-armoured Courtenay, crashed onto the dusty ground. Blushing furiously, he nonetheless composed himself and presented Mary with a beautifully wrought golden pomegranate that opened to reveal portraits of Henry VIII, Catherine of Aragon, and their beloved little princess, "Mary of the Marigold Hair", as Courtenay called her. He then proceeded to recite a poem he had written of the same title, about which the less said the better. He then fell thrice more trying to remount, then shouting curses at his horse and calling it "a sulky brute" he raised his gilt-armoured foot to kick its rump and fell with a great crash onto his own. Embarrassed and agitated, he got to his feet, seized his horse by the bridle, and stalked off the jousting field.

But he was not done humiliating himself. When he was again in the saddle and ready to compete in the first joust, he dropped his lance in terror, hugged tight his horse's neck, squeezed his eyes shut, prayed, and held on for dear life as it galloped towards his opponent, who didn't need his lance to unhorse Courtenay. Left to his own devices, he tumbled off himself. In the tiring tent afterward, I heard it said, when his squires stripped him down, Courtenay's linen reeked of urine.

Undaunted, Courtenay, having heard of the sugar-candy and marzipan fairyland Henry VIII had created for his beloved daughter on her sixth birthday, wanted to give Mary a fairyland of his own devising and continued his wooing that night with an open-air banquet and pageant. I was amongst the maidens dressed in diaphanous flowing gowns of pale gold-spangled rose, green, and cream, with diamond-dusted fairy wings strapped to our backs, and our hair cascading down our backs, glistening with diamond dust, and crowned with wreaths of gilded rosemary and bejewelled silken wildflowers who danced before the Queen with gold ribbon sandals laced round our naked feet, while Mary and her most favoured ladies sat in a flower-bedecked fairy bower upon a great heap of silken cushions illuminated by jewel-hued lanterns.

Courtenay himself made his entrance mounted on the same white horse he had ridden – for lack of a better word – at the tournament, somehow managing not to drop the silken cushion with an elaborate crown of gilded rosemary and jewelled flowers with which he meant to crown "The Queen of My Heart". A pearly horn was strapped to the horse's forehead to transform it into a unicorn and, when Courtenay grandly made his way to the Queen and bowed low before her, the horse also bowed low and charged.

Mary and her fairy-gowned ladies fled hastily, some tittering in amusement, others shrieking in alarm. But Courtenay did not know anything was amiss until he found himself floundering face-down in the Queen's hastily vacated bower, the gaping hole in his torn breeches showing more than was proper to Her Majesty and her court, as he burst into tears and began to scream for the royal physician to come and save him from the cold embrace of Death.

Showing Courtenay the same compassion she would have shown a wounded child, Mary knelt upon the cushions beside him, modestly turning her face away from the red rose welt now blooming on the bare bottom of "The Last Sprig of the White Rose", and held his hand as the royal physician applied ointment and a bandage. She stroked his fair hair and begged him not to cry any more and gave him a diamond ring that had belonged to our father, which Courtenay promptly mistook for a betrothal ring and threw his arms around her neck and kissed her.

Blushing hotly as she floundered upon the heap of fat cushions in Courtenay's eager embrace, Mary struggled free, gathered up her skirts, and fled back into the palace.

Back in his apartments, Courtenay proceeded to get gloriously drunk on elderberry wine. He ripped the gold fringed and embroidered blue velvet curtains off his bed and draped them round his body and, despite the late hour, sent his manservant running to fetch his tailor to come cut the fabric to fashion his coronation suit. He then decked his wild and rumpled golden curls with dandelions and bluebells to simulate a gold and sapphire crown and snapped the gilded leg off a chair to serve as a makeshift sceptre.

Then, still swathed in the blue velvet curtains, he climbed up onto a table to make a rather explicit speech about what he would do to his queenly wife on their wedding night, the sum of all the knowledge he had acquired visiting the Southwark whores several nights a week since his release from the Tower to make up for lost time and his lack of carnal knowledge. And when the diamond ring slid off his slender finger and down a rat-hole in the floorboards, Courtenay tried to dive in after it and knocked himself unconscious and spent the rest of the night snoring on the floor. He appeared the next day with a royal purple lump the size of an egg protruding through his golden curls only to discover Mary turning a distinctly cold shoulder to him when he ran up to her and tried to embrace his "wife-to-be".

Pining for his lost love, and lost chance to wear a crown, Courtenay moped around for days weeping and wearing deepest black mourning. He even sent Mary a little black coffin with some sort of animal's heart inside it as a symbolic gesture, albeit a gruesome one, of his grief. Then he made the foolhardy decision to accept an invitation to dine with the French Ambassador, who urged the gullible young man to shake off his gloom and take heart; if the Queen herself would not marry him, perhaps her younger, prettier sister would. He went on to captivate Courtenay by painting a pretty word picture about what a beautiful couple we would make, me with my Tudor-red tresses and milk-pale skin, a vibrant living reminder of Henry VIII, and he the very image of the tall, majestic blue-eyed golden-haired Plantagenet kings, comparing him to the great Edwards who had ruled before, when in truth his character was more like that of the weak and foolish, volatile and unstable, Edward II, who had let his kingdom go to wrack and ruin while he frolicked with Piers Gaveston. And when the Ambassador painted us with golden crowns on our heads, and Mary deposed or dead, and us sitting on a pair of golden thrones in robes bright with jewels and edged with ermine, the susceptible Courtenay realized he was in love with me and rushed straight out to pick a bouquet of buttercups and then rush breathlessly to throw himself at my feet and declare his love for me.

Every time I turned round there he was doffing his feathered hat and bowing to me, sending me childishly written verses so gushing and sugary they nearly brought on a bilious attack of indigestion or gave me a toothache, and trinkets and gifts he either bought off street pedlars or picked up about the court and my servants later had to discreetly return to their rightful owners. Once he even knelt with his lute outside my window and serenaded me all through the night though the poor lad couldn't carry a tune even if some obliging soul had put it in a box for him. Ever afterwards he would have the court musicians play that same melody and ask me to dance, always making sly reference to his serenade. "That song has been haunting me," he would loudly proclaim, then turn to me and ask, "Do you know why, My Lady Princess?" To which I invariably replied, "Perhaps it is because you murdered it, My Lord? It is a common belief, I am told, that ghosts often return to haunt their murderers." Other times he would creep up close behind me and whisper in my ear that red hair denoted passion and how he longed to put a gold ring on me so he could lead me to his bed for a game of stallion and mare, asking me did I not think as the last remaining Plantagenet heir and a Tudor princess we were "fated to be mated". "I want to ride a young filly, not an old maid," he said, with an unsubtle jerk of his head towards Mary.

He was supposed to be Mary's suitor, not mine, yet he now made it plain that his affections had changed course, tempering it with neither kindness nor tact, flaunting it in Mary's face that he preferred me, the younger and prettier sister. And even though Mary no longer favoured him, declaring she could not love a man who disported himself with whores and lost his dignity so utterly when in his cups, she was nonetheless upset that he had transferred his affections to me and had cast off his mourning robes and mended so quickly the heart he vowed that she had broken and, I fear, blamed me for it, though anyone with eyes could see that I did nothing to encourage him.

Every time Mary saw us together I felt my blood freeze and the back of my neck prickle as if the headsman's axe was poised to strike. I saw the anger in her squint-narrowed eyes, and I felt the flames of her jealousy reach out and scorch me.

I knew that those who opposed the Catholic regime saw me, their beacon of hope, and young, addle-brained, easily-led Edward Courtenay, and the pretty picture we made together, as the perfect figureheads for a Protestant rebellion. There were whispers all about, so loud sometimes that they were practically screams, giving voice to all manner of schemes from the careful and cautious to the flamboyantly bold and brazen to dethrone Mary and put Courtenay and me, such a pretty Protestant pair, on the throne as king and queen. But I would have none of it; I blocked my ears and walked steadfastly on, pretending that I did not hear. I wanted no part in any of their plots. If I ever became queen it would be by God's will, and the people's, not through any rebellion or conspiracy. I would not have my sister's blood shed for my sake to forever stain my conscience.

But Mary heard the whispers and they fed her fear and mistrust. She refused to grant me leave to retire from court, to go back to Hatfield or one of my other country manors. She wanted to keep me close, so she, and her spies, could keep an eye on me. She wanted to know all I did and whom I spoke with and even what letters I sent and received. She began to snub me publicly, to show that I had offended and disappointed her. Once when I stood ready to accompany her, albeit unwillingly, to Mass, she passed me by, openly shunning me, as if I did not even exist, and bade our cousin Margaret, the Countess of Lennox, a loyal and favoured lady-in-waiting whose devotion, both personal and religious, was never in doubt, to walk into chapel with her and even sit beside her.

And she was still trying to turn back time. She had Parliament declare the marriage of Henry VIII and Catherine of Aragon legitimate, thus reaffirming and emphasizing her own legitimacy and my bastardy. She ordered a large painting of her parents, clad in black, gold, and ermine, sitting side by side on a pair of gilded thrones, holding hands, and sharing fond and loving glances, whilst their loving and devoted daughter, and lawful successor, Mary, sat at their feet, between them, also clad in black and gold, gazing up at them in rapt and worshipful adoration as if she knelt at an altar in veneration of a pair of saints, and beside her lay that eternal emblem of fidelity – a dog, her svelte little Italian grey-hound.

After it was completed, there were many occasions when she would ask me to walk with her in the gallery where it hung, prominently displayed, and have us pause before it, to admire it, to comment on the beauty of the carved Spanish pomegranates and Tudor roses, the entwined initials, *H&K*, that adorned the gilded frame, or what fine, accurate likenesses the artist had wrought. "They seem to live and breathe!" Mary would sigh, clasping her hands over her heart as she stared up at the idealistic portrayal of the loving couple and the smiling, fresh and radiant-faced little girl with the wealth of marigold curls, sitting at their feet. It was a child's memory, not an adult's reality.

It was a portent, I think, of the blindness of her madness. Mary would blunder and stagger her way through her reign like a blind woman, so short-sighted that she would never see what she needed to see until it was right in her face and far too late to avoid collision and calamity.

But my own eyes were wide open and I saw it all. Mary was already alienating her Council. She made it clear as the finest Venetian glass that she trusted the Spanish Ambassador more than any man living, except her cousin the Emperor, for whom his ambassador stood proxy. But in her idolization of Charles, Mary forgot one crucial fact – a monarch *always* acts in his, or her, *own* best interests, as does, by extension, any ambassador in their service; they are servants dedicated to serving their monarch's and country's best interests, even though they smile and behave with kind deference and concern to those whose favour they are courting; it is all part of the game. Renard was a velvet-tongued liar who would have happily seen Mary turned out of her kingdom in her petticoats if it would have benefited his master, but Mary believed every word he said because she wanted to believe, and sought his advice over that of her own Council when, regardless of religion, whether they were Protestant or Catholic, those men were all first and foremost Englishmen, and even though they might act out of ambition, self-interest, and greed, they would *always* serve England before they would Spain, or any other country. But Mary was too blind to see that, and whenever she desired advice or wanted to confide in someone, there sly Renard would be, with the pearly nacre of his smile agleam and the loyalty of a devoted lapdog shining in his dark serpent's eyes, walking by or seated at her side, from which he never strayed for long. It was as if they were bound together at the hip by an invisible tether.

Thus, the people of England gradually came to believe that their queen, born of a Spanish mother, loved Spain more than she did England and its people, and they began to look to someone else – to me – to give them what was lacking. And when the whispers began that the Queen lusted for a Spanish bridegroom it was as if Mary had taken a keg of gunpowder into her bed; she had fallen into full and blinding love with self-destruction and had lit the fuse herself and none could dissuade or stop her.

That was one of the few things Mary and I had in common; a time came in each of our lives when lust made blind fools of us both, and passion pushed us into the arms of danger. When I fell over the chasm, I pulled myself back up, I fought to save myself, to become like a phoenix and rise again. I could only pray that Mary would be able to do the same, for if she married Philip, she *would* fall. I wished my sister and I were close enough that I might sit down beside her, take her hand in mine, and tell her all about Tom Seymour, and all that I had learned dancing in the arms of danger. But, had our positions been reversed, had she sat down and bared her heart to me, would I, blinded by passion and folly, have listened? No, I think not. Bold and confident in my new-found sensuality, I would have fancied that I knew better. So I kept silent, for this reason, and also out of fear that if I bared my heart and exposed the naked truth about myself, I might also be giving Mary a weapon to use against me. The loss of trust is the Black Death to any relationship; whether it kills it fast or kills it slow, the end result is always the same.

❧ 25 ❧

Mary

My Council tried to dissuade me. My subjects were openly hostile to the marriage, fearing England would become a province of Spain, yet another coin in the Hapsburg purse, as a wife's property becomes her husband's upon their marriage day. They also feared that Philip would embroil us in his costly foreign wars, that he would bleed our nation dry of money and men to settle disputes in which England had no part, and bring the dreaded Spanish Inquisition, and its torture and burning of heretics, with him. And the common, uneducated masses harboured a deeply entrenched but erroneous belief that all Spaniards were cruel and haughty and given to drunkenness, lechery, and thievery, and even murder at the slightest provocation. Catholics and Protestants alike forgot their differences and united in their opposition to my Spanish bridegroom, and raised their voices as one outside my palace or whenever I passed, to shout, "No Spaniards on England's throne!"

But my heart was set on Philip – I would have no one else. The very thought of any other husband was torture to me. And I had given my word; I had solemnly laid my hand upon the Holy Scriptures and sworn that I would be Philip's wife, and I could not go back on it, nor did I want to.

In my heart, I was already his, body and soul, and waking and sleeping, my mind teemed with dreams of our life together. It had already been noted by my court – some brash gentleman had even dared tease me about it – that whenever I sat I would gaze to the side as if a certain someone already sat beside me. I would gaze at his fantasy-conjured figure with yearning and a wistful, faraway look in my eyes and a dreamy little smile upon my lips, and my fingers would rest tenderly upon the arm of my chair and ofttimes caress as if another's hand lay beneath mine and our fingers intertwined in a loving flesh-and-blood knot. And my ladies, who took it in turns to sleep on a pallet at the foot of my bed, had reported that often in my sleep I would breathe the name "Philip!" in a long, drawn-out sensual sigh, and hug and caress the pillow beside mine and extend a leg as if I meant to drape it over or entwine it with another's.

I spent hours every day staring at his portrait and I had confided to Ambassador Renard that the very mention of Philip's name was poetry to my soul and filled my heart with ecstasy, whereupon he kissed my hand and said, "Ah, Madame, there can be no doubt, you have come to understand what love is."

"Oh, Señor Renard, I *know* I have!" I breathed as I felt my entire person lit from within by love. "I *know* I have!"

But my Council simply could not or would not understand.

"I consider myself His Highness's wife," I heatedly informed them in a storm of tears as I leapt up from my chair at the head of the Council table, "and I will *never* take another husband, *never!* I would rather lose my crown and my life! And if you force me to take another husband I shall *die*, I tell you. I shall be dead within three months, and have no children, and then you will all be sorry!"

Unable to control the storm of emotion raging inside me, I ran from them, sobbing loudly, stumbling over my skirts, and nearly colliding with the wall, in my wild, tear-blinded haste. Behind me I knew they were murmuring and shaking their heads, no doubt comparing me to a greensick girl in the throes of her first love, but I could neither help nor change what I felt. The truth was, hurtling over the bounds of reason and common sense, I had fallen in love with a painted face in a gilded frame and a paragon spun from the good reports of others, a man I had never even met, and I could not bear the thought of losing the chance to be with him and belong to him.

Elizabeth

At last she relented and allowed me to leave court, to go to my house at Ashridge. But I knew the eyes of Mary's spies would follow me wherever I went, never would I escape their scrutiny, and I must take care not to walk into any of the traps they laid for me. I knew that the Spanish Ambassador was doing his utmost to turn Mary against me, adding fuel to the bonfire of her suspicions and mistrust, and urging her to send me to the scaffold. He was also ardently campaigning for the unwilling Protestant usurper, Lady Jane Grey, to be put to death, even though she was in truth the innocent tool of ruthless and power-hungry men. Like Mary, Renard was determined to see Catholicism flourish again in England as the *only* religion, and to kill any and all weeds that might choke or overtake those fragile, beautiful blossoms of faith and grace.

Mary herself came out to see me off despite the coldness of the day. Before I climbed into my litter she removed my russet velvet cloak and fastened a rope of lustrous white pearls round my neck; then, even as I breathed my thanks and admiration of her gift, she replaced my old cloak with a new one of fine sable lined with flame-coloured satin. And after clasping them in a sisterly farewell, she tucked my hands into a matching muff adorned with a large crucifix brooch encrusted with rubies. I felt something cold and metallic inside the muff. It was an ornate gold picture frame of the sort that holds two portraits, face to face, and opens and closes like a book. This one was all done in Spanish pomegranates and red and white enamelled Tudor roses, so I was not at all surprised when I opened it to behold the faces of Henry VIII and Catherine of Aragon, angled so they seemed to gaze lovingly and longingly at each other, painted no doubt by the same artist who had done the larger black and gold portrait that hung in the gallery.

I forced myself to smile. "How lovely!" I exclaimed. And, in truth, the frame was fine and the artist was talented. "Thank you, Mary." I leaned in and kissed her cheek. "I cannot tell you what this means to me."

And indeed I could not. It would not do to tell her it made a great din and clamour like an alarm bell ringing inside my mind warning me, "Be wary, oh be wary of sister Mary!"

Just as I started to climb into my litter, I impulsively turned back and grasped Mary's hands. Intently, I looked into her eyes, trying with all my might to make her see that I meant her no harm, only goodwill, and wished most fervently that suspicion, jealousy, and religious differences had not erected this icy wall between us.

"Mary . . ." A lump rose in my throat as I tried to find the right words. "Dear sister, I know there are many who would speak ill of me, and, seeking to make mischief, run to you bearing tales about me." I knelt then in the snow before her, still holding her hands. "All I can do is assure you that you are my sister and my sovereign and as both I wholeheartedly give you my loyalty and my love, as, despite the differences between us, I always have. May I presume upon your generosity and humbly beg one favour of you?"

"You may," Mary said softly, her voice a tremulous whisper, and I saw upon her face wariness jousting against her innate desire to believe as she looked down at me.

"Thank you!" I said most fervently, and kissed her hands, before I looked up at her again, begging her with my eyes and all my heart to believe and trust me again. "I humbly implore you, should you ever hear any evil spoken of me, that you withhold your judgment and do not condemn me unheard; allow me first to speak to you so that I may kneel before you, as I do now, in loyalty and love to my sister and sovereign, who are one and the same, and clear my name of any stain others might try to sully it with."

Mary nodded mutely and raised me to my feet, tears shimmering in her eyes, and her lips aquiver, as she embraced me and kissed both my cheeks.

"I promise," she whispered, clasping my face between her hands. "I give you my word as your loving sister and queen that I will do as you ask." She hugged me close again and said into my ear, "You were such a sweet, precocious little girl, I used to pretend you were my own. It breaks my heart that we have come to this" – she drew back and held me at arm's length – "that there are times when we face each other almost as . . . enemies!" A sob broke from her at the last word.

"Mary!" I impulsively drew her to me. *"Never, never* think that! Though we do disagree upon matters of faith, I am not, and never have been, and never will be, your enemy! No matter what others may say or do, what schemes they may devise and fly the false banner of my name over them to lend them credence, they will *always* be *lies!* I mean you and your throne no harm. *You are Queen* – by the will of our late father, and our Heavenly Father, and the people of England – *you are Queen*, and I would *never* try to take that from you! *Never!*"

"I *want* to believe you!" Mary sobbed, her heart shining in her grey eyes as she looked at me, so fearful and uncertain. They were the eyes of a woman who no longer knew whom to trust or what to believe. Charles and his emissary Renard were the only ones it never even occurred to her to distrust or doubt, and they were snakes in the grass who would bite her if she took one false step.

"Then *believe*" – I squeezed her hands – *"believe!"*

"Go with God." Mary pressed a coral rosary into my hand and, with a choking sob, she turned away from me and hurried back inside the palace, hugging herself against the cold.

Ambassador Renard gave me a curt nod and then, like the Angel of Death, his black velvet cloak flapping like wings behind him, turned and followed her.

As I rode away, I impulsively called one of my retainers to me and bade him ride back to Whitehall with a message for the

Queen, requesting that she send me adornments for my chapel –
candlesticks, chalices, copes, and chasubles, and everything else I
might need – so that I could continue to hear Mass. I also asked
that she send books to further instruct and enlighten me, and told
her that in the peace and quietude of the country I planned to
probe my conscience and make a deep study of the Catholic faith.

As he rode back to deliver my message, I worried that Mary
would see my request for what it was – another move to buy me
more time. But I knew that she, wanting to believe that I would
indeed embrace her religion, would grant it just the same, even if
she suspected hypocrisy; she would still comply as it was for the
service of God. I knew that she doubted me, but it was that kernel
of doubt that was keeping me alive, and so I nourished it as best I
could.

Though I knew I was not free of danger, I felt a respite from it,
the same sense of release and temporary relief I felt when I removed my stays each night.

One dreary December day as I walked beneath a grey sky, huddled in my furs, amongst naked trees that stood out starkly like
black embroidery on a ground of shifting greys, a stranger accosted
me. I started as he flung himself in my path and knelt at my feet, a
big, auburn-haired and bearded, broad-shouldered brute of a man.
He introduced himself as Thomas Wyatt, son and namesake of the
poet who had loved my mother, and, kissing the hem of my skirt,
vowed he would accord a like loyalty to me.

He wanted to talk of an audacious scheme to pull Mary from the
throne and put me in her place. He mentioned Courtenay, and
how much the people feared and detested the coming of the Spanish bridegroom, but I would not hear him. It was as if Tom Seymour had come back from the dead to torment me, this time laying
all his cards upon the table instead of holding them close to his
chest to prevent me from truly seeing the fool he truly was with all
his mad brainsick jealousy and ambition-driven folly.

I put my hands up over my ears and ran from him, my hands
clasped tight over my ears until distance rendered him mute. I did
not slow my steps until Ashridge was in sight.

As I opened the door, I saw him standing still in the distance; he cupped his hands around his mouth and shouted, "Your sister puts Spain and the Pope before England, but you . . . you are not just Elizabeth, you *are* England and the people love you for it!"

After that there were notes left and taps upon the windowpanes at night, but I refused to heed them. The notes I burned unread, the knocks and taps I ignored, rolling over in bed, pulling the covers up over my head to muffle that damning tap-tap-tapping that could, if I responded to it, send me to the scaffold. Letters also came, trying to draw me in, asking me to do this or that, go here or there, but I threw them into the fire after no more than a cursory glance.

My heart was torn. I wanted to warn Mary that Wyatt was planning a rebellion, but I knew that if I did I would find myself accused of treason. I could not trust Mary, especially with the Spanish Ambassador whispering words against me into her ear like a sinister black parrot perched upon her shoulder. I could not trust her to believe me if I came to her with such news, so though it rent my heart and mind with fear and worry, and kept me awake at night, I kept silent.

But knowing he was out there plotting, and a rebellion was brewing, ready to boil over at any moment, made me so uneasy that I fell grievously ill. Pains assailed my stomach and head, and I could not keep down even a sip of broth or a morsel of food, and my body began to bloat and swell, my joints ached unbearably, and my skin turned yellow-green with a terrible jaundice, and passing water caused me great discomfort.

I lay there tense and wakeful, pretending to sleep whenever Kat or Blanche Parry came to look in on me, for I had learned from the Tom Seymour scandal that I must keep my own counsel and confide in no one, not even those closest to me. Even though I knew they loved me, I must say nothing and trust no one. So I lay in my dark-shrouded bed and waited, hoping that my illness would save me from suspicion, and knowing it was my penance, the price I paid, for keeping silent.

❧ 27 ❧

Mary

Thomas Wyatt the younger, the son of the poet who made Anne Boleyn immortal in his sonnets – pathetically portraying her as a frightened doe fleeing from my father the mighty hunter, when in truth it was she who was the huntress – the even more foolish son of a foolish father, incited a rebellion against me, to put a Protestant queen, Elizabeth or Lady Jane, on the throne. With a mob seven thousand strong he marched on London, with many who feared and deplored my coming marriage falling into step behind him.

My Council pleaded with me to flee, to barricade myself behind the thick, impenetrable walls of the Tower, but instead I donned my crown and regal robes of crimson and ermine and rode boldly through the streets of London to the Guildhall. And there, I delivered a rousing speech to my people.

"I come to you in my own person," I began, staring out nervously into the sea of faces before me, "to tell you that which you already see and know; that is, how traitorously and rebelliously a number of Kentishmen have assembled themselves against us and you. What I am you right well know: I am your Queen, to whom, at my coronation, when I was wedded to the realm and laws of the same, you promised your allegiance and obedience. My father, as you all know, possessed the same regal state, which now rightly is descended to me, and to him you always showed yourselves most faithful and loving subjects; and therefore I do not doubt that you will show yourselves likewise to me.

"I say to you, on the word of a prince, I cannot tell how naturally a mother loves her child, for I was never the mother of any; but certainly, if a prince and governor may as naturally and earnestly love her subjects as the mother loves the child, then assure yourselves that I, being your lady and mistress, do as earnestly and tenderly love and favour you. And I, thus loving you, cannot but think that you as heartily and faithfully love me. And then I doubt not but we shall give these rebels a short and speedy overthrow.

"But for marriage, I will not, for my own pleasure, choose where I lust, for I am not so desirous that I need a husband. For God, I thank Him, I have hitherto lived a virgin, and doubt not that with God's grace I am able so to live still. But if, as my progenitors have done before me, it may please God that I might leave some fruit of my body behind me to be your governor, I trust you would not only rejoice thereat, but also I know it would be to your great comfort. And, on the word of a queen, I promise you that if it shall not probably appear to all the nobility and commons that this marriage shall be for the high benefit and commodity of the realm, then I will abstain from marriage while I live.

"I am minded to live and die with you, and strain every nerve in our cause, for this time your fortunes, goods, honour, personal safety, wives, and children are all in the balance. If you bear yourselves like good subjects, I am bound to stand by you, for you will deserve the care of your sovereign lady.

"And now, good subjects, pluck up your hearts, and like true men face up against these rebels, and fear them not, for I assure you I fear them nothing at all!"

The people greeted my words with resounding cheers, and a volley of caps flew up into the air. And I knew, yet again, they, like God, were on my side, and would fight for and with me.

"God save Queen Mary! There never was a more steadfast and true queen!" they cheered.

And as I walked out, fearlessly, head held high and staring straight ahead, never letting it show that the fear of assassins lurking in the crowd ready to burst out and plunge a dagger into my breast or back was very much in my mind, my people fell to their knees, and those nearest reached out to reverently touch or kiss the hem of my robe as if it were a holy relic being paraded past them. I was God's anointed sovereign and they knew it was by God's divine will that I reigned and against that a rebellious poet's passion was *nothing!*

My people did not disappoint me. And to reinforce their fighting spirit, I sent heralds out with copies of my speech to be read from every street corner and every square in the city to give the people heart should their courage falter. And I gave orders that whoever captured the traitor Wyatt, whether it be dead or alive, would be rewarded with a landed estate to be held in perpetuity by his heirs.

There was one moment when those about me feared all was lost, when the rebels penetrated the palace courtyard. My ladies raced about like chickens in a barnyard frightened by a fox, weeping and shrieking, "All is lost!" And Edward Courtenay wet his pants in terror and crawled under a table to hide, but I held my ground and ordered my people to "Fall to prayer, and I warrant we shall hear better news anon!"

To set an example for them, I dropped down onto my knees with my rosary in hand. Faithful Susan Clarencieux and devoted Jane Dormer followed my lead and knelt down behind me in a puff of velvet skirts, bowing their heads over their clasped hands and rosaries, and my other ladies dried their tears and followed suit.

"If God is for us, none can be against us!" I stoutly repeated the phrase that had become my battle cry. And I was right; soon word came that the rebels had been beaten back and cornered, and Wyatt himself was taken.

But I knew who was *really* behind it – *Elizabeth!* When I sent for her she claimed to be too ill to travel, just as she had when I had to fight for my throne. But I didn't believe her; she had played that card too many times before. When things were difficult or uncertain Elizabeth took to her bed rather than make a definite stand. I *knew* she was behind it! When rebellion exploded, like a lit powder keg, in my kingdom, I *knew* that Elizabeth was the guiding spirit that lit the fuse and tried to blast me off my throne. She was more accomplished at feigning sincerity than any play-actor; she was false and insincere. And I knew they wanted her. I saw it in their eyes whenever they looked at her, when they cheered her, the affection in their voices and in their eyes, the way they noted with approval her resemblance to our father. "There goes Great Harry's daughter!" they would say, ignoring me as if I were no more than a maidservant privileged to ride at her side and not the reigning and rightful Queen of England. I knew it was Elizabeth they loved, it was Elizabeth they wanted. They were only waiting for me to die – I knew they prayed for it. I had found broadsheets printed with prayers for "The Ascension of Elizabeth" shoved underneath my door, even on the altar of my private chapel and in my sewing basket; they wanted me to know, they wanted me to see them. Perhaps they thought grief would sicken me and I would die from it. But the throne was *not* her right and, by God and all His saints, I would *not* let her take it from me! Her minions would not snatch the crown from my head and put it on hers!

But even though they wanted her, the English could always be counted on to stand up for what is right, and they knew that *I* was right, God had chosen *me*, and Wyatt and his rebel army were wrong. So my people rose up to champion me, and the rebellion was quickly put down, and the leaders locked away in the Tower to await their just end upon the scaffold. Wyatt went to his death proclaiming Elizabeth innocent of any involvement, but I *knew* he was lying. He was in love with her, just as his father had been with that whore Anne Boleyn. Poor naïve Edward Courtenay, who had been gulled into being a part of it, believing that Elizabeth would marry him and make him king, suffered pangs of conscience and came and threw himself weeping at my feet and confessed all. I pardoned the poor fool, of course, and bestowed a dukedom and income upon him with the stipulation that he live out the rest of his life abroad, and thus rid myself, and my court, of him once and for all.

In order to save myself, and my throne, and assert my authority, I could no longer be "Merciful Mary". I could not let a certain rebellious and misguided element think I was just a weak and feeble female at the mercy of her own heart. Those who had rebelled against me must die, lest others think they could do the same and not suffer the consequences. They must not think me womanly and weak, that I would shrink from sending traitors to the scaffold. And that, sadly, would now have to include Lady Jane. Renard was right. After this rebellion it would not be safe to let her live. Her father had lent his support to Wyatt's rebellion on condition that Jane be restored to the throne. He was captured caked with mud and quaking with fear hiding inside a hollow tree. He too must die, and die with the knowledge that his actions had sealed his daughter's fate.

His wife, my cousin Frances, came to see me to plead for his life, though she said not a word about her daughter, languishing in the Tower, an innocent traitor condemned to die though guilty of no crime.

Frances was dressed in vivid shades of pink, crimson, and orange, all spangled with gold beads, fringe, and pearls, which the truth behoves me to admit ill became her; with her dark red hair, beady little eyes, florid face, and ample figure it made her appear alarmingly like a pig dressed up in fine array. As she paced nervously before me, she slapped her riding crop against her meaty pink palm, rough and calloused from years of hard riding despite the ladylike gloves she always wore, and her brisk bow-legged stride and the clacking heels of the gold-spurred riding boots she always wore further betrayed her nervousness.

In discreet words, comparing her husband's moral and carnal weakness to an occasional craving for quince pie, Frances confided in me about her husband's sin, for which the Lord would surely punish him, explaining that from time to time throughout the years of their marriage he had sometimes strayed, as men often do, when Frances was with child, or left him too long to his own devices, or the urge just like lightning struck him. But instead of turning to a petticoat, serving girls and the like, to slake his lust, Henry Grey had upon rare occasions followed another fancy when he found himself drawn to breeches and the handsome figures that filled them instead, usually grooms and stablehands, men both handsome and rough, never effete pretty boys. Afterward, repentant and contrite, he had always come back to Frances, weeping and bearing gifts of jewellery; to illustrate this she flourished a plump diamond-laden pink hand and gestured to the icy glitter of her necklace. "He has always been a weak man," Frances said with a contemptuous snort. Thus when Tom Seymour came a-wooing, singing of cakes and ale, and bearing a platter and flagon of the same, Henry Grey was powerless to resist and had all too readily succumbed to his blandishments, big dreams, and promises of wealth and glory, when Tom promised that, if given a free hand, he would marry Jane to Edward and make her Queen of England.

"He approached me in the same manner," Frances added, further confirming that Tom Seymour was singularly unimaginative when it came to wooing. "He followed me out when I went riding, skipping along after me with a basket of cakes and a flagon of ale, belting out that ridiculous 'Cakes and Ale' song over and over again until I thought I would go mad. Finally, I reined in my horse and put a stop to it. When he caught up with me, I kicked the cakes from his hand with the toe of my riding boot and slapped the ale from his hand with my riding crop, and galloped off, leaving him sucking his smarting fingers. I am not some little milkmaid ready to flop on my back when a handsome gallant comes calling with a song on his lips and the makings of a picnic in hand!" To emphasize her indignation and scorn, as she spoke she paced back and forth and repeatedly slapped her riding crop against her palm.

When Tom Seymour died, she had thought the whole silly scheme was at an end. And then, when King Edward died, Northumberland, who had replaced the Seymour brothers – and was a greater villain than either "that fool Tom or his chilly brother, or the pair of them put together" – proposed a way to make Seymour's scheme come true in an even greater and grander way, and Henry Grey was all too ready to listen. He had become accustomed to thinking of his daughter as the someday Queen and was loath to relinquish the dream.

"And here we are." Frances sighed. "My lack-wit fool of a husband is in the Tower and my daughter was Queen of England and sat on a stolen throne wearing a stolen crown for nine days, and both of them shall die for their presumption, unless it pleases Your Majesty to show mercy."

I took Frances's hands in mine and bade her kneel and pray with me. Then I sent her away with a kiss and a loving embrace, promising I would take all she said into consideration. I just wanted to be rid of her; I felt her confession about her husband's forays into the sin of Sodom had sullied my soul and I just wanted to be alone to pray and cleanse myself of it. And I did not want to tell Cousin Frances to her face that her husband had to die; he had supported a rebellion to pull me from my throne and place his daughter upon it, and even if my heart cried out for mercy, as a monarch I must stand firm and send him, and poor little Jane, to a traitor's death upon the scaffold. Afterwards, it was up to God to deal with his wicked, weak, and wayward soul.

Though Henry Grey wept, for his feckless self, and perhaps even shed a tear or two for his daughter, Jane herself took it well. When the verdict was pronounced and they turned the axe heads towards her, she did not break down. Calmly and resignedly she announced, "I am ready and glad to end my woeful days."

Only afterwards, back in her room at the Tower, with her devoted Mrs Ellen, did she let her tears flow and her fear show, clinging to her nurse and sobbing, "I am innocent, and I do not deserve this sentence, but I should not have accepted the crown."

Renard was beside me, to lend his support, when I had to sign her death warrant. When I hesitated he reassured me, saying, "God will not allow you to condemn unjustly."

Still hoping against hope to save her, I sent the kindly Dr Feckenham to offer her a reprieve; I would spare her life if she would renounce her heretical beliefs and convert to the true faith, but she refused. I knew she would. Her religion, however blasphemous and false her beliefs were, was the only thing Jane had to cling to; I could not imagine her letting go even if it meant falling straight into the fiery pit of Hell. And she was not sad to die. When urged to grasp this opportunity to save herself, she turned to Dr Feckenham and said dolefully, "Alas, Sir, it is not my desire to prolong my days. I assure you, my life has been so odious to me that I long for nothing so much as I long for death." Then she asked him to leave her alone to make her peace with God.

"Death will give pain to my body for its sins, but my soul will be justified before God. If my faults deserve punishment, my youth at least, and my imprudence, were worthy of excuse. God and posterity will show me more favour," Lady Jane announced stoically as she looked out upon the scaffold being built below her window on Tower Green.

Touched by her bravery, Dr Feckenham humbly begged leave to attend her on her last day. And, courageous spirit aside, the frightened little girl that she really was mutely nodded assent then turned away, back to the window, lest he see her chin quiver with the tears she was fighting to hold back.

I sat in my room beside the portrait of Prince Philip and held her miniature in my rosary-wrapped hand and wept as she mounted the scaffold. As penance, I bade Dr Feckenham, who had walked with Jane every step of the way on her final journey, come to me afterwards and made myself listen to a full account of her death. I closed my eyes, hugged Jane's picture and my rosary to my heart, and drank in every word as tears poured down my face as I imagined it. I wanted to feel as if I were actually there, bearing witness to it; that would be my punishment, my cross to bear.

Early that most saddest of February mornings, before she dressed, I sent a panel of matrons to examine her, even though Jane reacted with angry tears and considered it a grave indignity and humiliation to have to lie down on her bed and lift her shift and spread her legs to their probing and prying fingers and answer their equally intrusive questions. I know she thought I did it out of spite, and I am sorry for it. I'm sorry I could not have been there to hold her hand and stroke her hair and try to make her understand. Poor little thing, she could not know that I was grasping at that little wisp of cobweb-slender hope that even though she was a most unwilling wife, if the examination showed her to be with child I could tear up her death warrant and stay her execution and buy us both more time – time for Jane to think, time for Dr Feckenham to try to persuade her, time in which I could delay signing the death warrant that would stain my hands with my sixteen-year-old cousin's innocent blood. But she was not with child. How could she be? She loathed Guildford Dudley and hated his touch and had not shared his bed in months. And since she would not renounce her religion, not even to save her life, Jane had no choice but to dry her angry, humiliated tears and prepare herself to die. So, really, it was not my fault; it was her own decision. My signature on the death warrant was just a formality.

After watching, weeping, from her window as Guildford walked to the scaffold, pale as the ghost he would soon be, trembling but trying to be brave, elegant in black velvet with not a strand of his golden hair out of place, and after his corpse made the return journey by cart wrapped in a bloodstained sheet, it was Jane's turn.

In a plain, black silk dress that left her neck and shoulders bare, with her hair pinned up tight so as not to impede the axe, she walked to the scaffold, her head bowed over a small black-velvet-bound prayer book suspended from a cord about her waist. She was accompanied by the faithful Mrs Ellen, the nurse who had seen her into this world and would now see her out of it, Sir John Bridges, the Lieutenant of the Tower, who had grown quite fond of her and had begged her little prayer book as a remembrance, and Dr Feckenham, who still hoped fear would at the last moment sway her to grasp at this last chance to save her life.

"There is a time to be born and a time to die and the day of our death is better than the day of our birth." Jane spoke the words aloud as she inscribed them with a pencil of black charcoal inside her little black prayer book before handing it to Sir John and thanking him for his great kindness to her.

From the scaffold, in a timorous little voice, she bravely and very formally addressed the crowd that had come to watch her die. Some were actually presuming to call her a Protestant martyr!

"Good people, I am come hither to die, and by law I am condemned to the same. The fact, indeed, against the Queen's Highness was unlawful, and the consenting thereunto by me: But touching the procurement and desire thereof by me, I do wash my hands in innocency before God and the face of you good Christian people." She wrung her hands and swallowed hard before continuing. "I pray you all to bear me witness that I die a true Christian woman. And now, good people, while I am alive, I pray you assist me with your prayers."

And then she knelt and in a tear-choked voice, recited in English the 51ˢᵗ Psalm, the *Miserere Mei Deus*. Then she rose and went to Dr Feckenham and gratefully embraced him and kissed his cheek.

"Though true it is that we shall never meet in Heaven unless God turns your heart, I beseech Him to abundantly reward you for your kindness toward me. Although I must needs say it was more unwelcome to me than my instant death is terrible."

They stood together, embracing, for a long time, then Jane sighed resignedly and turned away, squaring her shoulders, and trying to be brave as she faced the black-hooded executioner.

He knelt down and asked her forgiveness for what he was about to do, and Jane readily pardoned him.

"I pray you dispatch me quickly," she said, and he nodded his consent. When he started to turn away, panic seized her, and she grasped his arm. "Will you take my head off before I lay it down?" she asked fearfully.

"No, Madame," he reassured her most kindly.

Mrs Ellen came forward then and tied a blindfold over Jane's eyes and her nimble fingers made quite sure the pins restraining her hair were secure.

But when she knelt in the straw and reached for the block, Jane's hands found only empty air.

Only then did she give way to panic, whimpering over and over again with rising panic, "What shall I do? Where is it? Where is it?" until Dr Feckenham, moved to pity and unable to bear her suffering, stepped forward and took the blindly groping, flailing hands in his and gently guided them to the wooden block, his hand lingering reassuringly over hers for a moment to give what comfort he could.

"Thank you!" she breathed. And with a deep breath, Jane laid her head down.

"Lord, into Thy hands I commend my spirit," she said as the muscular arms of the headsman raised the axe up high.

A single stroke and a great gush of blood ended Jane's life. The headsman bent and caught her head up by its hair and held it high as he cried out the traditional words, "So perish all the Queen's enemies! Behold the head of a traitor!" though it was noted by some, the honest Dr Feckenham among them, that his voice was lacking in both volume and robustness.

After Dr Feckenham left me, I retreated to my private chapel. I prayed for her soul, fasted, and wept for what I had been forced to do even when my heart cried out to be merciful and lenient to this poor, misused little girl who wanted only to be left alone with her beloved books. Now she lay rotting, headless, in the musty crypt beneath the floor of the Tower's chapel, St Peter ad Vincula, with Anne Boleyn, her brother and lovers, the dainty harlot-queen Catherine Howard, and her bawd Lady Rochford. Poor Jane, I thought, to lie entombed with such a lewd company.

As I knelt in prayer suddenly the stained-glass window nearest me shattered in a shower of rainbow prisms and sharp shards of jewel-coloured glass. A dead dog, its body still warm, landed beside me, the pink ribbon of its tongue unfurling to lick the hem of my skirt. I screamed and clasped my chest as I saw that its head had been shaven in a gross parody of a monk's tonsure and it was dressed in crudely sewn robes cut from a rough cloth sack to mimic a monk's habit. The noose that had strangled it was still around its neck.

Alarmed by my scream, my ladies, led by Susan and Jane, rushed to my side, as the guards streamed in and then just as quickly out again in pursuit of the culprit after first ascertaining that I was all right. I was seated and given a cup of warm wine while Susan and Jane rubbed my hands and feet, trying to calm me and slow my rapidly racing heart, and another sponged the dog's blood from the hem of my garnet velvet gown. Then Ambassador Renard was there, kneeling beside me, whispering urgently, now that Jane was gone there was still the threat of Elizabeth. The people loved her, the Protestants loved her, she was their flame-haired white-clad candle of hope, and something *must* be done about her . . .

I knew he was right. Elizabeth had always been more dangerous than our poor little cousin Jane. It was Elizabeth who should have died upon that scaffold, not Jane. So I sent my own doctors and my personal litter to convey her to London, for, sick or not, Elizabeth had much to answer for. . . .

❧ 28 ❧

Elizabeth

Kat shook me from a light and restless sleep, her face a gaunt, ashen, red-eyed mask of fright all wet with tears, to tell me that Lady Jane Grey was dead. Mary had signed the death warrant and sent our harmless, guiltless little cousin to the block, to pave the way for her Spanish bridegroom's safe arrival.

I sat up in my bed and hugged my knees, letting my tears drip down on them, as I bowed my head and remembered the shy little scholar I had known, and not always been kind to, at Chelsea, the little mouse who wanted only to stay holed up with her beloved books, burrowing into them to feed her hunger for knowledge, who, even during her confinement in the Tower, pursued her study of Hebrew so that she might read the Old Testament in its original tongue.

I could see her shy, intent little face back in the schoolroom at Chelsea as she answered me when I asked why she was so passionate about her studies.

"I will tell you, Cousin Bess," she earnestly confided, sitting down opposite me in the window seat. The pale golden sunlight streamed in through the diamond-shaped panes to cast a beatific nimbus about her chestnut hair and plain grey gown embellished with but a little black silk braid that her nervous nail-bitten fingers constantly tried to unravel whenever they were not occupied with writing, reading, or sewing. "I will tell you a truth which perchance you will marvel at. One of the greatest benefits that God ever gave me is that He sent me, with such sharp, severe parents, so kind and gentle a schoolmaster. When I am in the presence of either Father or Mother, whether I speak, keep silent, sit, stand, or go, eat, drink, be merry, or sad, be sewing, dancing, playing, or doing anything else, I must do it, as it were, as perfectly as God made the world, or else I am so sharply taunted, so cruelly threatened and tormented with harsh words, pinches, slaps, and other chastise-ments – which I will not name for the honour I bear my parents – to such a degree that I think myself truly in Hell, till the time comes when I must go to Master Aylmer, who teaches me so gen-tly, so pleasantly, imbuing in me such joy in learning, as he has himself, that I think of nothing else all the while I am with him. And when I am called from him I fall to weeping, because what-ever else I do but learning is full of great trouble and dislike for me. And thus my books have become so much my pleasure, and more, so that everything else is but trifles and troubles to me."

Remorse filled me now at the memory. I had seen Jane un-dressed once, when I came into her room just as she was emerging from her bath to be wrapped in the sheet Mrs Ellen held up for her. Jane had just returned from a visit to her parents, and I saw the bruises, ugly blotches of urine-hued yellow, grey-green, brown, and purplish-black all up and down her arms, buttocks, legs, and back, and silvery-white scars as if the skin had split dur-ing a brutal caning, all places that when she was properly dressed would never show. I had been so preoccupied with Tom then, I let it go. It did not properly register; I did not feel the outrage that I should, as I did now when it was too late. I wished now I had been kinder and the true friend Jane never had but always needed; per-haps I could have helped her. I should have done something! I should not have let my head become so soggy with lust that I failed to render aid to a soul in need, a little girl who lacked my own strength. I had learned the art of self-preservation early, to rely on and fight for myself, when my mother died and my father could not stand the sight of me, but Jane had not; she had been beaten down since the day she was born, she never had a chance, she never learned to fight, only to hide like a frightened rabbit in a den of books. Now she was dead and beyond all mortal help. Poor little soul, she never had a *real* chance to truly live!

"Godspeed, Jane," I whispered fervently through my tears. "May you find with God in His Heaven the love and tenderness you were always denied here on earth."

"Merciful Mary" had just spilled the blood of our kinswoman, a delicate girl she used to dress up like a doll, whose abundant waves of chestnut hair she used to brush, and whose now-severed neck she had decked with rubies for her wedding day, a girl she *knew* to have been innocent, the forced and bullied pawn of ambitious, greedy men jockeying for power in a real-life game of chess where the throne of England was the ultimate prize. Jane, whose only crime – and it was only a crime in fervent, fanatical Catholic eyes – was her unshakable devotion to the Protestant faith. She had been true to her conscience even as Mary had always been true to hers; even though they disagreed, they had that mule-stubborn devoutness in common, and Mary had killed her. That day I was ashamed to call her my sister. And if she could sign away the life of our cousin, what would she do to me, her own sister?

That night I dreamt of a small army of woodsmen striking the tops off the trees growing in a fine park. At each strike of the axe, blood spurted from their trunks, and as their verdant heads toppled they gave off bloodcurdling screams as the blood gurgled and spewed out. And in their midst, wandering frantic, frightened, and lost, hands outstretched as she staggered and stumbled, flailing and groping blindly amongst the falling, bleeding green branches, was a small, slender white-gowned ghost, the only colour about her the bright red blood bubbling from her neck, trickling down to stain her gown. "*Where is it? Where is it?*" a hysterical little voice sobbed over and over, even though she had no head and thus no lips to speak the words with, just as Jane herself had done when she knelt blindfolded in the straw and reached out, groping blindly for the block.

I bolted up in bed screaming and did not dare close my eyes again for the rest of the night. Later, Kat would tell me that the woodsmen at Bradgate Manor, Jane's childhood home, upon hearing of the death of their poor little lady, had taken it upon themselves to behead the trees in the park as a gesture of mourning for her.

They came for me soon afterwards. I knew they would. Knowing and fearing that, and the uncertainty of the outcome, made me even sicker. Disbelieving my physician's letter that I was far too ill to travel, Mary had thoughtfully sent two of her own physicians and her personal litter to bear me back to London with the utmost care and comfort.

For three days the learned doctors poked and prodded me; they scrutinized and sniffed my urine, felt my pulse, and noted my pallor, and finally diagnosed an imbalance of the watery humours, but nothing serious enough to keep me from travelling. One of them made so bold as to tell me that he thought fear or perhaps even – he begged forgiveness for the presumption – a guilty conscience was the root from which my illness stemmed.

The fear that death awaited me at the end of my journey made me even sicker, and my escorts slowed our pace to a mere walk lest they arrive in London bearing my corpse. As I lay back against the soft velvet cushions, my head and joints an aching agony, and my vision wavering as if I looked up and out at the world from under water, I fought down wave after wave of nausea. Sometimes it became unbearable and I had to shout for them to halt as I leaned over the side of the litter, Kat holding me so I did not tumble out, and gathering back my hair, as, dignity be damned, I vomited into the road until, exhausted, I slumped back against the cushions again, the bitter bile burning my throat and tears stinging my eyes.

At my insistence, I travelled with the curtains open wide, to give me air, contradicting Mary's orders that they stay closed. The people saw me lying there pale and wan, as white as my gown, my flame-red hair glowing all the brighter against my deathly pallor, and shook their fists at my escorts, and shouted, "Shame!" and called the wrath of God down upon their heads.

Word quickly spread that I was being taken to London as a prisoner of my own sister, and the people rushed to line the roadsides. They tossed bunches of flowers and sweet-smelling herbs onto my litter and, hearing I was ill, more than one country housewife ran out to humbly bob a curtsy and present some tried and true remedy to me, assuring me that it would do me "a world of good".

"God save our Princess Elizabeth!" I must have heard it shouted ten thousand times before I reached Whitehall, and every one was a shot of courage to my heart. The warmth of their love banished the deathly chill of fear, and my nausea eased. I sat up a little straighter as I returned their smiles and waves. I knew that I was loved and that I was not alone.

The London I returned to stank of death, starting with the rebels' severed heads impaled on pikes adorning the city gates like grotesque gargoyles. I gagged and had to clutch my pomander ball to my nose, but the sweet, spicy scent of oranges and cloves was a poor defence against the stink of death. And on every street corner stood a gibbet with the rotting body of one or more rebels hanging from it like rotten fruit. I felt nauseous and faint. It took all my will not to order the curtains drawn, but I could not disappoint the people. They needed to see me, and I needed to see them, and hear their voices. We gave each other heart, and the strength to go on and face whatever lay in store.

When I arrived at Whitehall I was taken under guard to my apartments. The guards crossed their halberds behind my back the moment that I crossed the threshold. Further proof that I was indeed a prisoner. I pleaded to see Mary, I tried in vain to remind her of the promise she had made me when we parted, but my every request was denied. Instead, I was informed that I would be taken to the Tower upon the morrow, and must be ready at dawn, for the tide tarries for no one, not even a princess.

One hundred guards in white coats arranged themselves in attentive, straight-backed rows in the garden below my window, their white coats glowing ghostly in the moonlight. It was Mary's way of telling me that escape was impossible. And every time I heard the rattle of armour, the clank of swords, the thud of booted feet, or a shouted command, four panic-filled words rang shrilly inside my head: *There is no escape!*

I did not sleep at all that night. I could not, for above my head was a terrible din. My spiteful cousin, Mary's pet, the Countess of Lennox, had established her kitchen directly above my rooms, and the whole night pans rattled and banged, clattered and clanged, as the smells of fish and meat and smoke seeped through the floorboards to further add to my discomfort and turn my fragile stomach until I had no choice but to keep a basin close beside me. I sat up the whole night through, dressed for travel, but in white to proclaim my innocence, waiting to greet the dawn and the fresh horrors it would bring, knowing that soon I would be locked up inside the Tower where my mother had spent her final days before she was taken out to the scaffold on the green to die. I watched the orange sun bounce off the silver armour and halberds of the guards standing at attention in the garden below my window and wondered how many sunrises I had left.

When the Marquess of Winchester and the Earl of Sussex came to me, I threw myself on their mercy, imploring them to let me write a letter to the Queen, my sister, before they took me away to a prison from which I might never return.

I watched them anxiously, pacing, gesturing, and murmuring as they conferred. I heard only bits and snatches of their conversation, but it was enough to tell me that they were both keenly aware that if my sister died without issue I would be the next Queen and might well remember any favour or courtesy they did me or failed to render me when I needed it most. Finally, the Earl of Sussex decisively stepped forward and said I would be allowed to write my letter and he would personally convey it into the Queen's hands.

I thanked him profusely, then ran to my desk. I murmured a quick prayer, then took up my pen, knowing that this would be the most important letter I would ever write.

March 16, 1554.

If any ever did try this old saying, "that a king's word was more than another man's oath," I most humbly beseech Your Majesty to verify it to me, and to remember your last promise and my last demand, that I be not condemned without answer and due proof, which it seems that I now am; for without cause proved, I am by your Council from you commanded to go to the Tower, a place more wonted for a false traitor than a true subject, which though I know I deserve it not, yet in the face of all this realm it appears that it is proved. I protest before God, Who shall judge my truth, whatsoever malice shall devise, that I never practised, counselled, nor consented to anything that might be prejudicial to your person in any way, or dangerous to the state by any means. And therefore I humbly beseech Your Majesty to let me answer afore yourself, and not suffer me to trust to your Councillors; yea, and that before I go to the Tower, if it be possible; if not, before I be further condemned. Howbeit, I trust assuredly Your Highness will give me leave to do it before I go, that thus shamefully I may not be cried out on, as I now shall be; yea, and that without cause. Let conscience move Your Highness to take some better way with me than to make me condemned in all men's sight before my desert is known. I have heard in my time of many cast away for want of coming to the presence of their Prince; and in late days I heard my Lord of Somerset say that if his brother had been suffered to speak with him he had never suffered; but the persuasions were made to him so great that he was brought in belief that he could not live safely if the Lord Admiral lived, and that made him give consent to his death. Though these persons are not to be compared to Your Majesty, yet I pray God that like evil persuasions not persuade one sister against the other, and all for that they have heard false report. Therefore, once again, kneeling with humbleness of heart, because I am not suffered to bow the knees of my body, I humbly crave to speak with Your Highness, which I would not be so bold as to desire if I knew not myself most clear, as I know myself most true. And as for the traitor Wyatt, he might peradventure write me a letter, but I pray God confound me eternally if ever I sent him word, message, token, or letter, by any means, and to this truth I will stand in till my death.

    I humbly crave but only one word of answer from yourself. Your Highness's most faithful subject, that hath been from the beginning, and will be to my end,
Elizabeth

As I neared the end I noticed that a goodly portion was blank below my signature, tempting and fertile ground for any forger seeking to put incriminating words into my mouth and "prove" my guilt so that Mary might have sure and certain evidence to condemn me, so I took up my pen again and drew wavy diagonal lines down the length of the page.

By the time I had finished the tide had turned, and it was too late to safely embark, so I must wait another anxious day and night, praying that Mary would remember and keep her promise and send for me so that I might kneel and plead my case directly before her.

Mary was furious when she found out what had occurred. She railed at Sussex for disobeying her, but he took it well, knowing he had done the right thing, and earned my everlasting gratitude.

But my words failed to soften her heart and she sent not one single word to me in response.

"My Lord of Sussex, I have a good memory," I said softly, laying my hand on his arm and fixing him with a meaningful gaze when he returned the next morning to convey me to the Tower. *"Thank you!"* I added in a fervent whisper.

He nodded and bowed his head deferentially, to show me he understood, as he draped my grey velvet cloak about my shoulders.

We departed at dawn even though the wind howled and the rain shot down from the pewter sky like arrows, pelting and piercing us, stinging any exposed skin it touched. We had barely set foot outside before we were soaked to the skin, but still we made our way to the barge, trudging through the mud, our pace hampered and slowed by our waterlogged clothes. The weight of water in my skirts caused them to slap and cling to my limbs, and more than once nearly caused me to fall. Kat and Blanche Parry, who accompanied me, had the same difficulty, and Winchester and Sussex, and our guards, were all most solicitous, reaching out each time to catch and steady us as we tripped and trudged our way to the jetty.

The oarsmen had to fight the raging current, and more than once the barge came close to capsizing; it was as if the swirling brown waters of the Thames were loath to take me to Traitor's Gate and would rather drown me instead. Kat, Blanche, and I clung fearfully together as the barge pitched and rolled, and Winchester and Sussex debated what to do, whether to make for shore or continue, expressing concern that we would be dashed against the piers of the bridge, but in the end we made it safely to that grim and foreboding fortress and docked at Traitor's Gate, where Sir John Bridges, the Lieutenant of the Tower, and six yeomen guards waited to receive me.

I could not bear to pass through that portal, knowing that most who entered there never came out except to lay their head on the block on the hill or the green. To do so seemed to be an admission of my guilt, and in despair I sank down upon the steps, even as the water rushed over my shoes.

"Your Grace, you must not sit here!" Sir John Bridges implored, concern etched deep upon his kindly face, as he held out his hand to me.

Sniffling, I turned my head away from that kind face and proffered hand. "Better to sit here than in a worse place!" I said, with a defiant toss of my head.

I shivered and wept and thought about my mother. Eighteen years ago she had passed through this portal, to a prison she would never emerge from except to die. Even now her headless body lay mouldering in the crypt of the Tower's chapel, St Peter ad Vincula, St Peter in Chains. Some even believed her ghost still walked the Tower, an unquiet spirit protesting the injustice that had robbed her of her life. Would I catch a glimpse of her phantom shade, I wondered as I sat there shivering, chilled to the bone, on the cold, wet, slimy stone steps. She also had worn a white gown and a grey cloak when she was taken by barge, I suddenly remembered hearing, and, glancing down at my own attire, shivered all the more.

Suddenly an ineffectually stifled sob intruded upon my miserable reverie and I turned to see one of the yeomen, a fair young fellow with hair the colour of straw, snivelling, with his eyes full of pity as he looked down upon me from his great gangling height.

It was like a sudden slap across my face.

"Don't cry for me!" I commanded. "No man need ever weep for me!"

I shot up, as fast as my sodden skirts would allow, trying not to stumble as they tangled themselves around my limbs, and walked boldly through Traitor's Gate, into the Tower of London, with all the majesty and dignity I could summon, defying my resemblance to a drowned red rat, and vowing that I would hold my head up high until the instant the headsman struck it off, but it would *never* droop or fall of my own free will!

Framed by the dark yawning mouth of Traitor's Gate, I paused suddenly and spoke in clear, ringing tones, my eyes commanding all who heard me to believe each and every word: "Here landeth as true a subject, being prisoner, as ever landed at these stairs. Before Thee, O God, do I speak it, having no other friend than Thee alone. O Lord, I never thought to come here as a prisoner!" Then I turned and looked at each of the yeomen guards one by one, meeting each man's eyes. "I pray you all, good friends and fellows, to bear me witness that I come in as no traitor but as true a subject to the Queen's Majesty as any as is now living."

One of the yeomen muttered approvingly that I was indeed Great Harry's daughter. "Aye, the livin' spit o' him!" he said proudly. "God preserve Your Grace!" he called after me, and I could hear his heart in every word, and those of the other guards as they took up his cry.

I paused a moment to face him, to nod my thanks. "Great Harry's *and* Anne Boleyn's daughter as well!" I said proudly; I could never forget the woman who had, out of her own tragedy and proud, defiant spirit, taught me never to surrender.

"Lead on, Lieutenant Bridges!" I said with feigned bravado. "Take me to my dungeon!"

"Oh no, Your Grace!" he hastened to assure me as he caught up with me. "We have a nice, comfortable room all prepared for you, with a fire to chase the chill out of your bones!"

The room was indeed pleasant for a prison cell – a goodly sized circular chamber with a vaulted ceiling and a great fireplace. There was a bed for me and pallets for my ladies, and there were three tall, arched windows with seats set deep into the thick walls where I might sit and take advantage of the light to sew or read, and also breathe in a little fresh air.

I was told, somewhat abashedly, by Sir John, that my mother had lodged there before me. And for a few moments, curiosity overcame my fear, and I walked around touching the furnishings, hangings, and walls, wondering if she too had touched these things. Had she sat in this chair, had she leaned her forehead against this glassy pane as she looked out, had her fingers idly caressed this tapestry, perhaps lingering to fastidiously pluck away a piece of lint or stray thread, had she lain awake and restless, her mind consumed with worry, in this very bed, had her anxious, restless, pacing footsteps worn at this very floor?

There were inscriptions carved crudely into the walls.

> *To mortals' common fate thy mind resign,*
> *My lot today tomorrow may be thine.*

and

> *While God assists us, envy bites in vain,*
> *If God forsake us, fruitless all our pain –*
> *I hope for light after the darkness.*

I ran my fingers over the words, reading them with my fingertips, and wondering if she, or some other doomed soul, had carved them. It might even have been poor Jane.

For the first time in many years I felt my mother was close to me. It gave me a strange sort of comfort to know what had been her prison was now mine. That I now walked where she had walked and slept where she had slept. Though I knew the floors had been swept many a time since she had walked here, I was sorely tempted to kneel down and lay my palms upon the floor, as if that senseless gesture could make me feel even closer to her. And I wondered if these feelings were a portent that I would soon be very close to her indeed, that I would follow in her footsteps up the thirteen steps of the scaffold. I thought I heard a rustle of skirts beside me then, and a voice from out of my past whisper urgently into my ear, *"Never surrender!"* The memory was so real it made me shiver. And seeing this, Kat and Blanche hurried to shoo me over to the fire and into some warm clothing, and with a weary sigh I gave myself over to their ministrations and soon found myself sitting bundled in a fur-trimmed robe by the fire as Kat vigorously towelled my hair and Blanche brought me a cup of warm spiced wine.

That night as I slipped wearily between the cold lawn sheets, the first of many nightmares in which the axe loomed large came to plague me. The headsman's axe swooped down on me, and I heard the flap of the ravens' wings, like a dark angel's, as they cackled and cawed. I saw my own head, grey and ghastly with blind, clouded eyes, impaled upon a pike, my red hair whipping in the wind, as the ravens ravenously picked at me, tearing at my rotting flesh, until the bone showed pearly white beneath. Each time I would bolt up in bed with a scream on my lips, shivering as if the cold of death had already invaded my bones; try as I might, in the Tower, I simply could not get warm enough.

I spent many days sitting listless and morose in one or another of the three window seats, watching the ravens, or else beside the fire, staring without seeing into the heart of the flames as if they held the answers I sought, wondering how long I had left. I told Kat and Blanche that I had decided, when the time came, to ask Mary to grant me the favour of the swift and sharper sword, to send to France for an executioner as my father had done for my mother. If he could do that for the woman he had once loved after that love had turned to hate, then so too could Mary for the sister she had once loved and used to pretend was her own little girl.

And yet . . . despite my despondency, somehow I felt I was not alone. There was a benevolent, protective presence that hung about me in that grim place of bloodshed, tears, and tortured souls.

One night, when I lay in darkness after the candle I had left burning had gone out, I saw a spark out of the corner of my eye. I watched as that lone spark multiplied into many, and wondered if I were dreaming or if a horde of fireflies had invaded my room. And then, out of the thick stone walls, seemingly walking upon the air, appeared two beautiful naked, golden-haired little boys walking hand in hand. They were surrounded by a dazzling brilliance that lit up the room and their very skin seemed to glow with an inner rosy-gold radiance of such a startling beauty and innocence it brought tears to my eyes. They came to stand, hovering, beside my bed, smiling down at me with such indescribably sweet smiles lighting up their cherubic faces. There was nothing lewd about their nakedness; they were just beautiful, innocent children, far too beautiful for this world. The elder one seemed to be about twelve, and the other, his little brother – I instinctively knew that they were brothers – appeared to be a year or two younger. Both had eyes the colour of bluebells and thick, curly shoulder-length golden hair.

Suddenly my heart leapt in my chest, and for a moment I feared it would stop and cease to beat for ever. In that instant, I *knew* who they were – the boy-king Edward V and his brother Richard, Duke of York, who had been foully done to death here in the Tower in the year 1483, smothered as they slept, it was said, their bodies buried at the foot of the stairs, upon order of their fiendish uncle Richard who coveted the throne for himself.

Still smiling down at me, they began to slowly fade away, the brilliance dimming, until I was left in darkness once again and fell into a deep sleep. I awoke late the next morning with a slight fever, feeling troubled and uncertain. I knew I would never know for certain if I had truly seen the ghosts of the murdered princes or if it had all been just a dream wrought by my troubled mind and this terrible blood-drenched place.

I continued to brood over it all that day, reliving that encounter, or dream, whichever it had been, over and over again, until, finally, I could stand it no longer and, when they continued to press me about what troubled me, I told Kat and Blanche about the pair of glowing golden naked boys who had come to visit me during the night.

Kat immediately set to weeping and wailing, hugging me so close I feared she would snap my ribs.

"Oh pet, it was a pair of Radiant Boys you saw, and the sight of them *always* means doom and gloom, and death coming soon to the one who sees them!"

"Stuff and nonsense!" sensible Welsh Blanche Parry declared.

"Dry your tears, woman, and don't frighten our princess with such drivel! My own grandam told me about Radiant Boys, and My Lady" – she knelt beaming at my feet and took both my hands in hers even as Kat continued to snivel – "you have *nothing* at all to fear! Rather, you should rejoice! The one who sees a Radiant Boy will rise to the summit of prosperity and wield great power! And you didn't see just one, My Lady, but *two! Two Radiant Boys!* Oh, just think what great things shall come to you!"

"Which is it to be then – death or prosperity?" I wondered as, shrugging them both off, gesturing for them to leave me be, I went to stand by the window and watch the antics of the ravens while, in whispers, they continued to debate what the sight of a Radiant Boy truly meant. All I knew was that, whether it had been a true visitation from a boy who had been cheated of his chance to be king, or just a fever-dream, I would never forget it, but a part of me liked to think that one who would have been a great king but had been robbed of his destiny had come to smile down on and bless me, to show me that even though I felt lost in the dark now, a bright future lay before me, and he, hand in hand with his little brother, had come to be the candles to show me the way, to illuminate my destiny.

❧ 29 ❧

Mary

But why did he not write to me? It seemed so strange that I had as yet received no letter from the man I was to marry. Talebearers gossiping within my hearing – I *know* they *wanted* me to hear them, they *wanted* to hurt me! – archly suggested that perhaps he was too busy, and with great glee and relish imparted tales of his amorous excesses.

They claimed he had mistresses, some liaisons of some duration, others only for one night, and numerous bastards born as a result of both. They said he sometimes exchanged clothes with his groom and went into low, common taverns to consort with the kind of women who frequented such places, his servant pretending to be the Prince, and the Prince enjoying a taste of freedom in the guise of his own servant.

I also heard tales of a golden-haired Spanish girl, an alluring little nymph, a bud rather than a full-blown rose, who rarely left her couch of satin sheets, upon which she lay naked, except for the jewels Philip gave her, and whose exquisite little toes Philip liked to kiss and suck.

Another scandalmonger told of a pair of twin sisters who shared a bath and washed each other most erotically while Philip and a few chosen friends watched. They were said to have had their portrait painted fondling one another's breasts, and the painting was rumoured to hang in Philip's bedchamber in a cunningly devised frame that also contained a religious painting by Señor Titian which could be manoeuvred via a lever to conceal the lascivious canvas if Philip so desired it.

There was also talk of a dancing girl who performed at private parties for men of wealth and means and in a haze of incense rose up out of a black enamelled red-velvet-lined coffin wearing only a corset, stockings, and tall leather boots, sometimes black, other times white, to dance seductively around the man she intended to offer herself to while sultry Moorish music played, ending her dance lying flat on the floor at his feet with her knees up and her legs spread wide so that her naked feminine parts were fully exposed to his gaze.

The talebearers also spoke of a cinnamon-skinned girl, with hair like raven silk and a ruby in her navel, from some heathen land, plucked from the jade green stone temple where she used to dance before a golden idol and given as a present to the Prince to console the bereaved young man after his wife died in childbirth.

Blushing in embarrassment and blinded by tears, I fled from such tales in horror, with my hands clasped tight over my ears, screaming at these "well-meaning" and "concerned" purveyors of slander to be silent if they could speak no good reports of my prince. But the damage was done. I could not outrun what was already inside my head; I carried these wild and lewd tales with me wherever I went and sometimes had lurid dreams about them at night.

I tried to quash the jealousy raging like a stormy sea inside of me, but I just could not do it. And, finally, in blackest despair, I sent for Ambassador Renard.

I ran to him the moment he came through the door, looking, I am sure, quite wild and frenzied, a very hag, with my hair and clothes all unkempt and my face red and swollen from crying.

"I cannot marry His Highness," I blurted out, "for he has been amorous! I am told he consorts with courtesans and dancing girls and has bastards too numerous to count!"

"*Madame!*" Ambassador Renard took a step back, a pained expression on his face, and his hand rising to clasp his heart as if my words had hurt it. "I can scarcely believe it! I *knew* those who opposed His Highness would try to discredit him by slandering his good name, but . . . Can it be? Have you actually *believed* these ludicrous tales?"

My heart leapt in my breast, eager to grasp at this newborn hope.

"You mean these wicked, lascivious tales are not true?" I asked hopefully.

"Madame, may I be so bold as to act as – dare I suggest it? – your uncle by proxy since you have no living male relative who can speak candidly and advise you on such matters?"

"Oh yes, *please* do!" I cried, grasping at his arm as if only he could save my heart from drowning in grief.

"Then come" – he led me to the window seat – "sit beside me, and dry your tears," he said kindly, "and I shall explain. Madame, they have told you these things in an attempt to poison your mind against Prince Philip. He married young, at sixteen, to a lovely young girl, the Princess Maria of Portugal; though an arranged marriage, as royal matches always are, it was also a love match. Sadly, she died two years later giving birth to their only son, Don Carlos. His Highness has been a grieving widower ever since. A handsome widower at the age of only eighteen, heir to Spain, the Low Countries, and the gold-rich Americas, Madame, it is no vainglorious boast that for some years he has been accounted the greatest catch in Europe, and I cannot begin to count the number of princesses who have been paraded before him as prospective brides, but he has rejected *all* of them, until you; he wants *you*, Madame, *only you*."

"Oh! Oh, Señor Renard, you are like unto a tonic to my heart and nerves! How can I ever thank you?" I cried, smiling through my tears.

"That is simple enough, Madame." He smiled. "You can thank me by drying your tears and stopping your ears to any more of this base slander."

"I will," I promised, "I will! And may God bless and preserve His Highness and speed him soon to me!"

"Amen!" Ambassador Renard said, smiling also as he bowed gallantly over my hand and took his leave of me.

God had well and truly blessed me; He had given me the prince of my dreams, and I must not let those gossipmongers acting as the Devil's agents succeed in taking him away from me!

❧ 30 ❧

Elizabeth

Sir John Bridges was unfailingly courteous, ever mindful of who I was and what I might someday become. Had I met him elsewhere I would never have taken him for a gaoler. He did everything in his power to make me comfortable and to set my mind at ease. He even had me to his home, a fine cottage within the confines of the Tower, to dine each evening with his family. And as we passed the Lady Jane's scaffold, which had not yet been dismantled, he did his best to distract me. And when I complained that I was sickening for want of fresh air, he allowed me to walk every afternoon in the little walled garden adjoining his house.

One day he even allowed me to visit the chapel, St Peter ad Vincula, and withdrew quietly, leaving two yeomen guards stationed discreetly outside the door to escort me back when I was ready.

My footsteps produced a ghostly echo as I traversed the dimly lit chapel. I sank down over the stone that covered my mother's mortal remains, and then, impulsively, I lay down, resting my cheek upon it as I had once rested my head upon her breast and listened to the soothing sound of her heartbeat. In that instant, memories of my mother came rushing back to me, so vivid and intense they took my breath away. It was as if I were standing in a doorway watching those within a chamber.

I saw my mother in a gown of apple-green brocade, shot through with glimmering golden threads, her bodice and the half-moon-shaped French hood that perched upon her head edged with pearls, and her black hair cascading down her back, all the way to her knees, as if she were a carefree maiden instead of a wife and mother. And about her neck, the pearls with the golden *B* I remembered so well. She threw her head back and laughed as she swirled and spun to the music.

And I was there; I must have been about three, in a russet velvet gown trimmed with gold braid and a cream satin kirtle and cap embroidered with golden butterflies. Patiently she instructed me in the steps, lifting up her full skirts so that I might see her dainty, green satin-shod feet deftly executing the steps.

"*Oui, chérie, très bien!*" She nodded brightly, smiling her approval at my childish attempts to emulate her steps, clasping her hands together as she smiled down at me. "You shall be the finest dancer at this court one day!"

And upon the window seat sat the man who might have been her twin, if she had one, my Uncle George. He strummed his lute and sang the haunting melody known as "Greensleeves", and his eyes followed my mother as his fingers caressed the lute strings.

And lurking in a corner was the one I secretly called "The Dragon Lady", the one with the beady eyes that burned with hate as she turned them first upon my mother and then upon her husband, my Uncle George. Even after my mother and uncle were dead and gone she would still be there, lurking in the shadows, vigilant and alert, always watching, poking her nose into other people's business, putting her eye to the keyhole or her ear to the door, until she also disappeared in the wake of the pert and pretty Catherine Howard, following her up the thirteen steps of the scaffold. Lady Rochford, I would later learn, had acted as go-between and helped my flighty and foolish stepmother to cuckold my father, and now they both lay entombed beneath the floor of St Peter ad Vincula, not far from my mother and Uncle George.

When the music stopped, my mother swept me up into her arms and sat down beside Uncle George on the window seat with me on her lap. There were coloured silk ribbons tied to the lute and my fingers reached out for them.

Laughing, Uncle George took me onto his lap and took my tiny hand in his big one and guided my fingers to pluck the strings. That day I played my first melody.

Then my lady-governess came to take my hand and lead me back to the nursery. As I looked back over my shoulder, my mother moved to sit closer to my Uncle George, and he began to tentatively pluck out the notes of a song he was composing, something about love, hesitantly singing, "and if the evergreen . . .", humming where the words were lacking.

My mother nodded and sang, ". . . should wither on the bough . . ."

He smiled and nodded back at her and replayed the notes as they sang together, "and if the evergreen should wither on the bough . . ." then paused to think, my mother tapping her chin and humming.

As I accompanied Lady Bryan down the hall, I heard their voices growing fainter, singing words that compared the stars to little candles in the sky. Did they know even then, I wonder, that their own lives were fated to be snuffed out like candles?

I would, I think, see them only once more, that day in the garden at Greenwich when my mother told me to "Never surrender!" Then they were both dead, their headless bodies entombed without ceremony beneath the cold stones upon which my cheek lay and my tears now dripped.

I do not know how long I lay there, trying to hold on to the memories, to my mother's laugh, her quick smile, and lively dark eyes. She was *so* alive! And the fine, masculine voice that sang, "I called my lady Greensleeves" as she danced, holding up her skirts so that I might see her feet, as her full hanging sleeves, of a design she had made famous to conceal a slight deformity on her left hand, swayed to the music.

When I emerged from the dim interior of the chapel, blinking my red-rimmed eyes and whisking the tears from my cheeks, the night had already begun to push the sun from the sky, like a mother impatient to shoo her child off to bed, and the stars were vying with the dying orange-tinged light to come out to show off their diamond-bright sparkle, like a jewel merchant opening his case to display his wares on a bed of tufted midnight velvet.

I looked back over my shoulder, back into the dark chapel, the wavering orange flames of the candles barely penetrating the gloom and, raising my hand to my lips, blew a kiss to my mother. Then I drew my back up fully erect, held my head up high, and walked back to my prison, determined, come what may, to do her proud.

Some nights I dreamed that the dead surrounded my bed. The radiant spirits of the two little murdered princes, my mother, Uncle George, and the friends who had died with them, the men Kat told me my mother had called her Evergreen Gallants on account of their loyalty, flighty Catherine Howard, vengeful Lady Rochford, and poor little Lady Jane – they were all there, thronged round my bed, staring down at me, but not to frighten me, to warn me to be careful lest I meet their fate, but also to give me heart, to give me hope. And sometimes at night as I tossed restlessly in my bed, one foot in and one foot out of the dreamland between sleeping and waking, I would hear the mischievous laughter of two little boys, and feel their little hands tugging at my hair and bedclothes, tickling the soles of my feet, suddenly uncovered and exposed to the cold, or soft breath blowing on my face in the dark. The kinds of tricks little boys played upon their big sister. Yet I still did not know if they were real or just figments of my imagination.

❧ 31 ❧

Mary

Why did he not write to me? He sent me jewels, but no letters! A smiling Ambassador Renard knelt and laid them one by one in the lap of my plum and gold brocade gown.

There was a dainty gold filigree necklace, as lacy and delicate as a cobweb, set with eighteen twinkling diamond brilliants, and a great table diamond as big as my thumb, and hanging below it, a large white teardrop pearl known as "La Peregrina", "The Wanderer", because it had travelled first from the Americas, and then to Spain, and now to England to be my bridal gift, but . . . no letter.

"No letter," I said mournfully as the tears began to flow, "when a few tender words written in his own hand would be worth more to me than all the jewels in Christendom!"

"But, Madame," Ambassador Renard said, "His Highness thinks a message carried from one set of lips to another is much more romantic than words written upon a page, thus he bade me tell you that these are the most lovely pair of gems in the world, barring two others – your eyes!"

"Oh! How romantic!" My heart melted like butter inside my breast. "Did he *really* say that?"

"Madame, having seen your eyes and how they shine with the love that fills your heart, I know *exactly* what he meant," Ambassador Renard gallantly asserted as I clasped my beloved's gifts to my galloping heart and lay back, almost swooning, against the soft cushions of my chair. I glanced over at Prince Philip's portrait and impulsively held out my arms to it and in a breathless whisper sighed, *"Come to me, my beloved!"*

❧ 32 ❧

Elizabeth

The hour I spent each fine, fair day in the little walled garden adjoining Sir John's cottage brought a bright spot to my otherwise dull and dreary, fearful days. Indeed, it soon became the hour I looked forward to most of all.

Two little children, a boy of five called Christopher, and a tiny tottering tot, his little three-year-old sister, Susanna, came, at first shyly, then more boldly, to visit me, bringing me bedraggled bunches of flowers, some with dirty roots still trailing below their stems, picked by their clumsy but well-meaning fingers.

Susanna would settle herself, sucking her grimy thumb, upon my lap, and I would tell her stories. And her brother would take up a stick and brandish it like a sword, pretending that he would slay all my enemies, be my knight, and kill the dragons that threatened me, just like St George. Sometimes he would creep close and whisper in my ear a message of greeting from "the dark-haired young man who wishes to be remembered to you as your gypsy."

I knew at once whom he meant. Robert Dudley, my Robin, my childhood friend, born on the same day in the same year as myself. When Catherine Parr had brought me back to live at court, he was among the boys who shared my brother's schoolroom where he was clever at mathematics but a poor study at languages. We had become fast friends, united by our love of music, dancing, and, most of all, fast horses. I had dubbed him "my gypsy", because of his dark good looks, free spirit, and bold ways, as well as his magical affinity with horses. Like the gypsies who performed daring feats of horsemanship at the fairs, Robin possessed an innate understanding of horses; he knew instinctively how to gentle the most wild and troubled mount, and could soothe away their fears with a touch of a hand and words gently whispered in their ears.

Each time Christopher whispered in my ear, I would send back a greeting to "my dear gypsy". We had not seen each other for ever so long, not since I had left the court after my father died to make my home with Kate. How queer that we should be united here though divided by thick prison walls. Robin's father, John Dudley, the power-mad Duke of Northumberland, had been the mastermind behind poor Lady Jane's brief, ill-fated reign; he had married his youngest son, Robin's vain and petulant brother Guildford, to that poor little bookworm; and now, though the mighty Duke, pretty posing Guildford, and poor Jane had all gone to their deaths, Robin remained a prisoner in the Tower, still awaiting his fate, always wondering, just like me, if each day would be his last.

One day Susanna toddled up to me in her primrose-pink frock and pressed a sticky bunch of dirty, old, rusted keys into my hand, prattling in her baby talk "go free, Lady, go free!" and clapping and giggling at her own cleverness and pointing at the lock upon the gate.

Snapping to attention, my half-dozing guard rushed over and snatched the keys from my hand. Susanna instantly burst into tears, and I gathered her in my arms and stroked her straw-straight yellow hair while chiding that churl of a guard that any fool could see that the child meant no harm. She was far too young to understand, and any fool could see that the keys were of utterly no use at all; they were more likely to unlock a cupboard than the sturdy lock upon the gate, though in their degraded rusted condition, I doubted they could be used at all.

But that was the last I saw of my little friends. They were borne off by the guard, kicking and screaming, to be questioned by the Constable of the Tower, Sir John Gage, instead of the genial and understanding Lieutenant, Sir John Bridges, and given a stern rebuke. Henceforth, they were forbidden to come near the garden during my daily walks. Sir John Gage, that beastly man who would do his best to curtail my few liberties, had threatened to "flay the skin off their bums" if they ever dared speak to me again.

But bold little Christopher was still my brave knight, and the next day, when my guard was distracted, guffawing over the antics of a pair of the Tower's ravens bickering over a worm, brave little Christopher crept up to the gate, caught my eye, and whispered, "I can bring you no more flowers, Princess," as he stealthily tucked a folded paper into the flowering hedge that bloomed fragrant and pink beside the gate, then crept away as silently as he had come.

Casually, I stooped down to sniff the flowers and discreetly palmed the square of paper.

> *Dine with me tonight at nine o'clock.*
> *I have arranged all with Sir John Bridges.*
> *He will bring you to me.*
> *– Your Gypsy*

Oh how my heart soared at those words! For the first time since I had walked, an unwilling prisoner, through Traitor's Gate, I felt alive, truly alive! And, like any woman with a shred of vanity, I began planning what I would wear, considering each gown I had brought with me to the Tower and weighing its merits. Oh to see Robin again! I felt as if my impatiently thumping heart would burst clean out of my chest and gallop straight to his door, defying all locks and stone walls to be with him, the one I had always called my best friend.

I spent over an hour fussing before my mirror, trying on first one gown and then another, nearly driving Kat and Blanche to distraction, before finally settling on a gown of lion's mane tawny embellished with gold tassels and braid.

For some reason I couldn't quite understand, I did not want to go to Robin wearing virgin white. Perhaps it was merely because I was pale enough from imprisonment and worry, or perhaps it was something more. Perhaps some part of me wanted him to see me as a flesh-and-blood woman and not a plaster saint evoking chastity. I do not pretend to know or understand, I only know that, that night, I could not bear to wear white.

I trembled with nervous anticipation as I followed Sir John along the cold and clammy torchlit corridors until he paused before a door and took the keys from his belt and unlocked it.

I did not even hear the door close behind me, or the key turning in the lock. I flew like a falcon, diving in for the kill, straight and true into Robin's arms, nearly knocking him off his feet with the fervour of my embrace. Oh how we clung! Neither one of us ever wanted to let go. He clutched me tight and covered my face with kisses. It was as if we had never been apart – the distance that had been between us instantly dwindled away to nothing. It was as if we had been together each and every day of our lives.

Wordlessly, hand in hand, we went to sit on a pile of red velvet cushions laid out before the fire. Robin's nimble fingers lifted the French hood from my head and rippled through the flaming waves that streamed down over my shoulders. And with a blissful sigh I went into his arms, laid my head against his strong chest, closed my eyes, and let the rhythm of his heart soothe me.

Though Robin had spent extravagantly from his paltry purse to provide us with a fine supper, we touched not a morsel though we did partake freely of the malmsey. I felt it go straight to my head, to make me smile and giggle, and the room seem to glow, but I didn't care. That night I wanted to be free of all prisons, including the cage I had constructed around my heart, so every time Robin filled my cup I drank it down.

We sat thus for I know not how long, drinking and holding hands, gazing deep into each other's eyes, then Robin drew me to him again, enfolding me in his arms, and our lips met.

Though we had never shared such intimacies before, here in the Tower, where so many had died before us, with the shadow of the axe always looming above us, never knowing if each day would be our last, the day that a warrant would arrive signed by the Queen sealing our fate, it seemed only natural that we should grasp at what might be our last chance at happiness.

I sank back against the cushions, and drew Robin down with me, my legs rising to wrap around him, even as my arms rose and went round his neck. And then, as his lips moved down my throat, leaving a trail of hot kisses, and his hands reached beneath my petticoats, I felt a sudden inexplicable chill. My eyes shot open wide, and a silent scream filled my lungs, for over Robin's shoulder I saw the grinning ghost of Tom Seymour.

A frost instantly killed my reborn passion, which I had convinced myself was stone-cold dead, but Robin's kisses, the wine, and the threat of the axe had reawakened it with a new, vibrant intensity that made me want to grasp, fully experience, and hold tighter than ever to life.

I struggled free of him, hampered by my heavy skirts, stumbling and tripping, as I ran to the window and flung it wide, hanging over the sill and drinking in great gulps of the cool night air.

Robin came softly to my side, his brow furrowed with concern, and gently stroked my back, the way he would gentle a frightened mare.

"Frightened, my brave Bess?" he asked, his voice gentle and surprised. "This is not like you; you were always so fearless. Tell me, what has wrought this change in you?"

"Life," I stammered, "and Death."

I pulled away from him and went to the table and, with an unsteady hand that shook as if with palsy, poured myself another cup of malmsey and gulped it down. I spilled a goodly portion down the front of my gown, ruining the beautiful velvet, but I didn't care. I wanted the wine to chase away the vision that still haunted me, Tom Seymour standing there, leering at me over Robin's shoulder, as another man mounted me and my body gave in to the passion surging up inside me that I had tried so hard to kill. And over Robin's shoulder Tom smiled knowingly, as if he had known all along that I would never be free – passion's ghost would forever haunt me.

Again, Robin came to me, but I put out my hand to stop him, keeping him at arm's length, shaking my head at his murmured words, the concern vying with the curiosity on his face, and turned my back on him and went to the door and pounded on it as I called loudly for Sir John.

In silence, I followed him back to my cell. I waved off Kat's questions and stood in silent stillness as she undressed me, clucking dolefully over the wine stains on my gown. Then, with an absently murmured "good night", I climbed into bed even though I knew it was no use; even behind the drawn bedcurtains, I could not hide from my private demons and the salacious ghost of Thomas Seymour. Would I never be free of them, I wondered as I tossed restlessly upon my pillows, haunted by the ghost of an ambitious fool's caresses and the newer, fresher memory of the kisses of a tender, loving friend, even as the urgent, adamant "Never surrender!" rang like an alarm bell inside my brain. I felt as if I were a woman torn apart by wild horses, forever at war between the burning desires of my body, the crypt-cold reason that ruled my head, and the icy fear that came with the red-hot passion of surrender. I could not reconcile them all, and I knew deep down that I never would. I would always be a soul in conflict, torn between weak and blissful womanly surrender and absolute control. I could never win, because even when to all the world it would seem that I had triumphed, a part of me would always feel the loser.

And as I drifted off to sleep I heard a phantom voice softly sing, imbuing each word with such intimacy it was like a lover's caress gliding over my body:

> *I gave her Cakes and I gave her Ale,*
> *I gave her Sack and Sherry;*
> *I kist her once and I kist her twice,*
> *And we were wondrous merry!*

> *I gave her Beads and Bracelets fine,*
> *I gave her Gold down derry.*
> *I thought she was afear'd till she stroked my Beard*
> *And we were wondrous merry!*

> *Merry my Heart, merry my Cock,*
> *Merry my Spright.*
> *Merry my hey down derry.*
> *I kist her once and I kist her twice,*
> *And we were wondrous merry!*

I bolted out of bed, snatched up the nearest cloak, and went to spend the rest of the night sitting by the low-burning fire. Did I only imagine it, or did the glowing embers truly resemble burning hearts?

The next afternoon, my eyes dark-shadowed, I went to walk, with my guard trailing after me, upon the wall-walk instead of in the garden. Robin, followed by his own guard, was already there, lost in thought, the wind running playful fingers through his curly black locks and tugging at his black cloak as if to say "pay attention to me!"

I started to turn away, but he saw me and called to me.

"Don't go!" he pleaded. "Stay. Walk with me." He held out his hand entreatingly.

I silently fell into step with him. After what had happened the night before I found it hard to meet his eyes.

"I do not pretend to know what has happened to you, Bess," Robin said at last, after we had walked in silence for a time. "I see a fear in you where there was none before; a fear to let anyone get too close to you. I have a suspicion it has to do with the Lord Admiral, but," he added hastily when I made a sudden move as if I meant to bolt, "we shall not discuss it, for it really has nothing to do with us. I have a plan, Bess; would you like to hear it?" I nodded, and he moved to stand directly before me, keeping a distance of a little more than arm's length between our two bodies. "If I stay with you, Bess, being your friend as I have always been, making no sudden moves, never pouncing on or pawing you, patiently nurturing your friendship, winning your trust, then, perhaps, after a time, one day when I stand before you like this, and hold out my hand to you, like this" – he reached out his hand to me – "perhaps, you will come to me."

"You would gentle me as you would a wild horse, my gypsy?" I smiled and said softly and teasingly.

"I want your trust, Bess, and to be able to touch you, to hold you, without seeing fear in your eyes," he said seriously.

I closed my eyes and sighed at the thought of being able to let down my guard again, to be able to trust someone, to feel so safe in his company that I could let all my defences crumble and just be me for a while, not a princess, watchful and alert, or the even greater vigilance and wariness that would come with the crown if I ever inherited it, to just be myself, to just be me, Elizabeth.

"Perhaps," I whispered, "someday, my Robin, perhaps . . ." And with those words of possibility hanging between us, I turned, glancing back at him over my shoulder and, with a smile and a gentle jerk of my head, indicating that he should walk beside me.

Robin's lips spread in a wide smile and he bounded over to take my arm, and as the ravens circled overhead and our cloaks billowed about us, flapping like dark wings themselves, we continued to walk along the Tower walls, gazing out at the city, but trying never to look down to where the Lady Jane's scaffold still stood upon the green.

Robin glanced up at the ravens and squeezed my hand and smiled at me. "Have patience, Bess. Someday, we too shall soar and fly free as the birds in the sky."

His voice was so confident and reassuring, I could not help but believe him, and in my heart a part of me recognized the truth in his words and aimed for it, like a falcon going in for the kill, determined to prevail.

❧ 33 ❧

Mary

Sometimes I thought they were all against me. Though I gave them assurances aplenty that they had *nothing* to fear from my marriage to Prince Philip – only good could come of it, including the blessing of an heir – my people still continued to protest, as did the members of my Council.

Even my dear old friend, Reginald Pole, now a great learned and esteemed Cardinal serving His Holiness in Rome. The son of my beloved governess, he had fled abroad to avoid Father's wrath when he spoke out against his infatuation with The Great Whore and callous treatment of my mother; even he put pen to paper and wrote cruel and stinging words to me. "You will fall into the power and become the slave of your husband," he warned. "And at your advanced age," he said with cruel bluntness, "you cannot hope to bear children without peril to your life." How could he be so mean and hateful? I wept over his letter until my tears broke through the paper.

Even the children were against me! When the weather warmed and the grass was green, dozens of them turned out to play a game they called "Queen and Wyatt". When I found out that the most popular part of the game was when the Prince of Spain was captured and hanged, it made my blood boil. I ordered the little offenders whipped and, despite their youth, sent briefly to prison to teach them a lesson lest they, as they gained in years, turn rebels for real and become an even greater threat to my beloved. I could not bear that the children of my kingdom might grow up harbouring thoughts of harming my beloved. Indeed the reports said that so enthusiastically did they play at hanging the Spanish Prince that some of the boys enacting his role had been strangled almost to the point of death. I could not have it! I simply could not have it! They must *never* play "Queen and Wyatt" again! For weeks I lived in terror that Philip would learn of it and the antics of those beastly children would prevent his coming even after on my knees I assured the Spanish Ambassador that I would lay down my life if need be to keep Philip safe. "I would rather not have been born at all than that any harm should befall His Highness!" I threw myself down and sobbed at Renard's feet.

But it was even worse. Ragged gangs of dirty barefoot street boys gathered outside the Spanish Embassy to pelt any who entered or exited, including dear Ambassador Renard, with rocks and offal, chanting, "We'll have no Spaniard for our King!" and "Spaniards go home!"

And when I heard that even the ladies of the court were protesting my bridegroom's arrival with the very garments on their backs, favouring gowns the colour of sun-bronzed skin and calling the shade "Dead Spaniard", my heart broke and I could not stop the torrent of weeping it unloosed. I took to my bed, unable to sleep or eat, and the flesh began to melt away from my bones, while the doctors stood over me and shook their heads, at a loss for what to do.

"Only Prince Philip can cure me!" I told them repeatedly, waving aside their leeches and lancets. "He must come to me if I am to live, otherwise I shall most assuredly perish!"

And still Ambassador Renard continued to shake his head, and express his and the Emperor's fears for Philip's safety on English soil and concerns about Elizabeth. She must go the way of Jane to pave the way for my beloved's safe arrival. But my Council held fast – they would not allow me to condemn her without absolute, indisputable proof of her guilt. She was too popular with the people and they feared they would rise en masse to save her, and the traitor Wyatt had gone to his death swearing from the scaffold that she had played no part in his rebellion. Furthermore, it was unjust to keep an innocent person imprisoned, my Council claimed, and the people clamoured night and day for the release of "Our Princess". That was what they called her: "Our Princess". Even from her prison cell Elizabeth was still able to exert the witchlike wiles she had inherited from The Great Whore and turn my people against me.

I wept and felt torn apart inside. I loved Philip so much, and longed for him more than I had ever imagined possible, yet a part of me still remembered the baby sister I had loved and cared for, the little red-haired girl I had held on my lap, dressed, bathed, sung lullabies to, and rocked to sleep, and pretended was my very own child. I had horrible nightmares in which I would see myself guiding that tiny tot by her leading strings up the thirteen steps of the black-draped scaffold and I would start awake with a scream upon my lips, my face bathed in tears, and my heart pounding as if it were about to shoot like a cannonball out of my heaving breast. I just could not do it; I could not sign her death warrant. Finally, after one such dream, in which I stood calmly by as that dainty red-haired tot knelt in the straw staring defiantly, despite the fearful quiver of her chin, at the scarred wooden block while the tall menacing figure of the headsman in his black hood towered over her with his axe held high, I bolted from my bed, ran to my desk, and ripped the death warrant into shreds.

At last, fearing for my life, the Emperor gave in, and Ambassador Renard came to my bedside to deliver the happy news that Philip was preparing to depart. But, as a precaution against poison, he stipulated, he would be bringing his own cooks, apothecaries, and physicians.

It was as if God Himself had laid hands on me to effect my cure. The moment I heard those words I was cured. Heedless of the immodesty of appearing before the Imperial Ambassador in my nightgown and bare feet, with my greying and faded hair hanging down my back in a long, limp and bedraggled braid, I sprang from my bed. I laughed from sheer joy and leapt and clapped my bare heels together in the air. I grabbed my startled doctors and Susan and Jane by their hands and danced round in circles with them, ignoring the physicians' warnings about my pulse and heart. Then, laughing, I broke free, leaving them staggering dizzy and startled, amazed at my behaviour and sudden, miraculous recovery, and began to rush about, hither and yon, summoning servants and palace officials, issuing orders to prepare for my bridegroom's arrival. Everything *must* be *perfect!* There was so much to do and so little time!

I ordered that beneath every canopy of estate in every palace a second throne must be erected beside mine. And I began to name courtiers to serve in his household – there must be 350, and not one less, and they must all be made to swear an oath of loyalty and allegiance to My Prince; the Earl of Arundel should have the honour of presiding over them all as Lord High Steward. And I must send a deputation of noblemen to Spain to escort him, and a fleet of ships to patrol the coast to alert us when his ship was in sight and to shepherd it safety into the harbour. A hundred-gun salute must be fired the moment his ship was sighted. I wanted it to feel as if the very earth shook the way my knees did at the thought of him. The Earl of Arundel himself must row out on a golden barge to greet him and kneel at My Prince's feet and fasten a specially made Order of the Garter, encrusted with diamonds, rubies, and pearls, about his calf, then invite him to partake of a fine banquet on the barge and, standing proxy for me, drink a loving cup with him. Welcoming speeches, songs, and poems in his honour must be composed, and a children's choir assembled to greet him with their angelic voices on the docks of Southampton. And he must have guards to keep him safe; with this in mind, I began to select the best men from my personal guard, skilled archers who were also adept in foreign tongues so language would pose no barrier, men who could be counted on to keep my beloved safe. And a splendid horse must be procured as a gift for him, a mount fit for a prince. It should be white as snow and caparisoned in crimson velvet embroidered with golden thistles, with rubies sparkling on its reins, and Philip should have a pair of golden spurs set with rubies; the goldsmith should see to it without delay. Sir Anthony Browne should lead the horse to Philip when he disembarked, so that he would not have to suffer the indignity of walking through the crowd of slack-jawed, craning-necked people who would no doubt gather to catch a glimpse of him. I would not have my beloved being stared at like a freak in a country fair! So Sir Anthony would gently boost my beloved into the saddle, then kneel and humbly, reverently, as if it were a holy relic, kiss his stirrup and inform him that he did so in proxy for me. Then he must kiss Philip's hand and place upon his finger a magnificent diamond ring set in a golden nest of acanthus leaves and pin a brooch crafted like a great golden lovers' knot upon his shoulder, explaining that both were love-tokens from me. Only then would he take the ruby-studded bridle in his hand and lead my beloved in stately progress through the streets of Southampton to the Church of the Holy Rood for a Mass of thanksgiving for his safe arrival, then on to the Lord Mayor's palace, where he was to lodge. His rooms there should be hung with tapestries depicting the might and majesty of the Tudor dynasty and my Spanish forebears, the great Catholic sovereigns Ferdinand and Isabella. And he must be presented with the keys to the city, of course. The Lord Mayor, decked out in his ceremonial robes, should meet him before he formally entered the city.

I gave orders for the best tailors in London to craft splendid garments to adorn my beloved, and for the decoration of his rooms, fine tapestries and beautifully carved and gilded furnishings, and for the adornment of his private chapel, there must be jewelled crucifixes, statues and stained glass, golden chalices and candlesticks, and the altar cloth that I had been embroidering ever since I had agreed to take him as my husband. He must have fresh flowers every hour, and a deep crimson velvet canopy, curtains, and coverlet, and silken sheets, all embroidered in gold with lovers' knots and our lovingly entwined initials, for his bed. And there was the wedding to plan, the ceremony. There must be incense and *thousands* of tall white candles of perfumed wax, and the walls lined with shimmering sheets of cloth-of-gold in which the dancing candle flames would be reflected. And the wedding banquet! There must be wondrous subtleties sculpted out of sugar and marzipan so elaborate they would make the guests gasp in awe.

And my gown! What had I been thinking all these months? The

dawning horror of it nearly felled me. I stood there in the centre of the room swaying with both my hands raised to clasp my head. All these months I had lavished so much thought upon my bridegroom but not given a single thought to my wedding gown! I must have the dressmakers in immediately! I must look my best for him! I must, even if it was for only one day in my life, be beautiful! I must have creams and lotions for my skin, to ease the lines of worry from my brow and about my mouth and eyes, and to soften my hands and make my nails shine. And my hair! Surely there were special washes that would make it shine with a newfound lustre to match the glow of happiness within me, and perhaps even give the illusion of thickness? I would entrust this to my faithful Susan; I *knew* she would not fail me; she would want me to look as beautiful as I was happy on my wedding day.

And amidst all this planning every few moments I ran back to Ambassador Renard to embrace him and clasp and kiss his hands in humble gratitude, thanking him again and again for making my dreams come true. "My friend, I shall forever bless you!" I promised, hugging him again. "You shall be the godfather of our first child!"

Weeping with joy, I took him by the hand and led him into my private chapel adjoining my bedchamber, where the Holy Scriptures lay upon the candlelit altar, and laid my hand upon it and promised him that something would indeed be done about Elizabeth. I would send her away, under strict and stringent guard; she would be kept under house arrest, deep in the country, somewhere remote where she could work no mischief and was well beyond the reach of those who would work it on her behalf. Every move she made, every breath she took would be observed, every word she spoke would be written down. She would see no one alone and be allowed to neither write nor receive letters, and if even the barest hint of suspicion brushed against her again she would be brought to trial for treason and I would not hesitate to condemn her to ensure the happiness and wellbeing of my beloved. I would bury Elizabeth alive in the country, I vowed, and do my best to forget about her and pray that everyone else would as well.

I ran out into the gallery, heedless of the shock my appearance would cause, running through the corridors in my flapping white nightgown and bare feet. I stopped short, panting, before my sister's portrait. Levelling an accusing finger at her likeness I said in a loud and commanding voice, "*That* comes down!" And I stood and watched until my orders were obeyed and Elizabeth, in her bare-shouldered harlot-scarlet gown and pease-porridge and gold kirtle, was carted away to the attic.

And then I seemed to awake from a *beautiful* dream and found myself kneeling at the candlelit altar in the royal chapel at Whitehall in a golden gown with my hair, like a bride's, unbound, crowned with a wreath of gilded rosemary.

With my hand upon the Holy Scriptures, I swore a solemn oath before my assembled court.

"I call upon God and all of you to witness that I am marrying Prince Philip not out of any carnal affection or desire" – I stiffened my back and ignored the titters and whispers these words provoked – "nor for any motive whatsoever but the honour and prosperity of the realm. I call upon all those present to pray that God will give me the grace to accomplish this marriage, and that He will look upon this union with favour."

With a smile of pure delight, Ambassador Renard stepped forward, to stand proxy for Philip, and placed upon that most special finger of my left hand, the one with the vein leading directly to my heart, a rose diamond set in a nest of golden petals from Philip that was especially dear as it had belonged to my beloved's own mother and had in fact been her own betrothal ring. The moment it slid onto my finger our marriage was considered binding.

Smiling jubilantly, I looked out into the sea of faces and vowed, "I will wholly love and obey His Highness, my husband" – oh how I savoured those two words upon my tongue! – "Prince Philip, to whom I have given my heart, and myself, following the divine commandments, and I will do *nothing* against his will."

I pointedly ignored the stir of unrest these last words caused, for I knew that many needlessly feared that Philip would interfere with the governing of the realm. I wish I could have gone to each and every one of my subjects who felt this fear and taken their hands in mine, looked into their eyes, and assured them that they had nothing to fear, and urge them to smile and be happy for me. But I doubted that even such warm reassurances would dissuade them. They were all determined to believe the worst of my beloved, the prince of my dreams. So I ignored them and held my head up high, walking boldly and confidently towards the fulfilment of all my desires and dreams.

As I left the chapel, a double row of two dozen little girls in angelic white dresses, with shimmering silver lace angel wings on their backs and halos on their innocent fair heads, showered me with red and white rose petals, while a choir of little boys sang. As I walked through that rain of fragrant petals I felt like a young girl again. I felt like dancing. I wanted to swirl and spin and show the whole world my betrothal ring and shout out so everyone could hear me, "I am a married woman! Praise God, I am a spinster no longer!" I felt like doing it, so I did; that is one of the advantages of being a queen, and that day I felt like I was Queen of the World! The only thing lacking was my bridegroom. Had he been there to run through that fragrant shower of rose petals and dance with me, my happiness would have been complete.

❧ 34 ❧

Elizabeth

While Mary planned to marry, I spent my days in dreary boredom and a state of constant worry; the anxiety gnawed like a ravenous rat at my mind every hour of the day and night; it never deserted me. I feared the dark circles, like violet bruises, beneath my eyes and the slight nervous tremor of my hands would become permanent parts of me. I thought she was a fool to proceed with her stubborn plan to marry Prince Philip when her people clearly abhorred and feared the thought of Spanish dominion and showed their displeasure with outbursts of violence and riots. Even from my own prison I knew the prisons were full of street-corner firebrands whose only crime had been to speak out against the Spanish bridegroom.

Mary was throwing away her subjects' love with both hands, but so in love was she with the prince in the portrait that she was too blind to see that. But even if I had been at court, I knew I would never dare tell her so; mistrust of me had crept into and sickened her brain until she suspected me of being behind each and every act of defiance and conspiracy in the realm. And it hurt my heart that it should be so. I still loved my sister, even though I did not like her, or approve of her policies and actions as Queen, but I would never have tried to pull her from her throne or snatch the crown from her head. If that was to be my destiny it would come to me in time, through the grace of God, and I was content to wait and bide my time, and at present I was in truth more preoccupied with the business of just staying alive.

I was sitting at the window, drumming my fingers irritably on the stone sill, and watching the ravens, when a knock sounded upon my door. Sir John Bridges entered with a bright and cheery smile, saying he was the happy bearer of glad tidings, and gesturing to the fat, grey-haired fellow who followed puffing in his wake, cradling his great protruding belly as if he were a mother-to-be cradling her unborn child. He was the sort of man who should have looked jolly, the sort whose apple-cheeked face was always wreathed with smiles and whose every word burbled with good cheer, but, alas, Sir Henry Bedingfield was a dour-countenanced man who rarely if ever smiled. He was a stickler for the rules and followed them to the very letter, meticulously dotting all the *i*'s and crossing all the *t*'s and never overlooking a punctuation mark. He was precise and exacting even when it came to the tiniest trivialities. He was one of Mary's most ardent supporters.

Sir John smilingly informed me that my time in his custody had come to an end and I was to be released from the Tower and given over into the care of my newly appointed guardian, Sir Henry Bedingfield, who had come to escort me to my new home at the old palace of Woodstock in Oxfordshire, a former royal hunting lodge with a most romantic history. Henry II's beloved mistress, the Fair Rosamund, had once lived at Woodstock, losing herself in the twists and turns of the maze her lover had created for her to evade his jealous queen, and a later king, Edward II, had passionately sported with Piers Gaveston in its perfumed bowers while another angry and jealous queen fumed in frustration.

As I prepared to take my leave, I fought down the fear rising within me. I could not stop thinking about the two little princes who had disappeared quietly within the Tower, the bright candles of their young lives cruelly snuffed out by an assassin who crept into their chamber as they slept. I kept seeing their radiant, beatific little ghosts as they had appeared to me that night. Would such, I wondered, be my fate when I reached the quiet, secluded environs of Woodstock? Would I myself become an unquiet spirit revealing my phantom shade to others in the night decades or even centuries after I had died? I feared it so much I dared not sleep. Far from London it would be so easy to do away with me – a poisoned cup, a silken noose, a pillow over my face as I slept. A malignant fever could be given out as the cause, and though there might be whispers and rumours of murder, given my history of illness, none could really dispute it.

Dressed for travel, with Kat and Blanche close beside me, I left my cell for the last time, glancing up at the wall-walk to wave farewell to my dear gypsy.

He doffed his plumed cap and fell to his knees, holding it over his heart, and blew me a kiss. "Till we meet again!" he called down to me.

Sir Henry Bedingfield himself came forward to hand me into my litter. As he took my gloved hand, I turned to him, taking him completely unawares, and bluntly asked, "If my murder were committed to your charge, would you see the deed was carried out?"

With an appalled and wounded gasp, Sir Henry let go of my hand. "Certainly not!" he indignantly exclaimed. "My Lady, I swear on my immortal soul that I have been charged with nothing but to protect you and keep you safe from all harm, whether it be from Catholics or Protestants. I would not harm a hair on your head nor allow it to be done by any other!"

I travelled, once again by litter, with Sir Henry astride his horse, riding at the head of the procession, and a number of guards surrounding me, to protect me, or so they said, though I knew it was to prevent any from attempting to rescue me.

As we made the journey a wonderful thing happened that made hope spring to vibrant rosy life again. The good people of England, honest and true, thronged the dusty roads, hailing me with warm words and showering me with blessings. They tossed bouquets of wildflowers and bunches of herbs onto my litter, and country housewives ran up to bob their curtsies and give me gifts of home-baked cakes and bread, tarts, and even rounds of cheese and jars of jam and honey. They shook their fists and railed against Sir Henry and the guards. And in every village through which I passed, the bells began to ring. In strict defiance of the edict that they be rung only for the sovereign, they rang their bells for *me!* Sir Henry was beside himself, sending riders dashing off to protest, shouting for them to silence those bells at once, threatening the villagers with the pillory and stocks, but they ignored him, and the bells continued to chime, and even when we had passed through and were but a speck upon the horizon, still the people cheered, "God save our Princess Elizabeth!"

And when it was time to dine or sup, to Sir Henry's horror, the local gentry insisted on hosting banquets in my honour, treating me with all the deference and respect as if I were myself a queen.

When we passed through Windsor, the schoolboys at Eton came rushing out in their flapping black scholars' gowns, shouting, *"Vivat Elizabetha!"* and tossing their caps into the air. Laughing, I conversed with them in Latin, quizzing them about their lessons, and doled out cakes to them, sharing my bounty.

"Tamquam ovis," I said to the throng of young scholars, "I am taken like a sheep to the slaughter!" and the word quickly spread of the grave injustice being committed in their midst; the Queen was sending her own sister away, perhaps even to die, in obscurity, and yet more abuse was hurled at the flustered and irate Sir Henry and his men. To calm the crowd, some of the guards even declared that they were for me, and meant me no harm, only to safeguard me, swearing that they would lay down their lives in my defence.

Sir Henry continued to protest, swatting at the boys with his round feathered cap and riding crop, pulling at their black scholars' gowns when they clustered round me, trying to shoo them away, but they, like the rest of the villagers, ignored him, nor would the bell-ringers obey his demands for "Silence!" either, and so we continued all the way through Windsor in a shower of blessings, flowers, cakes, love, and good cheer, all to the tune of church bells.

Nearly weeping with despair, again and again I heard Sir Henry bewail, "I was to take the Lady Elizabeth as a prisoner into private confinement, not upon a triumphal progress! What will Her Majesty say when she hears of this? She will think me remiss in my duty!"

But I just laughed at him as my heart surged with love, a warmer, deeper love than I had ever felt before. It made the hot passion that had roused me in the arms of Tom Seymour and Robert Dudley seem cold as the grave in comparison. These people, this country, I knew would be the great loves of my life, and I must do all that I could to sustain myself, to preserve my life, so that, someday, God willing, I could serve them.

I saw the hope burning bright in their eager eyes. They were frightened by my sister's Catholic regime and the Spanish bridegroom who was soon to arrive – they feared greater harshness, another Spanish Inquisition, this one on English soil – and they were looking to *me* to save them. And I made a promise then and there, to the people of England, and myself, that I would never disappoint them.

All the way to Woodstock people lined the roads to see me pass, pelting me with posies, and even thronged outside the rusty sagging gates through which I must pass. And with one last rainbow shower of wildflowers and blessings upon me and a violent volley of hissed and shouted boos and shames and shaken fists directed at Sir Henry and the guards, my litter was carried through the crowd of well-wishers, and the gates of my new prison clanged shut behind me, and, with a sigh of relief, Sir Henry mopped the sweat from his flushed face which I thought, smiling to myself, looked rather like a giant strawberry drenched with dew.

❧ 35 ❧

Mary

Of course I could not go down to the docks of Southampton and welcome him personally – that would not have been fitting – but with a spyglass trained to my eye, to remedy my shortsightedness, and my cloak, skirts, and full, hanging over-sleeves whipping wild and flapping about me, being pulled this way and that most vexingly by the wind, which had already presumed to snatch the hood from my head and the pins from my hair, I stood beneath an alarmingly grey sky dotted with dark roiling clouds, and watched it all from the rooftop of the Bishop's palace with Susan and Jane beside me, holding fast, as if they feared I too might be blown away.

Never before had I seen anything more magnificent than his flagship, the *Espíritu Santo*. It was an enormous twenty-four-oared galley, painted all in vivid red and sunny yellow, with a beautiful blue-mantled Virgin mounted as a serenely smiling figurehead upon the prow, holding out a candle to light the way. Its hull was painted like the most beautiful flower garden imaginable. It was a true paradise! There were flowers of every kind and colour, and heavily laden fruit trees, all accented with gold; there were even bees, birds, and butterflies hovering over the blossoms, even proud strutting peacocks. The forecastle was draped with red cloth sewn with golden blossoms, and from the mainmast fluttered the flag of Spain and the Prince's coat of arms. Every bit of rigging was adorned with little alternating red and yellow silk pennants that waved gaily in the breeze. This awe-inspiring, gigantic marvel of a ship led a flotilla of 125 smaller ships, carrying an entourage of 9,000 Spaniards – grandees, their ladies, thousands of servants, priests, the Prince's personal physicians and apothecaries, and fine Spanish mules and horses, of course. The ships were all painted either red or yellow, with their riggings aflutter with thousands of tiny silk pennants of the same two colours.

But upon the deck of the flagship was a sight even more magnificent to behold than the ship itself, a sight which even if I lived for a hundred years I doubt I would ever see equalled, much less surpassed. Upon the wide expanse of the deck – I am sure it was as big or even bigger than the largest palace Great Hall ever built – were musicians in extravagant costumes of striped and slashed red and yellow, sewn along the seams with tiny gold bells, with long ribbon streamers flowing gracefully back from their shoulders as they played their instruments, and parti-coloured hose and tasselled boots with long pointy toes reminiscent of those that had been worn in bygone days, and felt caps with red and yellow plumes. As they played, fifty – or maybe even a hundred, or somewhere in between that number – couples danced. Each man wore a costume similar to the musicians, very elaborate and form-fitting to show off his virile, masculine physique, with short jackets that ended at their trim waists, flaring out over their hips, and figure-hugging hose and mammoth codpieces that left nothing to the imagination, and tasselled ankle boots of red or yellow Spanish leather. And each woman wore a gown trimmed with silk roses and ruffles of the same sunny yellow and vibrant red, and mantillas of red or yellow lace, with their feet encased in high-heeled slippers of either yellow or red with roses of the contrasting colour on the toes and satin ribbons wrapped about their shapely ankles and tied in bows. As they swirled and shook their ruffled skirts, displaying their shapely limbs, their dancing partners beat beribboned tambourines. On another part of the deck, sailors in uniforms of the same red and yellow, sporting wide-legged breeches, danced a boisterous hornpipe. And there were jugglers expertly displaying their art with red and yellow balls, and there were ugly little dwarves in outlandish red and yellow spotted and striped costumes sewn with bells, who tumbled, capered, and danced, rolled their eyes, stuck out their tongues, and made funny faces. And up high in the rigging, all aflutter with red and yellow silk pennants, acrobats, as agile as monkeys swinging from tree to tree in the jungle, performed feats of daring. The sight was so dazzling and alive with motion and colour the eye hardly knew where to look. I wished Father's master painter, Hans Holbein, were still alive, so that he might capture it on canvas; one could look at it a hundred times and notice something new every time. Each one of the performers had somewhere about their person a perfumed silken rose of either red or yellow, so exquisitely crafted they looked at first glance real, and when the ship docked they tossed these out into the crowd of gaping and dumbstruck onlookers. It was such a dizzying, magnificent sight that it would later be said by many that never before in their life had they seen so much yellow and red at one time and hoped never to again; some even claimed it gave them blinding headaches that lasted three days.

Then he was there. My handsome, golden-haired and golden-bearded bridegroom clad all in white velvet delicately embroidered with pearl and diamond flowers springing from golden foliage swirling across his chest. His fine legs were encased in white silk hose and tall white leather boots with tops that flared about his thighs. As he disembarked he removed his white plumed cap and held it humbly in his hands.

As he started to falteringly speak the unfamiliar English words of a speech he had learned, to thank the good people for turning out to welcome him, the storm broke with a vengeance. Thunder boomed loud enough to rattle every glass windowpane in town, and blinding white lightning streaked across the sky, as a dense torrent of needlelike rain poured from the black clouds overhead.

Shrieking, the Spaniards ran for cover as the red and yellow dyes on their costumes began to run off in rivulets of rainwater. Sir Anthony Browne quickly brought forward the white horse that was my special gift to my beloved and boosted the poor startled Prince into the saddle without first apprising him of his intentions. And as he bent his head and hunched his shoulders and determinedly led him towards the Church of the Holy Rood, where they could take shelter against the raging rain and celebrate Mass, I noticed with dismay that the crimson velvet that adorned that beautiful white horse had bled onto my beloved's beautiful white hose and boots. Oh what a *dreadful* welcome for my bridegroom! I had wanted everything to be perfect, and now it was ruined! And it had all been so beautifully planned, right down to the tiniest, most minuscule detail! All the lovely ceremonies and gifts and presentations had been drowned out. Oh the indignity inflicted upon my darling! Soaked to the skin and his beautiful clothing all ruined and stained the moment he set foot on English soil! Even the weather conspired against me!

I flung aside the spyglass, letting it roll off the roof and smash onto the street below and, ignoring the pleas of Susan and Jane urging me to go inside lest I catch my death, stood bareheaded being pelted by the relentless rain that felt hard enough to bruise me down to my heart, letting it plaster my clothing to my skin, as I wept to rival the downpour.

The storm raged and howled and wept all through the night, but by dawn it had cleared. Bundled in a warm cloak, with only a small entourage, I stole quietly away at first light, returning to Winchester and the Bishop's Palace, where I was lodged, to officially meet my beloved face to face for the very first time.

When my beloved set out later that day, in a suit of black velvet embroidered with silver, diamonds, and pearls, again astride the white horse that was my gift to him, at the head of his enormous entourage, their number further swelled by the 350 Englishmen I had appointed to serve him, the storm erupted again with renewed vengeance. The entire party were again soaked to their skin and their fine clothing, made new for the journey, was ruined once more, and they were left floundering in the muddy quagmire of the road. Oh how I wept when I heard and then, when Susan and Jane cautioned me that my face would be all red and swollen and I wouldn't look a bit pretty when my darling came to meet me, I instantly ceased and rushed to lie in a darkened room to have my ladies apply cold compresses and soothing creams to my face while

I fingered my rosary and prayed that my prince would find me pleasing.

I arranged for us to meet at twilight in the Bishop's torchlit garden. Still feeling anxious about my appearance, and the eleven years between us, I hoped the gloaming would be kind and flatter me.

In a high-collared black velvet gown with a kirtle and plump padded under-sleeves of rich sapphire and silver brocade, with icy diamonds and sapphires dark as midnight adorning the crucifix at my breast and bordering my hood, I awaited my beloved surrounded by flowering jasmine, seated on the rim of a plashing fountain in which silver fish darted like lightning against the blue marble bottom. I know it was rather vain of me, but I arranged to be attended by my four oldest and plainest ladies, all clad in severe, unadorned black gowns, standing back as unobtrusive chaperones, melting into the darkness, with their backs straight like sentinels, and their hands folded modestly at their waists.

I saw my reflection mirrored in the water's glassy black surface and frowned. It looked like a death's head, deathly pale, pinched, and haggard, with my eyes set in deep, dark hollows. My brows were so pale I seemed not to have any. As she helped me with my toilette, Jane Dormer had brought out a pair of false brows made of dark hair and a little vial of a glue of some sort to hold them in place. But when I learned they were made of mouse fur I shuddered in horror and ordered her to take them away; I could not and would not wear them. Lest I cry, I had to look away. I rose and plucked a sprig of jasmine and closed my eyes and endeavoured to calm myself as I breathed deeply of its fragrance. But at the sound of approaching footsteps, I started and my heart began to race, and I hurried back to resume my placid but, I fancied, romantic pose seated on the marble rim of the fountain, idly twirling the sprig of jasmine between my diamond- and sapphire-ringed fingers.

Carrying a torch, Susan Clarencieux led my bridegroom to me. *Oh he was exquisite!* How he made my heart beat! He was wearing another fine suit of black velvet, this one with a ruff of silvery lace about his throat and smaller ruffles ringing his wrists. And a large crucifix set with diamonds and three large dangling pearls hanging from a heavy silver chain about his neck. His cloak was lined with cloth-of-silver and his high black leather boots flared out above the knee to call attention to his firm, handsome thighs. When I caught myself staring at them I blushed and made myself look away, scolding myself, and hoping he had not noticed and conceived an ill opinion of me.

Please do not let him think me a foolish old maid, harbouring secret lustful fancies. *Please*, God, do not let him think me wanton or ridiculous, I prayed.

Then, in spite of myself, before I even realized what I was doing, I sprang to my feet, forsaking all dignity, dropping the jasmine and crushing it underfoot in my haste, as I ran to him. As I sprinted across the garden, bold and brazen as a harlot, my skirts gathered immodestly high so that my ankles in their black wool stockings and silver slippers showed, I pressed my fingers to my lips and kissed them. I hurled myself onto my knees before him and took his hand in mine and, staring up at him in unabashed adoration, with eyes that proclaimed "I will worship you; I will be your slave!" I brought it to my lips in a kiss of hungry devotion.

"My Lord, Your Highness, my husband." The words poured out of me in a breathless rush. "I am much beholden and thank God that so noble, worthy, and famous a prince would vouchsafe so to humble himself by uniting with me in marriage. These words are spoken from the depths of my heart. They are not just idle flattery or a pretty speech composed to welcome you."

"Then they are even more precious to me," Philip said as he reached down and raised me, then bent his face down to mine and kissed my lips, giving me the first *real* kiss of my life.

"We are married in the eyes of the law," he said, referring to the ceremony by proxy, "so it is permitted." He spoke to me in slow, careful Spanish that was like a velvet glove caressing my naked spine, making my knees tremble, though I know he intended only to make sure I could understand him clearly as his accent was stronger, and his pronunciation slightly different, than Ambassador Renard's.

My voice had forsaken me and all I could do was nod eagerly as he took my hand and led me back to sit beside the fountain.

Still speechless, I intently searched his face for some sign that he liked what he saw when he looked at me. But Philip's face was a cipher that kept his true feelings a mystery.

There was a nervous awkwardness between us; I had lost my composure and wits to such an extent I could only sit and gape at him, while he stared blankly back at me. It seemed we had nothing to say to one another; how unbearably awkward! For is there anything worse than a strained and awkward silence between a pair of lovers?

Finally I blurted out, a trifle too loudly, "I hope you had a pleasant voyage."

"It was neither pleasant nor unpleasant," Philip replied.

"Oh." I nodded, struggling to think of something suitable to say. "M-My m-m-mother . . ." I frowned at my unexpected stammer, the way the words seemed to stick in my throat. "My mother was very seasick when she came from Spain." I finally managed to get the words out.

"I have never been seasick," said Philip.

"Oh I am so glad!" I smiled, for the thought of him suffering even a momentary discomfort pained me.

"I am sorry the rain spoiled your arrival, I had such lovely things planned to welcome you," I said.

"It was God's will." Philip said with a slight shrug of his shoulders.

"Yes, it was God's will" – I nodded – "but I am still sorry."

"Shall I present you to my gentlemen?" Philip asked, gesturing to the four dark and handsome young noblemen standing in the background just as my own ladies did.

"I would be honoured if you would," I said, and let him take my hand and lead me over to them.

As he named them to me, each came forward and bowed low over my hand. Then it was my turn to introduce my ladies to Philip. Gallantly, he took from inside his doublet a black velvet bag and from it poured into his palm a number of loose diamonds, rubies, emeralds, and sapphires, and as the introductions were made he held out his hand so that each lady might choose a jewel for herself to have set however she pleased.

And then he turned to me and in Spanish asked, "What is the English word to say good night?"

"Good night," I said slowly and clearly, enunciating each syllable with great care.

Philip nodded and bowed to me and my ladies. "G-ood Ni – hi-ite" – his tongue struggled to coax out the unfamiliar syllables – "lay-dees all." He finished with a bow, then he turned and strode briskly away, with his gentlemen, bowing and bidding us good night first, falling into step behind him.

I watched until the garden gate closed behind them, then I turned to my ladies and demanded, "Did you ever see such a man?" and without waiting for an answer I began to dance, spinning round and round around the fountain, singing out to the heavens, "I'm in love, I'm in love, I'm in love!"

We were married at Winchester Cathedral on the 25th day of July 1554. It was the feast day of St James of Compostela, the patron saint of Spain. Crowds thronged the streets to see us arrive in our golden chariots.

Philip was again all in white velvet with a surcoat lined in gold, edged with pearls, and embroidered with golden thistles. I was a little hurt to see that he had chosen not to wear my wedding present. That morning I had sent him a surcoat to wear over his wedding clothes, a magnificent garment made of crimson velvet lined in cloth-of-gold, with eighteen large table diamonds to serve as buttons, the whole thing embroidered with Tudor roses, Spanish pomegranates, lovers' knots, and our initials entwined like lovers in an embrace, all embellished with pearls and diamond and ruby brilliants and gold and silver bugles and beads. I would later discover that Philip had pronounced it "too ornate and garish".

The people neither blessed nor booed, cheered nor cursed him; they merely watched, curious and intent, as if he were some strange animal in a menagerie the likes of which they had never before seen. But at least they did not hurl stones or excrement at him, and for that I was most grateful.

When I dismounted from my gilded chariot, oh how they

cheered. "God save Queen Mary!" they cried, and threw their caps in the air, showing me by their words and deeds that they still loved me. And the women were agog at the grandeur of my gown – a high-collared, deep black velvet so thickly encrusted with gold embroidery and precious gems that the black could scarcely be seen beneath it all. When the sun struck it I seemed to be robed all in light. It had a train so long and heavy that Susan and Jane, gowned all in gold, as the first pair of fifty ladies, half clad in silver and the other half in gold, had to ride behind me in a silver chariot and hold it up lest it drag in the dust and filth of the street. It had provoked my dressmaker to insolent exasperation, causing her to forget herself, and that it was the Queen of England whom she served, and cry out in vexation, "God's teeth, My Lady, if you wanted a gold gown, why did you not just order one of gold brocade instead?" And there were rumours afoot that one of the sewing women who had slaved over the embroidery, working all day then far into the night by candlelight to have it ready in time, had gone blind and, no longer able to ply her trade, was forced to beg alms in the street and sometimes even sell her body for crusts of bread. Others said she slit her throat or threw herself in the river in despair. But I am sure it was just a story invented by my enemies to show me in a bad light, to slander me. They were trying to taint my joy, but I refused to let them spoil it! I *knew* they were all against me. Elizabeth herself, tucked out of sight and bored out of her mind at Woodstock, might even have started the rumour herself, but God was for me, and Prince Philip, and soon we would make a son, a saviour for the true religion, to keep the faith shining bright in England long after I was gone, and that was all that mattered. Elizabeth and the heretics would *never* win!

Despite the heat, the church was crammed to bursting, and many women in their sumptuous and weighty finery fainted. The walls were hung with long shimmering sheets of cloth-of-gold, just as I had commanded, and thousands of tall white perfumed wax tapers lit the church. As I walked slowly and proudly up the blue-velvet-carpeted aisle, with my head held high despite the painful weight of the heavy jewelled coronet that sparkled and flashed and made me feel as if a rainbow tightly embraced my head, the choir sang and censers swung before me, so that I walked through thick bluish clouds of incense that made me feel nauseous and dizzy all at the same time.

At the altar, I knelt beside my beloved. And when he slipped the ring, the plain hoop of gold I had requested because that was how maidens were married in olden times, onto my finger, it was the happiest day of my life. I smiled broadly, forgetting that this would expose the bare places on my gums left vacant when the agonies of toothache forced me to submit to the dentist's forceps until I had only a few teeth left at the very front of my mouth, which I tried very hard to preserve for my appearance' sake.

We left the chapel hand in hand, deluged by a shower of rose petals and blessings; even those who deplored my choice of a bridegroom could not resist the good cheer and hope a wedding inspires. I could not tear my eyes from my husband, and I felt as if my whole body and not just my face shone with the rosy glow of love, and there was a lightness to my steps despite the weight of my gown that made me feel as if I were walking on air. We were surrounded by smiling faces and engulfed in blessings for our happiness and fertility, some of which were so brazenly spoken they made me blush and lower my eyes modestly; though I was a married woman now I was certain I would never be able to hear such things spoken of without blushing.

At the wedding feast that followed, a dozen sailors from Philip's flagship, dressed in wide-legged trousers made from a patchwork of silver and gold, danced a lively, energetic hornpipe that made me feel breathless and exhausted just to watch. The performance ended with them falling to their knees and each in turn presenting to me an oyster shell which opened to reveal a large, perfect pearl; strung together they would make a beautiful necklace that I would wear often in fond remembrance of my wedding day.

And to honour the Spaniards I had my confectioner and her helpers, and every helping hand the kitchens could spare, slave day and night to construct from sugar and marzipan a series of subtleties recreating the wedding flotilla in painstakingly authentic detail, led by the magnificent *Espíritu Santo*, sailing into harbour with her colours flying and the red- and yellow-clad performers, all crafted out of marzipan, on the deck, and the acrobats high up in the rigging. It gave me great pleasure to see the looks of amazed delight upon their faces as each of the 125 ships was carried in upon golden platters by my servants clad in the red and yellow livery of Spain.

Then in came a procession of Philip's servants clad in liveries of the Tudor colours, white and green, bearing great wooden casks of English beer on their shoulders and trays of golden cups, which they filled and distributed amongst the guests, English and Spanish alike. And my beloved, my husband, kissed my hand, and stood. "Henceforth, we are all Englishmen!" he declared, raising his cup to the company before he drained it in a single gulp.

Though it disappointed my court, I had chosen to dispense with the traditional and lewd and indecorous practice of putting the bride and groom to bed, wherein the ladies undressed the bride, and the gentlemen the groom, and then saw them into bed together, to drink a loving cup, whilst the wedding guests made bawdy jests and comments and drank one last toast to the happy couple before leaving them alone to consummate their marriage. I knew my court delighted in such things, but I just could not bear the thought of it; it was more than my nerves could stand.

Instead, after the Bishop had blessed the bed with holy water, Philip and I were left alone in my candlelit bedchamber, standing on opposite sides of the bed, facing one another, still fully clad in our wedding clothes. Given the many and complicated fastenings and layers we would have no choice but to help each other disrobe unless we chose to spend the night in our clothes.

Philip held out his hand to me and in a commanding tone spoke a single word: "Come."

Dutifully, I walked round the bed. He put his hands on my shoulders and stared down hard and intently into my face before he turned me round and began to unlace my gown. With brisk fingers that were disturbingly skilled at navigating the manifold intricacies of a woman's attire, Philip undressed me until I stood blushing before him as naked as a newborn babe. Tears pooled in my eyes and I could not decide where to look, either down at the floor in shame, or at Philip's face in the hope that I would see some show of emotion there so that I would know if he admired me even a little. Repeatedly, I moved my arms to try to cover myself, to shield my breasts and privy parts, but each time Philip stopped me, making me stand with my arms straight at my sides, "like a soldier," he insisted, "arms down, back straight, head up!"

"Now," he continued, "undress me."

With nervous, fumbling fingers, I played the servant, and unlaced, unpinned, and unbuckled. I lifted garments over his head, pushed them from his shoulders, pulled them over his arms, and eased them down over his hips and legs, and struggled to tug the tight-fitting high leather boots from his feet, until he also was naked. But Philip felt no shame. He stood straight and proud before me with his hands on his slender hips and his head held high, his blue eyes commanding me to admire him.

There was another part of him that stood straight and proud, and to behold it made me blush all the more, if that were possible, for my cheeks were already flaming, and want at the same time to look my fill and run away. I had seen nude male babies and classical works of art that showed undraped male figures, but never before this moment a living, breathing, full-grown adult male with his virility so evidently displayed.

A quick twist of amusement contorted his lips but was there and gone so fast I was not entirely certain I had truly seen it. His eyes never left my face as his hand descended to languorously stroke and caress the long, thick shaft of his male organ. He did this repeatedly, like one stroking a favoured pet. And I, with my mouth hanging open, and my eyes so wide I feared they would tumble from their sockets, watched entranced, unable to look away even though I knew I should.

He chuckled softly, and I frowned, uncertain of whether he was mocking me.

Like a general issuing orders to a mere footsoldier, Philip pointed at the floor. "Down," he said, and when I hesitated, he added, "kneel."

Trembling, I sank to my knees and gazed up at him questioningly, though his image was blurred by the tears that filled my eyes.

"Before she was a Queen of England, your mother was a Princess of Spain," my husband said to me. "I want you to tell me what she taught you about wifely obedience."

"I was raised to regard a husband as his wife's lord and master, as Christ's earthly representative, and she is to honour and obey him as such." I recited the long-ago but well-learned lessons of my childhood. "A woman is clay in first her father's and then, upon marriage, her husband's hands; and he is the sculptor who will mould and shape her and make her his creation, whatever he wants her to be. A woman without a husband is incomplete. When she is blessed with the gift of a husband she should give him her complete devotion and do whatever he asks or commands of her. His every wish and whim is law to her."

"And will you honour the teachings of your childhood?" Philip asked.

"Yes," I nodded, swallowing down my tears, "yes, I will."

"Then I think we shall do well together," Philip announced as he walked past me to stand before the mirror that had been his gift to me.

It was such a beautiful mirror, the most beautiful one I had ever seen, oval and set in a heavy silver frame engraved with the most wonderful inscription, *"Cuando miras en este espejo estas viendo a mi persona preferida,"* which when translated into English read, "When you look into this mirror you are seeing my favourite person." The day before our wedding, Philip had sent it to me with the request that I hang it on my bedchamber wall with a table and candles beneath.

"Bring more candles," Philip said. "I want to see myself better."

I did as he asked and took a branched candelabrum with four lit candles from a nearby table and brought it to him and stood back as, by the light of six candles, Philip admired himself from head to waist. Reflected in the glass, he could see Titian's portrait of him hanging behind him on the opposite wall. "A magnificent likeness," he observed. "It *almost* does me justice."

"It is a very fine portrait," I agreed.

"Fine enough to make you fall in love with me?" Philip asked.

"Yes," I admitted in a soft voice scarcely above a whisper.

"That is to be expected." Philip nodded. "When the portrait was first completed and hung in my father's palace for all to admire, a servant girl stabbed herself in despair before it because she loved me but could not have me. She was quite right to do so; she was an ugly little thing."

"Oh, the poor child! That is so sad!" I cried.

"You are too softhearted, Mary," Philip rebuked me, "too sentimental. These things happen; it is the way of the world. It is a good thing that I have come to you; you need a firm hand to guide you."

"Yes, I am too soft," I readily admitted. "I have always dreamed of having a husband who would be a strong, firm, and commanding presence at my side, to walk through life with me, to help, teach, and guide me. Too often, I let my heart rule me, though I try not to. I cannot seem to stop, and that is not a good policy for a monarch, to be so swayed by sentimentality."

"Well, I am here now," Philip said, "and I am strong, so we will have no more of that. Emotion is the enemy. To show it is to show yourself weak; it is a mark of failure."

Philip bent and lifted the heavy, fringed brocade cloth that covered the table and tucked it back so that the bare space beneath showed. He glanced over at me, then back again at the dark, shadowy space.

"Come here and kneel down," he directed, "here, before me, beneath the table but not so far that you cannot reach me."

"But . . . *why?*" I asked, my brow furrowing with confusion. I did not understand what he wanted of me.

"Because I am your husband and that is what I have told you to do, and it is your duty to obey, not question," Philip answered sternly. "I am your husband, yes?" And at my nod, he continued. "And as such I am like Christ on earth to you?" he asked, and again I nodded. "Then come here, kneel down, and worship me, Mary!" he ordered. "Worship me on your knees! Worship me with your mouth!"

My face blanched and my knees nearly buckled with horror as understanding suddenly dawned on me. He meant for me to put . . . *that* . . . in my mouth!

"But surely I cannot beget a child that way? Or . . . can I?" I hesitantly inquired with an uncertain quaver in my voice, for in truth I knew little of such things and was not entirely sure.

"This" – Philip took his organ in his hand again and stroked it – "what we are to do right now, is not about conception. This is for *my* pleasure. Later, we will do our duty as King and Queen and attend to the other business."

"But conception is the purpose of marital relations!" I exclaimed. "A man's seed should *never* be spilled in vain!"

"It will not be spilled," Philip impatiently retorted, "unless you fail me. Let us come at once to an understanding. Hear me now. Henceforth, my seed will be to you like mother's milk is to a baby. I want you to suckle greedily, as hungrily as an infant. And I will look at myself in the mirror and together what my eyes see and what your mouth does will give me *great* pleasure. Then when I am ready to spend myself I will look down at you. I want to watch you swallow every drop, and then beg for more, grovel, kiss my feet, and beg and plead as if your life depended on it, and, perhaps I will be generous and grant your request."

"No, oh no!" I cried as, one by one, all my illusions about love and marriage shattered.

I ran past him into my private chapel and slammed the door.

I hugged my arms about me and doubled over, feeling so ashamed to stand before the crucified Christ in all my nakedness, even though it was with great compassion that His dark eyes gazed down on me.

The door flew open, banging hard against the wall with a sharp retort like a gunshot, and Philip roughly seized hold of me. He thrust me face down upon the altar and struck me hard across my bare buttocks several times, hard enough to make me cry out, before he roughly pulled me up, put me over his shoulder, and carried me out and threw me onto the bed.

Everything went black as he snuffed the candles out, and then I felt the warmth of his body upon mine and his fingers probing, questing and inquisitive, between my thighs, provoking such lovely sensations that I instantly lay back, sighing, blissful and content. So enraptured was I by his touch that I quite forgot the shocking peculiarities and violence that had preceded this. Then his hand rose up to cover my mouth, to stifle my scream, as I felt a sharp pain like a lance being driven into my womanly parts. And then . . . *Oh!* Then the most exquisite sensations, so wonderful they defy words to describe and, out of modesty, I dare not even try. Suffice it to say that in my beloved's, my husband's, arms I discovered to my astonishment, and immense delight, that my body, which myself and others had so often thought of as a wizened old maid's perpetually pure, chaste, and virgin carcass, had been made for love. I arched my hips and sighed and clutched his body close to mine, wrapping my arms and legs tight around him. I could not get enough of his touch, this marvellous expression of his love, this special, sacred union that God had created just for husband and wife to enjoy together as they strove to achieve the miracle of conception. God had given me yet another miracle! Philip's touch lit a fire in my soul and my flesh harkened to his. I lost myself in his embrace and found a new part of me I never knew existed.

And then he gave a great groan and a shudder and he lay heavily upon me, with his head resting upon my shoulder, whilst the warmth of his seed flooded my womb. I stroked his hair and back tenderly.

"I never knew it could be like this!" I whispered into the dark.

"Pray that your womb will be fruitful," Philip said, perfunctory now that his passion was spent. He rolled off me and, obediently, I got up and knelt, heedless of my nakedness, beside the bed and fervently prayed to God that it would indeed be so, that his seed would anchor in the safe harbour of my womb and bring forth God's most precious miracle of all – a child.

Philip was gone when I awoke the next morning. Soon afterwards, a group of Spanish gentlemen and their ladies came to my door, singing and bearing gifts of fruit and wine and pretty baubles.

Horrified, Susan and Jane shooed them away, explaining, as best they could as they knew little Spanish and the Spaniards knew little English, that in England it was customary for the bride to remain in seclusion, and not show herself in public or receive visitors, until the second morning after her wedding. The Spanish lords and ladies were greatly perplexed – in their country it was the tradition to greet the bride when she awoke with music and gifts – but they respected my wishes and retreated.

Secure in the knowledge that no one would be allowed to disturb me, I ignored the babble outside my bedchamber, and drew on my nightgown, blushing at the memory of Philip's passion. Rather than ring for a servant, I went myself to fetch my lap-desk, and settled myself comfortably with my back propped against a mound of pillows to write a letter to my cousin, now my father-in-law, the Emperor, thanking him "for allying me with a prince so full of virtues that the realm's honour and tranquillity will certainly be thereby increased. This marriage renders me happier than I can say, as I hourly discover in my husband so many virtues and perfections that I constantly pray God to grant me grace to please him, and behave in all things as befits one who is so deeply beholden to him."

The next morning I emerged from my bedchamber and went in search of Philip. I was wearing one of my favourite gowns and I wanted Philip to see me in it. It was made of quilted gooseturd green velvet latticed with seed pearls with a kirtle of green and gold stripes, profuse amounts of gold parchment lace, and a high gold lace collar that hugged my throat like a second skin. I knew I looked my best in it and I hoped Philip would like it as much as I did.

I was surprised to find him in the gallery, standing in a state of absorbed contemplation before the portrait of Elizabeth, the very portrait that I had ordered taken down and consigned to the attic with its face to the wall. It must have only just been restored; even then two servants were fussing over it with dust cloths, straightening the frame and polishing the gilt until it gleamed. Philip was staring most intently at Elizabeth and stroking the gold silk of his beard with a movement of his fingers that was rather sensuous and reminded me of the way I had seen him caress another part of himself in the privacy of my bedchamber.

"Good morning, my dear husband," I said, reaching out to gently touch his arm and turn his attention to me.

But Philip did not look away from Elizabeth's portrait, nor did he return my greeting.

"Why was your sister not invited to the wedding?" he demanded. "Appearances are very important, and her absence did not look right. Ambassadors and gossips alike take note of such things; it will be remarked upon. You must invite her to court at once."

"*I will not!*" I cried, stamping my foot as anger filled me and my head felt like to explode. "And she is *not* my sister! She is the bastard of that whore Anne Boleyn and the lute player Mark Smeaton, and I would not dishonour you by having you meet a woman whose soul is as dark and foul as . . . a . . . an overused privy! She is a traitor, always scheming against me, spinning plots against me like a spider spins its web, hatching them like eggs, and I cannot bear to have her near me!"

Philip turned and regarded me with eyes so cold they froze my heart. "Curtail your emotions, Madame. You speak with the frenzy of a madwoman, and Philip of Spain does not converse with deranged persons."

Wounded to the core, and instantly contrite, I fell to my knees and caught desperately at his hands. "I am sorry! I will do better! I promise! Please, forgive me!" I implored, saying these same words over and over again as I wrapped my arms round his waist and clung to him as if I were drowning and only he could save me. "It is her fault! She always brings out the worst in me!"

Philip thrust me from him and I fell backwards onto the floor.

"That is no valid excuse and is not grounds for absolution either!" he said sharply. "*You* let her do this to you; *you* let a girl young enough to be your daughter get the better of you by provoking you to behave thus, to cry, and rage, and weep, and carry on like a madwoman instead of comporting yourself like the queen you are."

Calmly, as if nothing were amiss, he folded his hands behind his back, and resumed his absorbed contemplation of Elizabeth's portrait.

"Until we have a son, she is second in line to the throne, and as such must be treated with respect. Send for her. I am curious, I want to meet her. Now go to your room and dry your tears and take off that *hideous* dress; that collar makes you look like the giraffe in my father's menagerie."

And, without giving me a chance to answer, he turned his back on me and walked away, leaving me sitting on the floor before Elizabeth's portrait.

"*I rue the day you were born!*" I hissed at it, and it was all I could do not to fly at it, screaming my hate, and rip the canvas to shreds with my fingers.

But my husband was right. He was harsh, and brutally honest; he barked orders at me as if he were a general and I a common foot-soldier, but he was right to do so, to teach me and help me learn, to make me a better woman, and, God willing, a better queen. I could not continue to dispense mercy with such largesse; it grew commonplace and people came to expect it of me. It made me appear predictable, as well as womanly and weak, but with Philip's help, if I could grow a callus on my heart, when I deigned to show mercy the gesture would be much more precious and seem all the more spectacular. It would also be more appreciated for its rarity. Philip was right – appearances really were important. I *must* do better. Then he would be proud of me and love me. His love would be my reward. And with those thoughts in mind, I stood up, dried my tears, and went to change my gown. When I reached my room Philip was waiting for me, naked, before the mirror. "Creep to me on your knees, Mary, just as you would creep to the Cross at Easter," he directed.

❧ 36 ❧

Elizabeth

At Woodstock, I languished in boredom. Upon arrival we discovered that the old palace was too decrepit to inhabit, and were forced to make do as best we could crammed into the two-story, four-room guest house, itself in none too good repair.

I chafed at being kept in such close confinement. Sir Henry was a man entirely lacking in leniency and imagination. He governed me strictly by the rules that the Council and my sister had laid down, denying himself the liberty of interpretation.

If I asked for anything that was not explicitly allowed or denied me in their instructions, he would dutifully write a letter of inquiry, and then would begin the long dull, dreary delay while we waited for an answer.

I was allowed nothing to read except books of Catholic instruction and prayer sanctioned by Mary. When I asked for an English Bible I was given one in Latin instead; Sir Henry ventured that since I was so skilled in reading Latin I might prefer to read in that language lest my skills grow rusty. My servants were separated from me and forced to lodge elsewhere, most of them taking rooms in a nearby tavern. And I was allowed no writing materials so that I might directly address my sister and the Council, nor was I allowed to speak to anyone, not even the maid who was charged to attend me, out of Sir Henry's hearing. And when my laundry was returned to me he himself searched it meticulously for hidden messages. And I was compelled, by Mary's orders, to attend Mass, said in Latin, twice daily.

I festered with fury, boredom, and impatience. It seemed my life was being wasted and whiled away. My days were spent waiting for night so that I might retire to lie restless beneath the blue ceiling painted with silver stars above my bed, and my uneasy nights were spent in restless waiting for the day to arrive. All I was doing was waiting and marking time.

"I am only following orders, Princess, nothing more and nothing less!" Sir Henry would wail each time I rounded on him and railed at him for being overly strict.

Time and again I would point an accusing finger at him and scream, *"Gaoler!"*

And in response, Sir Henry would, despite the difficulty presented by his great bulk, drop to his knees and implore me not to call him such a harsh and deplorable name. "For I am your officer, appointed to take care of you and protect you from any harm."

I was allowed to walk in the orchard daily, but only with Sir Henry trudging along, puffing and blowing, red-faced and panting, struggling to keep up with me. He was a man clearly unaccustomed to brisk exercise. In angry frustration, I would quicken my pace and lash my riding crop at the high-grown weeds.

As spring rolled into summer, word reached us of the Spanish bridegroom's arrival and, at summer's end, an announcement that Mary was expecting a child.

In deep despair, fearing that the rest of my life would be spent in captivity and the crown would never be mine, I opened my copy of *St Paul's Epistles* and upon the flyleaf wrote, "I walk many times into the pleasant fields of the Holy Scriptures, where I pluck up the goodlisome herbs of sentences, that, having tasted their sweetness, I may less perceive the bitterness of this miserable life."

One rainy afternoon, when I must stay inside, I took a diamond ring from my finger and used it to etch onto the windowpane a little verse of my own making:

MUCH SUSPECTED OF ME,
NOTHING PROVED CAN BE.
QUOTH ELIZABETH, PRISONER

Seeing it, Sir Henry frowned and, for the umpteenth time exclaimed, "I am only following orders, Princess, nothing more and nothing less!"

"*Gaoler!*" I screamed shrilly at the top of my lungs, putting all my anger, fear, and frustration into that solitary word, and flung my book at his head.

❧ 37 ❧

Mary

And then God chose to vouchsafe me another miracle, the greatest a woman can receive regardless of whether she be commoner or queen. My monthly bleeding had always been painful and erratic. It was not unusual for me to go one, or even two, months without bleeding whilst I suffered the bloated agony of the pent-up blood that refused to flow. "Strangulation of the womb," the doctors called it, and often had to resort to bleeding me from the bottom of my foot to bring on my courses. But *three* whole months without that agony or even a cramp or the tight pressure and ache in the small of my back? I sent for my doctors; they quizzed me about my symptoms. Was there any tenderness or swelling about my breasts? Had I been sick of the mornings upon rising? They felt my pulse and stood huddled by the window with their heads together over the urine in my chamberpot to scrutinize and sniff. And then they confirmed it – I was with child, and they expected me to be delivered in May.

God had given me the most precious miracle of all and the means to vanquish all my enemies. I wished I could see Elizabeth's face when she found out that she was to be supplanted, that now she would *never* be queen. Thus far, I had managed to put off bringing her to court. The truth was, I did not want Philip to see her. I did not want him to look first at her and then at me and make comparisons that were not in my favour, to gaze at her smooth, flawless white face and then at my lined and yellowed countenance, and her thick and glossy mane of brazen harlot red hair as bright as the flames of Hell and then compare it with my own limp and thin rusty-grey tresses. Already he had a hurtful habit of reminding me that I was old enough to be Elizabeth's mother and I didn't want to make it worse. Every time he said that it was like a stab through my heart that kept on bleeding and aching without killing me, condemning me to live in perpetual pain. Anne Boleyn's daughter had inherited her mother's witchlike wiles, and I was afraid that he too would fall under her spell; Elizabeth had a way of harnessing men's hearts. But now, in my womb, I had the means to break her!

She was making quite a nuisance of herself at Woodstock, and it was time to put a stop to it. Nearly every day brought some new request submitted to the Council by Sir Henry Bedingfield, as plodding and diligent in his duty as a plough horse, and I myself must rule whether to accede to her request or deny it. Every day it was Elizabeth wants this, Elizabeth wants that! And Sir Henry, a careful and capable gaoler he might be, but I swear the man was utterly incapable of making even the smallest, slightest decision, no matter how trivial, on his own. He must instead defer all to me. I was a new wife, and now, by the manifold blessings of God, a mother-to-be, and I should not have been bothered with such things. But none of them cared, none of them wanted me to be happy, they were all against me, they *all* wanted to spoil it for me, to slap my hands as if I were a naughty child and wrest all my joy away from me, and many wanted to take my crown too, and Elizabeth was the mastermind behind it all, even though my Council protested there was no evidence, not a shred of clear and certain proof. But I didn't need evidence, I *knew*. Elizabeth was like a great spider sitting at the heart of her web, spinning her schemes, concocting ways to rob me of my happiness and steal my crown away from me. She thought she was clever, but I could see through her as if she were made of glass!

But first, before I dealt with Elizabeth, there was something even more important I must do. I took up my pen and wrote to my old friend Cardinal Pole, beseeching him to return to England as Papal Legate and officially mend the break with Rome that The Great Whore had brought about. Now that I was with child, it was more important than ever that England be reconciled with Rome. And I begged him to come quickly and help me bring my greatest work to fruition; I wanted my son to be born in a land that knew no other religion than the true one.

I wanted the people to share my joy, so I donned my royal robes of crimson and ermine, and put on my crown and, with heralds to announce my good fortune, I rode through the streets of London, carried gently upon a well-cushioned golden litter, at a pace no faster than a walk in deference to my condition. I reclined against the velvet cushions, my hands protectively clasping the gentle swell of my stomach, with my robe open to let the people see that within my body I was carrying their saviour. Philip rode beside me on the fine white horse I had given him, and from time to time I reached out to take his hand in mine and a smile of triumph would pass between us. Together we had made a son who would be heir to the greatest empire in the world. In fact, he would rule half the world, and I expected before his hour came to leave it he would have conquered the whole of it.

Many of the people cheered us; there seemed this time to be less opposition to Philip, and I heard many comment on what a handsome man he was. But there were some heretics in the crowd who cried out to God to "either turn the heart of Queen Mary from Papist idolatry or else shorten her days." I gave orders for my guards to arrest them, but in the dense crowd that had assembled to watch us pass, it was impossible to ascertain who the offenders were and none were willing to betray them.

Philip and I had our portrait painted together, clad in black and gold, reminiscent of the portrait I had commissioned of my parents sitting lovingly together, though ours was less sentimental and Philip insisted on standing. He thought it would appear weak and unmanly for him to sit and hold hands with me, like a pair of lovers. If he stood while I was seated, Philip explained, he would appear as a pillar of strength beside me. And I agreed, for he truly was my pillar of strength. He helped me atone for my womanly weaknesses and made me seem and feel stronger. He also decreed that the painter should disregard the signs of my condition, my undone laces and the extra panels of material inserted into my skirts, and paint me as though I were not with child. This was an official portrait about power and appearances, Philip said, and it would be inappropriate to portray something so intimate. Such things were better left to allegorical or mythical paintings, if they must be painted at all, but were certainly not appropriate for formal, dignified portraits of kings and queens. But he agreed with me that space should be left in the foreground where our child, or, God willing, children, could be painted in later as family portraits bespoke power and we, God willing, were laying the foundation for a dynasty.

Philip still persisted in asking to meet Elizabeth. "Bring her to court. I want to meet this brazen red-haired heretic," he would say. But I continued to delay sending for her. Every time I stood before my mirror I thought of Catherine Parr and wondered if she too had stood thus and compared her age and appearance to that of vibrant, young Bess, the stepdaughter whom she had trusted and lavished so much fond attention upon, who would nonetheless scheme to steal her husband and hard-won happiness from her. With Elizabeth it was "All or Nothing", just as it had been with her mother. Would Anne Boleyn's bastard brat do the same to me? I could not help but wonder.

Philip and I were there to welcome Cardinal Pole at the top of the grand staircase at Whitehall as all the church bells in London chimed to welcome the first Papal Legate to set foot in England since Cardinal Campeggio had come to try to persuade Father to honour his vows to my mother and cast off The Great Whore.

The moment he set his red-slippered foot upon the first step I felt my child leap for joy within my womb. I felt as if an invisible angel had just whispered in my ear, "Fear not, Mary, for thou hast found favour with God." I *knew* it to be a sign, certain proof that I was carrying the son who would be England's, and the true religion's, saviour.

With my face wreathed in smiles, I reached out my hands to my dear old friend, remembering that our mothers had once fondly cherished the hope that we would grow up to marry. Now we would form a different sort of alliance, a union devoted to restoring the Church to its former might and glory here in England and, holding both his hands in mine, I impetuously confided what had just occurred.

"My friend, the moment I laid eyes upon you I felt my child move for the very first time!"

A smile brightened his careworn features. "Blessed art thou amongst women, and blessed be the fruit of thy womb. It was the will of God that I should have been so long in coming. God waited until the time, and your womb, was ripe. Now, God willing, you shall have a son to carry on your great work so that none can ever again undo it."

My head swimming in elation, I sank to my knees and brought the hem of his scarlet cardinal's robe up to my lips and kissed it to show my humility and respect. He had come here as the Holy Father's true representative, and I must welcome him as if it were the Pope himself who stood before me.

Cardinal Pole knelt down before me. "As is only fitting before the sovereign lady of the realm," he explained as I continued to smile and clutch the hem of his red robe to my heart.

With an air of impatience, Philip bent and took each of us by the arm and gently urged us to our feet, saying it was more fitting that we both should stand as equals now that we had paid our respects to one another. Philip *always* knew the right and proper thing to do; he really was my tower of strength, and I knew I would be lost without him. I loved knowing I could always rely on him whenever I was in doubt or my emotions threatened to get the better of me.

Together, the three of us walking side by side, with me between these two great men, we went to hear Mass and then on to Parliament, where Cardinal Pole made a stirring speech about forgiveness and reconciliation.

"I come not to condemn but to reconcile, I come not to destroy but to rebuild," he said in a firm but warm and reassuring tone like a benign and forgiving father. "Touching all matters past, they shall be as things cast into the sea of forgetfulness." He went on to assure all those who had profited by the dissolution of the monasteries that they would not be punished or forced to make restitution. The Church would not take back their lands; what was now in private hands would, in the spirit of forgiveness, stay in private hands. We would now move forward, and only faith and the Pope's authority would be restored, for these were far greater treasures than any lands or riches. And what Henry VIII's lust had destroyed his daughter's pure heart and courageous spirit would now rebuild.

The following Sunday in St Paul's churchyard Cardinal Pole presided over a public absolution "to welcome the return of the lost sheep", wherein all who had forsaken the true faith, for whatever reason, were free to come without fear of punishment and kneel before him and be forgiven and received back into the Church. Nearly twenty thousand people came to kneel and receive his blessing.

For the first time since my father's wicked lust and Anne Boleyn's witchlike ways had plunged our nation into darkness I felt as if the sun were truly shining down on England in warm, golden, healing rays. And as I watched, tears of joy poured down my face. Never before had I felt such pride in my people. I hugged my unborn child and let the warm balm of happiness fill my heart.

Now, when the time came, I could withdraw from public life into the safe, warm cocoon of my confinement chamber to await the birth of my child, knowing that everything would be all right. God and the Pope were both smiling over England and my people had come running back into the warm and loving embrace of Our Lord and His Church. I could sit back and take my ease and embroider little gowns and caps for my baby knowing that all was right with my world and I had fulfilled my divinely appointed destiny.

❧ 38 ❧

Elizabeth

At last, my hopes and prayers were answered – a summons came from Mary, bidding me come to court; she wished to see me before she withdrew for her confinement, as was the English custom. I danced a jig for joy, spinning round and round the unsmiling rotund form of Sir Henry Bedingfield, singing out, "To court, to court, I am going to court!"

We set out for London on a blustery April day. A mighty gust of wind ripped my hood right off my head. Laughing, carefree as a child, I ran after it, skipping and dancing, my violet velvet skirts fluttering and billowing about me, being tugged in all directions by the wind, as I pursued my windblown hood, snatching at it and laughing when I missed and the wind carried it farther beyond my reach, with Sir Henry huffing and puffing after me, red-faced and panting from the exertion. I stopped and laughed, with my hair whipping about my head in a wild sea of flame-red waves, and laughingly called back, "Sir Gaoler, I hereby dub thee Sir Huff and Puff!" before I turned and ran on again in pursuit of my hood. When I had caught it, I took shelter under a roadside hedge to tame the wild riot of my tresses and replace my hood while the ever vigilant Sir Huff and Puff stood by, bent over, bracing his hands upon his thighs, and caught his breath, begging me to have mercy on him, and declaring that he was far too old for antics such as these.

"And fat," I added helpfully.

"Aye, Princess." He nodded. "And fat."

"Nonsense!" I leapt up. "Brisk exercise is *marvellous* for slimming the physique! Come, Sir Huff and Puff, let us run!" And seizing his hand, I began to run again, just for the sheer joy of it, along the road to London, leaving the guards and litter to follow in our wake.

"Princess, *please!*" Sir Huff and Puff cried, "have mercy on me!"

The London I returned to was a very different place from the one I had left. The burnings had begun; to give the condemned heretics a foretaste of Hell in the hopes that they might repent and be saved even as they breathed their last, and to frighten those who bore witness back onto the right path – the Catholic road to salvation. I could smell the singed hair and roasted flesh in the air, and see the ashes wafting down like grey snowflakes. It made me gag and my eyes smart, and I clutched my pomander ball to my nose, inhaling deeply the commingled scents of oranges and cloves.

When the people saw my litter they fell to their knees and reached out to me, and I saw hope leap like flames inside their eyes.

"English to the core that one is," I heard many a man or woman say as I rode past. "A *true* English rose, not half a Spaniard in body and *all* Spaniard in heart like her sister is!"

It both gladdened my heart and saddened it, knowing they wanted me, but that I was powerless to stop the burnings that made every English man and woman live in terror, fearing that an overzealous priest or heretic hunter or even a vengeful neighbour might denounce them and send them to a fiery death.

Time and again, the ignorant were punished for their lack of knowledge or simple misunderstandings; people who did not even understand what a sacrament was were sent to the stake because they couldn't name the proper number. Some of them died with their eyes turned to Heaven calling out my name, imploring God to keep me safe and send me soon to reign; they were looking to me as to a light at the end of a tunnel, they were looking to me to save them, to deliver them from this evil. Out of the three children my father had sired, I was the most like him, and they knew that this would never have happened in Great Harry's time. I, the princess who he always said should have been a prince, was the only one to inherit his power to reach out and touch people's hearts. With just a look I could inspire loyalty, I could give them courage and hope.

As for my sister, the woman who had once been their beloved "Princess Marigold", whose rights they had always championed, and who had begun her reign being hailed as "Merciful Mary", she had forfeited her popularity and thrown away her subjects' love to have a Spanish prince's ring on her finger and his body in her bed. Some claimed now that they had been mistaken when she began her reign in believing that she was God's divine instrument sent to sit upon England's throne, but in truth the virgin queen named Mary was actually the Antichrist in disguise. How it must have hurt Mary to hear such things said of her, to know that people prayed for her and the child she carried within her to die, but she was queen and as such must take responsibility for the acts and laws of her realm, and it was her signature on the death warrants that sent those people to die in agony amongst the flames.

When we reached Hampton Court, Sir Henry Bedingfield walked me to the door of my apartments. Hat in hands, he humbly took his leave of me, apologizing for any offence he had given me, and reminding me yet again that he had only been following orders.

Impulsively, I took his hand and gave it a reassuring squeeze, and with a smile I said to him, "If ever a day comes when I am in a position of power and require a prisoner to be most strictly and straitly kept, rest assured, my good Sir Gaoler, I shall send for you."

"Oh My Lady!" He blushed like a bashful boy and, lowering his eyes, bowed to me and bade me a hasty farewell.

Alone in my apartments with Kat and Blanche Parry to attend me, I donned my finest virgin white gown and brushed out my hair until it rippled and gleamed in bold and brazen scarlet waves down my back. Then Kat crowned me with a white French hood edged with pearls, and Blanche hung ropes of pearls about my neck, and I took a deep breath and steeled myself to face my sister.

There was a sharp imperious tap upon my door and it opened instantly to reveal a short but nonetheless handsome golden-haired man with a little pointy-as-a-dagger beard and cold, dead eyes that sharply contrasted with their warm, oceanic blue colour. He had a distinctly regal bearing and was dressed grandly in the fashion of Spain, all blood-red crimson and gold embroidery and lace, all asparkle with bloody rubies and icy diamonds. Here was a man both hot and cold.

Prince Philip of Spain. I had no need to wait for an introduction, I recognized him at once. I knew him for a foe but I would feign to be his friend. I felt as if the Devil himself had walked into my bed-chamber, but I knew better than to let him see or sense my fear; he would glut and gloat and feed on it and turn it into a weapon to be used against me.

I dropped at once to my knees, the virgin supplicant begging mercy of the mighty monarch; I knew instinctively that these were the roles and that was the game we would be playing tonight.

"Your Highness," I said, letting conviction sear every syllable, "no matter what you may have heard said of me, I am entirely loyal to my sister, the rightful queen of this realm, long may she reign." I saw the scarlet rosettes on the toes of his golden shoes as he came to stand before me, and I could feel the burn of his eyes upon the exposed white flesh of my bosom as he stared down my low, square-cut bodice.

I did not flinch as his hand reached down and caught my arm and pulled me up, his fingers biting hard through the rich stuff of my gown. He stood and stared for a long time, his eyes boring hard into mine. Suddenly, he pulled me close, tight against his chest, and his lips came down over mine, in a bruising and crushing con-queror's kiss.

Though I wanted to push him away, to spit in his face, kick and slap him, and rake my nails down his face, I forced myself to close my eyes and go limp in a swoon of surrender, letting my head flop and loll back, making my breasts appear all the more prominent above my low pearl-bordered bodice. He shifted me, as limp in his arms as if I were a poor child's rag-poppet, and I felt the strength of his arms beneath my back and knees as he lifted me and carried me to my bed.

Flushing and fluttering, wringing her hands, Mrs Ashley hovered indecisively nearby, not daring to intervene yet afraid to go, as he lowered me against the pillows.

He leaned down and pressed a lingering kiss onto each of the exposed half moons of my breasts, then turned on his heel and strode purposefully out with all the confidence and supreme arrogance of a man who has come to conquer and succeeded ... or thinks he has.

When he was gone, I sat up, threw my pillow at the door through which he had gone, and laughed until tears rolled down my face at the overweening vanity and arrogance of the man. He actually thought he had staked his claim to me as Spain had to the New World! Did he *really* think he could conquer me and treat me like a puddle at his feet? Oh yes, he did!

"Oh, Philip, Philip," I sighed through my convulsive glee, "you don't know me very well, and you *never* will, you will never see the *real* me until it is too late! You are *not* my master, or England's master, and you *never* will be either!"

At ten o'clock that night, "Faithful Susan", Mary's favourite and most trusted lady-in-waiting, came with a lighted torch in hand to lead me across the dark garden and up the backstairs to Mary's private apartments.

The reunion with my sister was a tense and frosty one. She stood straight-backed and harsh-faced before me, with her hand constantly caressing her swollen belly as if it were a talisman or good luck charm. She wore a blinding silver and gold gown with a dizzyingly dense and intense design of silver and gold embroidered pomegranates, the symbol for fertility, which had also been her mother's personal emblem and thus was doubly dear to Mary, trimmed with copious amounts of gold and silver parchment lace, and accented with a whole treasure chest of diamonds and pearls, with an enormous diamond-encrusted crucifix at her breast and her treasured ivory rosary and a gilded and bejewelled Book of Hours dangling where her waist should have been. She was so weighed down with jewels, upon her headdress, about her neck, wrists, and gown, rings on every finger, and tugging cruelly at her ears, I marvelled that she could even walk or stand upright beneath the weight. She looked like a woman who had drenched herself with glue and then jumped and rolled in a jewel merchant's chest. And yet . . . all the finery could not hide the fact that her face looked gaunt and haggard, with dark shadows around her eyes, almost like a ghastly yellowed skull in the candlelight. And beneath the richly decorated headdress I could clearly see the curve of her skull through her hair.

And there beside her, in his scarlet and gold conqueror's clothes, was Prince Philip, with thinly veiled irritation lurking just below the surface as he suffered the touch of her hand, with the talonlike nails, possessively grasping his arm. I could see it was all he could do not to slap it away. I watched him watching us, taking careful note of the coldness between us, and I knew I must play this scene for his benefit. I needed him. I could see it in her eyes that Mary wanted me dead, and now I must look to the combined forces of the lust of a Spanish prince and my own wits to save my life.

I could see at a glance that things were not well between Mary and her Spanish bridegroom, and the servants' gossip that Blanche and Kat had collected confirmed it, though my wilfully blind sister was so besotted with Philip that she could not see his genuine contempt and callous indifference. He had not a shred of love for her, or even liking; any scraps of affection he gave her were feigned and false. I could see him grimace every time she spoke to him, fighting not to flinch and pull away each time she touched him, which she did often, forever clinging, begging for his attention and affection like a dog for table scraps. It sickened me! I knew he was here only for one reason – to give Spain a foothold in England, to make our proud little nation another jewel in the Hapsburg crown. You fool – I had to bite my tongue not to laugh in his face and tell him – we English will lay down our lives before we suffer you to rule here; you may be Mary's consort but you will *never* be king, but the vain and pompous flash of your diamond-brilliant pride will not let you see that. You are as blind in your own way as my sister Mary is in hers!

In my best white gown, I knelt at Mary's feet, feeling Philip's lingering and admiring gaze scorch and burn my bosom, as I humbly hung my head and waited for her to address me.

"Well?" she asked, her voice impatient and gruff. "What have you to say for yourself? My Councillors tell me that even after a stay in the Tower and a dreary exile in the country with nothing much to do but think, you *still* refuse to confess your guilt."

"I cannot confess a crime I have not committed. Mary, you are my sister, and my queen." I met her eyes boldly as I continued to kneel at her feet. "And I will *not* lie to you. I have had no part in any rebellion or plot against you. Those who have used my name have done so entirely without my sanction or support. I am your *true* and *loyal* subject, as well as your loving sister."

"Oh you are clever!" Mary hissed. "You excel in the art of dissembling! You have covered your tracks well and left no evidence against you, knowing that my Council will not allow me to condemn you without it!"

"There is no evidence to conceal, Mary," I told her, my voice calm and level. "I have always walked the path of a loyal and loving subject, thus I have no need to cover my tracks. In searching for proof of my dishonesty and betrayal, you are looking for something that cannot be found because it does not exist."

"Liar! Heretic!" Mary screamed, clasping her hands about her head, digging her fingernails hard into her temples. "You have always been a gifted student of languages, and are as fluent in the language of lies as you are in English!"

"Mary," – calmly I reached for her hand even though she snatched it away as if my touch burned her – "you have let our differences in faith sour and cloud the love that was once between us. I can worship God in my own way without being party to plots, rebellions, and conspiracies. Just because I, like you, follow my conscience and remain true to the faith I was raised in, even though it is a different faith than your own, does not make me disloyal, dishonest, or in any way a threat to your person or your crown. I am not a traitor. If any sought me out with such in mind I would turn them away. Why must religion always come between us? Why can we not agree to disagree? There is but one Jesus Christ and Ten Commandments, the rest is but a dispute about trifles!"

"Blasphemer!" Mary screamed and swung out her hand, striking me so hard that the metal and jewels of her rings stung my face and I fell backwards, flat on my back at her feet. "And do not lie and say that you are my sister, for that is the most foul lie of all! You are the bastard brat of that whore Anne Boleyn and her pet lute-player, that creature Smeaton, and you will *never* be queen, for you are *not* my father's daughter. You are *not* a Tudor even by half, and you do *not* deserve it – you are a bastard. God Himself is against you; He has shown *me* His favour by blessing me with a son!" She hugged her belly triumphantly. "And when he is born you will be *nothing*. You will be forgotten, and, proof or no proof, the Council will not be able to stop me from . . ."

"Madame!" Philip's voice crashed down like an executioner's axe onto her words, cutting them off. *"Control yourself!"* This is *not* queenly behaviour, and I will *not* have *my* wife behaving like a brawlsome tavern strumpet who leaves a corset off her emotions as she does her loose body!"

With a cry like a wounded animal, Mary, despite her burdensome belly, dropped to her knees and took Philip's hands in hers, covering them with kisses and tears, begging for his forgiveness.

"She always brings out the worst in me!" she sobbed, glaring at me with accusing, reproachful eyes.

"No one should *ever* be able to make a queen and a *true lady* with even a *drop* of *Spanish blood* in her forget her dignity!" Philip reproved her coldly, and I saw his leg twitch as if he longed to kick her like he would a dog that vexed him.

"Husband, *please*, *forgive me!*" Mary sobbed, clutching frantically at his fingers and rubbing her wet cheeks against them, bathing them with her tears.

Coolly, Philip pulled his hands away. "I think you should retire now, Madame. In your condition it is not meet that you should let emotions so overwhelm you. Mistress Clarencieux!" he barked. "The Queen is distressed and will retire now; you will assist her!"

And weeping, Mary leaned against "Faithful Susan" and let herself be led away.

I lay still upon the floor, leaning back upon my elbows, and watched it all.

As soon as the door closed behind them, Philip came to me, and raised me to my feet. "She *will* apologize," he promised. The steely cold anger in his eyes guaranteed it. "She will kneel at your feet and humbly beg your pardon; I shall see to it. Henceforth, she will treat you with kindness and respect. I as her husband shall command it and she *will* obey; that is what wives do."

He caressed my smarting red cheek as if his very touch could heal me, and then pulled me close, crushing my breasts against his chest, as he buried his lips in the curve of my neck.

"*Mi Elizabetha!*" he murmured hotly against my skin.

"*Algún día, Philip, algún día!* Someday, Philip, someday!" I sighed with wistful, fervent ardour in Spanish, although what I actually meant and what he thought I meant were two very different things entirely. I clutched him close, pressing my body into his as though I meant us to fuse together into one person, digging my nails into his back through his splendid clothes, while over his shoulder I smiled and bit my lip to keep from bursting out laughing.

An hour later, Mary sent for me, and under Philip's watchful and commanding gaze, cumbersomely lowered herself to her knees and knelt before me in her silver and gold embroidered nightgown and cap and humbly begged my pardon for striking and insulting me.

"Sister, of course I forgive you!" I said with a reassuring smile. "We all forget ourselves at times when the heat of the moment takes our tempers from a simmer to a boil. Here, let me help you up. In your condition you should not kneel." And I bent to help her.

But there was a quiet, cold anger blazing in Mary's grey eyes. I knew she resented what she had just been made to do, which I could well understand. I felt sorry for her; I knew what it was like to be under a man's spell, wilfully blind to the truth and his faults, and to behave in ways that flew in the face of reason. I wished I could sit down, take her hands in mine, and confide in her, and make her see, and set her free. But Mary had always been short-sighted. It taxed her eyes just to read a book or write a letter, she could not recognize faces across a room, and lived always in a blur with no clear or true sight of who or what lay in wait for her. And her mind was equally short-sighted; time and again she consistently failed to see beyond her own nose. She chose to see only what she wanted to see and believe only what she wanted to believe. And just as she chose to believe that England longed for a return to what she considered the true religion, she now chose to believe that Philip loved her, that his strictness was proper husbandly conduct, meted out for her own good, moral enrichment, and improvement, and that God had sent her a fairy-tale prince and together they would live happily ever after while the Pope, happy to have his power restored, not to mention his tithes, smiled down upon them like the sun, as the good shepherd and shepherdess who had brought his flock back to him.

"I am tired and wish to retire. Leave me," Mary said, pulling away from me and, turning her back to me, going to her bed and sitting upon it while Susan Clarencieux knelt to remove her slippers, then helped raise her legs and tucked her into bed.

"Philip!" Like a beggarmaid, Mary entreatingly cried and stretched out her hand to him.

Begrudgingly, Philip went to her and bent and pressed a passionless kiss onto her brow as he stoically endured her clutching hands and the arms that reached up to twine like a strangling vine around his neck.

"Good night, sister," I whispered as I drew the door shut behind me, "and may the scales fall from your eyes and remedy your blindness before it is too late."

⊱ 39 ⊰

Mary

I lay patiently, in my hot, dark-shrouded lying-in chamber, with my hands folded across my belly, resting quietly, and waiting for my son to be born. The silver cradle prepared for him glimmered in the candlelight. Though I could not from my bed, or in this dim light, make out the inscription, I knew it by heart.

THE CHILD WHICH THOU TO MARY,
O LORD OF MIGHT HAST SENT,
TO ENGLAND'S JOY IN HEALTH PRESERVE –
KEEP, AND DEFEND!

The ermine coverlet was already turned back in readiness for the joyful moment when he would be laid down upon the ivory satin sheets and his delicate head would rest upon the plump little satin pillow stuffed with the softest goosedown.

Sometimes I passed the time sitting propped up in bed with my lap-desk writing letters to foreign rulers to announce the birth of my child, leaving the name, gender, and date blank for a secretary to fill in after the blessed event. Whilst all about me my ladies sat with their hands busy over dainty little garments and layettes, and preparing the swaddling bands. They read the lives and teachings of the saints aloud and perfumed the air with rosewater for, with the fires roaring and the windows nailed shut and covered over with tapestries, as tradition decreed, it was ripe and roasting, like being trapped inside a kitchen without the clatter of pots and pans, and the smell of sweating bodies rather than food. And, with the chief midwife standing by to guide me, I interviewed wet-nurses and cradle rockers. And to allay my fears, for I was at nine years past thirty, very old to be having my first child, a woman of forty, of petite and slender build just like I, who had successfully given birth to a set of thriving rosy-cheeked triplets, was brought in with her little angels to visit me and bank my courage up. We sat on my bed and cooed over and caressed those darling tots, and she quite candidly told me what I could expect the birthing to be like. "It's like shitting a pumpkin out of your cunny instead of your arse, Your Majesty," she most crudely described, before the chief midwife, fearing that she would unduly alarm me, hustled her and her beautiful little brood out.

But even in the seclusion of my birthing chamber, those who wished me ill would not leave me be. They slipped anonymous notes and broadsheets printed with crude woodcuts and drawings under my door. They all, in one way or another, some more coarse and crude than others, implied that Philip had betrayed our marriage vows and was unfaithful.

The most popular was a rhyme about my beloved and a baker's daughter.

> *The baker's daughter in her russet gown,*
> *Better than Queen Mary without her crown.*

A series of drawings depicted Philip copulating with the baker's daughter on a stack of flour sacks and being caught and chased off by her outraged father, who irately brandished a rolling pin as Philip fled while trying to pull up his breeches to cover his buttocks at the same time. They claimed that Philip himself had composed that scurrilous little rhyme when, having outrun the irate baker whose daughter he had just despoiled, he stopped at an ale house to refresh himself. The last picture showed him holding a tankard of ale, as if making a toast, and declaring:

The baker's daughter in her russet gown,
Better than Queen Mary without her crown.

There were so many rumours of his affairs that I could not keep count of them. They said he coupled with common women, both respectable and whores, as well as grand ladies both from the English court and of his Spanish entourage. There were tales of spy holes he had drilled into walls so that he might watch certain ladies he fancied in the act of dressing or undressing, relieving themselves at their chamberpots, or even coupling with their husbands. But the most persistent, and cruellest, rumour of all was that he was courting Elizabeth, and that she was encouraging him, and that, should I lose my life in childbed, they had already made a pact to marry. Philip would, I knew, master her, break her like a wild horse, and preserve the true faith in England, but I could not bear the thought of him in Elizabeth's arms and in her bed. It made me even more determined to be rid of her. And I prayed to God that she make one careless slip that would result in the evidence I needed to condemn her, or, if He did not desire her death, that He would show me some other way to be well and truly rid of her.

❧ 40 ❧

Elizabeth

I did not see Mary again privately before she withdrew, as per English custom, into a world of quiet seclusion, attended only by women, with the exception of her doctors, to await the birth of her child. And while she sat in her quiet, warm tapestried sanctuary, praying and sewing baby clothes, Philip bade me stand proxy for his absent wife, though it was noted he spent far more time with me than he ever had with her. We began to spend nearly every waking hour together. We dined and danced and walked and talked and rode together, he gave me gifts of jewels and furs, and took me to sail upon the Thames by moonlight, and all with eyes could clearly see that he was courting me. Soon bets were being laid as to whether I would inherit my sister's husband as well as her crown if she died in childbirth. But the common people knew what the nobles did not. They smiled and chuckled behind their hands, "Best that Spaniard; play him, Bessy, play him!" They knew their true English rose, their Tudor rose, Great Harry's daughter, would have none of Spanish Philip, and if she came to the throne whilst he was still within the realm she would quickly send him packing; a clod of dirt in the face was all he would ever get of England.

I knew those with gossiping tongues who despised my sister

made sure she heard all about it. She sat and stewed in her jealousy for a time, and then, when she could bear no more of it, she sent for me.

She looked bilious and ghastly in a high-collared gown of goose-turd green that looked unbearably tight, straining at the seams over her bloated belly even with the laces undone and the extra skirt panels. She put aside the little gold lace and scarlet-ribbon-festooned baby gown she was embroidering with the golden pomegranates of Spain and red and white Tudor roses, and bade me sit beside her on the window seat.

"I have come to realize that I will never know peace of mind as long as you inhabit my realm." She bluntly came straight to the point. "I have discussed this matter with my husband, and we wish you to marry a good Catholic prince, who will take you to live in his own kingdom and teach you proper wifely obedience, and exert his husbandly rights to make you conform to his will, and his religion, by which, of course, I mean the *true* religion. You may choose either the Duke of Savoy or Philip's son, Don Carlos . . ."

"But Mary, Don Carlos is only ten!" I interjected, shuddering at the very thought of him; a vicious little hunchback who, despite his youth, already had a reputation for heartlessness and cruelty. He once went on a rampage and blinded every horse in the royal stables and was known to take fiendish delight in throwing live hares into the fireplace to be roasted alive.

"Then you had best take the Duke," Mary said, undaunted as she fidgeted with the great heavy emerald and gold crucifix at her throat.

"Sister" – I turned to her entreatingly and tried to take her hand – "please understand that my experiences and observations have been such that I have resolved never to marry. The heat of passion only leads to a cold grave."

"*Nonsense!*" Mary scoffed. "I don't know who has put these ridiculous ideas into your head! Matrimony and motherhood are woman's natural state. I admit that I too had reservations; I am not a woman of amorous inclinations so I had certain . . . trepidations about this . . ." She hesitated, groping for the right word. "Aspect of wedlock, but my fears were groundless, and I find myself happy and well-contented, as I am sure you will also when you are married to the Duke."

"*No!*" I shook my head adamantly.

"*Yes!*" Mary insisted. "You *will* marry the Duke of Savoy! Now go; I will hear nothing more about it, I will not have you vex and gainsay me in my condition! And this gossip about you and my husband *must* cease. Do not think I am unaware of it just because I am absent from the court!"

"Mary . . ." I started to speak again.

"*Out!*" she screamed, pointing to the door. "Susan! Show my sister out and do not admit her again. She is not welcome here!"

Even as Susan tried to usher me out I turned and grasped the doorjamb and shouted back at Mary, "England is the only lover and husband I shall ever have. I will *never* accept any other!"

But Mary just ignored me and began to sing a Spanish lullaby, a song I remembered her singing to me when she used to rock me on her lap, as she took up her sewing once more. It grieved my heart to remember how close we had once been, and how cold, distant, and far apart we now were, even when sitting right beside each other upon a window seat. We might as well have been in Heaven and Hell, we were so opposite and far apart.

On the final day of April, saying he would like to procure a wild boar for Mary's table, that being her favourite meal and knowing how well such a gesture would please her, Philip bade me bring my bow and quiver and ride out into the forest with him.

We had only been riding a little time before Philip reined in his horse, dismounted, and came to lift me down from my own saddle. I laughed as the spray of speckled green and tawny feathers on my round russet velvet cap tickled his nose. Impatiently, he snatched it from my head and flung it away, his fingers inadvertently catching the golden net that held my hair and causing it to tumble down about my shoulders in a riot of flame-coloured waves.

"*Marry me!*" he breathed as he clutched my waist and held me close against his fast-beating heart, ardently grinding his loins into mine as he began backing me towards the nearest tree.

"Perhaps." I shrugged with a silky noncommittal purr. "But my sister tells me that it is your wish, as well as hers, that I marry the Duke of Savoy."

"*Hang the Duke!*" Philip cried angrily, ripping open the emerald and russet velvet jacket of my riding habit, causing the ornate gold lacings and buttons to tear and pop as he wrenched it from my shoulders.

"Your son, Don Carlos, though he is but ten, has also been suggested as a suitor for my hand," I added as he slammed my back against the tree and I felt the rough bark bite painfully through my white linen shirt.

"*Hang that vicious little fiend too!*" Philip exclaimed as he tore open my shirt, heedless of the laces, ripping it down to my waist, then tearing and tossing it away.

"Why so cruel, My Lord?" I asked, gasping as he spun me round to face the tree and, fumbling for his jewelled dagger, slit the laces of my leather stays and flung them aside, into the brambles.

"*I want you all for myself!* Before I met you, I would have happily married you off to one of them. It wouldn't have mattered because if I wanted you I could still have had you; they would have been so grateful to me for arranging the marriage they would have been willing to share. But now that is not enough for me. Now I want you all for myself! I know you like this," he added, his voice rough with desire as he cut away the top portion of my shift, causing me to shiver at the exquisite agony of my stiff pink nipples grazing the rough tree bark as he ripped it down to hang in jagged white tatters about my narrow waist. With sudden violence, he spun me round again, slammed my back against the tree, and lifted my leg, his fingertips digging into the tender flesh behind my knee, below my black ribbon-gartered stocking and high black leather boot. He pushed up my russet and emerald-green velvet skirts and starched white petticoats and ground his loins hard against mine. "I know *all* about you and Tom Seymour," he whispered in my ear, biting the tender lobe so that I gasped and cried out at the unexpectedly fierce pressure of his teeth, "and how he once cut the clothes from your body in the garden, right in front of his own wife! I should like to do that one day, just to see the look on Mary's face!"

Despite the warmth of the day, I shivered at the memory, and I thought for a moment that I saw the ghost of Tom Seymour leering at me over Philip's shoulder and had to close my eyes and give my head a hard little shake to clear it, though this gesture went unnoticed by Philip with his head then bent to bite my breasts.

"*Marry me!*" he repeated insistently.

"My sister is still alive," I reminded him, gasping as the press of his body increased the bite of the bark and I felt blood begin to trickle down my back.

"She is as cold as if she were already dead," Philip told me. "Her womb is like a tomb. And she is old to be carrying a first child; it will be a miracle if she survives it."

"Mary would remind you that she is no stranger to miracles," I said, tightening my arms about his neck and arching my back as he lifted me off the ground and my legs wrapped tight around his hips. "But we must not speak of this now; it is treason to predict or discuss the sovereign's death."

"I won't tell if you won't," Philip murmured, his lips hot against my throat. "Marry me, Elizabeth, when she is dead, and together we will rule the world! Together we will be another Anthony and Cleopatra, only we will *not* fail. We will have the most passionate marriage the world has ever seen and together we will conquer the world!"

"*Algún día*, Philip, *algún día*; someday, Philip, someday!" I cried as I arched my neck and breathlessly gasped as I clung to him, reaching down to grasp his manhood in my hand before he could push into me and learn my most closely guarded secret – that I was no longer a virgin. There were many rumours about Tom Seymour and me, but no one knew for certain, and I meant to keep it that way. "But not now . . . Now you must wait. . . ."

"Soon," Philip whispered hotly against my neck. "Our someday will come soon!" he promised.

"*Sí*, Philip." I caressed his cheek and nuzzled my breasts against his chest. "And then you will know the *real* me!"

"*Oh the passion and the power!*" Philip groaned as his seed spurted onto the ground between my feet and he leaned hard against me, pinning my back painfully against the tree, as he lay his head upon my naked shoulder and breathed heavily.

Suddenly there was a great clanging din and we nearly jumped out of our skins as the sound of church bells assailed us from all sides. It could mean only one thing – Mary had been delivered of her child.

Philip froze. Our eyes met, and his whole body stiffened. Abruptly, he let go of me and ran to his horse and bolted into the saddle and dug in his spurs.

As he galloped away, I was left alone. I felt as if my life had ended. If Mary had given birth to a son, and I was not to be England's queen, that left me stripped of my destiny and without it I was nothing, naked to my enemies. What was to become of me?

Alone in the forest with no one there to see, I let myself grieve. I let my tears flow, free and unchecked, and sank to the ground, and lay curled on my side, like a child in its mother's womb. I stuffed my skirt into my mouth and bit it to stifle my noisy, wracking sobs and cried until I had no tears left. Then I stood and went to collect my scattered and torn garments and make myself as presentable as possible so I could ride back to Hampton Court, alone amidst the sounds of rejoicing, hoping that, caught up in the celebration of the heir's birth, none would take notice of my disarray. If anyone did I would claim I had been thrown, as indeed I had in a way, thrown down from the proud heights of the destiny I thought would be mine.

But it was a false alarm. All was not lost after all and my tears and grieving had been in vain. Somehow a rumour had started and rapidly spread that Mary had been delivered of a son, when in truth she still lay in quiet seclusion, embroidering baby clothes, signing death warrants to send yet more heretics to the stake, and praying to be delivered soon.

That night, supplementing my white gown with deep cherry-red velvet sleeves and a matching kirtle worked in swirls of gold embroidery as a conciliatory nod to Mary's continued complaints about the plainness of my clothing, I waited for Philip to come and escort me into the Great Hall to dine. He slipped a necklace of weighty gold all spangled with rich blood-red ruby drops about my neck. He covered my shoulders with kisses as he fastened it, and apologized for abandoning me in the forest so precipitously.

"When you are mine, I will never leave your side," he promised.

"Someday, Philip, someday!" I smiled, as I threw back my head and laughed and laughed, before he pulled me close, into his arms, again.

❧ 41 ❧

Mary

When my child didn't come in May, the doctors patted my hands and said I had muddled my dates, as women often did, especially with a first baby, and said I should most likely be delivered near the end of June. When that month also passed I began to despair that something was well and truly wrong. I knew then that I must put myself wholly in God's hands.

"A miracle *will* come to pass!" I insisted as I put on one of my fine pleated Holland cloth birthing smocks with the wrists, neck, and hem edged with gold braid, and tucked my hair up in a matching cap. Then I wound my precious ivory rosary around my hand and fastened round my neck the cross my mother had given me containing a splinter from the True Cross. Having these dear, precious things made me feel like my mother and grandmother were right there in the birthing chamber with me. I clasped an ivory and gold inlaid crucifix to my breast and lay back on my bed with my legs wide and my knees bent and waited for my pains to begin. I had the midwives bring their instruments and stand poised in readiness at the foot of my bed, and issued orders for the swaddling bands to be brought out of the chest where they were kept, and for the wet-nurse and cradle rockers to be ready to assume their duties; I was about to give birth. At my command, all my ladies and a number of nuns from an abbey I had recently restored arranged themselves in neat rows and knelt in prayer around my bed. Whilst outside in the courtyard I could hear a procession of monks in rough dung-brown robes walking round and round in circles, the soles of their leather sandals slapping against the flagstones, as, with their tonsured heads bowed, they chanted:

> *O Almighty Father, which didst sanctify the Blessed Virgin and Mother Mary in her conception, and in the birth of Christ Our Saviour thine only Son; also, by thine omnipotent power, didst safely deliver the Prophet Jonas out of the whale's belly: defend, O Lord, we beseech Thee, thy servant Mary, our queen, with child conceived; and so visit her in and with Thy godly gift of health, that not only the child Thy creature, within her contained, may joyfully come from her into this world, and receive the blessed sacraments of baptism and confirmation, enjoying therewith daily increase of all princely and gracious gifts both of body and soul; but that also she, through Thy special grace and mercy, may in time of her travail avoid all excessive dolour and pain, and abide perfect and sure from all peril and danger of death, with long and prosperous life, through Christ our Lord. Amen.*

I closed my eyes tight and prayed with all my might, harder than I ever had in my life, beseeching Our Lady to show mercy and bring on my good hour.

> *Truly, you are blessed among women.*
> *For you have changed Eve's curse into a blessing;*
> *and Adam, who hitherto lay under a curse,*
> *has been blessed because of you.*
> *Truly, you are blessed among women.*
> *Through you the Father's blessing has*
> *   shone forth on mankind,*
> *setting them free of their ancient curse.*
> *Truly, you are blessed among women,*
> *because through you*
> *your descendants have found salvation.*

For you were to give birth to the Saviour
who was to win them salvation.
Truly, you are blessed among women,
for without seed you have borne, as your fruit,
him who bestows blessings on the whole world
and redeems it from that curse
that made it sprout thorns.
Truly, you are blessed among women,
because, though a woman by nature,
you will become, in reality, God's mother.
If he whom you are to bear is truly God made flesh,
then rightly do we call you God's mother.
For you have truly given birth to God.

For hours I lay thus waiting for my pains to begin, repeating my prayer, feeling the wooden edges of the crucifix I clutched bite into my hands. It comforted me to know that I was surrounded on all sides by prayers – the monks outside chanting in the courtyard, walking round and round, wearing out their soles, and inside the palace, at my command, when I lay down and opened my legs and drew up my knees, everyone had stopped whatever they were doing and knelt where they were, and prayed for me and my safe delivery.

My voice grew weary and hoarse and in the heat of the late afternoon I fell into a torpor. I drifted as the voices droned and I know not how many more hours had passed before a heavenly light so bright it hurt my eyes appeared beside my bed. Within it I saw a bright angel gowned in blue with flowing gold hair.

Though her eyes were kind, her lips were downturned in sorrow. She told me that God was not pleased with me. Heresy still flourished in my realm. I had failed to uproot the weeds from my garden – though some had been plucked and others had perished, many more still remained to breed and multiply and spread their blasphemy like a Black Plague of the soul – so He must withhold my miracle. My child could not be born until every heretic in England had been burned or converted to the true faith.

Heretics were the worst kind of criminals, worse than any ordinary murderer or thief, and much more dangerous, for their crimes were not only against man but God as well. They were the worst kind of thieves, for they stole the souls of the innocent and ignorant and cheated them of salvation, condemning them to damnation and denying them the kingdom of Heaven.

I opened my eyes then and sat up. God, through His angel, had spoken to me, and I knew *exactly* what I must do.

❧ 42 ❧

Elizabeth

Mary had been pregnant nearly ten months with no sign that the birth was imminent. Many believed that it was a physical delusion wrought by the mind of a brainsick woman because she wanted a child so very much, or else a tumour of the womb that caused her stomach to swell in a grim parody of pregnancy. But her women, her doctors, and even the midwives who were the wisest of the lot, were quick to defend Mary and insist that she had shown every sign of being with child. Her courses had stopped, her breasts were tender and swollen and milk had even flowed from them, and her stomach had expanded with the passing months exactly as it should during the course of a normal pregnancy.

A crudely printed but much circulated drawing predicted that Mary's pregnancy would end in a great wind and nothing else and showed Philip on a ship being blown out to sea, back to Spain, by the force of a massive fart issuing from Mary as she lay in an attitude of birthing, whilst on the deck of the ship Philip fastidiously held his nose. And there was a rumour that a woman named Isabel Malt, who had just been delivered of a son, had been visited discreetly after dark by men in the Queen's service who had tried to buy her child so that it might be passed off as the Queen's.

The burnings had taken on a whole new intensity. From the

bed where she still lay, praying and waiting to give birth, Mary spent her days, and sat up far into the nights, signing death warrants. Mary signed them without weighing the merits of each case. There was no time to fully investigate them; the merest hint of suspicion was enough to send the accused to the stake.

Untold horrors reached my ears of people dying in choking agony upon piles of damp, green faggots, and of bags of gunpowder tied about their necks to give them a quick death either failing to explode or doing so but failing to kill and instead maiming horribly so that they died in even greater agony as they waited for the smoke and flames to consume them. One woman went pregnant to the stake – How could Mary do it? Did she even know? Did she miss that crucial fact in her haste to sign and send another alleged heretic to Hell? – and in her agony her womb disgorged the child right into the grasping hands of the flames, thus claiming two lives, one entirely innocent, and the other guilty only of being a poor uneducated woman with a muddled understanding of Catholic dogma, unable to name or number the Sacraments correctly. If any tried to help or intervene or spoke out in protest, they were also subject to arrest and punishment in the stocks or pillory, or even the stake itself if they too were suspected of harbouring heretical beliefs.

Lists of those who had died at the stake were sold in the streets of London as "Names of The Martyrs". Their ashes and belongings were preserved and displayed as holy relics. And verses and prayers for "The Ascension of Elizabeth" were printed on broadsheets on secret presses that changed locations regularly and operated only in the dead of night, the printers knowing full well that if they were caught it was jail or death, or even both. One of the most popular went:

> *When raging reign of tyrants stout,*
> *Causeless did cruelly conspire*
> *To rend and root the simple out,*
> *With furious force of sword and fire;*
> *When man and wife were put to death:*
> *We wished for our Queen Elizabeth.*

There was also an even shorter and more direct verse that was upon many of the common people's lips.

> *When these with violence were put to death,*
> *We prayed to God for our Elizabeth.*

To them, I was the living embodiment of Hope; I was the virgin queen whose coming to the throne would put out the flames. That, more than anything else, kept me alive. When I grew weary of struggling to stay alive, of flirting with Philip, of battling with Mary and trying to combat and disprove her suspicions, it was their hope and belief in me that sustained me and kept me going to live and fight to preserve my life for one more day. Because I knew that my day would come, and that my people had need of me.

Another month came and went. And it was apparent to all except Mary herself that there would be no child. A rumour arose that the Queen was dead and to prove it false she made a point of showing herself each afternoon at her window overlooking the courtyard, where monks, intent on their prayers, walked round and round even in the deluge of rain that was rotting the crops in the fields and bringing famine upon the country. Some persisted in believing that it wasn't truly Mary at all but a wax figure held up by Philip.

Mary refused to believe that she was not carrying a child and insisted that every day a long winding procession of clergy trudge through the streets of London praying that England be delivered from heresy and that God send the Queen a goodly hour soon. And the doctors and midwives, too fearful to tell her the truth, continued to reassure her and murmur about miscalculations and such.

Instead of warmth and abundance, the summer of 1555 was a summer of cold and want. Incessant rains drummed down upon the fields and turned the soil to a muddy, mushy mire in which nothing could thrive. The crops were pelted and pounded mercilessly, and when the rains stopped, they lay broken and rotting in the feeble sun. None had seen the like of it in human memory. The people lived in fear of famine and the burnings that continued unabated. And with no grain to be had, prices soared, and people went in want of bread and beer. There was no grass and oats to feed the cattle, sheep, and horses, and many sickened and died, and before summer's end the price of one scrawny sheep could, in better times, have bought a small house.

In August, everyone, except Mary, admitted that if she were delivered of a child it would indeed be a miracle, for she had by then been pregnant an entire year.

Finally, with the air of Hampton Court grown unbearably foul and ripe, with the rushes in dire need of changing, and the courtiers surly, ill-tempered, and bored from want of fresh air and outdoor exercise, and the gardens a rotting, muddy mess, pounded into a pulp by the pouring rain, and fear of the plague running rampant, Mary emerged from seclusion with her belly deflated and her face defeated.

She made no mention of her pregnancy, and no explanation was ever given out either publicly or privately. She simply declined to discuss the matter; she merely announced that they would be leaving for Oatlands Palace so that Hampton Court could be cleansed.

I was not invited to accompany them, but told to go back to Hatfield or Hell or wherever I would. "You are at liberty to go where you will," Mary said to me when we parted. "All I know is that I will never trust you again."

So I took myself back to the peace and quiet of Hatfield and left Mary to play beggarmaid-queen, weeping, whining, and grovelling for scraps of affection from her cold-hearted husband's table.

❧ 43 ❧

Mary

The August morning I awoke to find blood on my nightgown my heart broke. I knew it was God's judgment upon me. I had failed to deliver England from the vipers injecting my people with the venom of heresy, so He had failed to deliver me of a son. It was a hard but fair bargain, and I knew I *must* do better – it was the *only* way I would ever hold my miracle in my arms – and it must be soon, for the hourglass that holds the sands of a woman's fertile years was, for me, fast running out.

Crossing the threshold of the room that was to have been my birthing chamber to confront the curious faces of my court was one of the hardest things I have ever had to do, but I held my head up high as I regally sailed past them in black velvet and diamonds, offering no explanation.

And as I rode to Oatlands in my litter, with my resumed monthly blood seeping into the cloths between my thighs, and the great cramps that seized and wrung my womb making me gasp and bite my lip not to cry out, I watched Philip through a gap in the velvet curtains riding straight-backed in the saddle of his white horse and knew that very soon he would leave me. He didn't have to speak to show me his displeasure; his silence was my punishment.

Other men might have shown compassion, they might have held and kissed and comforted a wife who had lost a baby, but not

Philip; such was not his way. When I held out my arms and begged him to hold me, he turned his face away and said coldly, "It is not when you need me to hold you, Mary, it is when I want to hold you." So I was left alone to bear my personal cross – the knowledge that I had failed my husband, my Christ on earth, just as I had failed God.

And then he left me, after we moved to Greenwich. I knew that he would. At the top of the stairs he bowed formally over my hand, his lips barely brushing my feverish flesh that trembled and yearned for his touch, before he turned his back and walked away from me, leaving me wringing my hands and helpless as the tears poured down my face. He never once looked back even though my eyes followed him, like a drunkard, never able to drink their fill. Each tap of his boot heels on the stairs was like a nail being driven into my heart.

The moment the palace doors closed behind him, I burst into tears, loud keening sobs that startled even me, and caused my court to start and stare horror-stricken and appalled at me. They were too callous to care that my heart was breaking, and I knew more caricatures and jests would soon follow and be left for me to find.

Wailing like a wounded animal, I sought solace in my private chapel and the compassionate face of the Holy Virgin, who understood so well the hearts and sorrows of women. I threw myself on my knees before the candlelit altar and prayed that my husband would come back to me soon and safe.

I cried until my eyes were as red and dry as autumn leaves. Then, staggering blindly, I made my way down to the kitchens and gave orders that a batch of my beloved's favourite meat pies be prepared at once, then taken, by the fastest ship in our fleet, to Calais, the first stop on his journey, and presented to him with my love and most heartfelt wishes for his "health, long life, and speedy return". Then I staggered back upstairs to my bedchamber and sat down at my desk to pour out my heart to him in a letter. I vowed I would write to him every day until he returned to me, and I am proud to say that I kept that vow; I never gave cause for anyone to ever doubt my devotion.

❧ 44 ❧

Elizabeth

The burnings continued as Mary's heart burned for Philip. The great men of the Protestant Church, Latimer, Ridley, and even gentle, soft-spoken Cranmer, who had been my mother's friend and my father's instrument, all went to the stake and martyrdom, dying heroically with courageous words that would never be forgotten.

Whilst Ridley suffered the full horror of burning at the hands of an inept executioner and died screaming in agony, Latimer seemed to glory in it. With a beatific, saintly smile, he washed his hands and bathed in the flames, calling out encouragingly to his friend, "Be of good cheer, Master Ridley, and play the man, for we shall this day, by God's grace, light such a candle in England as I trust shall never be put out!"

Fear and the false promises of Mary's heretic-hunting lackeys had persuaded the sensitive Cranmer to embrace Catholicism to save his life, but he had not counted on Mary. She could never forget or forgive the role Cranmer had played in the divorce drama of our parents' lives, and she gladly signed his death warrant.

As he walked to the stake, Cranmer repented his cowardice and reaffirmed his faith, asking the crowd to forgive him for fearing the flames and in consequence trying to save his life. Proud to die a Protestant, he boldly thrust his right hand into the flames, loudly proclaiming that since it had signed his recantation it should be the first part of his body to suffer the flames.

Mary haunted the halls of her palaces, a gaunt, white-faced, skeleton-thin, walking wraith, caring for nothing but the persecution of Protestants and the return of Philip. She left her court to its own devices, and neglected affairs of government, while she fasted and prayed and spent long sleepless nights straining her weak, bloodshot eyes by candlelight writing love letters that were almost as lengthy as books to her beloved until the shadows encroached on her vision and her sight, always poor, worsened and dimmed, but still she kept writing. She thought if she kept trying, her devotion would be rewarded, and she would eventually find the right words, like a magical charm, that would bring Philip back to her.

She was too blind to see that he simply did not care. His father, the Emperor, was ailing badly and on the verge of retiring to a monastery. Philip was about to come into his inheritance. He would rule Spain and the Low Countries, and it was expected that he make a tour of the lands he was to govern, to stake his claim and win his people's loyalty and respect. He didn't need Mary, or, for the moment, at least, England, either, with the adulation of his new subjects and the welcoming fetes and festivities, and the beautiful women who threw themselves at his feet, to distract and occupy him, and it broke Mary's heart to find herself unloved and unwanted by the one she loved and wanted most.

My sister had so much love to give, I am sorry she never found anyone truly worthy enough to receive it. That, I think, is the greatest tragedy of love, that those who love and long to be loved are not always loved in return, that the warm love that fills a human heart is sometimes left to curdle and dry up or turn bitter and sour for lack of anyone to give it to, or else it is lavished in vain upon someone who does not want or even deserve it.

⤙ 45 ⤚

Mary

He left me alone, surrounded by heretics, traitors, and enemies, to fend for myself, and live in fear for my life and crown, hardly daring to eat lest someone slip poison into my food or cup, and afraid to sleep. For when I did sleep, an incubus in Philip's form would come to visit and ravish me in lewd dreams that made my body gasp and groan and sigh and go through all the motions of passion, making my heart beat fast as if I had climbed to a great height and then leapt blindly, not knowing whether I would land on a soft feather bed or be impaled upon the sharp rocks below sticking up like phalluses to taunt me. I always awoke with a start to find my nightgown pulled up to my chin, my legs spread wide and wet between, and my fingers wet from touching myself. Some of my ladies always slept on pallets in my bedchamber when I was alone, and they saw and heard these wanton displays the Devil tricked and coaxed out of me, and ran giggling to tattle, and soon word spread throughout the court and whenever I appeared before their knowing eyes I felt as if I were being burned on a pyre of shame.

He was not with me on my birthday. He was not there to smile and drink a loving cup with me when Susan and Jane presented me with a goodly supply of Dr Stevens's Sovereign Water, a potion made of exotic and mysterious spices mixed into Gascony wine, promising "death-defying longevity well past the normal span allotted to mankind".

He was not at my side on Easter Sunday when upon my knees in a linen apron I humbly washed the feet of forty-one poor women, one for each year of my life, and kissed with ecstatic devotion the sores of one-and-forty more suffering from scrofula.

He was never there when I was ill with "menstruous retention" and "strangulation of the womb" to hold my hand when the doctors had to bleed me from the sole of my foot to bring on my courses and bring me relief. He was never there when I suffered toothaches, heart palpitations, and megrims.

When he bothered to answer my letters at all, there were no words of love or tenderness, only clipped and curt businesslike phrases. They said he did not welcome my letters and each day when yet another one arrived was wont to exclaim, "The Queen of England is nothing but a nuisance!"

They said he was busy dancing in Antwerp, and getting drunk on Flemish beer, that he had cast off his rigid sense of decorum like a winter coat when the weather warms and given himself over to debauchery and pleasure. They said he had developed a passion for masked balls and was likely to attend, whether invited or not, any wedding celebration he could find. They said he was likely to hammer at any hour on any door of any Flemish nobleman and demand beer and to be entertained and to exercise his *droit du seigneur* to bed any woman he desired, even the wives and daughters of his hosts or just a pretty maidservant.

I wept and howled and screamed like a madwoman and took a knife to his portrait. "God often sends bad husbands to good women!" I raged as I slashed it to ribbons. Then I sat on the floor for hours, weeping with remorse, as I tried to piece it back together again. "The Lord giveth and the Lord taketh away!" I sobbed.

And everywhere I went people seemed to be singing a mournful ballad of lost love that began:

> *Complain my lute, complain on him*
> *That stays so long away;*

He promised to be here ere this,
But still unkind doth stay.
But now the proverb true I find,
Once out of sight then out of mind.

Ceaselessly, relentlessly, my enemies tormented me with crude drawings, pamphlets, broadsheets, and doggerel verses about Philip's antics and excesses in the Low Countries. They pictured me as a wrinkled old hag suckling my young Spanish husband at my sagging breasts and labelled me "Mary, the Ruin of England. She robs England's coffers to send money to her faithless husband."

They said marriage had aged me ten years; they feared that sorrow would drive me to take my own life. Some even prayed that I would. They said that after I was dead Philip would marry Elizabeth, claiming that he had already secretly petitioned the Pope and been granted a dispensation.

He said he would come back to me if I would finance his war with France, if I would overrule my Council's adamant "No!" We had no quarrel with France, they said when I begged and pleaded with them, and England had no reason or responsibility to pay for Philip's warmongering. Furthermore, it would bankrupt the nation. But the only way I could get him back was to provide him with money and men. If I did, then he would come back to me and be my loving husband and share my bed again. Why couldn't they understand?

And I, in my desperate love and need for him, was willing to bleed England dry as Philip's faithlessness had bled my heart, if only he would come back to me. To feel his touch again I was willing to do *anything*. I sent him £150,000 and after eighteen months of waiting, hoping, begging, pleading, and yearning, he, at last, came back to me.

❧ 46 ❧

Elizabeth

Wearing a ghastly gown of blood-red and gold stripes trimmed with heavy, dripping gold fringe, and delicate pink satin ribbons and bows, with a collar so high and tight, topped by a tiny white ruff, it made her look as if her head were overly large and teetering on a plate balanced on top of a pillar, Mary ran out to meet him.

As every church bell in London rang and the choir from the royal chapel sang "Hallelujah!" and the Tower guns fired a welcoming salute, she bunched up her skirts, hitching them high above her knees, and ran to him, looking for all the world like an eager dog scampering to lick her master's face when he returned home after a long absence. She flung herself at his feet, like Sappho hurling herself off the cliff, with all the passionate force of a cannonball, kissing first the toes of his dusty boots, then clutching at his hands and covering them with ravenous kisses and bathing them with her hot, salty tears.

All the time Philip stood there stiff and straight as a soldier at attention, calm and imperious in his gold-trimmed garnet velvet. I watched as, over Mary's hunched and kneeling figure, he shared an amused glance edged with the intricate lace of cruelty, with the woman everyone knew was his latest mistress – the beautiful and worldly, voluptuous, full-hipped and ample-breasted, golden-haired

Christina, Duchess of Lorraine. She had once been a reed-slender widow of sixteen, who, whilst posing for Holbein, had quipped that had she been born with two heads she would have gladly placed one of them at my father's disposal, and thus declined his invitation to become his fourth wife.

It maddened me to see him standing there, calmly accepting Mary's devotion as if he were a golden idol meant to be worshipped and adored. Mary did not see the flame of gloating triumph blaze up briefly in his cold serpent's eyes, nor did she, I think, notice the twitch of his leg, as if he were holding himself back, striving not to kick her. I turned away then, sickened and saddened, to see my sister, the Queen of England, debasing herself so before this most unworthy and callous man who cared nothing at all for her.

It also sickened me to know that later that night, in just a few hours, at the flower pageant Mary had devised to welcome him, behind the diaphanous curtains of a barge, in a gown bedecked with honeysuckles, pink roses, and buttercups, with golden shafts of wheat in my hair, I would be lying in his arms. The look in his eyes when he turned them my way told me so. And that was indeed what happened, but as I lay back against the silken cushions, listening to the water lapping gently against the barge, while Philip eased down my bodice and kissed my bare breasts, I was haunted by the memory of Mary down on her knees kissing his dirty boots as if they were a holy relic, and had to close my eyes against my rising nausea. When I could stand it no more, I pushed him away and struggled to my feet, claiming I was taken of a sudden ill by the onset of my courses. I went alone, back to my apartments, and sat on the window seat and hugged my knees and stared up at the stars, reflecting upon how love makes slaves and fools of women, and we are, in truth, better off without it and the meanness of men and the misery it brings.

Of course the maliciously minded made sure that Mary found out who and what the Duchess of Lorraine was. And Mary made a fool of herself, ordering the Duchess's possessions carried out of her rooms and taken down to the ground floor of the palace, as far away from her husband as she could decently lodge a noblewoman and honoured guest from a foreign land. At table she seated the voluptuous, golden Christina as far away as possible from Philip, trying to block his view of her with lavish subtleties created in his honour by the royal pastry chef. And whenever there was dancing, Mary did all she could, making a complete fool of herself, to keep Philip and his "Fair Christina" apart, even digging in her heels and tugging at his arm to make him stay with her. And when her efforts failed and Philip spoke sharply to her, publicly reprimanding her for her rudeness and behaving like a barmaid jealous of the attentions her favourite patron bestows upon another instead of like a queen, she burst into noisy, wracking sobs and fled the Great Hall, leaving us all to stand in stunned and silent amazement until Philip clapped his hands and called for the musicians to play and led his "Golden Duchess" out to dance a most sensual and provocative rendition of the volta.

Sickened, I turned my back and walked away; I could not abide to see my sister so humiliated in her own palace. I tried to go to Mary but found her door barred against me. She would not let me in or deign to talk to me and I heard her tear-choked voice, muffled by the thickness of the oaken door, shouting at me to go away.

❧ 47 ❧

Mary

I gave him the money and the men he demanded but he wanted more – to share my government and wear the Crown Matrimonial. He wanted a grand coronation to publicly proclaim him England's King.

"A woman ruling absolute and alone is an absurdity, a perversion and abomination in the sight of God and man," he said to me, pacing before me, with his hands clasped behind his back, like a stern schoolmaster delivering a lecture. "God sent me to you, Mary, to lift this burden from your shoulders; you are clearly not capable of bearing it alone."

"But, husband, the people fear Spanish rule!" I protested.

"How else should I rule but as a Spaniard?" Philip snapped back at me. "I *am* a Spaniard, *not* an Englishman!" He said this with such pride for his Spanish heritage and such obvious contempt for the English that I could not ignore or mistake it.

"But at our wedding banquet you drank a toast of English beer and said . . ."

Philip snorted derisively. "I know perfectly well what I said. That was for appearances only, to win the people's good regard. Have you not learned the power of appearances by now? Even Elizabeth, a woman young enough to be your daughter, understands. . . ."

"Why must you always say that?" I petulantly demanded.

"Why should I *not* say it?" Philip countered. "It is the truth. Are you so cowardly that you must shrink from it?"

"I don't want to talk about Elizabeth!" I cried. "I cannot give you the crown you desire, my love, for my people . . ."

"Are stupid, blundering sheep who need the firm hand of a good and skilful shepherd to guide them," Philip interrupted. "Someone like me. But if you cannot give me what I ask" – he sighed and spread his hands – "then I must depart. My pride will not allow me to stay in a country where I am not respected and have no authority. . . ."

"*No!*" I ran to him and flung myself at his feet, grasping his hands. "You *cannot* leave me again!"

"You have humiliated me, Mary; I serviced you like a stud does a brood mare, I gave you a child that *you* failed to deliver, which is not my fault, but where is my reward? Your love and gratitude are insufficient. For all that I have endured, I deserve the crown and have earned it many times over. But if you will not give it to me, then I shall have no choice but to leave and never return." With those words he pulled his hands away from me and started for the door.

"Beloved, *please*." I ran after him and caught at his sleeve. "I need a little time to persuade the Council, but I promise, when you return, victorious from your war, I shall crown your head with a wreath of golden laurels, and then, at Westminster Abbey, the Bishop shall bestow upon you England's crown so that you can feel pride in being my consort. Your wish and will are commands that I will dutifully follow until the day I die!"

"Very well" – Philip nodded – "then I shall stay a little longer."

"*Thank you!*" I bowed my head and fervently kissed both his hands. "*Thank you!*"

And that night, in the privacy of my bedchamber, when Philip stood naked before the mirror looking at his favourite person, I swallowed my shame, and put my pride aside with my clothes, and did all he asked of me.

In truth, I would have gone naked, clothed only in God's love, if it would have pleased him. I would have done *anything* to make him stay. There were moments when I thought Philip made me weaker instead of stronger as he claimed, but he was my husband, my lord and master, my Christ on earth, and his word was law. And, God help me, oh how I loved him and oh how I sometimes hated him for it! I begged for his favour like a dog begging for a bone, and I hated myself for it, that I was willing to grovel and stoop so low. I was the only daughter of Henry VIII and Catherine of Aragon, I should not have had to beg anyone for anything, but I did, outwardly shameless but inwardly filled to the brim with shame. I was a beggarmaid in brocade and diamonds, begging for my husband's love, or even just a token, some sign of affection, and everyone knew it. I saw the pity and contempt in their eyes when they looked at me, and I saw it in my own when I looked at my face in the mirror.

❧ 48 ❧

Elizabeth

He stayed only long enough to get what he wanted – money and men to fight his war with France – then Mary was left alone again standing on the crumbling precipice of a country she had brought to the brink of ruin.

To provide the money he demanded, coins had to be newly minted, which caused a panic as the value of the currency dropped alarmingly. With threats to take away their titles, lands, and estates, or even sentence them to death, she bullied the Council into doing Philip's bidding, and seven thousand English men were sent to fight a war that was not of their making. And when Philip wrote to her demanding even more money, Mary sold Crown lands and her jewels to raise funds for Philip.

I was of the party that accompanied them to Dover and watched in sad and pitying silence as Mary, dressed in dramatic black and trailing veils, extravagant mourning for the imminent departure of her love, stood on the icy quay and declared, "My heart is already in mourning for your absence," as she made her passionate and tearful farewells to the husband who, I knew in my bones, would strike her if she asked of him one more time, "You will come back to me?"

I could see the impatience and irritation twitching his cruel little mouth and simmering in his cold blue eyes, dangerous as a shark-infested sea. I watched her cling to him, anxious for reassurance, her voice and chin all aquiver and her face swollen and red beneath the ceaseless cascade of her tears. But even she, in her besotted blindness, I think, could see that he would never return to her no matter what words his lips spoke.

Before he boarded his ship, he took her aside, reminding her that, since she had failed to give him a son, I remained her lawful successor, and as such I deserved to be treated with respect, and if he should hear otherwise . . . He left the rest unsaid, a threat hanging like a sword on a frayed rope above her head.

Mary stood on the docks of Dover and waved until his ship was not even a speck on the horizon that even the most sharp-eyed amongst us could discern, and then I went to her.

For once, she did not push me away. She looked at me with such sadness in her face, before she burst into tears and fell into my arms, weeping on my shoulder and clinging tight to me as if she were a brokenhearted child, which, I realized then, in a way, for all her forty-one years, she was.

I stroked my sister's sob-shuddering back and held her close, but I said nothing, for there was really nothing that I, or anyone except Philip, could say, and he was gone for ever.

We returned to London and I watched my sister go through the motions of life like the Shadow of Death. She would sit at the head of the Council table without hearing a word. She would just sit there, lost in thought, and stare at Philip's portrait on the wall, or else sign death warrants by the score to send yet more Protestants to the stake.

She wore black mourning and her eyes were always swollen and red-rimmed from weeping. She did not sleep but sat up the whole night through writing passionate letters to Philip, pouring out her heart and soul to him; letters I daresay he didn't even bother to read and hardly ever answered. When he did deign to write it was always requests for more money, men, and arms, and reminders that he should have the crown. She kept messengers standing by at all hours, stationed all along the roads, and ships at the ready in the harbour, to carry forth her letters. She even kept the kitchens busy baking batches of Philip's favourite meat pies, then rushed these culinary offerings of her love out to him on our navy's fastest ships.

Whenever word reached her of Philip's adulteries – as it invariably did – she would lash out like a madwoman, seizing a dagger and attacking his portrait, or else tearing it from the wall and ordering her servants to take it out, kicking and screaming at it as they dutifully carried it away to the attic. Later in the night, holding a candle aloft, clad in only her white nightgown and bare feet, with her red-grey hair hanging down her back in a frightfully thin, wispy braid, she would emerge from her bedchamber like a ghost and go in search of the banished portrait and kneel down before it, reverently, as if it were an altar, or Philip himself, and tearfully apologize and worship it with tears and kisses until, exhausted and in sore need of rest, sleep mercifully overwhelmed her. Many a time the morning light found her thus, curled up like a puppy at the foot of Philip's portrait.

I could not bear to see her in such a state and, as soon as I could, I left for Hatfield. Listless and distracted as she pined and dreamed of Philip, Mary let me go, either forgetting or choosing to ignore the Spanish Ambassador's sage injunction that one should keep their friends close and their enemies even closer. She was so tired by then, I don't think she cared any more, though I wish I could say instead that she had learned to trust me again, and knew that I was not, and never had been, her enemy.

Before I left, I went to her to say goodbye, dressed in my wine-dark velvets for travel. I found her sitting listlessly upon the floor in her nightgown and robe with her knees drawn up to her chin and her ivory rosary clasped in her clawlike hand. I was horrified to see her face close up, so heavily lined and wrinkled, more like a woman of seventy than a year past forty, her bleary grey eyes so red and swollen and with such a vacant, lost look in them I thought even her own soul had fled and abandoned her.

Kat and Blanche had told me that Mary now avoided sleep as much as possible, for when she did sleep she was tormented by such vividly real dreams of Philip's love-making that she, to use her own words, "disgraced herself in her dreams". Thus she chose to spend her nights either writing to her absent husband or kneeling in her private chapel imploring the Blessed Virgin to help rid her of these unclean distractions and deliriums, this "incubus sent by Satan" in the guise of Philip, and begging her to send a swarm of angels to surround her bed and guard her so she could sleep in blessed peace.

"Mary," – compassion and worry flooded my heart as I knelt beside her and took her hand in mine – "you must take heart! You must try to get well!"

With a long, heart-heavy sigh, Mary shook her head. "Only his return can cure me." After that she would say no more except to absently murmur, "Safe journey," before she turned her face away from me and went back to staring longingly at the portrait on the wall, that devilishly handsome likeness of the haughty Spanish prince that had first made her fall in love with him.

There was nothing more I could do, so with a heavy heart I left my sister and went home to Hatfield, wondering if I would ever see her alive again.

❧ 49 ❧

Mary

God is merciful. He took my husband, and let him sail away to war and into the arms of another, but He left me with a baby in my womb.

This time I waited six months before I let my people know. I was afraid they wouldn't believe me and would laugh and remember how it had been before. But this time, I knew it would be different; this time God would smile and give one more miracle to His good servant Mary. When Philip returned to me I would greet him smiling with our baby in my arms.

❧ 50 ❧

Elizabeth

No one believed her or gave much credence to Mary's announcement that she was with child. The announcement provoked more pity and laughter than genuine belief. Philip had been gone from her six months and as impressively large as he thought his cock was, it was not long enough to stretch across the English Channel to impregnate his wife. This time, everyone knew it was just her imagination, a lovely illusion she wanted so badly to believe. She wanted to believe that Philip had not entirely forsaken her, that he had left her with something tangible, some little part of himself, a miracle that they had made together. But she was pregnant with hope, nothing more, and everyone but Mary knew it.

Then he lost Calais and it broke the already broken pieces of Mary's heart into still more pieces, so shattered they could never be mended and put back together again. Calais was England's last remaining foothold in France; it never would have happened if Philip had not embroiled us in a war we had no cause to fight. Our proud nation smarted with the humiliation, for there was not money enough in the Treasury to raise and equip an army to go out and try to win it back. The people blamed Mary; they called her a traitor to her own country, and accused her of loving Spain more than England. Philip had now taken everything from her. He would never come back. What was left for him to come back for?

Finally, she sent for me. As "Faithful Susan" took me to her, she confided that Mary had not left her chamber in weeks. She spent most of her time sitting on the floor, too afraid to face her people, and too cast down in spirits to even think of trying. Susan paused in the corridor and looked into my eyes and told me that she feared for Mary's life. Sorrow was strangling the life out of her heart and, if that deathly grip could not be broken, soon it would cease to beat. As for the child Mary still believed she carried as God's gift to her, with tears brimming in her eyes, Susan said the doctors and midwives now suspected it was a tumour partnering with the sorrow to leech away Mary's life.

When I walked into the candlelit bedchamber and beheld that poor brainsick woman, mired deep in darkest sorrow, I started in amazement. I hardly recognized this devastated wreck as my sister, so greatly had she altered.

When she looked up at me, her grey eyes squinting hard, straining to pierce the shadows and blurriness that encroached upon her vision, her tear-damp face was a wrinkled red and swollen mask of despair surrounded by a grizzled silver cloud of hair with just a few rusty streaks running through it. In the flickering candlelight I fancied I could see the skull beneath the lined yellow flesh, like a gruesome, parchment-pale death's head. She sat huddled upon the floor, tucked into a corner, where she must have felt safe, rocking back and forth, crooning a Spanish lullaby and cradling her grossly swollen belly. Her robe hung open to reveal that she was wearing one of her birthing smocks made of pleated Holland cloth, and beneath its gold braided hem her bare feet peeked out to reveal long, cracked and brittle yellow nails. She was surrounded by exquisitely stitched and beribboned little baby garments, lovingly embroidered by her own hands, that the ghost-child in her womb would never wear. Her sewing basket sat beside her and her prayer book lay open at a page so stained with tears that the ink had run and entirely obliterated the words written there.

I knew I was looking at a dying woman, a woman who had lost everything that mattered to her, and with it the will to live. She was old and tired and sick, her body, heart, and soul worn out. Raw and aching, and utterly naked and vulnerable in her grief, she was suffering pain to rival the agony of the childbirth that she would never herself experience. When she raised a trembling hand to reach out for me I saw that the rings hung loose and spun around on her fingers and the skin was almost transparent, like old yellowed parchment, and I could see every vein and bone beneath.

"Mary . . ." Tears filled my eyes as I took her hand and knelt down beside her.

I gathered that wasted and forlorn figure in my arms, remembering all the times when I was a motherless child in need of comforting and she had held me and rocked me gently and sung Spanish lullabies to me. As she laid her head on my shoulder I stroked and tried to tame that wild riot of rust-streaked silver hair. The whole story of Mary's life was written in her hair – the white and grey of woes, the hair of a broken and defeated woman old before her time and dying of an illness that cruelly mimicked her greatest desire, the auburn of a mature woman ripe for life and love, and a few wispy orange-gold strands to recall the beloved little princess who thought her life would always be as golden as her hair and that love always lasts for ever.

"When I die . . ." she croaked in a feeble and raspy whisper. "When I die and they open my body they will find the word *Calais* written on my heart."

I could think of nothing to say, nothing to assuage or vanquish her guilt or grief, so I just held her.

"Philip . . ." she whispered against my shoulder. "I was" – a shuddering sob broke from her – "I was . . . *wrong!* I should not have married him, I should not love him, but, God help me, I do, I do!"

I clutched her tight as the tears convulsed her, trying with my embrace to hold her body and soul together.

"There is a reason they say love is blind, Mary," I said gently. "Sometimes it wilfully or unwittingly fails to see the things it should see."

"But I . . . I was warned! They tried to tell me, they tried to stop me!" she sobbed.

"Mary, my dear sister" – I cradled her to my breast and stroked her wild, wispy and matted hair – "this I have learned from both observation and experience – there are times in our lives when we find ourselves standing on the edge of a cliff. Sometimes you stand there, looking down, for a *very* long time. Sometimes you find the strength, and the courage, to turn back, but sometimes you go over the edge; you jump. Sometimes you jump because you believe you cannot go back or that there is nothing to go back for, that your soul is lost in a long black tunnel with not even a glimmer of light at the end of it to guide you and give you the hope you need to go on. Sometimes you jump just because you are tired of being afraid. And sometimes you jump just to find out what it feels like to fall, to test your strength, to find out if you can claw your way back up again."

"Why did I fail?" she rasped, gazing searchingly into my eyes. "I tried *so* hard! Why did it all go so wrong?"

"Because you shut your ears to the *real* voice of God," I said gently.

"No! I didn't!" Mary tearfully insisted. "I was *always* true to God, I always followed . . ."

"Mary," I spoke gently but firmly as if she were a child, "you did. You were always true to your faith, to the teachings of your Church, but to a monarch, the voice of the people is the *true* voice of God. It is their love and will that puts a king or queen upon the throne and keeps them there. As God's anointed queen, you were His candle on earth, sent here to light the way, to guide and inspire, but you *cannot* compel and force people's consciences with torture and threats as if they were wild horses in need of breaking. But you tried to do just that, and when you began to burn those you branded heretics you also began to burn away your people's love. You didn't listen to them, you blocked your ears to their cries, and that is the reason you failed."

Mary stared at me for a long time as if she hadn't seen me before or didn't know who I was.

"Mary?" I prodded her gently.

She closed her eyes and took a deep breath and drew herself up straight.

"Promise me . . ." Her voice faltered and she tried again. "Promise me that . . . that the true religion will never die in England."

I took both her hands in mine and stared deep into her eyes. "*I promise!*" I put all the conviction I possessed into those two words. "I make no windows into men's souls, Mary. Loyalty to the sovereign is one thing, and faith in God and how one worships Him is another; there is no reason that the two cannot peaceably coexist in harmony."

"*Thank you!*" Mary closed her eyes and breathed a sigh of deep gratitude and relief. And then she opened them and asked falteringly, her words punctuated by sobs, "Will you . . . try . . . to find a way to . . . pay . . . my debts? There are . . . I fear . . . a . . . a great many."

"Of course I will," I assured her. "Do not trouble your mind over that."

"And will you . . . be . . . kind . . . to . . . m-my . . . my servants?"

"Those who have served you loyally and well shall be rewarded," I promised.

"While I live, I am Queen in name," she said to me, her voice firmer now, marred only by the slightest quiver, "but you are the Queen of Hearts. Go with God, His will be done." As the storm of tears broke anew she made an adamant gesture, waving me towards the door, and I dared not stay and intrude further upon her broken heart.

Those were the last words she ever spoke to me.

❧ 51 ❧

Mary

When the door closed behind Elizabeth I struggled to pull my-self up from the floor and, leaning heavily upon tables and chairs for support, pausing only when weakness and faintness threatened to overwhelm me, I made my way slowly across the room to the windows overlooking the courtyard. I collapsed thankfully onto the window seat and sat there feeling light-headed, dizzy, and breathless, clutching my heart and panting for air, fearing my sight would not be able to pierce the myriad of coloured stars and sparks that obscured it in time for me to see what I needed to see.

There was still snow in the courtyard and a young boy was busily sweeping the flagstones to clear a path when she came out.

She looked like a queen. She walked like a queen. Philip had been correct when he said she understood the power of appearances. All my jewel-bedecked, embroidery-encrusted finery could not mark me as a queen the way Elizabeth's carefully chosen white gown, covered with a black velvet surcoat, edged with white fur, and embroidered with silver snowflakes embellished with tiny twinkling diamonds and seed pearls, and matching white-plumed black velvet cap could. She wore her hair caught up in a net of pearls instead of loose and flowing as she usually did, I noted, the better to appear a mature woman rather than a green girl too young and inexperienced to rule. Black, silver, and white, her colours carefully chosen; elegant but not overdone adornments; the perpetual pearls; her Tudor red hair so none who saw her could mistake her heritage; and her confident, calm, and elegant bearing – she was sending a message of power, virginity, wisdom, and strength neatly tied into a bow with youth and beauty. She was telling the world that the last of King Henry's roses had grown stronger on the bush while the blossoms around her withered and died, but she, the last Tudor rose, had survived and imbibed the knowledge, through danger and hard lessons and the failings of those around her, that would enrich and empower her to rule England as none had ever done before; Elizabeth had within her the makings of a great queen.

The boy stopped his work and fell to his knees and caught up the hem of her skirt and kissed it. Elizabeth smiled and reached down to cup his chin. She spoke gently to him and caressed his cheek, and I knew then that even when, many years from now, he was a toothless old man, that boy would remember the day when he had touched and been touched by God's chosen one. He would grow old telling the story of the day he met Queen Elizabeth.

Others, alerted to her presence, came running, her name upon their lips like a prayer as they knelt around her, their fingers reaching out to reverently touch her skirts, with such love and unveiled hope upon their faces. She had a smile for every one of them, sometimes even a word, or a touch; a caress for a child's cheek or an elegant poised white hand extended for someone old and frail harbouring fond memories of our father to kiss.

I had been wrong; this was no lute player's bastard, this was the daughter of a king born to be a queen in her own right. I had let my hatred of Anne Boleyn corrupt and blind me. She had Father's gift for looking at a person and making them feel as if they were the most important person in the world, as if they alone existed for her, and it wasn't crude and common after all. I had been mistaken; I had been mistaken about so many things. She also had her mother's gift for winning against the odds. Elizabeth, daughter of Great Harry and The Great Whore, was a formidable combination to be reckoned with; she did not need a man like I did to be her pillar of strength, she was fully capable of steering the ship of state herself. She would not let England flounder or run aground or be dashed upon the rocks to shatter and drown. And even though the Blessed Virgin might disappear from England's altars, the people would not be lost with Elizabeth as the figurehead of the nation. She would hold the candle and light their way – no, she actually *was* the candle! She would be the virgin mother of her people, and when she walked amongst them and let them gaze their fill, reach out to touch her skirt and kiss her hands, through Elizabeth, the one God had chosen to wear England's crown, they would also be touching the divine.

I had lost. Everything I had aspired to, all my hopes and dreams, had been reduced to ashes, and I had lit the fires that rendered them thus. And Elizabeth was the phoenix who would rise from those ashes.

I had seen what I needed to see, and I knew what I needed to know. The true faith might not reign supreme as the only faith in England, but it would not perish.

I braced my hands against the stone windowsill to lever myself up, but as I turned, my head felt as if it were bobbing upon waves, and my eyes within my head felt the same, and then I had the most disturbing sensation that the floor was rising up to meet me, to slam into me with great force. And as it hit me everything went black.

I heard footsteps and voices all around me, a great bustle, a hurried preparation for a journey, servants running back and forth, trunks being dragged down from the attics, the bang of their lids, the snap of the locks. Why was everyone leaving? "Elizabeth" and "Hatfield" – I kept hearing those two names, sometimes spoken in normal tones, other times in whispers as if some didn't want me to hear them while others didn't care if I did. And then I understood. They were leaving me, like rats fleeing a burning building. My court was abandoning me, a dying and deluded woman. They were leaving me to die alone and running pell-mell towards the future and the flame-haired beacon of hope – Elizabeth.

I was in my bed now, I suddenly realized, feeling the softness of the mattress beneath me instead of the hard floor, and Susan was bending over to offer a cooling cup to my parched lips and to mop away the fever-sweat with a cloth dipped in rosewater.

"I have failed," I confided when Susan put her ear down closer to my lips. "All I ever wanted was to be loved, to find on this earth a love as true and everlasting as God's, but I have failed, and not through lack of trying; I prayed every day for someone to love me."

Susan was so overcome she could not speak, she had to turn away to hide her tears, but I could tell by the way her shoulders shook. A black-robed doctor was there at her side, patting her back and saying something that made her weep even harder. Somehow I just knew that he was telling her that there was nothing more that he could do for me. Jane Dormer came in carrying a tray and, seeing Susan's distress, set it down and went to take her in her arms, and they held each other and wept together.

I wanted to comfort them, but I was so tired. I will sleep for just a few moments, the better to gather my strength, to think of the right words to say, I promised myself, and then . . .

I called for Philip, I begged him to hold me. I needed to feel the strength of his arms about me; only he could make me well. I was poised to knock at Death's door and only Philip could pull me back.

Philip raised his head from the bosom of his "Golden Duchess". They were lying naked on a bed of buttercups and her hair, the colour of ripened wheat, was spread out, rippling all around her naked body in abundant golden waves so that she, with her ample, generous figure, seemed a very Goddess of Plenty. Annoyed at being disturbed, Philip glared at me with hard and angry eyes. "It is not when you need me to hold you, Mary; it is when I want to hold you," he said, and lowered his head to resume suckling at the bountiful breasts of his golden goddess – Christina. And she laughed and called him "Pompion", the French word for pumpkin, the name she had teasingly given him because of the round little belly he had acquired from too much drinking and debauchery.

I couldn't bear to look at them any more, to see them like that, naked and intent on their own private pleasures, so I slammed the door and ran away.

I was lost in a parched and barren landscape where nothing grew save sharp and ugly black thorns and nothing lived except horrid, slithering black serpents that hissed and looked at me with glowing red eyes. There was a cross in the distance. Our Lord was suffering upon it. I ran and threw myself upon my knees, hugging the cross below His feet. "I would die for you!" I cried as I looked up at Him and He looked down at me. And despite His suffering there was so much kindness and compassion in His face. All round me thorn trees sprang up, watered by the blood that dripped down from His pierced hands and feet, and the wounds caused by the thorny crown upon His brow. I hugged the cross tighter; I was surrounded, hemmed in on all sides, by thorn trees. They pinned me to the cross below Our Saviour's feet, and I felt His blood drip down to mingle with mine as the thorns impaled me. I felt the most peculiar ecstasy: a strange, beautiful, and bewildering blend of pleasure and pain so intricately bound together that I could not tell where one ended and the other began. And as the sharp black thorns pierced my heart I felt the urge to sing. I was past pain; nothing could hurt me now.

A priest was standing at the foot of my bed, and as he held the Host aloft, I saw a golden light as warm and bright as the sun, only it didn't hurt my eyes and make me want to turn away; I wanted to run straight into it and bask in that lovely golden warmth.

And God shall wipe away all the tears; and there shall be no more death; neither sorrow, nor crying, neither shall there be any more pain: these former things have passed away.

I was in a beautiful garden sitting on the warm green grass surrounded by rosy-cheeked tots with charming smiles and chubby little arms that reached out for me. When I swept them up into my arms they gurgled and smiled and laughed and hugged me tight. These were my babies, the babies I should have been bearing when I was a young woman, and the phantom children who had puffed out my belly with false hope when I was Philip's bride. Now here they were, safe in my arms, loving me and wanting me just as I loved and wanted them. They nestled in my arms and gave me hearty, smacking kisses and smiled and clung to me. I rocked them on my lap and sang them the Spanish lullabies my mother used to sing to me, and I used to sing to Elizabeth, but now I was singing them to my very own babies. God was good; I truly was blessed among women.

❧ 52 ❧

Elizabeth

It was a crisp November day, and I awoke thinking, strangely, of apples, their crispness and tart-sweet taste, longing for that crisp, juicy first bite all the time I was dressing in a simple white gown. I could not get them out of my mind. I felt so strange; I was unaccountably restless, I simply could not settle. For the life of me, I could not stand or sit still. Finally, without bothering to put up my hair or don a hood, I snatched up an old grey shawl and a book and went out into the park, heedless of Kat's concerns about the chill that nipped the air and the possibility of rain.

I walked aimlessly over the grounds and eventually settled myself on a bench beneath a great oak tree and tried to read. At the sound of hoofbeats my head shot up, and squinting into the distance, I beheld two horsemen hastening towards me.

Dismounting from their horses, the Earls of Arundel and Throckmorton came and knelt before me, the latter holding out his hand and opening it to display upon his leather-gloved palm a gleaming gold and ink-black onyx ring. It was Mary's coronation ring. I recognized it at once, and it could only mean one thing – my sister was dead.

"The Queen is dead, long live the Queen!" they said.

I turned my eyes heavenward, and clasped my hands in prayer and turned away from them. "Godspeed, Mary," I whispered. "May you find in Heaven what you never found in life!"

Then I turned round to face my destiny.

"This is the Lord's doing and it is marvellous in our eyes!" I announced as I took the ring and slipped it onto my left hand as solemnly and lovingly as if it were a wedding ring, which it was, for me, a sacred and eternal bond forged between myself and England.

Then a third horseman, this one leading a second horse alongside his, was approaching. Robert Dudley, his head a riot of unruly, windblown black curls, dressed in jewel-toned velvets, sombre yet gay, edged with a burnished gold braid. He was riding a black stallion, and leading alongside it a pure white horse caparisoned and saddled in silver and ermine. His hands made some sort of motion with the reins, and his lips moved in some soft, encouraging clucking sound perhaps, I was too far away to hear, and his ebony steed dipped its head low and bowed to me, then that magnificent virgin-white horse did the same, as Robin doffed his feathered cap, held it over his heart, and bowed to me from the saddle.

I clapped my hands in pure delight, as happy as a young girl beholding the wondrous tricks of the gypsies' performing horses at a country fair.

"God save the Queen!" my own dear gypsy cried out, putting his heart in every word. "Good Queen Bess; long may she reign!"

I smiled and went to him. My hand reached out to stroke the nose of that beautiful virgin-white horse, but then I was distracted by the sunlight catching the gold and black ring. The way the gold flashed around the onyx made it seem to be winking at me, conspiratorially and knowingly, like a secret lover discreetly from across a crowded room. I held my hand out before me, gazing at the ring, and thinking of all it stood symbol for, solid gold proof that I was wedded to England now, and, softly and solemnly, as if I were speaking my wedding vows, I began to recite:

> *Here is my hand,*
> *My dear lover England.*

I am thine with both mind and heart;
For ever to endure,
Thou mayest be sure,
Until death us two do part.

I knew in that moment that the future was ours – mine and England's, our destinies irrevocably entwined – and everything would be golden.

The white horse nuzzled the side of my head, startling me out of my solemn reverie, and I laughed and reached up to disentangle my hair from her nose. I glanced up at Robin, and our eyes met, and we smiled at each other, then Robin held out his hand to me.

POSTSCRIPT

Elizabeth ruled England for forty-five years as "The Virgin Queen" hailed as "Good Queen Bess" and "Gloriana".

In spite of having numerous suitors, and her grand passion for Robert Dudley, she never married.

Anne Boleyn's daughter, "the princess who should have been a prince", became the greatest monarch England has ever known, surpassing the deeds of even her own great father. She turned England into a power to be reckoned with, defeated Philip's bid to conquer and enslave England with his Spanish Armada, and ushered in a golden age of prosperity that gave the world such immortal talents as William Shakespeare and Christopher Marlowe.

She never lost her people's love or loyalty and died peacefully in her bed in 1603 at the age of seventy.

Mary and Elizabeth both lie splendidly entombed in marble in Westminster Abbey under the epitaph:

> CONSORTS IN BOTH THRONE AND GRAVE,
> HERE REST WE TWO SISTERS,
> ELIZABETH AND MARY,
> IN THE HOPE OF ONE RESURRECTION.

MARY & ELIZABETH

Emily Purdy

About This Guide

The suggested questions are included to
enhance your group's reading of Emily Purdy's
Mary & Elizabeth.

DISCUSSION QUESTIONS

1. Discuss the childhoods of Mary and Elizabeth. How were they different? How were they alike? How did their relationships with their parents, the loss of their mothers, the alternating periods of being in and out of their father's favour, and their father's multiple marriages affect and influence the women they grew up to be?

2. Discuss Elizabeth's dalliance with Thomas Seymour. What did she learn from it? Did it strengthen or weaken her? Did it make her wiser or leave her emotionally damaged? What do you think of Tom Seymour and his method of wooing women? Would you have fallen for him?

3. If Edward VI had survived, how would Tudor England have been different? What would have happened to Mary and Elizabeth? Would they still be remembered today, or would they have been virtually forgotten, their names known only to serious historians of the period? And would Edward have spent his entire life imitating his father, or would he have eventually discovered himself and become his own person?

4. Discuss the role virginity plays in Elizabeth's life. What does it mean to her? Why does she emphasize it by adopting white dresses and pearls? Is it symbolic, psychological, or propaganda, or are the boundaries blurred among all three?

5. Discuss the role Catholicism plays in Mary's life. Why does she cling to her faith as a drowning person would to a life preserver? And why does she try to force her religion on her subjects even when they resist? She believes herself to be God's instrument and that her life has been preserved to do His work; is this a sign of a delusional or unstable mind, or is she a sincerely devout person who means well but repeatedly makes bad decisions?

6. Discuss Mary and Elizabeth's relationship with each other and how it changes over the years. How are they alike and how are they different? Discuss the sources of friction in their relationship. Was there any way they could have got along and been loving sisters and friends, or were they doomed from the start to be rivals and adversaries?

7. Discuss Mary's relationship with her ardently Protestant cousin Lady Jane Grey. Why does Mary condemn her to death? Do you think she was right to do so?

8. Discuss Mary's and Elizabeth's beliefs about and experiences with love, sex, marriage, and childbirth. Are the decisions they make about these things the right ones? Why do they make the choices they do?

9. Mary sees Philip as a dream come true – but is he? Discuss Philip's character. Is the man himself as pretty as his picture? Despite her subjects' heated protests, Mary marries him anyway; was this a good decision personally or politically? Is the marriage what Mary expected it would be? How does it affect her emotionally and mentally?

10. Why does Elizabeth carry on a flirtation with Philip when she knows this will hurt and provoke her sister? Is there a genuinely amorous element to it, or is it a purely calculated act of self-preservation?

11. By the book's end Mary has either lost or failed at everything that matters to her and dies a lonely, broken woman. Do you pity her or do you believe she got what she deserved? What, if anything, could or should she have done differently to avert this tragedy?

12. At their last meeting, Mary realizes that Elizabeth is the phoenix that will rise from the ashes of her disastrous reign. What qualities do you think made Elizabeth England's greatest monarch? Why did she succeed and Mary fail?